How to Break an Evil Curse

Laura Morrison

ISBN Print – 978-1-7335994-8-1
ISBN eBook – 978-1-7335994-9-8

Cover Design and Interior Formatting
by Qamber Designs and Media
Edited by Lindy Ryan

Published by Black Spot Books,
An imprint of Vesuvian Media Group

DEDICATION

With infinite love, to Julia and Anna. So much of this book was written while you were babies sleeping on my lap while I typed one-handed. Thus, it will always be my favorite thing I've ever written.

CHAPTER ONE

The Forest of Looming Death was, as one might guess by the name, a dreary place. Through it ran the Brook of Dashed Hopes, which was as bleak a brook as one could imagine. The brook was where the coal mine upstream dumped all the byproducts of its mining operation. It was full of bony, inedible fish, which were the only creatures hardy enough to live there. Since the fish were the only creatures in the brook, they were cannibalistic by necessity.

Just beyond this brook, and over the Bridge of Misery, it was a hop, skip, and a jump to a cave, which (unlike most landmarks in The Forest) had no name. But if it had had a name, it would have been called the Dwelling Place of Mirabella the Traitor. The Forest was where banished criminals of the land were sent to live out their remaining days, and Mirabella had been a resident of its shades for nigh on twenty years. She was the sister of the Queen of the Land of Fritillary, and as if that wasn't enough distinction and rank for her, she was also the only person in all the land who did not have a soul.

At least, no soul that anyone could detect.

Most days since her banishment to the Forest of Looming Death, Mirabella spent her waking hours hunting, tending her vegetable garden, and fighting other criminals off her prime forest real estate. Most nights she plotted revenge. She had been plotting with her partner-in-crime since Day One of her banishment, so it was as nice a revenge plan as ever a villain could hope to concoct, full of twists and turns and heartbreak and sweet, sweet justice for all the wrongs she believed herself to have suffered.

ENT STUDIOUSLY OVER a piece of paper on the stone floor of her cave, large black quill in hand, Mirabella scribbled away industriously. She paused, pondered for a full minute or so, and then dipped the quill in the bowl of raven blood she used as ink. She had made the paper herself by hand out of plant pulp and water, and—since if you are going to do a thing you might as well do the thing well—she had decorated the margins of the paper with various pressed wildflowers and pine needles, so it was quite lovely.

Mirabella wrote a bit more, read it all over, and, with a pleased smirk on her gaunt face, breathed, "It is ready." Her soulless eyes turned to a crudely made sundial on a flat bit of rock just outside the cave entrance. "And just in time, too." She scooped up the paper and added it to a stack of others that sat on a small wooden table near the wall.

Then, she began preparations for her visitor. She pulled her only chair and an upended log up to the table, procured two mugs from her meager supply of kitchen goods, and tended to the fire that was heating a kettle for tea before stationing herself at the entrance to her cave to wait for her guest.

While she waited, she didn't fuss with her hair or worry about her appearance because, for one thing, Mirabella didn't care one iota about the opinions of others. And, for another thing, she happened to be one of those ladies who always looked good without trying.

Though she'd spent half her life in a in a cave while being harassed by murderers and thugs of all description, Mirabella had unnaturally good skin and long, wavy black hair unsullied by gray. Her face was a bit lined from all her brow-furrowing and squinting through late-night plotting sessions by the light of a single thin-flamed candle, her ratty old clothes were rather filthy, and she was concerningly thin since she'd never really gotten the knack of hunting even after two decades of banishment, but all in all, it could safely be said that she looked a lot better than one would expect, considering her circumstances.

If only she hadn't had those soulless eyes…

But, then, if she'd had a soul, she wouldn't have been banished to a cave in the middle of The Forest of Looming Death, and there'd be no need to be carrying on about how she looked pretty good all things considered.

At last, a great horrible swirl of smelly smoke appeared out of nowhere, startling a few chubby doves Mirabella had been eyeing hungrily, but not affecting Mirabella in the least. This was the visitor she had been expecting and his smoky mode of travel was nothing new. Her eyes still following the doves, Mirabella waved some smoke away from her face and turned her gaze from the doves to her visitor.

The great evil magician, Farland Phelps, strode from the depths of the smoke, too cool to cough. Mirabella had often wondered how long it had taken him to perfect that, the not coughing as he walked out of his big magic smoke column thing. Did he just hold his breath? Did the smoke seriously not bother him?

"Mirabella," he said in his sleazy voice.

"Farland," she responded, dryly. "The plans are complete."

"Excellent," he sleazed and followed her into the cave.

Mirabella the Traitor held out the stack of papers to her partner-in-crime.

He took them and began to read, cackling evilly at the contents. He laughed harder with each page, until he'd flipped too many pages for that to be sustainable, and then the laughs remained at the same intensity for the rest of the stack.

It was really a pretty big stack of paper.

So much evil cackling.

Again, Mirabella suspected Farland of pretension and guessed that those demonic chortles were, perhaps, rehearsed. It took him so long to peruse the papers that she had time to make a mug of tea for each of them, which she set down on the table just as he finished up.

"Well?" she asked.

"It's perfect. Perfect. These plans are all I could have dreamed of. And," he added, impressed, "the paper is quite pretty, too."

"Oh, thank you. Be careful not to touch the red flowers. They're poisonous. A little safety measure to keep the information between us alone."

Gingerly, he readjusted his hold on the papers. "Very clever."

"Tea?" she asked, gesturing to the table.

"Oh, lovely!"

They sat across from each other and sipped in silence for a few moments. Mirabella was thinking about her garden and wondering how the asparagus crop was faring. Farland was thinking about Mirabella. The closer they got to the completion of their revenge plot, the more acutely aware he was becoming of the fact that, over the span of these twenty years of plotting and planning, something had happened to him. He had fallen in love.

Or something like love, anyway.

Mirabella was smart, and pretty, and funny (if you liked mean-spirited sarcasm, which he did). He had not analyzed his feelings too much since paying too much attention to feelings is a sign of weakness, so he wasn't sure whether it was love exactly. But he knew for sure that he really liked being around her, that he would soon no longer have a reason to be around her, and that that knowledge made him gloomy. She had never expressed any interest in doing anything other than plotting revenge with him—no walks along the riverbank, no picnics, no anything—so he had a good feeling that, once their plans were completed, she'd be fine parting ways forever.

"Good tea," he said, wishing she were weak-minded so that he could read her thoughts. He could only effectively read the minds of people who were not very smart, and Mirabella was the exact opposite of not very smart.

"It's from my garden." *Ack. He was looking at her with that sappy expression she'd been noticing on his face more and more in recent months.*

"Ah." He paused. "Weather been good out here in The Forest?"

"Quite." *It had been a mistake to make tea and give him a reason to stay.* She sipped a small sip from her cup and stared witheringly at him over the rim.

"Because it's been raining like crazy in the capital."

"Mmm." Sip.

Farland shuffled about uncomfortably on his seat.

Mirabella tapped her fingers on the table and stared at the roof of the cave. *Stalactites.*

"Okay, well, I guess I'll be off then. Got get these plans moving," he said at last, looking toward the stack of poisoned papers.

"No time like the present," she agreed.

He set down his cup. "I'll come back in a week to keep you abreast of the developments." *Genius! He'd manufactured a reason to see her again soon!*

"No need," she responded, appraising him coolly.

"But won't you be curious to—"

"No."

"But—"

"I don't like you, Farland."

His face turned the same shade of red as the flowers in her paper. "I never said—"

"Your sappy eyes as good as said it."

He shot to his feet, embarrassed and angry. "I—I—"

"It's nothing personal, Farland. You know I don't have a soul. I can't *like* people." When she had been younger and hadn't known herself quite as well, she actually had considered him as a potential husband, but since her banishment, she'd had plenty of time to think it through and now knew that marriage (to him or anyone) was not for her, no matter how dreamy and smart the candidate might be.

"Yes, but I thought maybe, given time..."

She laughed. "Right. Look, you're a good-looking guy and I like the way you think, but I—"

He cut in sharply, unable to take the embarrassment of rejection a moment longer, and grabbed at the papers still on the table between them. "I'll be going now."

And he went.

Poof!

Mirabella gave a cry of frustration and made her way, coughing and bumping into things, out of the smoky cave. He could have at least had the decency to disappear *outside* the cave. Now it was going to take ages for the place to air out.

Chapter Two

At this point, you're probably wondering about the revenge thing, so let me give you some backstory. Come with me, back, back, back through the shades of time. Back just a bit further, to when Mirabella and her twin sister Lillian were wee toddlers. Lillian, chubby and sweet, and Mirabella, distant and (even at two years of age) gaunt, and with suspiciously empty eyes. Both girls were early talkers, Lillian's first word being "mama" and Mirabella's being "never". Sentences were soon to follow, and with language came proof of their parents' fears that something was not right with Mirabella. For with speech came nothing but insults, sassy comebacks, and unsettling observations—all things that cause parents worry.

Mirabella and Lillian's parents requested the assistance of the great wizard, Wendell, to see if he could find a glimmer of a soul in the empty-eyed little girl. When he had finished waving his wand, muttering under his breath, and sprinkling various sorts of shimmery powders, his results had proved inconclusive. However, considering that, in all her short life, Mirabella had never said a single kind word and caused nothing but heartache, calamity, and trouble wherever she went, the general public decided that for all practical purposes, Mirabella the Traitor was soulless.

Of course, at this point, she was not yet a traitor. That came about when she was nineteen. She and her sister lived with their parents on a small asparagus farm in the South of Fritillary. Their asparagus crops were known far and wide as being the most crisp, and the most pure. Even if you boiled them too long, they didn't go all mushy, which, if you've ever over-boiled asparagus, you'll have to agree is pretty neat. The reputation their asparagus enjoyed was a point of pride in a land where asparagus was as essential to the daily diet as grain products are today.

Also, asparagus tips, when dried and powdered, were essential elements in the highest forms of magic. So perfect were Mirabella's parents' asparaguses that the majority of their crop went straight to the Magical Commerce Division at the Capital, where it was numbered, cataloged, and distributed to wizards lucky enough to be able to afford such top-of-the-line goods.

The day that Mirabella earned her suffix "the Traitor" started out like any other day on the farm. Her twin sister, Lillian, awoke with the sunrise and hummed a contented tune as she prepared for the day, combing her long black hair until it shone, which didn't take much time because she was always brushing it. "Get up, Lazy Bones!" Lillian laughed with a musical trill that had been likened by many to the merry tinkling of fine crystal wind chimes. "How can you lay there abed while there is such beauty in the world waiting to be seen?"

She then flung open the window of their bedroom as if to prove her point. "Oh dear, dear sunshine, blessing us with your warmth!" she said as she spun around in its rays. "Lovely, lovely little robins serenading us with your sweet songs!" she added, spotting one representative of the species perched on a tree branch just outside their window.

It eyed her distrustfully and gave a small chirp.

"Mirabella, look! Look and hear! This little dear is singing us a song!" Lillian extended a gentle hand, crooning softly to it, her finger offered as a perch.

It flew off, alarmed.

No matter how kind you are, a wild animal is not going to sit on you.

Lillian gave a pout, then flounced to her wardrobe to find her apron.

Mirabella abandoned her pretense of sleep, opened her eyes long enough to give her sister a cold stare, then rolled over and contemplated the blank white wall, her back to the sunshine.

"Oh, Mirabella," Lillian sighed. "You silly dear. Well, if you don't care to see this beautiful morning, and if you don't want to go out and pick asparagus in the sweet sunshine, then it's all the more for me!" With that, she giggled and skipped out the door.

As the door swung closed behind Lillian, Mirabella rolled onto her back and regarded the ceiling as she eavesdropped on her sister's arrival in the next room. "Good morning, Mama! Good morning, Papa! No time for breakfast now. That asparagus won't pick itself!"

They all shared a good chuckle.

In a few more minutes Mirabella could hear, through the open window, Lillian singing as she went (probably skipping or dancing) over to the asparagus field. Mirabella shuddered and decided she might as well get out of bed. If she didn't, her mother would soon be knocking on the door, insisting that if her industrious sister was already up and picking asparagus then Mirabella should jolly well be doing the same.

She slowly got into her clothes for the day, but unlike her sister who wore her hair down, Mirabella braided hers tightly and wrapped it into a knot on top of her head, making her appear even more severe than she naturally did. Stalking out into the main living area that was combination kitchen, dining room, and family room, she gave a slight nod in response to her parents' greetings and went straight out the front door without touching the breakfast her mother had set out for her like she did every morning—no matter how often her daughter ignored it. Closing the door behind her, Mirabella picked up her asparagus basket from its place on the porch, then walked out to the field and started picking in a row far enough away from her sister that they wouldn't be able to speak.

The morning progressed uneventfully for two hours or so, Lillian and Mirabella harvesting asparagus while their parents took the wagon to the market. Mirabella worked mechanically, never once pausing to look up and admire the beautiful countryside that stretched out below their hillside farm or to appreciate the majestic mountain range looming behind them. Lillian, on the other hand, often took little breaks to enjoy the scenery and breathe the crisp air. In spite of all her shillyshallying, Lillian still somehow always managed to pick more asparagus than Mirabella. It was a great source of frustration for Mirabella that Lillian so constantly outshone her at every task, since the fact so often meant unwelcome comparisons from their parents and neighbors. *Why couldn't people just leave her alone?*

Eventually, Mirabella stood up to stretch her back and saw a regal procession making its stately way down the dirt road that led to the farm. Shielding her eyes from the glare of the sun, she detected tan banners with puce dragons embroidered on them. She smiled a creepy smile (the only kind of smile she had). It was the Prince, coming to visit her sister. And that meant...

She searched the procession again now that they were close enough that she could make out the faces of the individuals in the party, and sure enough, at the prince's right side was his personal wizard, Farland Phelps. Farland was, as usual, the very picture of dark and mysterious, with his black cape and his black hood casting a shadow over his face. At this point in our tale, Mirabella was still young and didn't yet know herself too well, and Farland hadn't yet lived long enough to get too pretentious. Mirabella already knew her dark heart was incapable of love, but if it had been, she would have pledged it to Farland Phelps. He was the second-greatest wizard in the whole Land of Fritillary (the first being, of course, Wendell), and he was intelligent, and—as was the talk of all the royal court—available.

All around, Farland Phelps was a prime slice of fella if you were a young lady of the court who was not quite so delusional as to hope to sink your talons into the prince himself, but still delusional enough to think you could sink one of his most powerful underlings.

Still, all these fine qualities of Farland's aside, the true reason Mirabella would have loved Farland if she could was that he was pure evil, and, if she was ever to pledge her affection to a man, he had to be evil. It was Number One on her list. A young lady should have a pre-set list of priorities when man-hunting so she can refer to it when her head gets clouded. Man-hunting is a most dangerous game, after all. (You're welcome for that advice, girls.)

Yes, Farland was pure evil. Even as he pretended to be the Prince's best friend, Farland was secretly planning to murder the whole royal family, saving the Prince for last. Farland didn't even want to take over as the king when the dust settled; he just wanted the Prince to suffer, consequences to the kingdom be darned!

The seed of his foul plan had been sown when he and the Prince had been mere lads—it had been some youthful dispute on the croquet field, something to do with the Prince picking the gardener's son, Walter, for his team instead of picking Farland. Over the years the initial reason faded until it no longer mattered, morphing from revenge for the Croquet Episode to various different revenges for all kinds of accumulated little wrongs both real and imagined. Then, eventually, when Farland was in his young twenties and fancied himself a revolutionary, his revenge became the takedown of the entire monarchy (because monarchy just wasn't the wave of the future, man[1]).

Mirabella knew his plans, and she was helping to make his dream come true. How did she know, you ask? Well, let me tell you. The reason she knew that he was evil when the rest of the kingdom thought he was a pretty awesome guy was because he needed her help: if Farland wanted to murder the entire Royal Family he needed a vast quantity of powdered asparagus tips. He couldn't just *buy* it, because the sale and purchase of asparagus powder was closely monitored by the Magical Commerce Division. He needed an accomplice on the inside of Big Asparagus—an accomplice who knew the best asparagus and could make the powder for him. An accomplice who, also, happened to be evil.

In his Evil Lair, Farland had gazed into his magical pool of raven blood and asked it to reveal to him the person who would assist in his evil plan. The magical pool of raven blood was quite temperamental and rarely condescended to divulge any information to Farland, so he was quite

---

1   Don't go thinking Farland some misguided progressive guy with the idea that the ends sometimes have to justify the means on the road to a greater society, because (1) his fancies ran more toward anarchy than democracy, and more important (2) killing people is pretty much never the best solution to a problem unless we're talking tyrannical monarch or poison-happy tower witch or some such. But in this case, we are not. While the Royal Family was quite self-absorbed and entitled, one must admit that those qualities seem to go with the profession—there is almost no getting around the fact that royalty thinks more highly of themselves than they probably should. The meaner members of this particular royal family could be rather oppressive to their subjects and had unreasonable taxes and laws, but no more so (and often less so) than their cohorts in neighboring kingdoms. Even the dungeon they spirited the particularly unruly citizens off to was smaller than most and stocked with fewer sadistic employees than might be expected. So, yes, the Royal Family of the Land of Fritillary was sort of bad, but not bad enough to justify all this hoopla on Farland's part.

surprised and pleased when, as he stared into its deep red depths, he saw a vision of Mirabella shimmer into sight. Then the magical bowl of raven blood had heartily warned him against confusing Mirabella with her twin sister who was the essence of all things good and not even a little bit evil.

And that's how the wizard Farland Phelps found, and then secured the help of, Mirabella. On his very first visit to the farm, Prince Conroy came along on a whim in order to do some mingling with the commoners—his PR guy had been hounding him about rubbing elbows with the peasants lately, saying mingling was a good way to keep public opinion high without having to actually mess with things like taxes or employment or whatever else goes into making a populace happy through competent governance. Conroy had no clue, really, since he'd zoned out when his private tutor had gotten into all that stuff. Boring! Anyway, Conroy came along with Farland, and there Conroy met Lillian, and *bam*! Love at first sight. Said love was deeply reciprocated, so the Prince kept visiting, handily supplying Farland with an excuse to continue coming to the farm to collect powdered asparagus tips from Mirabella. It all worked out quite nicely, actually.

*A*S MIRABELLA WATCHED the procession draw nearer, she became acutely aware of her sister beside her, hopping giddily from foot to foot and clapping her hands. "Oh, Mirabella! It's Prince Conroy!" Lillian squealed. "Oh, but Mama and Papa aren't at home! I cannot see him without a chaperone!"

"What are you blithering about?" Mirabella spat in her cold voice of venom, never taking her eyes off the handsome face of Farland Phelps.

"People would talk if word got around that Prince Conroy and I conversed without appropriate parental supervision!"

Mirabella doubted this. If that is what counted as gossip these days, then life in the royal court was dull indeed, but she didn't bother wasting her breath trying to convince her sister of this. For one thing, there was no point telling Lillian to do anything if she had already deemed it improper. And for another thing, Lillian was already making a beeline toward the house, probably with the intention of barricading herself inside.

Mirabella strolled to the stables and waited for the procession. The

Prince and the wizard were the first to reach her. They dismounted, and two pages who had been scampering along behind them scurried up to tend to their horses, who, in the presence of Mirabella, pawed nervously at the ground as if being circled by a predator.

Farland retreated to the shadows where he paced back and forth looking mighty out of place by a big bale of hay, waiting for the opportunity to speak with Mirabella.

Prince Conroy strode toward her with confident, royal strides, head of shiny hair held high, broad shoulders thrown back, hand on the hilt of his fancy sword. His hair and twinkling sky-blue eyes made Mirabella squint, even in the shade of the stable. His black boots shone, and his purple cape fluttered in the almost-nonexistent breeze. A cookie cutter prince if ever there was one, but no less impressive for the fact.

Grudgingly, Mirabella gave a shallow curtsy as the Prince halted before her. "Mirabella. Good morning," he said in a deep, smooth, manly baritone that was every bit as princely as the rest of him. "A lovely day."

She shrugged. "Eh."

The Prince raised a royal eyebrow. "Is your sister home?" he inquired, choosing (wisely) to switch from small talk to the real reason for his visit. As much as he tried for Lillian's sake to get along with Mirabella, he had to confess it was no cakewalk. He could find no common ground with her, and it wasn't as if he hadn't tried. Also, he just couldn't bring himself to look into those empty eyes of hers without shivering—eyes like those he had only ever seen on dead people. So it was, to say the least, disconcerting to see them in her head when she was quite obviously living.

"Yes, she's home. Locked herself in the house and will not see you," Mirabella said, trying all the while to snare his gaze. It amused her to watch him try to avoid her eyes. Most—possibly all—people she encountered were repelled by her gaze, but for all his manliness the Prince had an especially tough time of it. The big tough military captain couldn't even meet her gaze without quaking in his shiny boots? She sneered.

"Ah, your parents are out then?" he asked the space over her left shoulder.

She nodded slightly. "You must have passed right by them on the way here."

Conroy thought back and remembered that, not far from the turnoff to the farm, he had seen a wagon with two elderly people who were assessing some damage to a broken wheel—the wheel had sustained damage after being driven off the road and into the ditch by his procession. The moment they'd seen him, the couple had fallen to ground, groveling in the dirt like the peasants they were. Well, not dirt. Mud. He had smirked at them as he'd passed, thrown a few coins their way, and not bothered to stop to try to make out the words they'd been speaking into the mud (they were surely too afraid to look up at his Royal Glory to speak in his direction).

Now he wondered if those groveling peasants had been his future in-laws, and if they had been trying to tell him that Lillian and her sister were alone on the farm, and perhaps wondering whether they should abandon their cart and head back home. "Your sister is quite a proper young maiden," he said, his eyes glittering with love…or something. *Twinkle, twinkle.*

Mirabella winced.

"Indeed," she said and pushed at the dirt with the toe of her shoe. Her game had grown old. *Small talk, small talk, small talk. When would she get the chance to give Farland the latest pouch of powdered asparagus tips she had prepared?*

"Perhaps I'll take a walk through your garden and wait for your parents to return," the Prince said lamely, growing irritated with conversation with the soulless girl. *Small talk, small talk, small talk. Surely he had spoken with her long enough to come across as sociable should Lillian be watching through a window.* Yes, he was through, but it would be rude to leave Mirabella with no one to talk to, so he signaled to his friend, Farland. He was a wizard, after all, and thus probably knew about sticky issues like talking to soulless people with fathomless eyes.

As Farland glided toward Mirabella, arms folded and eyes glinting under the hood of his dark cape, Prince Conroy went off to pick some flowers for his love.

FARLAND'S BLACK EYES met Mirabella's empty ones, and they both grinned horrifying sorts of grins devoid of anything remotely related to normal smile-inducing things. Mirabella reached into the pocket of her gingham apron and drew out a small pouch, and then, with a cautious glance around, handed it to him, all overly-sneaky and covert. He would only need a bit more powder now. The batch of asparagus she currently had hanging to dry under her bed would be the last of it.

He took the pouch, inclined his head in the direction of the house, and began to move toward it, obviously wanting to speak to her out of earshot of the knights and pages and such who were milling about here and there waiting for the Prince's date to be over so they could go back home. Farland reached the porch and sat in one of the two matching rocking chairs, looking, again, amazingly out of place. He then proceeded to enhance the effect by actually rocking the rocking chair.

Mirabella joined him on the porch but wouldn't sully her creepy image by occupying the other chair. "My sister is in the house," she muttered. "We can't talk here."

"Nonsense," he muttered back. "This is the only shady spot on your whole cursed farm except the stables. You *see* this cape I'm wearing? I'm not going back out in that sun until I have to. Besides, listen." He cocked his head in the direction of the house. Mirabella crept to the door and listened. At the opposite side of the house, Mirabella could hear Lillian and the prince talking—they must be conversing through the (probably closed) window on the opposite side of the room.

"They won't be leaving that spot any time soon," Farland scoffed, as though Conroy and Lillian were hopelessly pathetic for being in love.

Satisfied they would not be overheard, Mirabella said, "One more pouch of powder should be more than enough."

"Excellent," Farland breathed. "Excellent. Just a week or two more and my revenge against Prince Conroy will be complete."

As Mirabella and Farland talked murder without, Lillian and Prince Conroy talked love within. Though really Lillian was the only one within. The Prince was, indeed, standing on the outer side of the shuttered and locked window, his ear pressed to the rough wood the better to make out the sweet voice of his most darling, adored dream. At that moment, he was exercising every ounce of his considerable princely charm, trying to coax her into opening the window just a crack so he could catch a glimpse of her dear, dear face.

"Of course not!" she gasped, scandalized.

"Please, my dear Lillian," he pleaded, having at this point abandoned eloquent reasoning and lapsed into whining. "Please, won't you open the window? Just a tad?"

"No!" she reiterated, then, feeling quite flustered, took flight across the room to distance herself from the temptation that was beginning to stir within her, battling with her desire to maintain her spotless maidenly honor. She would not give in and that was that! No princely wiles and snares would tempt her! Why buy the cow when you could catch an unchaperoned glimpse of it through a window? Or whatever the saying was.

Over the thudding of her goody-goody heart, Lillian heard her sister's voice through the front door she was now standing by. Then, she heard Farland answer. Farland was her dear Prince's best friend and had been ever since they were kids. Was there some romance blooming between Farland and her sister? Why, that would be perfect! Lillian fought a hard inner battle against eavesdropping, and the side that deemed eavesdropping wrong won out, so she was about to retreat to yet another part of the room when she heard something that nearly stopped her heart.

"—my revenge against Prince Conroy will be complete," the wizard said. Like lightning, Lillian darted to the door and listened intently.

"You have no idea," Mirabella responded, "how... happy... it makes me to be the one to supply you with the powdered asparagus tips that will kill the Royal Family. I'll be especially happy to know Conroy is dead. Those twinkling eyes are enough to make me scream, and that's even without having to listen to his inane babbling."

Lillian gasped and fluttered on wobbly legs back to the window where Conroy was still pleading. She might even have opened the kitchen window (such was the gravity of the situation), but her shaking fingers didn't allow it. One listen showed her the prince hadn't even noticed her absence. "—please, it would make my day! No, my week! No, my—-"

"Prince Conroy!" she broke in.

"Yes, my only?"

"Sneak quietly around the front of the house and see if you can hear what the wizard and my sister are talking about. Be cautious! For I fear they are plotting against you!"

OVERHEAR THEIR CONVERSATION Conroy did, and the long and short of what he learned from it can be summed up in one handy list:

(1) Mirabella and Farland meant to kill Conroy and his nearest and dearest

(2) Farland was *not* his best friend in all the world

(3) Lillian had saved his life and the lives of the rest of his family, cementing more than ever in his mind the fact that this was the lady he wanted to spend the rest of his life with

(4) Mirabella was a traitor and must be banished to the Forest of Looming Death

(5) He would have to return the friendship ring he had received from Farland in their youth

FARLAND AND MIRABELLA stood before Prince Conroy as he paced to and fro, agitated, confused, and, yes, a little broken-hearted for friendship dead and gone. Mirabella's hands were tied behind her back and she was held in place by a burly soldier about four times her size. Farland was unshackled, but only because it would have been pointless to try, he being a wizard and all. The only reason Farland was still there was because he chose to be, and everyone knew it.

Prince Conroy halted before the prisoners and said, "I never would have believed it if I hadn't heard it with my own two ears. Especially you, Farland!" His voice rang out with anger and disillusionment. "You were my best friend! Remember when we became blood brothers?" he added, hoping at least to elicit a tiny bit of guilt from Farland.

The wizard smiled a reminiscent smile as he thought back to the day he had talked the Prince into becoming his "blood brother[2]".

"Blood brothers? I only did that so I could have easy access to your blood when I needed to cast a spell against you!" he explained. He saw

---

2   A practice that, in case you are not familiar with it since you have been raised in a modern age with heightened awareness of diseases and cleanliness, involves both parties cutting themselves and then holding the cuts together, the idea being that one party would then have the other's blood flowing through their veins and vice versa)(never do that, by the way—it is disgusting).

Mirabella raise an impressed eyebrow at him and he felt a glow of pride at his cleverness.

Prince Conroy's jaw actually dropped as this was revealed. "Really?"

"Of course!" laughed Farland. He found, now that he'd been discovered, he wanted to get everything out in the open. He was disappointed that his lovely plans had been foiled in the eleventh hour by that irritating little harpy Lillian, and he wanted the Prince to know a thing or two before he (Farland) disappeared in a column of smoke. "As if a wizard of my caliber could pass up the chance to have your blood in my veins and thus hold power over you and your offspring for the rest of my life!"

"I—I—" the Prince stuttered, still in a state of surprise. "You can *do* that?"

Farland nodded.

"But—we were *seven years old* when we became blood brothers!" he spluttered. "Were we *ever* friends?"

A noncommittal shrug and an "Eh," were the only answer he received.

Prince Conroy looked at his ex-or-never-really-friend searchingly, then sighed, and said, "Enough of this. Down to business." He nodded his head sharply as if in response to some inner pep talk, then continued in a much more commanding tone, "Mirabella, traitor, as of today you are banished to the Forest of Looming Death. Set foot beyond its shades again and you shall be put to death!"

She blinked. Nothing more. No reaction in those empty eyes.

"And you!" Conroy went on, turning to Farland as he tried, unsuccessfully, to tug the ring that the wizard had given him—the one on which was engraved *Friends 4 Ever*—from his princely finger, "You!"

The ring didn't budge.

Farland sniggered as he watched the Prince struggle with the ring. He laughed aloud. "You dolt. Friendship ring, my eye! That ring is cursed and will never leave your finger!"

"Cursed? Cursed...how?" asked poor Conroy. What a horrible twist of fate! His best friend in the world was turning out to be maybe his biggest enemy. He had access to Conroy's blood whenever he needed it for a spell, and now there was a cursed ring too? Talk about overkill.

"Cursed how, you ask? Well—" and here Farland would have polished his nails nonchalantly on his cloak and surveyed them as he leaned casually up against something, if he weren't standing in the middle of a field—"Let me tell you. I was feeling rather creative the day I dreamed it up." He gave Mirabella a sidelong look; he knew she'd enjoy this this. He looked back to Conroy. "I'm sure you'd appreciate the cleverness if it weren't your life being mucked up. Yes, I was feeling creative that day—and vindictive. A nice combination of fuel to get the wheels of revenge turning in the engine of—" *The engine of what?* He mentally berated himself for attempting to use a metaphor he hadn't rehearsed ahead of time. "Whatever. Here's the curse: as long as you wear that ring, your firstborn child will never be able to let sunlight touch their skin. Not a single ray of sunshine. If your first child so much as walks past a curtain that isn't entirely drawn, death shall be the grand and immediate result." Farland studied the prince's reaction, frankly a bit disappointed the royal visage was not a mask of horror.

Conroy was by no means happy, but he had been bracing himself for worse. Farland hadn't taken into account the fact that, to most men, their children only become real to them on a true emotional level when they are actually holding them in their arms for the first time.

"It may not seem like a big deal now," Farland pointed out, "since you're not even married and the prospect of offspring is a bit down the road, but I assure you that once your child is born you will wish you'd never crossed me! You'll have to remodel the whole castle to accommodate the child. And no riding, no hunting, not even taking a walk! Family trips will be a logistical nightmare!"

Conroy mulled it over, and the more he thought the worse it did seem. But then something occurred to him and he brightened. "This only applies if the ring is on my finger?"

"Yes, but the ring will never leave your finger. It's stuck on. With *magic*."

Prince Conroy pulled a dagger out of his boot with a fancy flourish and held it, not to the wizard's throat as the slack jawed onlookers had expected, but to his own ringed finger. "And if I cut off my finger?"

"You will die."

"Oh..." Conroy's hands fell to his sides. Defeated, but not defingered. "Drat..."

Farland looked at Mirabella and raised his eyebrows with a look that clearly said, "Impressive, huh?"

She chuckled a soulless chuckle and nodded her approval.

Farland enjoyed a cozy glow of pride. Even if the murder wasn't panning out, this was a nice consolation prize: a bit of recognition from the lady he fancied.

"How do I know you're telling the truth?" Conroy asked, his voice affected a pleading tone. He was looking now at the house where his future wife was peeking out into the yard through a gap in the shutters. He met her one visible eye and saw there a horrified look that showed she had heard all. This was *her* future child they were discussing, too.

"There's no way of proving my curse short of testing it," Farland said dryly. "Cut off your finger, see if you live. Or, open a window during the day when you are in a room with your child." He grinned. "Then you'll know whether there's a curse. Maybe that ring is just stuck on your finger because you've put on weight living in the lap of luxury."

"I have not put on—" Conroy started defensively, but then snapped his mouth shut, not wanting to sound petty when Lillian was listening. "Is there anything that can break the curse?" he asked. "There's always *something* that can be done to break a curse[3]."

Reluctantly, Farland admitted this. "It is true that part of the procedure of concocting a curse requires the creation of a counter-curse. The key to success, however, is to make it really, really hard. Something so outrageous that it is almost impossible. *Almost* being the key word there, my friend. For if it were utterly impossible it wouldn't—"

"I get it. Go on, already," growled Conroy.

Farland blinked once in annoyance. "In order to break the curse, your child must fall in love with a person who has spent their whole life at sea, whose parents were once part of a traveling theater troupe, who can play banjo and accordion and harpsichord, and who is allergic to asparagus."

"Surely no such person can exist!" cried Conroy.

---

3   This is, indeed, true. For every evil curse that is created, there has to be an opposite and equal good that can cancel it out. A scientist said so and everything, sort of. The problem is that the creator of the curse is the one who also gets to choose the counter-curse, and so the odds of finding the good tends to be rather bleak.

"But it will be amusing to watch you search for this individual, because search you will. No matter how impossible you think the task. After all, the world is large, my *friend*—there was a sour tone on this word—"and full of people with all sorts of backgrounds, interests, and allergies. It is not *impossible* for such a person to exist, only *improbable*. But rest assured, if I ever do catch wind of someone who fits the description, I will kill them. That won't negate the curse, either, because there could always be another individual who fits the bill somewhere out there on the high seas."

Prince Conroy's shoulders sagged. What had he done to deserve this?

"You've annoyed me ever since we first met," Farland answered instantly. "All the annoyances over the years just started stacking up."

"You can read minds?" Conroy exclaimed, thinking frantically back to what must have been thousands of things he'd thought in the presence of the wizard that were better left unshared. If he could read minds then, Conroy had to admit, Farland really did have reason to think ill of him. Conroy tried to come off as a good guy, but there was a lot of stuff that went on in the ol' gray matter that was not so pretty. Also, some of the things Farland had doubtless found out by reading his mind were of a very personal nature. Conroy turned an un-princely shade of red.

Farland smiled, looking off into the distance in a reminiscent sort of way without bothering to answer.

"If you weren't a wizard who could vanish in a puff of smoke whenever you chose, I'd have you banished, too! No, I'd have you executed!" Conroy cried, totally losing his cool.

Farland laughed a final evil laugh, gave Mirabella a courteous nod, and disappeared in a puff of smoke. All assembled coughed, stumbled about, and staggered out of the smoke to get some fresh air.

The Prince, who had anticipated Farland's smoky exit with enough time to take a deep breath, recovered quickly. When he next whirled in a fit of regal rage on Mirabella, she was still coughing, and he enjoyed the feeling (rare when talking to her) that he was the one in control of the conversation. "You, traitor, have five minutes to collect your belongings and say your goodbyes. Then you will be escorted to The Forest of Looming Death where you will live the rest of your blighted days in darkness and solitude. Solitude except for the other banished criminals, anyway," he said vindictively, "but they're mostly murderers, so I can't imagine they make the best company."

He then turned his back on her coughing form, hoping never to set eyes on her again, and strode over to the house, hoping Lillian hadn't taken this whole affair too badly. One look into the eye he could see through the gap in the shutters showed she had been crying.

"Dearest!" cried he. "Poor thing, I have deprived you of your only sister! But surely—"

"Oh, I'm not crying about that!" Lillian blubbered. "I'm crying because…how *could* she! How could she…conspire to kill the man I love?" At this last, she gasped and covered her mouth (not that he could see that).

Conroy staggered backward a few paces.

"You—you—love me?" he stammered, all his troubles momentarily forgotten. "Oh, Lillian! Such joy! Such happiness! You have transformed this day from—" he thought "—from the worst day of my life to the best!" Not as flowery of language as he would have liked, but this situation had snuck up on him. Had he known words of love were going to be exchanged, he would have had the court poet whip up a little something for him, but as it was, he had to wing it on his own, which was not his forte.

What Conroy could see of Lillian's tearstained face broke into a grin of delight. "Conroy! Oh, Conroy!"

"Oh, Lillian!"

She opened the shutters a bit more, enough to stretch her hand through. He took her hand in both of his and gave it a gentle squeeze as he smiled at her, forgetting the guards and knights and pages and Mirabella fidgeting around behind him. "Lillian, will you tell your father to come to the castle tonight? I have something particular to tell him." He wiggled his eyebrows significantly.

Mirabella cut in from behind, "That you wish to apologize for banishing one daughter without giving him a chance to say goodbye, and on the same day taking his other daughter away to marry, thus leaving him and his wife on this farm in their declining years to tend the asparagus on their own?" Though in truth, she didn't mind at all that she'd never again see the parents who had cared for her all these years against the constant advice of friends and family to ship her off to an asylum.

A guard shook her roughly by the shoulder and whispered, "Quiet!" He was staring with rapt attention at Conroy and Lillian, a single sentimental tear trembling on his lashes.

Lillian didn't even spare her sister a glance. Mirabella would not ruin her happy moment with mention of the reality of the hardship their parents were now facing. Besides, Conroy would surely provide for them if this conversation were really going the direction it seemed to be. (He wouldn't really provide for them). "Of course I'll tell him, my only!"

Jubilation, cheers, happiness from all assembled (except, of course, for Mirabella).

With one last look that spoke volumes, the Prince turned and instructed two of his most trusted knights to see to Mirabella's banishment, and then he mounted his steed and trotted back home to the castle with the rest of his retinue trailing in his wake. He was happy as a clam, which I guess is pretty happy if we are to put our trust in the people who make up such expressions, though what a lonely little bottom-feeder scraping along the ocean floor eating fish excrement and decomposed plants and animals has to be all that thrilled about is beyond me.

CHAPTER THREE

The great castle where dwelled the Royal Family of the Land of Fritillary was the finest castle around. Top notch. Grade A. It was by far the largest and the most aesthetically pleasing, situated on a lush hilltop overlooking the coast of the ocean with nearby a preponderance of waterfalls and many a cave, inlet, and hollow.

The castle itself was beautiful beyond description, but let's give it a try, shall we? Wherever there was a place that would benefit from a nice pillar or a bit of carving, there was a nice pillar or a bit of carving. Wherever there was fabric (curtains, banners, upholstery, and so on) it was of the finest possible quality. Wherever there were doors, they were made of the best wood available, and their hinges never squeaked. The furniture was the grandest, the floors and ceilings tiled the most intricately, the ironwork the most curved and twisted, the nooks and crannies the most cozy, the gargoyles the most fierce, and the cherubs the most sweetly angelic.

But—

Come with me, dear reader, down a dark hidden hallway, through a dark hidden doorway, to a dark hidden staircase. Let us pause, summon our courage, and walk down, down, down.

To the dungeon!

Many a poor soul has disappeared in these depths, never to reappear again. The stone steps extend for an eternity and the torches are few, far between, and rarely lit. At the bottom of the dark and uneven steps, we find ourselves in a high-ceilinged chamber festooned with all manner of unpleasant-looking gizmos and machines whose purpose is plainly to inflict pain on the unhappy lodgers of the dungeon. Only two of the ten visible devices are in use at the time our story reaches this dreadful chamber, which says something for the head jailer and his boss the King, I suppose. Not much, but something.

Four dark passages lead off the main chamber, one north, one south, one west, and one east. Between the passages barred cells line the chamber walls.

The head jailer, Jim, was shuffling through some papers at his desk by the stairs, mumbling about the bother of paperwork and opining that they should get some dame down there to do the filing, thus freeing him up for more Man Work. But no, he'd put in a request to his boss for a secretary and he'd turned Jim down flat, saying the dungeon was no place for a woman, they being so delicate and prone to fits and things of that nature. Plus, they just get married and pregnant and quit, and you have to hire another one and start the whole darn process all over again. *Women! Bah!* Yes, Jim supposed it really was best if they stayed home and cooked and had babies and didn't get uppity ideas about employment and financial independence. So, when his boss had refused his request for a secretary, he had been annoyed but unsurprised.

Glancing up from some new admittance forms at the scene of blood and groaning before him, Jim had to concede that there might be some logic to the refusal. Dames didn't study the Secretarial Arts with this sort of workplace in mind. He allowed himself a moment of fun and spun around a few times in his swivel chair, then looked back down at his work, but the final sheet on the stack of long-postponed drudgery would have to wait, because just then something odd happened.

He cocked his head to one side, for he had heard something strange: footsteps coming down the stairs. Of course, footsteps are not, in general, strange, but these were. They sounded... female. *Those feet were wearing not boots but shoes that sounded as though they didn't even have hard soles. Slippers? And was that the swish of fabric against the wall? A gown?*

30

Closer and closer the newcomer came, and, after a few moments, voices could be heard. *Two women?* The visitors rounded the bend, and Jim found himself staring straight at the Queen. Despite the general spirit of shock that swept around the room like a cyclone, Jim and everyone else had the presence of mind to fall into the customary groveling bow. That is, everyone who wasn't affixed to a device that prevented it.

Oblivious of her prostrate subjects below, Queen Lillian was talking energetically to her maid, Eugenia, who was as always trailing a few steps behind her. Jim heard the last bit of what she was saying: "—never even knew there was a dungeon in the palace! Imagine my surprise! But I simply *had* to come down here and see it for myself, because I think it would be just the perfect place!" Here she took another step as her eyes scanned the room, seeing but not seeing. "Deep underground, no windows, quite sizeable. All we'd need is a good interior decorator…"

Her voice trailed off. Her gaze had fallen on a prisoner chained to the wall. A full minute of incoherent stuttering and stammering ensured, then she gasped, "Who is in charge here?"

"I am, Your Majesty," Jim said, still bowing.

She glanced at him and waved her hand distractedly. "Oh, do stand up." Her eyes drifted back to the room and she stared, momentarily waking from a lovely dream of a charmed life married to her handsome king to the nightmare of what truly went on behind the scenes of her fairytale castle she called home. "Does the King know about this place?" she asked in a low whisper. It was a silly question, but even now she was still inclined to believe the very best of her husband.

Before Jim could answer in the affirmative, Lillian gave a trill little laugh and continued, "No, he couldn't possibly," and of course Jim wasn't about to contradict the Queen.

But the truth was Conroy knew very well about the dungeon. As his father and his advisors had taught him, the dungeon was a key component in their formula for running a manageable kingdom. Scoop up just enough citizens for committing petty crimes or speaking ill of the King and imprison them for unreasonable amounts of time (or never release them at all) and you can bet your bottom dollar that gossip will spread like wildfire that you are not a ruler to cross. After centuries of trial and error

Conroy's kingly ancestors had worked the process out to a science. Take too many commoners at a time and you run the risk of the populace banding together and having riots. Take too few and no one really notices, but take just the right amount and the dungeon becomes a mysterious, fearful place whispered about before the fireplace on cold nights—a place that is possibly a rumor, maybe true, but certainly terrifying.

Yes, the key to keeping a populace under control was just the right amount of fear that they might be carted off for some minor offence and locked away forever. Once every few years, when his spies said that talk of the dungeon was dying down, the King would have a prisoner released—one who'd been driven crazy and thus couldn't give too many specifics—and rumors would begin to fly anew.

When Lillian herself had been a lowly peasant on the asparagus farm, she had never heard the gossip since she tended to block out all things unpleasant. But her parents had talked fairly often about a cousin's friend's uncle who had disappeared shortly after refusing to pay his taxes.

However, now that Lillian was standing in the very dungeon itself not even she could pretend it didn't exist.

In shaking slippers, she descended the rest of the stairs. She took one deep breath. Two deep breaths. Three. She was, as you'll have noticed, not that bright, but she was remarkably kind and good, and could be quite brave when confronted with something that went against her sense of what was right. "What is all this?" she squeaked.

"This is the dungeon, Your Majesty," Jim waved his arm about vaguely, since to him it seemed the answer was so obvious that the question was utterly unnecessary. What had she expected when she'd come down here? *Dames, who could figure them out?* "These are the prisoners," he added helpfully, pointing around to a few men, most of them looking just as confused as he was by their fancy visitor, but nodding or waving a hand as Jim pointed them out.

"What are their crimes?" she asked. "Surely, they must be murderers, or..." her sheltered existence failed her; she could think of no other really horrible crimes, the kinds that might come close to justifying the dungeon. Again, she asked, "What are their crimes?"

"Oh, this and that..." Jim shrugged, while at the same time feeling he should have a better answer available for the boss's wife. Yet another reason he should be more up on the paperwork.

She looked at him, appalled, and then transferred her gaze to the scrawny fellow hanging by his wrists from the wall. "Why are you here?"

He looked downright scared to be addressed personally by the Queen, but after a glance at Jim (who nodded that he should respond) he said, "I stole a loaf of bread."

She gasped.

"For my children." Really, he had no children, but he *did* have the good sense to milk this situation for all it was worth.

Her hand flew to her mouth and she swayed just a little on her slippered feet.

"Who have no mother." Of course they had no mother. They didn't exist.

"The poor darlings! And their father imprisoned for trying to feed them! How long have they been alone? How long have you been down here?"

"Six months. Little Gretel's birthday was two weeks ago," he added piteously.

Lillian held back a sob and looked around the chamber again through tear-filled eyes. She almost asked the prisoner on the rack what his crime had been but bit her question back before it left her mouth, sure she couldn't bear another story as painful as the last. (The prisoner on the rack actually *was* a murderer. If she'd known that she might not have done what she did next, but who knows?)

"This is ghastly. Ghastly!" She paused and rifled through her brain for something she'd learned from her royalty tutor during her betrothal period. She'd only been married three months, so the info was all still fresh enough in her head for her to say with some authority, "By my authority as the Queen of the Land of Fritillary, I pronounce these men free—to be released this very day!"

You could have heard a pin drop.

Especially one of the big creepy pins they used down there in the dungeon.

"Can she do that?" asked the murderer on the rack, whose thoughts flew to the man who'd turned him in and the revenge he might at last be able to dole out.

"Yeah, can she?" asked the guy chained to the wall, whose thoughts flew to his kids, who were, as previously discussed, not real, but could be some day if he was released! If he could just get out of there, he'd make some real changes in his life! Renounce his lazy ways, find himself a nice girl (one who'd make his mama proud for a change!)! He'd marry that nice girl and they'd have nice babies who he'd provide with the best of everything! Little Gretel's lavish dowry would land her a nice young man and then he (the prisoner) would have a brood of nice grandkids who he'd bounce on his knee on summer afternoons, regaling them with endearingly exaggerated tales of his ruffian past and subsequent reformation due to the kindness of the Queen herself. His dear wife would stand arm in arm with Gretel and they'd gaze with fond smiles at him as, in the background, his son-in-law would chop wood for the fire that would cook their nutritious and substantial dinner that he had provided them all. Ah, bliss.

"Yeah, can she do that?" asked a guard, whose thoughts flew to his job security.

All eyes were on Jim, whose own gaze darted around nervously. What was going on here? Release all the prisoners? Was this some sort of on-the-job training to test his handling of the situation? Covertly, he glanced up the stairs to see if there was someone in the shadows holding a scroll, checking boxes and marking down his every word.

But before he could speak, Lillian said imperiously, "Why are you asking him? I am the *Queen*. Does his word carry more weight in this land, or does mine?"

All present had the sense to recognize this question as rhetorical.

"But—but—" Jim said into the silence, quaking in his bloodstained boots. If there was a way to smoothly navigate this rocky workplace situation then he did not have the appropriate skillset. "But if we could perhaps, just *ask* your husband?"

The Women's Rights movement had not taken a firm hold in the Land of Fritillary at this point in its history, since anyone who tried to start up such unnatural nonsense was promptly burned as a witch, but with the jailer's last sentence, the cause of feminism gained a recruit too powerful to be silenced.

CHAPTER FOUR

About a half-hour later, down an alley in the shadow of the castle, Daisy was woken from a dead sleep by a very official-sounding pounding on her front door. She stumbled to the door and found she had been correct in her appraisal, for there stood a small troop of official-looking soldiers, one of whom demanded in an official-sounding tone of voice that she come with him, pronto.

That's how Daisy found herself, head spinning with all sorts of wild, horrible thoughts, stumbling through the midnight streets of the city on her way to the castle. She knew this was something bad because, as the Royal Interior Decorator, she had been escorted to the castle many times but always in the light of day with one friendly escort, not in the middle of the night with two surly soldiers in front of her and two surly soldiers behind her, boxing her in as though expecting her to try and escape.

Was the Queen unhappy with the new flower arrangements in the main hall? There had been some trouble with one of the new chairs for the banquet table, but she had thought the squeaking had been repaired. And, seriously, could troubles with the decor *really* get her in as much trouble as she felt sure she must be in? She had not held her position at the castle for very long, so she didn't know yet how things were handled when something went wrong, but this simply *had* to be excessive.

The guards were no help. They either hadn't been informed of the reason she was being summoned to the castle, or they knew and weren't telling. All they said was that the Queen had insisted it was urgent.

Daisy's anxiety increased when she arrived at the castle and was brought not through the main gates, but down a path around the side of the massive building and past the stables to a small, unadorned, heavily guarded back door. Then a short walk down a dark passage, and through another door, and then down, down, down an endless stone staircase worn with age and countless footsteps of the condemned. The longer she walked, the more convinced she became that there was only one place she could possibly be headed.

The dungeon.

And she was familiar enough with the rumors to know that people rarely left the dungeon.

What could she possibly have done to anger the Queen this much? Would she be given a chance to offer some sort of defense for whatever her crimes were supposed to have been? The Queen had seemed so kind and down-to-earth—there had to have been some ghastly sort of misunderstanding. Daisy wished she had at least been able to bid her family farewell. She hoped someone would inform them where she was so they wouldn't have to wonder, but that was unlikely considering the air of mystery surrounding the dungeon. How long would it take for people to notice she was gone? Would anyone think to water her houseplants and feed her bird?

Finally, legs shaking and on the verge of tears, she reached the bottom of the stairs and found herself standing in the high-ceilinged, huge main torture chamber. Appropriately gothic torches lit the perimeter and a slimy drop of condensation plinked down from the ceiling and onto the bridge of her nose. But, aside from the torches and the gross condensation, nothing about the dungeon was as she might have expected.

In fact, the scene before her eyes was confusing enough to jar her out of her despair and fear. There was an army of maids scouring the walls and floors, while a group of guards stood in one corner around an evil-looking device, scratching their heads. Daisy overheard one of them mumble, "Are we sure this thing *can* be disassembled?"

Another answered, "Well, it sure wasn't carried down all those stairs in its current state. There *must* be a way to get it apart. Look, I think we need an Allen wrench right there—"

A few more guards were removing some chains from the walls and dropping them into an open crate labeled, "STORAGE. Chains—Dungeon."

And there didn't appear to be any prisoners anywhere.

Then, just when Daisy thought things couldn't get weirder, the Queen herself bustled into sight, waving her arms about at this and that, dictating something to the woman trailing behind her who was scribbling frantically on a scroll of paper. Seeing Daisy, the Queen cried, "Ah! Perfect! You made excellent time!"

Daisy sank into a curtsy, and it was a good thing she'd recovered from much of her fear, otherwise her legs might not have permitted her to stand again when the Queen told her, "Yes, yes, up you get. We have work to do."

By the time Daisy had found her way back to her feet, the Queen was already on the move, so Daisy scampered after her, since she was obviously expected to be following.

"Of course, you're the professional here," the Queen was saying, "but I was thinking lots of rugs. Nice, thick rugs. This stone is just *so* cold. And tapestries. And paint. What do you think of paint?"

"Paint?" Daisy repeated through a whirl of confusion.

"For the walls, dear," Her Majesty said helpfully.

"But...what? I don't—"

The Queen looked at her for a long, baffled moment and then said, "Oh! Didn't anyone tell you why you are here?"

"No, Your Highness."

"Oh goodness! You poor dear! You must be rather confused."

Try petrified, Daisy thought, but only said, in a meek little voice, "Rather, Your Highness."

"You're here to turn this dungeon into a nursery!" she said with a glowing smile.

"I'm—Oh!" Daisy felt relief wash over her. She was not going to be imprisoned for a bad choice in decorating after all. "Oh!" she reiterated, this time in surprise—the relief had made her legs go weak all over again. There being no seating, she staggered back a few paces and leaned against the cold stone wall. Daisy took a few deep breaths. She would be all right!

Lillian watched Daisy's reaction for a few moments, apparently not understanding what was up with her decorator, then a look of comprehension dawned on the Queen's face. "Oh, you thought you were going to be *imprisoned!* Silly me! I've been so distracted lately."

Daisy gaped at her and then remembered just who it was she was staring at and instead looked at the ground, secretly fuming that she'd had to go through all that trauma just because the Queen was a flake. But Daisy was, as previously stated, the professional here, and she gathered she had a job to do. She tucked away her emotions to deal with later, cleared her throat, stood up tall, and said, "So, I'm here to turn the dungeon into a…nursery." Odd. Royal folks did have the strangest notions. And she knew the Queen was born a commoner, so inbreeding (the usual reason the commoners used to explain away royal craziness) was not to blame.

The Queen nodded and began to explain to Daisy all about the curse.

ELSEWHERE ABOUT THE castle, Conroy was just finding out that his wife had set free every prisoner from the dungeon.

"*WHAT?*" a red-faced Conroy exploded, flying out of his gigantic, ritzy throne and staring with bugging eyes at one of his advisors whose name he was always forgetting—they were all old and bald and crabby, and forever suggesting he do all sorts of boring stuff when he'd rather be hunting or playing croquet. (He was the King, for goodness sake! Of all people in the kingdom he should be the one who got to do whatever he wanted.)

"Yes, Your Majesty," returned the cowering advisor. "I heard a report that a hoard of emaciated and bedraggled men had descended upon the city saying they had been released from the dungeon. Released by, er, the Queen," he finished in a hesitant whisper. "I personally went down to the dungeon to confirm it, and it is—" *gulp*—"true."

Conroy spluttered and gestured wildly but no words came, so he just gave another roar of rage and then stormed down the steps of the royal dais. He had strode all the way down the vast, marble-pillared, gem-encrusted, gold-leafed throne room and reached the massive carved ebony double doors before the echoes of his yell had even died out. "Seriously, what in blazes is the woman thinking?!" he thundered.

His rage did not abate one iota as he stormed and stomped and cursed his way down toward the dungeon, sending maids and guards and other palace folks diving for cover. But the further he got down the stone stairs, and the closer he got to an ugly confrontation with his lady love, the more his steps slowed and his face drained of anger. He didn't like fighting with Lillian—well, he'd never actually fought with her so he didn't know for sure, but he was nearly one hundred percent sure that he didn't want to do it.

Let me, in my omniscient glory, let you know how a fight would have unfolded: She would have cried, he would have felt guilty, and they'd both just have ended up apologizing and nothing would have gotten accomplished except they'd both have been upset for a while. They were definitely one of those couples who should avoid screaming matches in favor of well-reasoned, respectful conversations, but unfortunately neither of them were really evolved enough to handle that either, so instead, in the future, they ended up bottling stuff up and exploding with passive aggressive comments every now and then.

"Darling," Conroy said nonchalantly (though inside he was still slightly fuming) when he finally reached the dungeon and saw Lillian talking to some lady not outfitted in a maid or cook uniform. "What's going on down here? I got a report that, um, you released all the prisoners? And, why are they cleaning?" He pointed around at the maids, though they had currently abandoned their cleaning to bend in low bows.

Lillian had been studying a sketch that Daisy had been scribbling on a scroll of paper, but when Daisy realized that she was in the presence of the King, she had collapsed into a bow, too, taking the scroll with her. Lillian gave Conroy a glowing smile and said, "Of course I let them go, darling! We need a place for—oh, but this is not how I would have chosen to tell you! I had been hoping to spring the news over a dinner of baby back ribs, baby carrots, and those darling little tiny corn cob things."

Conroy, as usual, looked confused.

"Dear," she said, rushing to him and clasping his hands in hers, "Dear darling love, we are going to have a child!"

Conroy stared at her for a moment, and then broke into a huge, genuine grin.

There was much laughing, hugging, kissing, and spinning of the queen around the floor of the dungeon. There was, in fact, more happiness condensed into the span of five minutes than had ever occurred in the dungeon before in the entirety of its existence.

After a time, however, Conroy became subdued as he looked at his surroundings once more and realized why all this bustle in the dungeon was going on. Farland's curse. His child was going to be stuck down here forever—or until the dratted curse was broken. "The dungeon," he murmured, "Yes, I suppose it does make sense. No sunlight at all."

Lillian met his eyes and produced a brave smile. "We'll make the best of it, Dearest. I have the greatest decorator on the job, so the place will at least *look* much better. And we must stop thinking of this as a *dungeon*. We must stop that mindset. Right now."

He nodded resolutely. *Yes.*

"Daisy is a simply splendid decorator—" she said with a gesture in the direction of where Daisy had been, only to realize that she was still prostrating herself before the King. Lillian hadn't yet been married to Conroy for very long, and so hadn't gotten used to one of those most annoying things about being royal: people were forever dropping to the floor at one's feet, *and* one had to remember to tell them to rise.

Conroy was used to it, though. "Ah yes," he said. "That lady who's not a maid or a cook." He peered at the top of Daisy's head.

"Oh, do get up," Lillian said, still vaguely embarrassed by being groveled at. "Everyone," she added to the rest of the room. Everyone popped up and got back to work. *Bustle, bustle; flurry, flurry.*

Daisy brushed off her dress (wishing she hadn't worn one of her finest, because it was going to be impossible to clean) then walked over to the Royal Couple in response to Conroy's beckoning finger. As she moved toward him, a man scurried between them chasing a rat, his thickly-gloved hands extended before him.

"You. Decorator." Conroy spoke to Daisy.

"Your Highness?"

"This place is to be perfect for my child. Perfect. You shall have no budget to concern yourself with. Spend whatever you need, hire whomever you think will perform the job best. Understand?"

Daisy nodded. "Yes, Your Highness."

He turned his back on her without another word, and said to his wife, "Darling, I'm sorry but I must go talk to my advisors. Urgently." He didn't add that the reason for this urgency was that he had a gigantic problem on his hands. There were now many violent criminals roaming the city—and lots of innocent people who had been wrongly imprisoned. He didn't know which group he feared the most, but he did know that he had a situation on his hands. A situation so serious he actually felt the need to address it himself, instead of ignoring it or pushing it off on someone else.

He hurried back up the stairs.

Lillian watched him go and sighed contentedly. "He will make a wonderful father," she said. Then she looked at Daisy, waiting for a response.

"Oh... Yes, very, Your Highness," Daisy responded automatically.

"Well then," the queen said, "I must go as well. You take a look around and report back to me with your ideas." Then Lillian and her maid were off.

Daisy looked around and squinched her mouth in distaste. Even empty of all its horrible apparatuses and its prisoners, the dungeon was horrible. So cold and dark and cavernous. And perhaps it was only because she knew it had been full of suffering for generations, but the very air seemed to her to be heavy with an oppressive *something*.

She could have no way of knowing that this oppressive something was a trio of ghosts who were at that very moment gathered around her, discussing all that had unfolded.

"No way will she be able to turn this place into a *nursery*," grumbled a tall, bald ghost wearing a pair of scraggly shorts held up by a rope tied around his bony hips. All three ghosts were scrawny, but this bald one was the most so. If he weren't a ghost and thus already deceased, I would be very concerned for him. Maybe invite him over for a pot pie and some cake.

"Oh Curtis, who knows..." said the short one in a guard uniform. "The real question is: why are we still here when all the other ghosts disappeared with the dungeon stuff?" There had been twenty-three ghosts in the dungeon before the cleaning crew had descended that morning, but now only these three remained. Twenty-two had been prisoners, and one (the short ghost who had just spoken) had been a guard who had been a victim of a failed prison break about a hundred years prior.

The third ghost watched Daisy as she hugged herself uncomfortably and muttered under her breath, "I bet this place is haunted."

"Perceptive, this one," the third ghost, Dexter, said, nodding his head in her direction. He had been in his mid-twenties when he died and hadn't been too long in the dungeon before he met his demise, so he wasn't as skeletal as his friend Curtis. He had a nasty cut running down the left side of his face from his forehead to his chin.

Daisy began to walk and they all followed, curious because this woman was going to transform their home into a place fit for a royal infant. The notion was quite jarring. As she moseyed around, taking notes and getting inspired thinking about color swatches, flower arrangements, and cribs, they moseyed along with her, peeking at her notes and testing her receptivity by speaking ideas into her ear and seeing whether she seemed to notice.

"Hang a swing from the ceiling," Dexter spoke clearly into her ear, and was pleased to see seconds later when Daisy wrote down in her notebook: *hang swing from ceiling.*

They saw she had heard him and the ghosts all moaned excitedly in unison, making Daisy shiver and look around nervously.

Over the days, weeks, and months that followed, the trio of ghosts watched the transformation of their home with great interest, supplying ideas to Daisy whenever they could, and generally trying to make the most of the situation.

Then one morning, Curtis was watching with interest as some day laborers (two of whom were former prisoners) laid intricate ceramic tiles down on the floor of the future bathroom, when the prison guard ghost (Montague) came in and said, "Hi, what's going on?"

Dexter and Curtis didn't often talk to Montague. Though Montague had not been a guard at the same time Dexter or Curtis had been prisoners, a guard was a guard, and they saw no reason to be friendly. This made things pretty lonely for Montague—the only other souls in this world who could see him would barely even speak to him. Even before the other ghosts had disappeared from the dungeon, it had been the same: since Montague had been the only guard ghost, the others had all taken a savage delight in making things as unpleasant for him as they could. And though Montague understood, on a purely rational level, why they acted that way, understanding didn't make things any easier as the years marched on.

Suddenly, there was a great ruckus from the main room. The ghosts floated out to join the workers and Daisy where they were gathered to watch a doctor bustling around, barking orders to a group of nurses. "Boil some water!" and "Get some clean cloths!" and other such labor-and-childbirth phrases. The nurses sprang into action.

"Oh," Curtis said.

"She's having the baby down here?" Montague asked.

Though they had no desire to witness it, they were stuck in the dungeon; you see, being ghosts, their spirits could not stray from the scene of their demise. So, much to their discomfort, the dungeon's ghosts could not escape the birth of Princess Julianna.

CHAPTER FIVE

Baby Julianna was a sweet kid. Not abnormally cranky, nor surprisingly mellow. She was just pretty much a normal newborn—except that she was a cursed princess. But that detail was surprisingly irrelevant in her early years. Conroy and Lillian had been obsessing about the curse and its implications since the beginning of the pregnancy, but now the new parents were so caught up in the joys of parenthood that at first the curse didn't even cross their minds.

It wasn't until Julianna started to become noticeably observant of her surroundings that her mother began to wish she could take Julianna outside to watch waves crash up on the shore, or look at the trees which were sprouting fresh green leaves. The best they could do was bring in fresh flowers and cuttings from tree branches, and put them in all the vases that Daisy had supplied for this exact purpose all over the child's living quarters.

Really, so what if their daughter couldn't go outside? That meant they knew where she was all the time, and that she was safe, which is a load off the mind of any parent certainly, but especially so for royal parents who have to fret about their kids being taken for ransom and revenge and those sorts of dreadful things. When Julianna got to be a teenager, Conroy in particular was glad his daughter was contained within the safe sphere of the palace instead of roaming about the city being flirted at by knights.

There is a little part of every parent that would like to keep their kids safe from the evils and temptations of the world, and Lillian and Conroy were living the unhealthy, overprotective dream. Every so often one or the other of them would comment in a vaguely guilty manner about how Farland had actually done them a favor.

And so it went until the fall of Julianna's nineteenth year.

IT WAS THE middle of the night and the Princess's living quarters were silent but for the snoring of her nurse and companion, Delia. The woman was fast asleep in a rocking chair in the central chamber that had once housed the torture devices, but was now lined instead with bookshelves.

As it did most evenings, peace reigned supreme this calm and tranquil night.

Unless you happened to be a person who could hear ghosts, as Julianna could. As far back as she could remember, she had been able to see the three ghosts who haunted her rooms. The ghosts had been really excited about this, especially Montague who at long last had a shot at being able to communicate with a person who didn't hate him. As Julianna grew, they had just as much, if not more, involvement with her upbringing than her nurse, parents, and tutors. When she was too small to understand that she should keep them a secret, the ghosts told her they were imaginary friends so people wouldn't think she was too crazy, since imaginary friends are acceptable for kids to have but seeing people who aren't there is schizophrenic. When Julianna got too old for imaginary friends, she started to pretend she didn't see them anymore, which was tough—imagine living in close quarters with three other people and not being able to acknowledge them.

But whenever Delia was gone and Julianna had no visitors, she was able to converse with the ghosts freely, and had a lot of fun learning all sorts of stuff that she'd otherwise never have learned as a severely over-protected princess.

This midnight found our long-suffering heroine crouched at the end of a tunnel she'd been digging as an escape out of the dungeon ever since Curtis had let slip that, when he'd been alive, he'd been digging a tunnel behind a loose stone in his cell. Horrified, the other ghosts had begged him not to let her know where the tunnel was, but at the time Julianna had been eight years old and thus highly skilled at the fine art of whining and nagging, and she hadn't give him a moment of peace until he finally folded and revealed to her the stone's exact location.

From that day onward, digging to freedom had been her dream and every night, she drugged Delia's nighttime tea and climbed into the tunnel with her digging implements. She had made so much progress with the tunnel over the years that her ghost companions could no longer accompany her to the end since their spectral tethers held them back.

So, if they wanted to speak to her, they had to yell.

And yell Curtis was doing.

The further along the tunnel Julianna progressed, the more he regretted letting her know it was there. It's not like he didn't want her to have freedom, and he knew she hated being confined down in the depths of the castle when there was a whole world to see, but he also didn't want to be the reason that she escaped to the outdoors. His biggest fear was not that she would finish the tunnel, but that the thing would cave in. She'd read a book on mining, and both Dexter and Montague could offer plenty of practical advice since they had had brief stints working in the country's infamous coal mines before moving on to safer professions—Dexter to thievery/poisoning and Montague to prison guardery. In theory, Julianna had the basics of digging a tunnel down, but Curtis still couldn't keep himself from fretting every night that she crawled into that "dark dangerous deathtrap" as he called it, quite alliteratiously.

"Seriously Julianna, you need to give it up for the night. You've been up there for hours! You're going to get sleepy, and then you'll make a silly mistake!"

Way up at the top of the tunnel, Julianna could barely make out Curtis' words, but she knew the gist of it because he'd been hollering the same stuff up at her for more than half of her life now. And, she had to admit, as she paused to scratch an itch on her nose, smearing it with dirt in the process, Curtis was right. No need to get stupid and cause a situation she couldn't fix. Sighing, she gently, almost lovingly, laid down her garden trowel. Her dear trowel had been her digging tool since one of the gardeners had come down to the dungeon a few years back to check on some of her potted plants. She'd managed to swipe it off his tool belt while the gardener had been distracted by an interesting fungus that had taken root in the soil of one of her plants. The trowel, a huge step up from the serving spoon she'd been using, had sped up her work by at least fifty percent.

She gave it a fond pat as though it were a pet dog and scooted over to a device she had constructed by putting the wheels from an old rolling toy horse on the bottom of a plank of wood she'd taken from the underside of her bed. Then, she rolled over so that she was on her back on the wheeled board. She reached up to grab the line made of tied-together bits of fabric and guided herself down to the bottom of the tunnel. The wheeled board saved her tons of crawling time and made it so she didn't have to build the tunnel too high, since she had to only accommodate her supine position.

Once at the bottom, she stood, gave Curtis a grin, stretched her cramped limbs, slid the two bags of dirt from that night's work off the board, and pushed the loose stone back into place.

"I've *told* you not to spend so much time up there!" Curtis fussed.

Julianna glanced at her still-sleeping nurse and grumbled back at him, "I *know* what I'm doing." She smiled apologetically when she saw his downcast expression. "Listen, I'm sorry. I know you're just worried. But, Curtis," she said, suddenly excited, "up there, digging those last few feet, I swear—" and she whispered the last bit, "I swear the air felt…different. The soil wasn't packed as hard. I—I *think* I may be close to the end."

Curtis scrunched his ghostly nose up disbelievingly. His expression was so full of doubt that he might as well have just said aloud that he thought she was crazy.

"Well, what's so crazy about that?" she asked, perturbed. "I've been working on that tunnel ten years now. I figure the thing's got to have an end at some point!"

Montague floated over and interjected, "Odds aren't *that* great you'll find the end. The dungeon's really deep. Really, really deep."

She glared. *Of course it was. It was a dungeon.* "But I've studied blueprints of the castle and topographical maps of the city," she sighed, explaining yet again how she knew there was hope, "and the castle is on a *hill*. And when I look at the castle blueprints and compare them to the layout of the building on the topographical map, it *clearly* shows that my tunnel is going the right direction to eventually end at the edge of the hill on the ocean side!"

"Geez, guys," Dexter muttered from where he was trying to read a book nearby, "let the kid have some hope." Then he asked Julianna, "Could you turn the page for me?"

As she walked over to the table where Dexter was hovering over an open book, she said, "Yeah, I need a project or I'll go mad, right?" to Montague, who had told her that very thing not too long ago, drawing on his observations from his stint as a prison guard as evidence. She gave Dexter a smile and flipped the page. Dexter continued reading. Of the three, he was the one most likely to side with and defend her against the others, probably because he'd led such a life of danger and excitement before he'd been imprisoned. He had had a lot of fun skirting the law and taking risks and thought that being daring and having as much adventure as she could was just the thing for Julianna to keep her mind off her troubles.

Montague nodded but said, "Yes, but it's just that the tunnel... well, it might cave in." He had a great skill for stating the obvious.

"You have no faith in me," Julianna sighed as she slung a bag of dirt over her shoulder and hefted it to the bathroom, then did the same with the other bag, turning a page for Dexter on the way. Once back in the bathroom, she started to run the tub, and then pried the grate off the floor—the grate she assumed led to some sort of sewer system. The only reason she hadn't crawled into it long ago to explore was because by the time it had occurred to her to do so, her shoulders had grown too wide to squeeze through. Peering wistfully down the grate, she asked, "Could one of you make sure Delia is still out?"

Montague floated over to investigate and Julianna began to carefully pour the bags' contents into the depths of the space below the grate. Once the bags were empty and each speck of dirt swept off the floor, Julianna went to hide the bags behind some books in her library, passing Montague as she did.

"She's coming out of it," he said. Julianna nodded. After hiding the bags, she went to another shelf and retrieved a thick book entitled, "An Unabridged History of Mulch." It was hollowed out, housing an array of glass vials wrapped in cloth to stop them breaking or clattering around.

These were the concoctions that she had brewed with Dexter on the sly. Some were for drugging her nurse and some were painkillers. The painkiller she had found to be quite handy when she got hurt in the tunnel and had to pretend that she was fine, since her injuries were unexplainable to people who thought she frittered her days away doing nothing more dangerous than cross stitching, playing her clarinet, and reading.

"One drop is all you'll need," Dexter said from his place by the book he was trying to read, though he had to rely on her to turn the pages, which was irritating because she was scurrying all around and he was just getting to a good part.

She nodded, grabbed the vial, and hurried over to her sleeping nurse. She tilted Delia's head back and dropped one drop onto the elderly woman's tongue.

"You'll need to lay off the drugs for a night," Dexter added. "You've used it five nights in a row. Another night and you get into the danger zone."

She sighed and nodded, having known from years of experience that he was going to say that. And he was right, of course. She didn't want to endanger Delia. Delia was a sweet, kind old lady. And heck, even if she was mean and crabby, one still doesn't drug people willy-nilly.

Her nurse duly neutralized long enough for Julianna to wipe all traces of her tunneling excursion from her person and the rooms, she turned another page for Dexter, took a bath, then scoured the tub of residual dirt. Julianna had, as a byproduct of the tunneling, developed much better house-cleaning skills than any royalty in the history of Fritillary. She was so proficient at sweeping, scouring, and scrubbing away any evidence of dirt around the dungeon that Delia had not found anything suspicious in years.

Even if Delia had found suspicious dirt on the floor, she might not have thought too much of it anyway since there were already so many odd things about Julianna. For one thing, the girl mysteriously exhibited knowledge and language that was shockingly inappropriate (all things Julianna had picked up from her ghost companions, but of course Delia couldn't know that). Then there were the odd quirks she had, like leaving books open on the desk and not reading them but at regular intervals turning the pages, and seeming to be watching something that wasn't there, and muttering quietly when she thought Delia wasn't listening. Also, in consequence of her never having once been touched by sunlight, she had a fierce vitamin D deficiency which resulted in depression, forgetfulness, and icky problems with her gums. The vitamin D deficiency also caused another quirk of hers, which was a constant craving for fish[4].

Yes, all in all Delia thought Julianna was a weird child and would not have been overly suspicious of a bit of unexplained dirt; she probably would have just assumed Julianna liked to play in the potted plants in the middle of the night.

Julianna hopped out of the tub, got into her PJs, turned another page for Dexter, and then succumbed to her exhaustion and went to her bedroom, where she collapsed into her four-poster canopy bed. She fell asleep quickly, dreaming of reaching the end of her tunnel. After a few hours, Delia woke her.

"Rise and shine, sweetheart," Delia trilled. "Remember your mother is coming down for lunch today."

The older Julianna got, the less her parents visited. It had gotten to the point where Conroy came down for a chat about once a week, and her mother visited once every few days for lunch. Julianna knew her dad was super busy dealing with an increasingly unhappy populace (they'd been getting more and more unhappy ever since Lillian had released that huge influx of prisoners into the city and thrown off the delicate balance) and Julianna knew her mom was really into being the figurehead of the women's rights movement, but still she felt that if they loved her like parents should love their kids they'd be down in the dungeon every single day playing chess, reading books with her, and asking what was going on in her life.

It didn't help that the visits had really dropped off since her little uncursed heir-to-the-throne brother, Conroy Jr., had been born seven years earlier, just when she'd been getting into her moody early teen years. Eventually, she had grown out of the resentment she had felt from that period of her life. Rationally, she realized that perhaps part of the reason

---

4   Fun fact: fish is pretty much the only naturally occurring source of vitamin D besides sunlight.) But nutrition science didn't really exist in Fritillary, since it and every other science were viewed with extreme suspicion by a populace that much preferred to explain away every ailment and trouble by saying it was because the sick person had angered some wizard. Consequently, everyone assumed it was Farland's curse that was causing all Julianna's symptoms.

they had stopped visiting so much was that she yelled at them and gave them the cold shoulder whenever they stopped by, but they were her parents, and if they weren't going to put any effort into helping her deal with her emotional distress, then who was going to[5]?

So, Julianna was sort of happy and sort of not that her mom was coming for lunch.

Another downside of the visits was that the older Julianna got, the more her mom talked about her future—a subject that made Julianna really, really uncomfortable. Would she languish away in the dungeon, a spinster to the end of her days? Would they find someone willing to marry her? Marriage was a chilling thought, because the way she looked at it, only a super-weirdo or a creep would consent to be all right with having a cursed wife who was confined for life to an underground chamber.

Over the course of her life she had met all the potential marriage candidates in the aristocracy pool and hadn't connected with any of them. They had been brought down to visit her whenever their parents had come to town for royal business, but none of them had been the types that she'd even want to be *friends* with, let alone marry. They tended to talk an awful lot about swords and archery and horses, and most of them had not read one single book in their lives that had not been assigned by their tutors. None of them had the slightest interest in philosophy or math or any of the subjects she'd developed a fondness for.

It wasn't so much that she didn't want to talk about swords and archery and horses, but that there was so much more she would have liked to discuss. Warfare and related subjects seemed to be *all* these noblemen's sons seemed to care about. It *did* make sense, since that was what they were going to be when they grew up, so it was the primary focus of their parents and teachers, but it sure made them boring. She couldn't feel too superior to them, though, because she supposed that if she hadn't been cursed, she might well have turned out to be just as one-dimensional, obsessed with dresses and hairstyles and parties and boys, since that was what a normal princess's life revolved around.

---

5   There was no psychiatry in Fritillary (yet another field that people looked at with suspicion and tended to burn its practitioners at the stake for).

But since she *was* cursed, she got to pursue whatever interest she wanted; her parents wished to do whatever they could to keep her from going stir crazy.

Thankfully, though, the subject of husbands didn't come up nearly as much as might be expected. This was, unbeknownst to Julianna, because her parents were still under the assumption they'd find the man who'd break the curse, that she would marry him, and that she would be able to live a normal life. They were still using every available resource to search for him, and wouldn't allow themselves yet to think about an alternative fate for her. Her parents had decided early on not to tell her about this mystery man who was the key to breaking the curse, because it would only cause her anxiety, and there was nothing she could do anyway to aid the search.

So, matrimony was not a subject that Lillian was likely to pester her about, but there was a lot more to Julianna's future than boys. Lillian's favorite topic lately had been how Julianna was going to fill her adult life in the dungeon. She was not a child anymore and was done with her formal education, and now, according to her mother, it was time to consider adulthood.

Adulthood is a stressful thing to consider for most young adults because of the myriad of options available to them; what if they make the wrong choice? It was stressful to Julianna for quite the opposite reason; it made her feel ill to think about languishing about in her dungeon contributing nothing, doing nothing of consequence, and pretty much leading a life that had so little impact on the world that (as far as the world was concerned) she might as well not exist at all. Julianna tried hard to block out all thought on the subject, but every time Lillian came to visit these days, she tended to talk of nothing else, thus forcing Julianna, for the duration of each visit, to dwell on what she felt was her meaningless existence. Lillian would totally depress her daughter with no notion that she was even doing so, then she would kiss her on the nose, flit off upstairs, and go live her life in the sunshine doing her queenly job of having well-publicized visits with peasants where she would distribute food and recite pre-written speeches about women's rights.

Julianna sighed and walked to the dining area—a space right off the main chamber that used to be a large cell where the new prisoners had lived until the guards had gotten around to processing them. Once the bars had been removed and Daisy had worked her decorating magic, it had been transformed into a lovely little alcove with tapestries of forest scenes on the walls, lush potted plants in the corners, a beautiful rug in earth tones on the stone floor, and a dining table and chairs that seated far more guests than Julianna had ever had down in the dungeon at one time, even counting when the ghosts sat, too.

She plopped down in her big golden chair with comfy green upholstery, stared down into her empty golden plate, twiddled her golden fork around distractedly in her fingers, and let herself daydream about the possibility that she really was about to reach the end of the tunnel. Her daydream-self was just digging out of the tunnel and taking her first breath of fresh air when Lillian finally came down into the dungeon more than an hour late.

"Sweetheart!" Lillian crooned.

"Mama," Julianna answered, happy to see her mother but also suddenly distracted because it had just occurred to her that she had to do some packing before going up into the tunnel. She couldn't just go scampering out into the world unprepared. Reading fairytales had taught her that princesses who ventured out into the world on their own tended to get into all sorts of trouble, and, while she knew those stories were fictional, she still saw some sense in them. She'd need food, money, a weapon of some sort, and probably tons of other things too. She'd do some brainstorming with the ghosts at night once Delia had fallen asleep.

They ate their dinner and chatted about what was going on in Lillian's life; they did not talk about what was going on in Julianna's life since Lillian always assumed (and usually rightly) that there was nothing to report. Their conversation shifted to small talk too boring to waste ink on and then Lillian left, but not before Julianna covertly reached into her mother's pocket when they hugged each other goodbye and found a little pouch of what felt like money. She had never held or even seen money before so she couldn't be sure, but the ghosts would certainly confirm it. Assuming it *was* money, then she already had one item to cross off her list of things to pack!

Feeling pretty good about herself, she went off to her bedroom to have a whispered conversation with her friends.

AFTER CHATTING WITH the ghosts about her escape plans, Julianna felt she had a good list of necessities to spend the day tracking down. She also decided it would be wise to take Dexter with her—a while back, she had discovered through some research on the paranormal that ghosts were thought to be tethered at the time of their death to something in the material world. This was what held her three ghosts to a clearly defined perimeter around the dungeon. This habit of ghosts' spirits to be tied to a physical thing that was nearby when they died was surely why the majority of the dungeon's ghosts had disappeared when the dungeon had been cleaned out. Since soldiers had hauled away the majority of the dungeon stuff to a waste management facility on the outskirts of the city, there must be a very haunted trash pile out there somewhere.

Through some trial and error exploring the dungeon and measuring how far the ghosts could go in each direction, Julianna had discovered that Montague's spirit was stuck to a big rock on the bathroom wall, Curtis was stuck to a big steel ring that had been anchored so firmly into the wall that the interior decorator had not been able to have it removed, and Dexter was tethered to a slightly protruding brick in the hallway.

Since the brick, when pried loose, was small enough to be carried around without trouble, it was only a matter of time before Julianna's curiosity got the better of her and she loosened it from the wall and found that, if she moved the brick around the dungeon, Dexter's perimeter changed from its usual one to a new one, always with the brick as the epicenter. Through the day she kept the brick in the wall, since it was right at eye level and Delia would surely notice its absence, but at night she sometimes removed the brick so that Dexter could accompany her up the tunnel. However, he rarely went up with her anymore since the novelty of being able to move beyond his usual range had worn off for him long ago and now he thought the tunnel boring.

Speaking of boring, while her plans and her gathering of supplies were quite important and essential to her imminent escape from the dungeon, they were not all that interesting from a storytelling perspective.

But, if we take our focus from the castle dungeon out across the Bay of Fritillary and then a few miles north into the ocean, we will be fortunate enough to find that which neither Farland nor Mirabella nor Julianna's parents have thus far been able to locate: the ship that was home to the strapping young lad who was the antidote to the spell that cursed Conroy's firstborn. The ship was, coincidentally, making its way into the Bay that very day.

Chapter Six

Warren Kensington was in the Captain's quarters, hard at work practicing the harpsichord and cursing under his breath because, due to either the humidity or the salty sea air or the jostling of the waves, the dratted harpsichord was *always* out of tune. Despite that fact, Warren had always felt a strange, inexplicable draw to the instrument that, up until the time he'd discovered it in the Captain's quarters a few years back, had only been used as a decoration the Captain had chosen in order to make himself look deep and well-rounded.

More practical for a life at sea were Warren's banjo and accordion, both of which he could rival the most seasoned professional at in a musical duel. Not so with the harpsichord, but still Warren plugged away at the thing with equal parts love and frustration. The Captain let him have pretty much unlimited access to the instrument throughout the day because it meant that at least Warren was out of his hair, which was more than the Captain could say of the rest of the Kensingtons.

You see, Warren's family was a traveling theater troupe, and they had been, for the past few years, paying the Captain to transport them about the seas; the money they paid was just enough for the Captain to overlook the fact that they were a very annoying lot. Warren's father, a tightrope walker named Bernard, was always climbing up into the rigging to practice his craft. His mother, Emily, a fire eater, was a positive menace on the deck.

The Captain had assigned a crew member with a bucket of water to follow her around whenever she was practicing; the very last thing they needed was to have the sail or mast or other ship bit burst into flames. And Warren's sister Corrine was very irritating due to the fact that she, as the playwright of the family, was always traipsing around reciting her poetry, or distracting the crew by asking their advice about whatever scene she was working on—and, since she was a young lady, much of the crew was so infatuated with her that they would drop whatever they were doing in order to help her out. It is a problem when crewmembers on ships will literally drop whatever they are doing while on the job; dropping a rope before a knot is properly secured can result in a boom or sail smacking another crewmember in the face; dropping a cannonball before it is in the cannon can result in a hole in the deck; and dropping one's hold on the helm can result in the ship meandering off course while the person in control of steering is instead helping Corrine find a good rhyme for "purple."

So, the Captain was more than happy to give Warren access to the harpsichord in his quarters since it meant that Warren was out of the way. And the general ruckus of the crew hollering and running around doing their ship sailing stuff meant that they could barely even hear the horrible sound, which was a bonus.

Over the discordant plinking of the keys, Warren heard the pitter-patter of rain hitting the deck above him and then some thunder off in the distance, which meant his family would be busy above.

Warren's family loved storms. His father would be climbing into the rigging because he liked to practice his balance in adverse weather, his mother would be practicing keeping fire burning in the rain, and his sister would probably be climbing into the crow's nest to soak up the feeling of the dramatic forces of the stormy sea—she found storms to be quite inspirational. Warren himself loved storms too; they were quite motivating for composing banjo music. He usually sat on deck as the rain poured down, playing frantic tunes that made the already-anxious crew downright jumpy. Thunder sounded again and Warren stood to go find his banjo.

Meanwhile, up on deck, it was apparent to Captain and crew that a storm was a'brewin'. A nor'easter. "Tell the passengers to stay down below!" barked the Captain to his first mate, Biggby. The Captain knew only too well how the family behaved during storms, and since this storm was looking like it was shaping up to be a pretty bad'un he didn't want his crew to have to deal with dodging a tightrope walker in the rigging, a fire eater on the deck, and a daydreaming poet in the crow's nest, all while being regaled by a wild banjo tune from the boy. The captain scanned the fast-approaching, menacing black clouds and yelled, "Move, Biggby!"

Warren was just exiting the Captain's Quarters when he was shoved back in by Biggby, who was walking past on his way to find his family. Biggby barked, "Stay in there!" then slammed the door. Warren narrowed his eyes with annoyance, but he knew better than to try to venture out again—Biggby was super scary when he was mad.

Warren sauntered over to the porthole to watch the storm. Then he heard the door open again, and turned in time to see Biggby fling his sister unceremoniously into the room before slamming the door shut behind her.

As she caught her balance and brushed off her dress, looking miffed, they both heard the door being locked from the outside.

"A storm's a'brewin'?" Warren asked.

"Must be," she growled with annoyance and sat down, glaring at him as though he was the one who'd pulled her from where she'd been basking in what little was left of the sunshine composing poetry, without so much as a "Sorry about that! Captain's orders!"

"Geez, don't look at me like that," Warren muttered.

"These people, Warren, are downright brutish," she grumbled.

"Well, they *are* pirates," he pointed out.

"Still, I mean, Mom and Dad are paying them good money to transport us around. You'd think it would be money enough to earn us a bit of respect."

"I think it has earned us *a bit* of respect," Warren said. "You know how they treat people who *don't* pay them." The deal they had struck with the pirates years back was simply this: the pirates attacked and raided the smaller ships and got all the spoils, but for the bigger ships (the ones that would be harder to raid successfully anyway) the pirates pulled down the Jolly Edmond (Fritillary didn't have a Jolly Roger), masqueraded as roadies (seasies?) for the troupe so the family could perform their plays and songs and acts, and the pirates got a 25% cut of those profits. In return, the family got room and board, and a much more streamlined mode of transportation than they would otherwise have been able to afford, thus enabling them to reach more ships, get more money, and gain a greater fan base.

Corrine was silent a moment, thinking back to what she'd glimpsed through her porthole as she watched what she could of the pirates' most recent raid. "True," she said at last with a shudder. "Good point."

Warren went back to studying the sheet music at the harpsichord and she ambled over to sit beside him at the bench. "Whatcha doing?"

"Oh, just trying to figure out this—"

The door was unlocked once more, and they both looked up to see their father being pushed into the room, balancing stick still in hand.

About a minute later, they were then joined by their mother, who, not knowing her children were in the room already, yelled some inappropriate things at the pirates on the other side of the door before turning, seeing she had an audience, and joining her family in a short, awkward silence. The kids burst out laughing, she said it wasn't funny, and then they were all silenced by a mighty crack of thunder which sounded as though it must be right above them. Seconds later, shouts of alarm and much scurrying from the deck suggested that something on the ship was amiss; a moment later, the mast cracking at its base and crashing into Captain's quarters, bringing down the ceiling all around them and covering them in splintered wood, debris, and rain confirmed their suspicions that all was not well.

When the dust settled and they'd all stopped panicking enough to take stock of the situation, it was discovered that their father, Bernard, had a cut across his forehead, Corrine had a pretty deep sliver in her left hand, their mom was okay if a bit flustered, and a bit of the harpsichord was smashed.

Warren was pinned to the floor under a fallen ceiling crossbeam. His right arm appeared to be broken. Bernard and Emily stayed with him while Corrine scurried off to ask for help, but no matter how much she begged the pirates, they said they couldn't help yet. They were all so busy with their own injuries or with discerning whether to save or abandon ship that they weren't available to help move the beam, which was too heavy for the family to deal with on their own.

"Get me the doctor!" Warren hollered, staring at his arm with horror.

The pirates didn't really have a doctor per se on board, more of a guy who had figured out through trial and error how to fix typical pirate injuries like stab and slash wounds and minor bone breaks. The pseudo-doctor was named Brock, and the Captain had christened him the doctor of the ship mainly because he thought it would be cool to be able to call him Doc Brock.

"Honey," said Emily as she sat beside her son, worriedly patting his arm. "That man is a quack. You don't want his help."

"But we have to do *something*, Ma!"

"Sweetheart, remember we're not in the middle of the ocean. We are in the Bay of Fritillary. Your father can take a lifeboat to shore once the water has calmed down a bit and he can find a *real* doctor."

"I want help NOW!" he yelled, wild-eyed and panicky.

Pacing around the rubble, Bernard said, "I don't think we're supposed to move the beam—I think it could make things worse. Son, we can't help you—we have to get a real doctor."

"Dad, sit down," Corrine said from her perch on some rubble nearby. "You're hyperventilating. Put your head between your knees and take deep breaths."

He nodded and did as she suggested, then she said, "Guys, seriously, let's stay calm. I think dad is right: we don't want to move that beam until a doctor is here. And I think we are all in agreement that Doc Brock should be kept far away from Warren."

Her mother nodded at her, her father (with his head still between his knees) said some muffled thing that didn't sound argumentative, and Warren looked at her beseechingly, hoping she was about to come up with some fabulous plan.

"I think Mom's right—the only thing to do is row to shore as soon as we're able and get a real doctor. Dad and I can go, and, Mom, you stay here with Warren and make sure Doc Brock doesn't come near him."

Bernard, Emily, and Corrine all concluded this was their only alternative. Warren was in shock at this point, so no one took it personally when he yelled at them and told them what a stupid idea it was. To the backdrop of Warren's addled ranting and the crew's yelling, the family sat back in the rain and made themselves and Warren as comfortable as they could as they waited for the sea to calm enough to row into the city.

But after just few minutes of that trash, Bernard hopped up and said, "Come on, Corrine, let's go. Those waves aren't so bad." But he wasn't looking at the waves; he was looking at Warren, who had stopped ranting and was looking way too pale and still as the rain fell steadily down onto his vacant face.

Corrine had been watching her brother the whole time too, getting steadily more and more concerned, so when her father suggested that they go she was on her feet in a moment, ready to put aside all reason and safety and row to the city even though the storm was still a'ragin'.

"The waves will make it so we'll barely have to row," Bernard said optimistically, "and then if we can just get to the city, we can wait out the storm while looking for a doctor, instead of waiting here doing nothing while things calm down."

Corrine nodded and looked to her mother who sat with Warren, looking indecisive. Sure, the waves would do most of the work getting them to shore, but the real problem was how to safely dock the rowboat once they got there. "I—I don't know..." Emily said, and bit her lip.

"Mom," Corrine said, looking significantly at Warren, "We don't have a choice. We can't wait."

After a long moment, Emily nodded a small, nervous nod. Bernard and Corrine gave her hasty hugs goodbye, and then they were off.

CHAPTER SEVEN

In less than a half hour, Corrine and Bernard were relieved and surprised to find themselves standing on solid ground with a mostly-undamaged lifeboat bobbing merrily away, tied to the docks behind them. "Yow!" Bernard gasped, "That went better than expected!"

"Indeed," Corrine responded, looking out at the rough sea they'd just crossed. They'd nearly capsized a half dozen times and had more smashed into the dock than rowed up alongside it, but what mattered was that it was done and they'd both survived. They gave the wild waves one last glance, then turned and walked down the road toward they knew not what. All they did know was that they were looking for a doctor and that there must be advertisements of some kind somewhere.

They both found it awkward to walk on land. Bernard had not set foot on dry ground in many years, and Corrine had actually never been off a ship before. If they hadn't been on a serious and time-sensitive mission, she would have liked to look around the city–she would have found even the scummy docks they were currently hurrying through quite fascinating after a life confined to one ship or another. She had been born on a ship and her family's livelihood was on ships, so there had never been any need to leave the sea as long as they made enough money to get all they needed. Which they did, because they were a rockin' traveling theater troupe, and one of the only ones that toured the ocean. When Bernard and Emily had become performers, it had been in the heyday of trouping, so it had been hard for a couple just starting out to get a gig. But Emily had always had a head for business, and so it didn't take her long to realize that there were all sorts of cruise ships and merchant ships and other ships in the ocean that were full of stir-crazy folks who would pay an arm and a leg for some entertainment.

Bustling through the city, Corrine and her dad inquired of everyone they could as to whether they could point them in the direction of a good doctor. However, the shady waterside characters who frequented the docks either couldn't afford health insurance and so didn't have a doctor, or were operating below the radar and had their own shady back alley doctors they didn't want to name, so Corrine and Bernard were not getting nearly as much help as they'd have liked.

In one neighborhood by the docks, they kept spotting flimsy signs posted at main intersections saying in a big, messy scrawl, "24 Hour Docktor. House Calls Available. 15 Pigeon Row." If it weren't for the fact that the docktor couldn't spell 'doctor', they might have been desperate enough to resort to visiting a doctor whose advertisements were flimsy intersection signs, but that misspelling was just too much for them. So, they left the neighborhood of the docks and found themselves getting into a fancier part of the city.

Unfortunately, though, they were soon to find that fancy doctors weren't inclined to climb aboard a pirate ship. The combination of the fact that they were already booked weeks out for first time patients and the fact that, not being in need of drumming up business, they saw no need to take the risk of going of their own accord under the shades of the Jolly Edmond, made it so Corrine and her dad found themselves–before the town crier had yet yelled noon–scouring back alleys for less savory physicians then they'd have considered even hours earlier.

And when that search proved both fruitless and more dangerous than they felt comfortable with (Warren would have no way of getting help if they got themselves murdered by some filthy gang of toothless vagrants) they found themselves back at the docks, standing in the middle of a busy intersection, staring down at one of the flimsy "Docktor" signs.

"Can't hurt to check," Bernard said. "A person doesn't need to spell to fix a broken arm," he added, as though he'd made a swell point.

Corrine gave him a skeptical glance, but decided to try giving the ol' man a break for a change and kept her mouth shut. Instead, she merely shrugged. After asking directions from a helpful old five-toothed crone, they found their way rather uneventfully to 15 Pigeon Row. It was a decrepit shack, of course.

"Dude," Corrine breathed as she raised a hand to knock on the door that had once been painted orange of all colors, "I can't believe we're really doing this." But Warren was trapped under a crossbeam, and an injury like that needed attention as fast as attention could be obtained. This docktor at least couldn't be worse than Doc Brock. So, in response to encouraging hand-flapping gestures from her forebear, Corrine gave the door a hesitant *knock-knock-knock.*

A skinny lady with short black hair answered the door so fast that her hand had to have been on the doorknob already. The surprise on the face of the black-haired lady showed that she must have been walking out the door just as Corrine had knocked. "Oh!" they both said in unison and took steps backward. Corrine tumbled down the stairs and landed in a pile of muck. Her dad and the lady hurried to help, but she swatted them away and regained her feet with an "I'm fine, I'm fine. Back off."

"I'm sorry about that," the lady said sincerely.

"It's no problem–"

"Here, come in and let me make you some–"

"We don't have time," Corrine snapped, turning down whatever the lady had been about to offer before she'd even heard what was on the table as a peace offering. "We need a doctor."

"What's your trouble?" the lady asked, looking Corrine up and down in an appraising sort of way that indicated she must be the doctor.

"It's my brother. His arm is crushed under a beam on a ship out in the Bay. Are you the doctor?"

"Yep," the lady said, signaling for them to follow as she darted back into the little building.

Inside, it was tiny and just as decrepit as the outside. But it was clean, and the bed that was presumably for the patients looked spotless, which was reassuring. From ceiling beams so low Corrine could have touched them without standing on tiptoe hung bunches of scrawny asparagus that looked like they must have come from a produce reject bin. As the short-haired lady grabbed a black bag off the rickety little table by the bed, she said, "My name's Jane." Then she grabbed a bundle of asparagus, tossed it in the bag, and snapped it shut.

"Mine's Corrine," Corrine said, so happy to see that Jane was going to help that she was finding it difficult to mention that the ship Jane's patient was on happened to be of the pirate variety. It would be wrong not to tell Jane at all, since setting foot on a pirate ship was quite risky, but it would also be wrong to let the only doctor willing to help Warren slip through their fingers. In the end, she decided to wait to divulge the information until they were rowing out to the boat and had had a chance to talk Warren up a bit; that way, Jane would be thinking of him more as a human being and less as a risk.

"I'm Bernard," said Bernard. He was also struggling with whether or not to tell Jane that they'd be taking her to a pirate ship, and his moral obligations took control of his mouth before his reason could shut him up. "Listen... the thing is... er... my son is on a pirate ship–"

Corrine stared at her father in disbelief.

Jane froze and shot him a suspicious look. "You're pirates?"

"No, just sailing with them. We're a traveling theater troupe."

Jane was quiet for a while, opening up her bag and rifling through it, more to kill time as she weighed the pros and cons of the situation than to actually check on the contents. At long last, she looked up at their expectant faces and said, "I suppose I'll still go... But only because I'm assuming you checked with every other doctor you could before you settled on me. I'm your last resort, right?"

Corrine and Bernard nodded guiltily.

Jane sighed. "Honestly, what will it take for people to be comfortable with a female doctor?"

They walked out the door.

Corrine said as Jane locked up, "Whoa there sister, you aren't our last resort because you're a lady. I can't speak for *all* your potential clientele, but you were *our* last resort because you're a doctor who can't spell 'doctor'."

Jane gave another sigh. She was one of those folks who was prone to sighing a lot. "Honestly, am I the *only* one in this city who has a sense of humor? I can spell D-O-C-T-O-R just fine! I wrote it with a 'K' on those signs because I am the *doctor* who works by the *docks*! *DOCKtor!*"

Bernard and Corrine exchanged looks behind her back, but composed themselves before Jane turned around and strode to where they were waiting beside the pile of muck Corrine had become acquainted with earlier.

"Right-o, lead the way," Jane said.

They walked toward the docks, dodging pickpockets and ticket scalpers and revolutionaries handing out trifold brochures about why the citizens should revolt against the Royal Family.

Finally, they made their way to their little lifeboat, which had a parking ticket stuck to its bow. Bernard grumbled and moaned like a textbook caricature of a dad, then he remembered this was a pirate lifeboat and no way do pirates pay parking tickets. He had another internal struggle with his moral obligations, but his morality muscle was plum tuckered out after his earlier struggle with whether or not to tell Jane about the pirate ship. With only minimal guilt, he tossed the ticket into the sea. "Let's blow this popsicle stand!" he said. How do they have popsicles in Fritillary, you ask? Good question. Icebergs are involved.

They were about to hop into the lifeboat when Corrine noticed an ad nailed to a nearby post advertising harpsichord repairs and tuning. A strange place for such an ad, but she didn't give it much thought. All she thought about was how, once her brother was patched up enough to notice that the harpsichord had been damaged in the storm, he would be heartbroken. It would be nice to be able to supply this name and address to him when he went ballistic.

She tore a little tab off the bottom of the sheet and joined her comrades in the gently bobbing boat, the oars of which Jane had already taken, insisting that just because Bernard was a man that didn't mean he was by default the only one capable of rowing a boat. She had been brought up by first-generation feminists who had joined the movement shortly after Queen Lillian had taken the helm as its spokesperson and declared the belief that women and men were equal was no longer grounds for being burned at the stake as a witch. Jane's mother and father had raised Jane to believe that she could do or be anything. So, she had become a doctor who, among other accomplishments, also rowed her own boats.

On the street corner across from them, a homeless guy who had been watching with interest as soon as he had seen Corrine looking at the harpsichord ad stood up, grabbed his hat full of change, and walked off with a purposeful stride.

THE ONE GOOD thing about how long it had taken them to find a doctor was that the storm had abated and the sea had calmed to the point where rowing out into the bay against the waves wasn't too difficult. Jane, Bernard, and a grudging Corrine (who only liked feminism when the boys still did the grunt work) all took turns rowing, and after just an hour in the boat they reached the pirate ship. Jane glanced at the Jolly Edmond as it flapped merrily in the wind, but then reminded herself that there was a patient in dire need of help, and climbed up without another moment of hesitation.

Corrine and Bernard led her straight to Warren, who had gotten nothing but worse in their absence. Seeing at a glance the gravity of the situation, Jane got down to business, barking orders and doing doctorly things that I won't get into the particulars of because it was an icky business. So, we'll just pick things up again at the point a few hours later when all beam removal and bone setting and stitching without anesthetic were done:

Jane put her hand gently to the forehead of a freshly patched up Warren and said, "Okay, that should do it."

Warren, who was pale, sweaty, and intensely cranky, couldn't bring himself to say thanks to the lady who'd had four pirates pin him down while she thwacked his humerus back into alignment. His family, however, extended thanks on his behalf.

Jane took their money and, with the invalid tended to, was more than ready to blow this popsicle stand...again. So, she asked Bernard if he'd be so good as to take her back to shore.

He courteously obliged, and they made their way toward the lifeboat.

However, they were halted in their tracks by Captain Maximus

McManlyman (the pirate captain had had his name changed legally from Pervis Collins after being laughed out of the Pirate Staffing Agency when they'd read his birth name on his pirate application. In a fit of youthful overenthusiasm, he may have overdone it a bit).

"Captain McManlyman!" Bernard gasped, alarmed to see the grizzled dude blocking their path with blade drawn. "I was just going to row her to shore."

"This nurse isn't going anywhere," McManlyman barked, jabbing a finger in Jane's direction.

"I'm a doctor!" Jane growled. "Why must you assume—"

"But you're a chick!" McManlyman said. "Or—are you a really puny dude?"

"I'm not a *chick*—"

"Then you're the most girly dude I've ever—"

"I *mean*," Jane sighed, "I'm not a *chick*, but a *woman*. And not a *nurse*, but a *doctor*. Get it?" She'd been too irked to notice the sword, but now she saw it and gasped, backing up a few paces.

If Max McManlyman had been thinking, he'd have said, "Well, I'm a *man* and a *pirate*. Get it?" But he wasn't thinking. "Whatever," he said instead, waving his cutlass about. "You're our prisoner now. We need another doctor."

Quick as a blink, before she'd had a moment to think, she followed her gut instinct and made to fling herself over the gunwale of the ship, which they happened to be standing near. But McManlyman had been pirating a long time and had taken many a prisoner. He knew a thing or two about escape attempts.

He caught her by the ankle mid-dive and even (since she *was* a chick after all) gallantly held her out far enough so that she wouldn't bash her head against the edge of the ship. Then he said in his best Pirate Captain Voice, "I am Captain Maximus McManlyman and you *are* my prisoner."

"Whozamus McWhatnow?" she asked as she swayed back and forth, trying to look up at him.

"Maximus McManlyman," he responded. "You're my prisoner."

"Pull me up," was her only response. It was exceedingly difficult to have a conversation while hanging upside down, and definitely took away any pretense that she might have any control over the situation. What she really needed was to be standing upright and having a rational talk with this bully, though really there was no point because there is no speaking rationally with bullies whether you're upside down or right side up. Bullies have deep issues that take more than one rational chat to sort out.

"I really must object," Bernard said from behind the Captain. He spoke as firmly as he could through his fear—this was the first time in all their years on the ship that he had ever come close to standing up to the Captain. "She was the only doctor in that entire city who was brave enough to venture onto this ship to help Warren. What sort of reward is it to repay such bravery and kindness with—"

"There is no way you're forcing me to be a pirate," Jane cut in, still hanging over the edge of the ship by her ankle. "Pirates *kill* people. I can't sail with you."

"Oh no, no, no," McManlyman said. "You wouldn't be *killing* anyone. You'd just be patching us up. I know you doctor types have a code. We pirates respect codes." He began at last to haul her up. "We have a code, too: Get Lots of Treasure at Any Cost. You respect our code, we respect yours. Easy Peasy." He set her on her feet.

"But I'm *not*—" she said, straightening out her disheveled clothes as she glared at him.

"But you *are*. You, as I have mentioned a few times now, are my *prisoner*. You can say 'Okay!' and go help some hurt pirates, or you can say 'NO!' and get sent to the brig, and we'll bring some hurt pirates down, and you can then *help some hurt pirates*. Your choice. The end result is the same, so I'm cool with whatever decision you make."

"No!" yelled Jane and Bernard in unison. McManlyman nodded as though this was exactly what he'd been expecting. Then he brushed Bernard aside and hauled Jane down into the bowels of the ship and locked her up. He ordered that some lanterns, doctor trappings, and injured pirates be sent down to her, assuming rightly that even though she'd said she wouldn't help she wouldn't be able to keep from doing so once she saw some real live injured human beings lying there groaning and bleeding on the floor of her cell. Doctors were so predictable.

Bernard waylaid McManlyman as the Captain was on the way back from locking up Jane. Bernard said, "Not cool, man. Not cool. What the heck was that? You can't—"

"I *can*. What is with all these people telling me 'you can't'? I'm a pirate captain, and this is my ship, and so that means I get to do what I want to do. You'd do well to remember that. I like the money you pay me to transport you and your weird family across these waters, but I don't like it enough to put up with any lip from you. Don't make me get all piratical on you and your family—because," he said, getting all up in Bernard's face, "I will. Just give me a reason, and I'll totally do it, man."

Quaking in his boots as he stared at the shiny blade of Captain McManlyman's cutlass which hovered steadily inches from his face, Bernard decided he'd done what he could to help. Jane seemed like a capable enough lady, he rationalized, and maybe, he thought hopefully, with her feminist leanings she might not want some guy jumping into the fray to fight for her. He didn't want to *insult* her or anything, he tried to convince himself as he found himself nodding mutely at the Captain.

Jane would certainly not have been offended by any help from Bernard—she would have seen him not so much as a man helping a distressed damsel but as one human being who had an opportunity to assist another human being in need, which was definitely more what the situation was. But, though Bernard tried to do the right thing whenever he could, he was no hero or soldier, or any good at protecting himself, and he couldn't go getting himself killed for a lost cause when he had a family that needed him. So, he stepped back with only a mild irritation at being bullied, but also with a firm knowledge that there was really nothing he could have done to win anyway (short of challenging the Captain to a tightrope walking contest or a tap dancing duel, and it was very far from likely that McManlyman would have ever consented to agree to that sort of showdown).

McManlyman gave Bernard an annoying 'That's *right*, you're backing down," look that Bernard tried to ignore as he strolled off to check on his son who was resting on the floor of the family's room.

Warren gave him a brave smile from his nest of pillows and quilts on the floor and said, "Did you see the doctor off without incident?"

"Yup." Bernard knew his son well enough to be sure that once Warren knew about the doctor's wrongful imprisonment, he would try to do something heroic and silly, and end up in a situation that, even in top form, he wouldn't be able to handle. In Warren's incapacitated state, he would stand no chance at all of defending Jane.

Warren had been raised from infancy acting in family dramas, reading books about knights and princesses, playing romantic songs on his banjo and accordion, reading poetry, and in his off time daydreaming while staring out at the sea. The lad was, consequently, a bit too starry-eyed for his own good. Thus, Bernard's desire to keep Warren in the dark about the fact that the brave woman who had risked venturing onto a pirate ship in order to give him medical attention was now being held captive. The injustice of it would drive Warren to do something stupid.

That night, the family was awoken by the sound of Warren yelling like a madman. They assumed he was in need of more of the pain tonic that Jane had left them. It took Emily a few minutes of listening to his fevered blathering, though, to realize that his arm felt okay and he was flipping out because he had just remembered the harpsichord had been smashed in the storm along with his arm.

"Mom, what am I going to do?" he asked frantically, clutching at her sleeve.

"Honey," she said, all soothing and maternal, "Let's get you fixed first, and then you can worry about the harpsichord."

"But what if the Captain throws it out? I *need* that harpsichord, Mom. I can't live—"

Corrine, who had been rummaging through her bag this whole time, pulled out the contact info for the harpsichord repairman. "Here," she said, thrusting the paper tab into Warren's hand and holding up the lantern so that he could read it. "I found this on the docks."

Warren read it, first distractedly, then intently, gripping it in his fingertips like a tiny little lifeline. "Ooh, Corrine! Could you track down this guy?"

"Sure thing, little brother. I'll head out tomorrow morning."

Chapter Eight

In his evil lair, Farland Phelps was plotting.

Much like Julianna's parents, Farland had been devoting considerable efforts to finding the boy who could break the curse. Part of his plan was to post fliers for harpsichord repair by the docks. He figured this approach was bound to yield fruit eventually, since it must be challenging to keep a harpsichord tuned and in good repair on the high seas what with all the humidity and motion of the ship and whatnot. He further figured that this seafaring curse breaker would eventually end up in the Bay of Fritillary, since the capital was one of the biggest ports-of-call in the known world. So, he had strategically positioned a few harpsichord repair ads, then paid some vagrants (it's super cheap to employ vagrants; they work for peanuts) to panhandle in sight of the fliers and report to him when they saw some seafaring person express interest in the ad. From there, he just left it up to time while he devoted his energies to other plots and schemes.

He was currently giddy with excitement because, earlier that very day, one of his paid vagrants had come by to report that, at long last, some lady had taken a tab off a harpsichord ad. Of course, there was no way of knowing whether this lady had any connection to the boy he was searching for, but it would be silly of him not to pursue the lead. The vagrant had said that the lady had gone out to a ship after taking the tab, so that was at least a positive sign, since it meant that the harpsichord in need of repair might be on a ship.

The plan was this: He would transform his evil lair into a harpsichord studio, then wait for someone to stop by and ask about harpsichord repairs. He would visit their ship, ask a few leading questions, and find out whether anyone on the boat fit the bill as the lad who could break the curse. If it was a dead end, he'd just say he didn't have the right tools to finish the job; but if he *did* find the lad, Farland would kidnap him and send word through one of Conroy's spies (Farland had a double agent working as one of Conroy's spies) that the lad had been located. From there, all he'd need to do would be to slip the lad some time-release poison so he'd die shortly after being collected by the king, but before meeting the princess and breaking the spell. It was essential to the plan that Conroy get his hopes up as much as possible only to have them dashed by the lad's death at the last possible moment.

Farland grinned, chuckled, then looked around his lair and muttered, "First thing's first. I have to make this place look like a harpsichord studio." He felt a bit daunted looking around at the heavy, black velvet curtains, tapestries of skeletons wielding swords, shelves full of colorful powders and liquids with alarming names and skulls-and-crossbones prominently displayed on the labels, big melty candles with black flames, and books with labels like *Really, Really Deadly Poisons* and *Mind Reading Can Be Easy!* and *Compendium of Poison Substitutions*. The only thing in the entire room that he wouldn't have to hide or disguise was his fern in the front window. It would have been easier just to rent a storefront somewhere for the week, but unfortunately, he'd put his own address on the advertisement. Plus, he'd been short on funds of late.

Farland wished he could devote his life solely to his revenge plots, but regrettably there was no money in vengeance (he knew this for certain because he had registered himself as a nonprofit and then written a grant to see if anyone would fund him) so he had to resort to scraping out a living doing black market black magic for nobles whenever necessary in order to keep himself housed and fed as he pursued his real dream: getting back at Conroy.

Farland gave a huge sigh and told himself that, tedious though transforming his lair from an evil kind to a harpsichord kind would be, it still needed to be done, and the sooner the better. He gritted his teeth and got to work. First, he packed up his books and put them in his bedroom. Then, he turned all his bottles around so the poison labels were facing the back of the shelf. Next, Farland put up a sign on the shelf that read 'Harpsichord Polishes and Oils'. Those details attended to, he scuttled off to a local music store to get some decorations.

Some time later, he came back with a few parcels and rolled up papers under his arms. The rolled papers were posters of harpsichords, fingering charts, and one big poster of Lonnie Green, the most famous harpsichordist around—Lonnie smiled out of his poster with nice teeth and long, curly brown hair. Lonnie looked most out of place in this room, Farland thought, as he hung the poster on the wall over the magical pool of raven blood and between a tapestry of a skeleton with a sword and another tapestry of a skeleton playing checkers with Death.

Next, Farland cleaned some poster putty off his fingertips and rolled up his beloved tapestries, then stuck up in their place some of the harpsichord pictures. The magical pool of raven blood informed Farland that he had better not move *it* anywhere, so Farland (not wanting to anger it) just covered it up with a big wooden board that he stored under his bed and usually used as a surface for working jigsaw puzzles. With the board resting atop the heavy stone basin, it looked sort of like a table. After throwing a plaid flannel sheet from his bed over the jigsaw puzzle board for a tablecloth, Farland unwrapped one parcel to reveal some sheet music and magazines which he arranged on the makeshift coffee table. Standing back and looking at the display, he had to admit it looked rather artfully done.

Next, he opened up another parcel and placed its contents (a metronome and a statue of a G clef) on the shelf in front of his magic powders and liquids. He gave the arm of the metronome a tap to get it moving, and the steady tick-tick of a calming 58 beats per minute permeated the room.

Farland finally stepped back and surveyed his work with satisfaction. It was not perfect, but certainly passable; anyway, it would easily convince anyone who had no reason to be suspicious. He reached into his desk for paper, ink, and a quill, and wrote on good sturdy card-stock 'Farland Phelps. Harpsichord Repairs and Tuning'. He took this makeshift sign outside, and used a bit more poster putty to affix the sign to the front door of his modest ground-floor Evil Lair in a cul-de-sac just off the textiles district of the city.

He rented in a building that housed a tailor to his right, a lady who spun and dyed yarn to his left, and a family with about a million kids by the sound of it above him. Back when he'd lived in the castle, his Evil Lair had been much more grand, but his free ride as Conroy's BFF was long over, and rent in the city was insane even with an income helping the lords and ladies with the black market black magic making truth serums and invisibility spells (the lords and ladies all seemed to have the same problem: not trusting their spouses).

Surveying the results of his redecorating project, he gave a satisfied nod. Then, having nothing else to do, Farland went to stretch out on his bed and maybe take a nap or something. He couldn't kill time doing a puzzle since his puzzle board was doubling as a coffee table, and he didn't want to leave the apartment for fear of missing the visitor who might or might not even show up, and might or might not lead him to the one who might or might not be able to break the curse. With a sigh, Farland snuggled up under a quilt and began to read a book.

BRIGHT AND EARLY the next morning, Corrine and Bernard sallied forth for the harpsichord studio. After their epic search for a doctor the previous day, they had a pretty good idea of how to get around the slippery, grimy, disgusting streets. So, they were able to locate Farland's lair—er, harpsichord studio—before the morning dew had even evaporated from the piles of muck that lined the city streets. Bernard knocked on the door, then noticed that the poster putty affixing the sign to the door had nearly come undone, so he pushed it back into place. Why did the owner of this store use poster putty instead of nails, he wondered, and why was the sign made of paper instead of wood?

The door swung open, and they were greeted by a smiling, attractive man of about forty. He had long, black hair and lots of jeweled rings on his long fingers.

Corrine wondered whether all those rings got in the way of his harpsichord playing.

"May I help you?" he asked in a sleazy voice that, when paired with the over-eagerness with which he asked the question, made Corrine's skin crawl.

"Yes, we need a harpsichord repaired," she said hesitantly, as he ushered them into the sparse storefront that was strangely devoid of actual harpsichords, though it did have a lot of posters and some sheet music and magazines. Corrine said, "The harpsichord is on a pirate ship. I hope that is not a problem?" Maybe she shouldn't have mentioned the pirate ship right off the bat, but part of her was hoping he'd say no—she had a bad feeling about this guy, but didn't know if the bad feeling was just because he sounded slimy, or if there was something else about him that was causing her intuition bells to ring.

He raised an eyebrow in surprise when he heard about the pirate ship, but said, "That shouldn't be a problem. Let's go." And then he headed toward the door. They didn't know it, of course, but pirates didn't scare him in the least since he could disappear at will. Getting into dangerous situations never fazed Farland Phelps.

"Wait—" Corrine said. "Don't you need to know what's wrong with the harpsichord? Talk payment? Anything?" Why was this dude flying out the door at the first mention of a broken harpsichord without getting any information or grabbing any tools?

Shoot, Farland thought, *I'm being too eager. Calm down, Farland. Calm down. You'll know soon enough if this lead is going anywhere.* He turned and said, "Ah, well, we can talk payment after I see what's wrong with it. And, er, as to what *is* wrong with the instrument, I never ask laymen to, er, diagnose. I would rather go in with a head unclouded by preconceptions."

"Wow, there must be more going on in the inside of a harpsichord than I thought," Bernard muttered. "You really have to worry about misdiagnosing?" As he asked this, his gaze began to travel over the various bottles of liquids and powders. There definitely was more to this whole harpsichord thing than he'd thought. *Just look at all those bottles of colorful stuff!* He reached out to touch a bottle with big shiny pink crystals inside.

"Don't touch that!" barked Farland with anger and alarm.

Bernard's hand froze an inch away from the bottle, and he stared at Farland with astonishment. "What--?"

"Fool! Do not meddle with things you do not understand!" Farland spat. "Imbecile!" he added for good measure as he swooped over to the shelf and laid a protective hand on the side of the bottle. It was only then, when it was far too late, that he remembered that the contents of the bottle were supposed to be mere harpsichord maintenance crystals, not potentially explosive minerals used to concoct an invisibility spell. He winced at his overreaction and turned to meet their shocked gazes. Farland cleared his throat, and, after an awkward pause in which he was painfully aware of the ticking of the metronome, he said, "I take harpsichord repair and maintenance very seriously."

"Clearly," said Corrine, looking at him with an expression that indicated what she thought of his sanity, or lack thereof. Every move Farland made and every word he uttered further convinced her that something was off with him.

"Look," Bernard said, "I have no doubt that a person who feels as deeply as you do about your art will be able to fix our harpsichord. You're a little loony, but I don't care as long as you can fix my kid's harpsichord. He's a sensitive boy, and I want him calmed down as soon as possible. You see, he's been injured and I want him to take it easy and relax so he can heal, but he's not going to do that until the harpsichord is repaired. He's got some strange connection to that thing that defies reason. So, if you are willing to come with us aboard the pirate ship, then I think we have a deal!" Bernard stuck his hand out to shake Farland's.

"A strange connection that defies reason?" Farland mused as he absently shook Bernard's hand. Now *that* sounded like something that could indicate magic was involved—when a thing defied reason, it could very well be because there was a spell or potion involved that was bending things in a way that was contrary to the norm.

Farland would have loved to read their minds right about then (assuming they were weak-minded enough), but he was currently out of his mind-reading powder (it was expensive to concoct), and even if he'd had the powder, he had to have been taking it for 48 hours, one dose every 12 hours, in order to effectively read minds at will. Without the help of the mind-reading powder, his skills were remedial at best; it was physically draining without the powder, and mostly he heard just a bunch of muffled rumbling, and jumbled up sounds, with only a hint of the subject's actual thoughts.

He missed the good old days in the castle when he'd had the ability to obtain whatever ingredients he wanted in whatever amounts he required. Currently, he only had one bottle left of his mind reading powder and he was saving it for a special occasion since he didn't know how he'd ever be able to get any more of the key ingredient: the pollen of a flower that grew half the world away at only a certain altitude on a particular mountain, and, of course, it bloomed only once every three years.

When he'd been pals with Conroy, he had sent expeditions to the mountain whenever he fancied.

Sometimes Farland wished that when he'd been younger, he'd have realized what a cost to his material comfort this whole revenge thing would turn out to be. If he had consulted the magical pool of raven blood, would it have told him that the path of revenge would lead him to a slummy little apartment and a pittance of an income? Would it have told him of cold winter nights with barely enough fuel for the fire to keep the chill at bay, and weeks where he had to get by with nothing more than sandwiches made of sawdust-infused bread and mustard? And, if the magical pool of raven blood had actually condescended to reveal this information (which was unlikely since the magical pool of raven blood was moody and peevish on its good days), would the knowledge have swayed Farland from following his dreams?

Probably not.

He had been so darn idealistic in his youth.

Fortunately, he had *another* plot brewing that would hopefully end up landing him back in the castle.

It took Farland a moment to realize he had zoned out in the middle of the conversation with his visitors. Oblivious, the dad was talking. Farland cut in, "What? I—uh—I lost track of our conversation just now. I was— uh—pondering the intricacies of the inner workings of the harpsichord... What were we talking about?"

Bernard blinked. "You were asking about my son's strange connection to his harpsichord. I was just saying how he's a born musician when it comes to his banjo and accordion, but with that harpsichord he touches it and it sounds like a rabid squirrel is running across the keys. But he keeps trying and trying."

Farland's eyes bugged out and his jaw dropped. He thought, *Banjo, harpsichord, and accordion?! Those are the instruments specified in my counter-curse! This is it!*

The girl was staring at him with a funny look.

Farland realized the expression on his face was pretty crazy. He shut his mouth, blinked his eyes, and tried to contain his excitement. But now that he was almost 100% sure he had found the one who'd break the curse, it took every ounce of his self-control to remain in character and not fly out the door demanding they take him at once to the pirate ship or suffer the consequences.

Then it occurred to him, why couldn't he just do that? Demand that they take him to their son/brother pronto or be cursed with some dreadful curse?

But no, if he did that, something could go wrong; they could try to be heroic and alert the lad once they neared the ship, or they might be wearing protective amulets--doubtful, but possible, and he had waited for so long that he didn't want to take the risk of messing it all up just because he couldn't be patient for a few more hours. No, it was best if he tried to play it cool for a bit more. He cleared his throat and said carefully, "How odd! Well, it sounds like this harpsichord is very important to him. Let's get it fixed up all shiny and new! The sooner the better, I say!"

"Indubitably!" Bernard said with a grin.

The two men capered out the door, one happy to have found someone who could help Warren and give him some peace of mind, the other happy to be shortly killing Warren dead.

Corrine watched them go, eyes narrowed with suspicion. She didn't like Farland one bit, but she couldn't put into convincing words what exactly it was that bothered her, so she followed at a distance, close enough to listen to him talking to her father, but far enough that he'd be disinclined to try to talk to her.

"So, have you always liked the harpsichord?" Bernard was asking, trying to strike up a conversation with Farland.

"Oh, yeah. Totally," Farland said, sounding like he was not paying much attention.

"What do you like most about it?"

"Oh—the—um—the plinky plinky things—you know, the black and white bits—"

"The keys?" Corrine supplied incredulously, finding herself unable to keep quiet.

"Yeah, them!" Farland replied. "They're what I like best about the harpsichord for sure."

"Ah, yes, they are nice," Bernard said, still trying to give Farland the benefit of the doubt. "But I didn't mean what part of the instrument do you like best—I meant, what drew you to the harpsichord as opposed to some other—"

"Dad!" Corrine roared. "This guy doesn't know what *keys* are! If it weren't for the fact that there is no conceivable reason a person would impersonate a harpsichord repair man and venture onto a ship filled with pirates, I would say he was not who he says he is! *Something is not right!*"

"You don't need to know what keys are called in order to fix them," Farland pulled out of the blue, and even managed to say it condescendingly.

Bernard nodded in agreement at this logic. "That does make sense."

"No it doesn't!" Corrine exploded.

Bernard said to Farland, "Will you please excuse me for a moment while I talk to my daughter?"

Farland said, "Indeed," then gave Corrine a shifty glance that Bernard didn't see and wandered down the road a bit to do some window shopping.

"What's up, kid?" Bernard asked her. "You're acting weird."

"*I'm* acting weird?"

"I'm not saying he's not weird, dear. I'm just saying that you are, too. So what if he's got some quirks? Like you said, there's no conceivable reason for him to be impersonating a harpsichord repair man. To get onto a pirate ship, no less. If he can fix the darn instrument and thus make Warren calm down and rest so he can heal, then that is all I care about."

She glared at Farland's back but said, "I guess you're right…" Farland was looking into the window of a gourmet dog food boutique, appearing to be surveying some baked-on-site bone-shaped biscuits and a pyramid of bejeweled food and water dishes "For that special pooch in your life!" as the sign in the window said.

As she watched him at the window, she caught his gaze through the reflection. Had he been watching them through the window's reflection? Creepy. There was definitely something more going on here than innocent harpsichord repair.

"Sweetheart, let it go. You're just stressed from these past few days. The storm, Warren's injury, your first time off a ship in your entire twenty-two years of life. There's been a lot going on."

Though she knew she was indeed a bit stressed, she also knew that stress didn't make her imagine things. However, she supposed she might as well ignore this Farland's weirdness and just keep an eye on him to make sure he didn't try anything stupid.

And of course, she didn't have to worry for long. Once they were back on the pirate ship surrounded by a hoard of murderous thugs, she'd feel worlds safer. This Farland didn't look like he would be able to hold his own in a fight against even the pirates' scrawny, asthmatic cabin boy, Frank. "Okay, Dad. I'll let it go. But once he's seen to the harpsichord and been paid, he is *off* the ship."

Bernard nodded in agreement and went over to let Farland know that they were ready to move on.

CHAPTER NINE

Julianna paced around her room, glancing at the clock on her fireplace mantle a few times every minute. She was making Curtis, Montague, and Dexter nervous as they hovered around watching her. Every so often they tried to talk to her, in hopes of snapping her out of her crazed anticipation, but she barely heard them, and didn't respond.

The previous night, Julianna had finally gotten so close to breaking through the end of the tunnel that the soil had been loose enough for her to push through with her hands. Though she had wanted nothing more than to break through that last bit of dirt and be free at last (if just for the night), she'd refrained since she didn't yet have all the supplies packed for her adventure. Also, she hadn't been sure what time it was, and there was no chance she was going to risk digging out into the world if it might be around sunrise. It was most certainly not her intention to finish her tunnel at long last only to bumble out at the wrong time of day and have the curse come to its culmination.

So, she had hurried back down the tunnel and continued her planning.

Now she was prepared at last and just waiting for sunset, which, according to her consultation of a chart of the Fritillary skies she'd found in her library, was going to occur at 7:06 pm.

For the third time in the past hour, Julianna pulled out from under her bed the bag she had filled with all the things she had packed for her escapade.

"You've looked through that bag a hundred times," muttered Curtis. "Julianna, just give it a rest. You're making me anxious."

Wordlessly, she pulled out the little pouch of money she'd stolen from her mother, some food scavenged off the table when Delia's back was turned, a steak knife from last night's dinner, and a heavy, thick blanket to cover herself with just in case she somehow got trapped out in the sunlight and needed to take cover.

She only needed one more thing: once Delia was in a drugged sleep, Julianna would pry out the brick that Dexter's spirit was tethered to. Part of her had wanted to be alone for her first adventure, but the closer the clock ticked to sunset, the more Julianna realized she wanted the company of a friend. She was at heart a cautious, worrying type, so it gave her comfort to have not only a friend, but a sneaky, criminally-minded friend who might be able to give her some advice on the off chance that she got into a sticky situation.

Dexter was very happy to be accompanying her but wasn't nearly as restless. He'd been a ghost for 83 years, and before that had been alive for 23, so he'd had plenty of time to acquire patience. "I wonder how much the town has changed," he mused as he lay stretched out on the floor. Surely things on the outside would look completely different from what they had last time he'd seen the city.

Montague grumbled something cranky, but Dexter didn't bother asking him to annunciate, figuring that he was just saying something about how it wasn't fair Dexter was going to be able to get out of the dungeon and not him.

"Oh, Montague, you know I'd take you if I could," Julianna said, "But there's no way I could pry that rock off the bathroom wall and lug it up the tunnel and outside!"

Montague shrugged.

Curtis was too nervous about Julianna's departure to think about what he'd be missing. He was fuming in the corner of the room, arms crossed over his chest as he glared at her. Earlier, they'd had a fierce fight where he had yelled as loudly as he'd pleased because he was a ghost, and she had whispered ferociously since she didn't want Delia to overhearing anything. What the fight had boiled down to was that he didn't want her to get stuck outside at sunrise, and she didn't understand how he thought for a moment that, now that she was so close, she would actually give up on the one dream she had ever had—the thing she had been working toward for more than half her life.

Of course, the fight had not changed her opinion one bit about finishing the tunnel. So, they had called a truce of sorts. He was still very mad, but she was too preoccupied with her preparations and with her excitement about what was to come to let it bother her too much. Besides, she was so used to Curtis hounding her about the danger of her tunneling project that she was really not as fazed as he'd have liked.

A consultation of the clock on the mantle told her she only had an hour to go. Julianna realized she hadn't had dinner and remembered that Delia had knocked on her door more than an hour earlier to let her know it was ready. Even though she was too excited to eat, she decided she'd better try anyway, if only to keep Delia from wondering if something was wrong with her. Also, dinner was a good time to slip some of the sleeping potion into Delia's tea.

Julianna wandered out, sat down, ate a dinner she barely tasted, paid just enough attention to Delia's questions to avert suspicion, and then drugged Delia's cup when the old woman left the room to refill the pitcher of water.

She finished her food, swiped a slice of bread and stuffed it in her pocket, and got up and walked in a giddy daze back to her room to change into the plainest dress she could find.

Then, she waited.

"LOOK, KID, JUST don't drop that brick," Dexter said from where he was hovering beside Julianna as she guided herself by her makeshift rope to the top of the tunnel.

"Of course I'm not going to lose the brick that your soul is tethered to," Julianna said as she grabbed up her trowel that was waiting for her at the top of the tunnel where she'd left it. "Give me some credit."

"Because," he went on as though she hadn't spoken, "If you drop that brick down some chasm or something and can't retrieve it, then I'm stuck in a chasm *forever*. And as boring as your dungeon is, a chasm would be worse."

She ignored him, then sunk the trowel into the dirt in front of her and began to dig. Almost immediately, what remained of the tunnel gave way and she was staring out of a hole into the real, honest-to-goodness night sky.

She gasped and stared.

Stars everywhere.

It was beautiful.

The cold breeze on the edge of the cliff tossed her hair around.

"Oooh!" she breathed. "Wow! Stars! Wind! Let's go!" and she scampered out the hole without a backward glance.

"Careful! That's a cliff!" Dexter barked, then sighed as he poked his head out the hole in time to see the princess careening down a thankfully-shallow bit of cliff that ended with a wide outcrop of rock. She rolled to a stop and gasped, then looked up at her friend as he joined her.

"Do you realize you could have just *died!?*" he screeched. "Working on that tunnel since you were eight years old, and then you fly right out like an idiot and nearly roll off a cliff to your death!"

Julianna winced at his rage, swallowed, and nodded. "You're right. I have to be more careful." She peered cautiously over the edge of the outcrop of rock and felt a horrible chill as she saw the sheer cliff below her and the ocean crashing up against its base far, far, far, far below.

"You have to pay attention to where you put your feet," he lectured, and floated down to sit beside her. "You're used to walking around on level ground. You've never walked on an uneven surface in your life, Princess."

She glared at him. He had a tendency to only refer to her as "Princess" when she was acting in an ignorant or silly way that was a byproduct of her pampered, sheltered existence. "I *know*." She shoved aside her apprehension about the cliff and looked up at the stars. "Look, there's the Great Bumblebee and the Lesser Bumblebee!" she pointed out, then proceeded to show Dexter all the constellations of the Fritillary sky, even though she knew that he didn't care and was probably only pretending to pay attention. She'd memorized them from a book as a kid, and was proud of herself when she realized how much of what she'd memorized had been retained in her brain.

"Great," he said after a while. "This is great fun. Kid, get up and climb this cliff. It's not too steep over to the left. Just climb on up to the base of the castle's foundation over there and let's see where that takes us. The ground's bound to level off somewhere up near the base of the castle."

Julianna looked at the castle towering above her, seeing for the first time the home she'd lived in her whole life. There was quite a bit of cliff to scramble up before she got to the foundation of the building, but she knew from studying maps of the grounds that, once she did manage to get to the top of the cliff, she could make her way to the left and end up in the gardens, where there were hopefully lots of hiding places amongst the shrubberies.

It was lucky that one of the moons was almost full, otherwise she'd never have been able to manage the climb. But after many a stumble and a few very close calls, she and Dexter finally emerged victorious from the edge of the cliff and stepped into the garden.

The Royal Gardener was, of course, awesome at his trade—the most awesome in all the land!—so Julianna's first glimpse of real live plants that weren't the sickly, sun-deprived potted ones in her dungeon was almost more beauty than she could process. She stared and stared and stared. Huge, colorful flowers, tiny colorful flowers, medium colorful flowers. Shrubs trained to grow in all sorts of wacky shapes. Trees everywhere. She went up to one little gnarly one with big, rounded leaves and touched its bark, staring up into its leafy shades with awe.

"Geez, you're seriously going to spend your first night out of the dungeon staring at the sky and petting plants?" Dexter moaned from beside her. "This whole kingdom is chock full of trees. No matter where we go tonight, one thing you can count on is that there will be trees."

"Simmer down, grouch. This tree is so pretty!" she said as she felt the rough, bumpy bark beneath her fingers. "Don't worry, I'll get moving soon, but do give me a few minutes of quiet. Or I'll drop your brick right here at the base of this lovely little tree and leave you to get to know it for a few weeks."

"You wouldn't," he said, but gave her the quiet she requested all the same, watching her as she left the tree behind and meandered down a dirt path. He had to keep reminding himself that, as much as he would have liked to just leave the castle forever and go exploring the city and the villages beyond, that was out of the question; the farthest they would be going was to the orchards on the outskirts of the ornamental garden—any further was too much of a risk because of that accursed curse. No matter how uneventful this night seemed to him though, he knew at least she'd be thrilled no matter how little they did, since however small it was, it was all new to her.

Dexter sighed a resigned sigh as he saw Julianna bend down in the path with a look of delight on her face, reach down, and pop up holding a worm. Meeting his eyes, she pointed at the worm with an enthusiastic grin. It was a very good thing no one was around, because she looked insane, especially since she was the only one who could see him.

"Simmer down, princess," he said and floated over to where she stood letting the worm slide around her fingers. "You look like a lunatic. Don't assume no one will be in the gardens at night."

As if on cue, they heard footsteps from the other side of a big bush. She dropped the worm and dove into a shrub on the side of the path. It was two guards, and as they walked by her hiding spot she heard, "—they don't understand the conditions the people really are living in! They're so out-of-touch!" The guard spoke with all the conviction of a ranting revolutionary.

"Keep it down, Larry. Geez Louise, you want to get overheard talking like that on the castle grounds?"

"I'm just so fed up with it!" Larry said, but more quietly. "I mean, I go visit my parents on days off, and I see how—" and they walked out of earshot. But Julianna got the gist of the conversation. She had already gathered long ago that the populace was getting pretty unhappy with how her dad was running things, but it was still especially disconcerting to find that the very men who were hired to guard the castle were talking about what a bad job he was doing.

She emerged from her shrub, feeling significantly less jolly than she had when she'd dived into it moments earlier. She looked at Dexter with unease but didn't say anything. For one thing, there was nothing to say anyway since he was every bit as in the dark about current events as she was. But also, even though Dexter liked her personally, he did not like royalty generally. Not at all. She had heard him ranting to Curtis so often about The Man that she knew he would side with that guard if she tried to talk about what they'd overheard. So, she kept her worries to herself and walked on silently, picking leaves out of her hair.

"Let's go to the orchard," he suggested mildly, watching her with concern. It was a shame she'd had to hear that and have her first night out clouded with apprehension. Maybe he could find some sort of little adventure for her to take her mind off of things.

In his flesh-and-blood life as a ruffian, Dexter had known of a hidden tunnel under the wall behind the orchard where people working in the castle had smuggled things in and out. Granted, it had been 83 years ago and the tunnel could have been found and filled in long ago, but it was worth a try.

Getting out and exploring the city was just the thing Julianna needed; all this quiet and moonlight and nature were too conducive to deep thought and the pondering of life.

R IGHT ABOUT THE time Julianna had been sitting down for dinner, Farland had at long last been stepping into the presence of the boy who could break the curse. Bernard, Corrine, and Farland had paddled out to the pirate ship and boarded, then Corrine had rushed off to update Warren.

Meanwhile, Bernard and Farland walked through the swarms of industrious pirates doing repair work to the ship and made their way to the harpsichord in the Captain's quarters. Farland had looked at it for a few moments and then said to Bernard, "What I really need to do in order to understand this instrument better is to talk to your son."

"Why?" Bernard asked. "I mean, the lid is bashed in and a few keys are knocked off. Isn't that all kinda straightforward?"

Farland looked at Bernard witheringly. "You, sir, are no musician?" Of course, the real reason Farland wanted to talk to Warren was not to gain greater insights into the harpsichord/player bond, but to make completely certain that Warren was the boy he was seeking out to kidnap and eliminate.

"No," Bernard said sheepishly. "No, I am not a musician."

"Then there is no point trying to explain."

"Right," Bernard mumbled. "This way."

As they walked, Farland reached into his satchel and felt around to make sure he had what he needed. There was the vial which he knew without looking held an orange liquid which, when combined with powdered asparagus tips, would create a gas that would knock unconscious anyone within a twenty-foot radius who wasn't holding their breath. It was Farland's plan to simply go into the room Warren was in, ask a few questions of the lad, and then hold his breath and mix the contents of the vial with the little packet of powdered asparagus tips he'd brought; everyone else would collapse to the floor and he'd disappear in a puff of smoke with this *Warren*.

But there was a problem. His hand searched around his satchel, but he couldn't feel the pouch of powdered asparagus tips. "Confound it!" he breathed and stopped in his tracks, peering into the satchel but not seeing the asparagus. He did, however, see a little hole in the satchel's corner. "Condratted-found it!" he roared.

Bernard turned and asked, "Is something wrong?"

"Yes, something is wrong!" Farland said. "Something very important has fallen out of my satchel!"

"Oh?" Bernard asked, backtracking and scanning the ground they'd just walked across. "What is it?"

"It's a very important constituent element for my—er—harpsichord, um… cream. Yes, my harpsichord cream." Farland winced inwardly at his clumsy save; he *really* should have done a bit of harpsichord research before getting into this.

But to Farland's relief, Bernard didn't find the idea of harpsichord cream suspicious, apparently, for he just said, "Well, you are going to have to go back to the mainland for your tools anyway, so you can just bring some of this cream when you return, right?"

Farland heaved a sigh. *This plan was going to take all stinking day to carry out at the rate it was going.* "Do you have a doctor on this ship?" he asked. "A doctor might have the ingredient I need." In the Land of Fritillary, the line between doctors and magicians was quite blurred. There were a few things doctors did that magicians didn't (surgery, for instance), and a few things magicians did that doctors didn't (like disappearing and reappearing somewhere else), but most of what they both did was actually more chemistry than anything—taking the same ingredients and mixing them up, just sometimes mixing in different ways for different end goals. Also, doctors were more progressive and tended toward science and reason, whereas magicians were more traditional, believing in the old ways and in supernatural explanations.

"Yup, we've got a doctor. I'll take you right over to the infirmary. Hopefully they've got what you need."

Bernard led Farland to visit Doc Brock and Jane.

CHAPTER TEN

Jane and Doc Brock were both in the infirmary when Bernard and Farland came in to ask for some powdered asparagus tips. Very soon after Jane had been thrown in the brig, she had begun to see her situation from a different perspective; resisting her capture had seemed like the appropriate decision at the time, but once the heat of the moment had cooled down a bit and she'd found herself stuck down in the bowels of the ship with three wounded pirates writhing around in agony on the filthy floor at her feet, with horrible lighting and no one to lend her a hand, she decided pretty quickly that it was time to set aside her righteous indignation about her treatment. Just because one doesn't like the facts, doesn't make the facts go away, and the fact was that she was stuck on this pirate ship whether she wanted to be or not.

If she just accepted it and got on with things, then at least she could be a captive in nicer surroundings. She could also have a better chance of patching up the pirates without them getting any number of disgusting infections one would expect to contract when lying with open wounds on a floor coated in rat droppings.

Not that the pirates deserved patching up.

She'd sent word to McManlyman that she was ready to accept her situation if he'd let her go up and work in the infirmary. He'd agreed and let her leave the brig, but not before throwing in an irritating jab about how he'd known the whole time that this was exactly how things were going to shake out in the end.

Into the infirmary traipsed Farland. He sleazed without preamble, "Asparagus tips! Have you any powdered asparagus tips?"

Jane looked up with surprise from the salty sea dog she was tending to. "*Excuse me?*" she asked. "What do you need powdered asparagus tips for?" Who was this stranger to come barging in here demanding she hand over one of the most potent ingredients in her cupboards? She wasn't about to start doling out asparagus without having a good reason.

"Sure. It's in the cupboard somewhere," Doc Brock said from where he was sitting in the corner, doing a very sloppy job of wrapping bandages—a task Jane had assigned him shortly after joining him to work in the infirmary. It hadn't taken her long to discover that he was not a real doctor at all. He had taken his demotion quite happily since he had never wanted to be a doctor in the first place.

Farland, who was absentmindedly fiddling around with the orange vial that was so important to his plan, gave her a contemptuous look. "Don't trouble your head with why I need it, little lady," he said dismissively. Then to the Doc Brock he said, "Many thanks, sir" and made his way toward the cupboard.

"Here, let me get it for you," Jane said quickly and darted to the cupboard before Farland had taken two steps. She had seen that vial in his hand. She had seen the thick, orange liquid within it. In medical circles, that orange substance was mixed in very small quantities with powdered asparagus tips to knock patients out for surgery; she had no idea what this guy could possibly be planning to do with such a large amount of the liquid, but one thing she *did* know was that he was not going to get his hands on any asparagus if she could help it.

However, if *she* could just get her hands on that vial of his, then she could use it herself to escape! Jane was somewhat alarmed at how quickly her brain had made this leap, but if she could just get that vial, then she herself could mix it with powdered asparagus tips when she was in close proximity to the pirates (maybe when they were all gathered in the dining room for brunch the following morning) and then she could hold her breath, mix the two ingredients, and there would certainly be enough gas released from the reaction to render them all unconscious. Freedom!

Jane looked suspiciously over her shoulder at Farland. That must be what he was planning—to knock out a room full of people! But why?

"What brings you to the ship?" she asked Farland, trying for mild curiosity.

"I'm here to meet with this man's son," the wizard disguised as a harpsichord repairman said irritably, then added, "Oh, and to fix a harpsichord, too. Now get on with it, nurse. The asparagus!"

If she had thought Farland's intended victims were the pirates, she probably would have just handed over a pouch of asparagus and stood back to watch what unfolded, ready to jump ship at a moment's notice. But it looked as though his target was not the pirates but Warren. Which made no sense at all.

Jane ignored his rudeness as she pretended to search through the cupboard. "Powdered asparagus tips for harpsichord repair? Well fancy that!" She figured it would be best to play the vacuous stereotype he obviously thought her, and not to inform him that she was a doctor; if he found out her true profession, he might realize she had the knowledge to be aware of what the orange liquid in that vial could do when mixed with the powder. The last thing she wanted was for him to put his guard up.

"It's for some cream," Bernard supplied when Farland didn't respond.

Some cream? Suspicious… At last she found what she had been searching for: a powdery green clay that, when mixed with water, was used to cover burns. Being lighter in color than the asparagus, it was not a perfect match, but certainly passable; anyway, it would easily convince anyone who had no reason to be suspicious. She emptied a bit of it from its storage jar into a little black pouch, then pulled the drawstring tight and turned, saying, "Here you go! I hear that stuff is pretty expensive, so don't waste it!"

"Oh, fear not, I'll be putting it to good use," he said with a sleazy cackle that was quite excessive for the situation. Then he snatched the pouch out of her hand and clutched it tightly in his fist.

Bernard thanked her for her help, and they left.

"Brock," Jane said to her assistant, "I'll be back in a few minutes." Grabbing some real powdered asparagus tips from the cupboard, she sneaked after them, not about to let that orange vial out of her sight.

○WARREN WAS CURLED up in his nest of blankets on the floor resting when his father, his doctor, and his maybe-kidnapper/ murderer strolled in. He had been having a quality chat with his sister, who had been filling him in about what a creepy weirdo this harpsichord repairman seemed to be, so Warren was already on guard. Upon hearing footsteps approaching, Corrine had grabbed her notepad and retreated to her hammock, trying to look as though she'd been working industriously on her latest play. She gave Farland a wary glance when he sleazed into the room, and he looked suspiciously from her to her brother and back again. But he merely said, "Why hello, lad. My name is Farland Phelps, and I fix harpsichords."

"Thank you for making the trip out to the ship," Warren said.

"Before I get down to business with the instrument, I need to know a bit about you[6]. The, er, repair stuff I use has powdered asparagus tips in it," he said, waving the packet he'd received from Jane about as proof. "I need to, um, know if you have any asparagus allergies, because you might not be able to touch the harpsichord if it has this asparagus cream on it." This was the first time in this whole endeavor that he'd had to talk to someone who actually knew about harpsichords, and he was suddenly painfully aware of how lame his story was. *Asparagus cream for a harpsichord? Why hadn't he given any time to thinking up a believable story? Why?*

He grimaced as Warren gave him a confused, disbelieving look. "Asparagus cream for a harpsichord?"

"Yes," Farland plodded on, because what else could he do? "It's a new thing. You may not have heard of it if you've been out here on the seas for a long time. Your harpsichord care tools may be out-of-date."

"Well, we *have* been out on the seas for a long time. My whole life in

---

6   In case you don't recall, dear reader, in order for Warren to be the one who could break the curse, he needed (1) to have spent his whole life at sea, (2) to be part of a traveling theater troupe, (3) to play banjo, accordion, and harpsichord, and (4) to be allergic to asparagus. Farland knew he had (2) and (3), and he was pretty sure about (1). That left (4).

fact—" (A-ha! That was (1) confirmed!) "—but I get *Harpsichord Quarterly* delivered to the ship by carrier petrel, and I've never heard of harpsichord cream."

Farland was so close. So close to getting the information he needed. "Are you allergic to asparagus?!" he cried. "ARE YOU!?" And he opened the pouch, took a pinch of the powder out of the bag, and rushed at Warren in a crazy whirl of black cloak and rage.

"Arg!" Warren cried, trying to both protect his broken arm from this madman and cover himself with a quilt to keep the asparagus powder off. "Don't get that stuff on me! It'll make me itch like crazy!"

Bernard, Jane, and Emily had all, after a few moments of utter shock at this turn of events, leapt forward to grab and subdue Farland. Corrine would have helped too, but she was in her hammock and was no good at extricating herself from the thing in a hurry. So, she just stared with amazed confusion. They pulled Farland away from Warren, which wasn't too difficult because he was done flipping out now that he had at last figured out that Warren was indeed allergic to asparagus.

"Let go of me!" he roared.

"No way, man," Bernard said. "There is something very off about you."

Corrine shot her dad a glare; if only he had listened to her back in the city, none of this would have ever happened.

"I think it's time we took you back to shore, Mr. Phelps," said Bernard.

"I think not," Farland said, switching from Harpsichord Repairman Voice to his fancy Wizard Voice.

Then, he disappeared in a big, smelly puff of smoke.

In the following pandemonium, there was much cursing and stumbling, and a few cries of pain from Warren as people stepped on him. Farland, from where he'd reappeared on the opposite side of the door, listened to the chaos for a few moments with a smile. Then, he rummaged in his satchel. He opened the vial and the pouch, poured the asparagus powder into the spare vial, poured some orange liquid into the vial too, and then covered the vial with his thumb so the reaction wouldn't start until he was ready for it. Once he heard things simmer down a bit inside, he opened the door and strode smirking into their baffled midst. "At last," he said with glee. "After years of searching, I've found you." He looked at a still coughing Warren, who was, of course, thoroughly confused.

"Me? You've been looking for *me* for years?" *Cough, cough.* "You've made some sort of," *cough*, "mistake," *cough*, "fella."

"Nope, my boy. You meet every single one of the criteria I set out when planning the counter-curse. That means you *are* the counter-curse for the King's firstborn child. And, further, that means you are coming with me!"

Blank stares and coughs all around.

"Um... No, I'm not... What?..." Warren stuttered as his parents both stepped in front of their son. Corrine began to ungracefully disentangle herself from the hammock in case she was needed.

From where she hovered in the doorway, Jane got ready to pounce should she see an opportunity to grab the orange vial. All was still and silent for a few moments, except for a few scattered coughs.

"You're a dead man, my boy," Farland cackled evilly.

"!!!?" said Warren.

His parents closed ranks tighter in front of their son.

Farland laughed at their pathetic, common attempts to bar the way of one of the greatest wizards in the land. Then he gave the orange vial a quick shake, took a deep breath, and removed his finger from the top.

A pop, a fizzle, and a little waft of lazy, purple smoke.

When he had laughed maniacally and begun to shake the vial, everyone but Jane had instinctively shielded themselves from whatever it was that was about to happen. Then, they heard the telltale fizzle of a spell gone wrong, and slowly all turned to look at him with varying degrees of fear, anger, and confusion.

"What in blazes is going on!?" Bernard roared, stepping forward with fists balled up.

Farland was about to disappear when Jane knocked him over the head with Warren's banjo case, which had been propped against the door frame.

The wizard collapsed into a heap, but not before Jane swiped the vial out of his hand.

Bernard walked over and gave him a shove with his toe.

"Dad, I *told* you there was something weird about that guy!" Corrine said, pointing down at the unconscious Farland.

"Honey, I know, I know..." he said, still looking down at Farland. "I'm sorry." A long pause followed. "I don't suppose there would be any use in tying him up? He can disappear."

"He's some kind of wizard, right?" Warren asked, not really needing to hear the answer. Then he asked a very important and obvious question, and one which he was insulted that a family member hadn't thought to ask first: "Why does he think he's looking for *me*?"

"That," Emily said shakily, "is an excellent question."

"And he called me a *dead man*. Is there any other way to interpret that, or does he want to kill me?"

"I think he wants to kill you," Corrine agreed.

"But—?" said Emily.

"We have to get off this ship," Bernard stated. "Fast. That guy is going to wake up and try to get Warren again, right?"

Everyone nodded.

"If he knows where to find Warren, he is going to just be able to appear any time he likes and *get* him," Bernard said, not finding himself able to say the word "kill" in reference to his only son.

Warren made to get to his feet, but Jane said, "Don't. Your legs will be wobbly from your medicine." She looked at this strange but somehow endearing family of traveling performers. "Okay. I have a plan." She then explained to them what she thought Farland's plans had been with the asparagus, and how they had only been foiled by her switching the asparagus powder for the clay powder. "We doctors use this orange stuff in conjunction with asparagus powder to keep patients unconscious during surgery. Judging by the amount I have here in this vial, I could probably keep him unconscious for about two days. That is plenty of time for you all to disappear into the city. How about I just keep him here until the medicine runs out? He can't disappear if he's unconscious."

"You would do that for us?" Emily whispered.

"Sure," said Jane. "You seem like really nice people, and you've gone to so much trouble to keep your son alive—I couldn't possibly just stand by and watch this Farland guy carry out his plan."

"Well then, just drug him quick and come with us. That way by the time he figures out it was you who kept him on the ship, you'll be long gone," Corrine said.

"I can't go. The drug needs to be administered every three hours. And besides—" She had been about to mention that McManlyman wouldn't let her go, but Bernard began to violently shake his head and then do a zipping motion across his lips.

Jane gathered quickly that for some reason Bernard didn't want her to mention that she was a captive on the ship. She shrugged and let her sentence die off awkwardly.

"Besides what?" Warren asked, looking from his dad to Jane while he processed his confusion about their sudden weirdness. "Hey wait, what are you doing on this ship anyway, Doctor? My dad said he returned you to shore..."

Bernard muttered, "Er, actually she is sort of–uh–a doctor on the ship now. Um, against her will."

"WHAT?" Warren exploded. "McManlyman is keeping you on this ship against your will?" He rocketed to his feet and flew to the door to do something well-intentioned but sure to end badly, but then the effects of the medicine he was taking for the pain made his legs go weak, and he crashed to the floor.

Jane hurried to his side and carefully examined his arm, saying as she made sure he hadn't damaged things again, "Look, don't worry about it. Seriously, in a lot of ways things are better for me here than in the city."

"Oh, yeah?" Warren asked. "Like how?"

"For one, I get regular meals. And the pirates appreciate what I do for them," she said, intending to add more to the list, but those two things were all she could think of. She smiled weakly.

"McManlyman is a big jerk," Warren grumbled as Jane and Bernard helped him up and guided him back to where he had been resting. He settled down again amongst the pillows and quilts and sighed. "We've got to help her."

"Warren," Corrine said hesitantly, "she's in no immediate danger. You, on the other hand, *are*. The pirates need her. They're not going to do anything to her."

"But it's *wrong*! They can't just take a lady captive!"

"They didn't take me captive because I'm a lady. They took me captive because I am a doctor. Don't worry about me. You only have two days in which to get as far from this guy as you can," she said, shoving the still-unconscious Farland with her foot. At her touch, he started to stir. She quickly crouched by him, took her real asparagus powder, knelt down, poured a bit of the liquid from the vial into his mouth, and then shook some powder in. Farland relaxed and stilled.

"But–but–you're on this ship because of me!" Warren cried.

"Don't worry about it," Jane insisted. "Seriously. This guy wants to *kill* you. Look, your family agrees with me, right?"

Everyone nodded.

"Okay, so if you don't leave, and leave *stat*," she said, throwing in some doctor lingo to sound more official, "I will drug you with enough of this stuff to keep you unconscious until you're safely to shore," she said, shaking the vial menacingly at him.

He set his jaw angrily. "Fine. But once we've figured out what's up with this fake harpsichord repairman, and once my arm is healed, we are coming back to rescue you."

Jane knew that, by the time those things had been accomplished, the ship would likely be back out on the open sea, but she said, "Whatever. Just grab your stuff and go. The clock is ticking."

Bernard, Emily, and Corrine set to work packing. Emily said as she worked, "What are you going to do when he wakes up here? He'll be really mad at you, dear."

"Oh, right after I give him the last dose, I'll just put him in a barrel or something and toss it in the sea. That'll give him about three hours to drift away from the ship. Once he wakes up, he can just disappear out of the barrel and reappear somewhere safe."

That settled it. The plan sufficiently ironed out for the family who was now on the run from a vindictive wizard, they finished their packing and fled.

At the last minute, Warren grabbed his banjo even though everyone pointed out it was silly because his arm was broken.

CHAPTER ELEVEN

Julianna and Dexter found their way to the edge of the castle grounds.

"Right about here is where the passage used to be," said Dexter as he scanned the tall stone wall. "See that orange star painted on the wall there? That star was a mark used by the resistance."

Julianna shuddered at the phrase "the resistance", since, after all, it was her family who they were resisting. She looked where Dexter was pointing and, sure enough, there was a star about as big as her hand, the paint faded, peeling, and barely discernible through the gloom of the orchard. An orange circle was painted around the star.

"So, where's the tunnel then?" she asked, looking around eagerly. She'd never even considered the option of venturing out into the city until Dexter had mentioned it, but the more she thought about it, the more she liked the plan. She could use the opportunity to talk to come real live commoners, maybe! See how real people lived! And perhaps she could get a feel for what exactly it was that the populace was so unhappy about, so she could mention it to her dad and maybe he could try to fix things.

"I don't know, kid. Somewhere around the base of one of those trees over there," he said, nodding straight out from the orange star. "Go stomp around and see what you can find."

"Okey dokey." She walked over to one of the big, gnarled trees and gave the ground a good stomp. "I wish I'd been able to get some outdoorsy shoes," she grumbled as a twig poked through her flimsy slipper. She tried the ground by another tree, then a third. At the base of the fourth tree, she stomped down and felt a hollow *thunk*. Julianna darted backward a few paces and started pushing leaves and dirt out of the way, soon revealing a small wooden door in the ground.

"Looks like fairly new wood," Dexter noted. "Must still be in use."

She swung it open without a word and jumped right in, down a well-worn slope that led to a tunnel much taller and wider than her escape tunnel, by the feel of it. She couldn't see a thing. "How far does this go?" she asked as she inched forward, arms outstretched. This tunnel was so big she could stand up straight. Over the years, the people who had used it must have had ample time to make improvements.

"Not too far. It ends in an alley just on the opposite side of the road that runs along the wall."

She walked cautiously on. "Did you use this tunnel when you were alive?"

"Yep. I worked with some people on the inside who smuggled things out for me. Food, medicines, potions, some big-ticket items."

She found herself suddenly wondering why it was that they had never spoken about the specifics of all the shenanigans that Dexter had gotten up to before he had been imprisoned. "You did some pretty crazy stuff when you were alive, huh?"

"Yeah," he said with a reminiscent smile. "I was probably one of the few prisoners in the dungeon who actually deserved to be there."

"Did you ever—oh!" she broke off and said, "The tunnel's going up!"

"Don't bump your head."

She proceeded carefully for a few more steps with her hands held above her head, then suddenly felt the rough wood of another trapdoor against her fingertips. "This is so cool!" she whispered over her shoulder to Dexter. Then, heart pounding, she took a deep breath and pushed the trapdoor up a crack, peeking out into a little slice of the real world for the first time in her life. She gasped and let the door drop again. "Dexter!"

"What?" he asked with alarm at the tone of her voice.

"Dexter! That is *not* an alley! That is a *room*! And I think I saw someone's *feet*!" she whispered in a panicky voice as she began to back down the slope away from the door.

"Did anyone see you?"

"I don't know!" she hissed.

They heard muffled voices from above, and she began to scamper backwards with her eyes still on the trapdoor. "Why did you tell me that was an alley?" she said frantically.

"Hey! Don't blame me! Eighty-three years ago, it *was* an alley! How was I supposed to know someone had stuck a house or whatever up there? If you'll recall, I was too busy being imprisoned by your ancestors, then tortured for years, then *killed*, to be keeping up with new construction projects in the city."

She had stopped listening to him, knowing that once he started ranting about injustice it could take a while. Instead, she was trying to make her way as fast as possible through the tunnel back the way she had come without running into anything or tripping. She was about halfway there when the trapdoor she was running from swung open and faint light shone down.

"Who goes there?" barked a man's voice.

Julianna froze and said quietly, "Oh no, oh no, oh no," as she hopped nervously in place.

"Don't panic," Dexter said with a calm that only a dead, invisible person could have in such a situation. "Just tell them you're a maid from the castle."

"Who goes there?" the guy asked again, this time with some annoyance. Legs appeared in the tunnel, then the torso and head of the legs' owner. He was maybe sixty, with a long white beard and no hair at all on his head. Julianna noted that though he was pretty old[7] he looked very tough. Julianna swallowed heavily. She glanced around the tunnel now that there was light and saw that it was lined with tidy rows of barrels, crates, and bags.

Light fell on Julianna from the guy's lantern. "Hi!" she said weakly and gave an awkward little wave.

---

7   The population of Fritillary had an average lifespan that was exactly what you would expect of a people that preferred to explain away health issues by saying it was the fault of magic instead of the fault of the pound of mostly-fat bacon they'd eaten for breakfast every morning for their whole life.

"Who in blazes are you?" he asked as he stomped over to her. "I've never seen you before."

"J—J—Jennifer," Julianna improvised. "I'm a maid," she added, though it came out more as a question than as a statement of fact.

The guy gave her a long, suspicious look, stepped a bit closer, and said, "Why so nervous, girlie?"

"Umm."

Dexter said, "Tell him you want to help them, but you're just nervous because you've never done anything illegal before."

"I—er—I've never done anything illegal before, you see. I want to help though. I want to help you smuggle stuff."

"Who told you about this tunnel?"

She toyed for a moment with giving the name of the guard she had heard complaining about her dad; but for one thing, this guy could easily check with the guard, who would deny any knowledge of Jennifer the maid, and for another thing, it was too big a leap to assume that just because the guard was complaining about the king that meant he was part of this smuggling thing. She was quiet long enough that Dexter opened his mouth to supply her with a story. But she cut him off with, "I was out a few nights ago and I saw someone sneaking into the orchard. I was curious, so I followed."

"Who? Who did you follow?" the guy snapped.

"I don't know. Whoever it was, he or she wore a hood. And I stayed far back."

"And why do you assume that we are a smuggling operation?" he grilled her.

"Well… I've heard rumors around the castle about the smuggling," she said, feeling her explanation was kind of weak, but trying not to let that feeling affect her delivery. "I guess I assumed. Because the person I saw was sneaking out in the middle of the night, and because this is a hidden tunnel."

He gave her a long, appraising look, and said at last, "I can't let you through. Come back tomorrow night with something valuable. Prove yourself. Show me you're brave enough to actually steal from the royal family. Because my first impression of you is that you are pretty wimpy."

She gave him a startled look. No flesh-and-blood person had ever been rude to her before. "Look here, sir, I am every bit as brave as any one of your other smugglers!"

"Well, prove it. What part of the castle are you assigned to?"

"The princess's rooms."

He raised his eyebrows and gave a low whistle. "Well now...You must be quite a maid to be assigned down there!"

"I *am* very good at cleaning," she agreed.

He looked at her with new interest. "How's this for a plan: you bring me something from the princess's rooms. Something that belongs to her. Something that is obviously hers and couldn't have come from anywhere else. You do that, and you can be part of our operation."

"It's a deal," she said with relief. He was going to let her go! She had been so afraid that, somehow, she would be found out. The last thing she wanted this guy to learn was that she *was* the Princess—these people were probably the types who would kidnap her and hold her for ransom.

"Great. I'll see you back here tomorrow night. Cover up the trapdoor again with some dirt and leaves on your way out."

She nodded, said, "Thank you so much!" and scampered back the way she had come, taking advantage of the guy's lantern light while she had it.

"Decent improvising," Dexter said as he trailed along behind her. "You may have the makings of a good smuggler, Princess."

She pushed up the trapdoor and took a deep breath of the night air, then hopped out and shut it quietly behind her. "Pfft. You don't mean you actually think I'm coming back here tomorrow night?"

"You mean you aren't?" She tried not to feel guilty at the disappointment in his voice.

"Of course not, Dexter. I just said all that stuff because I had to say *something* and that was the easiest story." She covered up the trapdoor as she spoke, then began to stroll back toward the ornamental garden.

He didn't respond. She knew he was mad. He had gotten his hopes up about seeing the city.

"I'm really sorry, Dexter. Going out into the city seemed a lot more possible when I thought that trapdoor just went to some alley and I could hop out and go exploring. But there are *people* on the other side. *Criminal* people."

"Aww, come on! Just think about it. *Try* to imagine how bored I am.

I've been stuck down in that dungeon for more than three quarters of a century. *You* were going stir crazy by the time you were eight years old, and you didn't even have a basis for comparison!"

"I'll think about it," she sighed.

W ARREN, CORRINE, EMILY, and Bernard stood on the dock staring at the city before them.

"Okay, you know where I live—*used* to live until I got doctor-napped by pirates, that is—so you can crash at my place if you want," Jane said from the lifeboat they'd rowed to shore, accompanied by McManlyman's first mate, Biggby, who had gone along to make sure Jane didn't escape. "My mom and dad will be happy to help you out, too. They live in the baking district at 67 Rye Road. Charles and Myrtle." She composed her face then because she was afraid that she would cry if she wasn't careful. "If you do track them down, please tell them my…situation. Tell them when I get away from the pirates, I will find them."

Biggby gave her a dark look. This talk of escape didn't sit well with him.

"We'll be sure to tell them, sweetheart," Emily said.

"We *will* rescue you," Warren said valiantly from where he stood propped between his sister and father (the medicine was still wearing off). "Please, know that we will not abandon you." He gave Biggby a stare that he fancied a hero ought to give a villain.

Jane smiled bravely up at them and said, "Thank you very much. But if a rescue doesn't work out, know that I don't blame you for my situation. I blame Captain Maximus McManlyman. *And* his crew." She shot a glare at Biggby. "One way or another, he will pay, and I will be free."

Warren nodded. "Thank you for everything. Really."

"No problem. If you do end up coming to rescue me, check with my parents first. Just to make sure I haven't rescued myself already."

"Will do. Best of luck!" Bernard said. He was feeling the need to wrap things up and disappear with his son into the city before too much time had elapsed.

A flurry of more goodbyes and thanks ensued, and then without further ado Jane started back to the ship. Almost as soon as she started rowing, they heard Biggby and Jane starting to fight. "*No way* are you escaping from a ship full of pirates, little lady."

"Whatever, dude. Tell me that again once I've escaped. Oh wait, you won't be able to because I'll be gone."

Biggby growled, but his response was lost in the sound of the waves and the flurry of activity on the docks. It was past sunset, and the family was surprised to see how busy the docks were even at night.

"Let's go," Emily said, eyeing squintly some unsavory-looking fellows who were in turn eyeing her daughter. "I think we should stay at Jane's place tonight, and then we can visit her parents in the morning. That will give us some time this evening to talk things over and figure out a plan."

Warren couldn't tell at this point whether his legs felt funny because of the medicine he had been given, or because this was his first time in his life walking on solid ground, or because the city streets were slick with muck. He was also finding that now he was on land, it was hard to retain the degree of fear he felt he should have; he was, after all, running from a wizard who wanted to kill him dead. But he was also just so darn interested in watching everything going on around him that he kept forgetting why they were in the city in the first place.

"This is so cool!" he said as he gaped at a half dozen dock workers trying to load a huge crate onto the back of a wagon. "Look! It is pretty neat to see real people doing real stuff."

His parents smiled fondly at him. Of the two of their kids, Warren had definitely retained more of a sense of wonder at the world as he aged.

Corrine sighed and said, "Warren, they're putting a box on a wagon. Focus, man. You're running from a crazy wizard."

Warren rolled his eyes at her as she forged on ahead, leading the family through the docks, proud of herself for remembering so well the route to Jane's house/office.

With only two wrong turns, they were there.

Bernard took out the key Jane had given him and unlocked the door. The main room was just like he remembered it: table, bed for patients, asparagus hanging from the ceiling.

There was a door in the back that led, they discovered, to Jane's living area. There was a small bed with a brightly colored quilt in the far corner, a chest at the end of the bed, a vanity with a brush and comb and a few little bottles of whatnot on it, a table with a bowl of shriveled fruit, and a little wood burning stove. A small window by the bed was covered with a striped green-and-brown curtain.

Warren laid down to rest, while Corrine went back to the front room to track down some medicine that Jane had told her to give him. Bernard and Emily sat down at the table to make some plans for the next day, periodically swatting at the fruit flies swarming around the bowl of rotting fruit. After a few minutes of that, Emily picked up the bowl, brought it to the front door, and tossed the bowl's contents into the street[8]; as she was walking back, absently running her hands over the surface of the fruit bowl, she felt something bumpy on the underside of it. She flipped it over and saw a key, apparently stuck on with poster putty. The key was small and plain, with an orange star painted onto the top part.

"What's that?" Corrine asked, looking up from a cupboard she was rummaging through.

"Oh, just a key. Whatever it is, it's none of our business."

Corrine shrugged and went back to her search.

---

8   There was, after all, no trash collection service in Fritillary, nor was there plumbing, so if folks had to get rid of old food, they tossed it into the street, which worked out great for the hardy-stomached street urchins.

CHAPTER TWELVE

The next morning, Warren, Corrine, Emily, and Bernard found their way to the doorstep of 67 Rye Road (the door of which was painted orange just like Jane's). Jane's parents lived in a much nicer part of town than their daughter; most houses on Rye Road had a little window box with a few flowers poking out, and not a single shutter was hanging loose, nor were there any broken windows in sight. The president of this particular neighborhood's homeowner's association must have been quite a despot, but the results sure were pleasant.

Corrine knocked, and a few seconds later a tall woman with a strong resemblance to Jane answered. "Hi!" Corrine said brightly to the woman, who was eyeing them all suspiciously, checking for clipboards or boxes of candy. All she saw in their hands, though, was a bit of luggage and a banjo.

"Listen," the woman said tersely, "We are not interested in whatever you're selling. Sorry." She made to slam the door, but Corrine halted the door's progress with her foot. The woman gave her a glare and called sharply over her shoulder, "Charles!"

"Your daughter, Jane, sent us," Corrine explained with a wince as the lady pushed the door against her foot.

The lady stared for a few seconds and then said in a rush, "You've talked to Jane? When did you last see her?" She stopped pushing the door against Corrine's foot.

"Just last evening," Corrine said.

The lady's eyes filled with relief, and she turned to tell someone, presumably her husband who must have been walking to the door in response to her earlier call, "These people talked to Jane last evening!"

A brown-haired man with glasses joined her and looked at them, saying eagerly, "Really? Oh, what a relief! Where were you? Where did you see her?"

"We—well, it's a bit of a long story," Corrine said.

"Of course. Listen, why don't you come in?" the woman said, much friendlier. "I'm sorry if I was rude just now," she added as she held the door open for them to pass through into a small foyer cluttered with an overcrowded coat rack, an umbrella stand, and a pile of boots. "You see, we've been worried sick about Jane. She always comes over Saturday for dinner, but that was two days ago and she never came, and we went by her place and she wasn't there. And, of course, the guards are of no use to us," she grumbled. Guards in the city had an unofficial policy of not going out of their way to help troublemakers and revolutionary types, and Jane's parents made no secret of their work in the areas of women's rights and general revolutionary stuff.

Jane's mom led them into a sitting room with a big red couch and a few mismatched chairs all gathered around a coffee table. There were four paintings of landscapes on the wall over the couch (one of each season) that all appeared to be done by an amateurish artist who might have some skill down the road if given proper lessons. Probably a project of Jane's from when she had been a kid. Emily immediately warmed to these people, since she was a fan of any parent who proudly displayed their kid's artwork front and center.

Everyone sat down, and Warren and Co. launched into the story of how Jane had helped them out and consequently become a captive of Captain Maximus McManlyman. They assured Jane's horrified parents that, even though their daughter was on a pirate ship, she was, in their opinion, quite safe since the pirates were so desperate for a good doctor. They further explained their intention to rescue her once they had sorted out their own troubles, if, that is, Jane hadn't already rescued herself by that time.

Charles and Myrtle had plenty of questions, and they needed quite a bit of time to process the information they'd been given by these strangers who had come calling to drop this bomb on them before they'd even had their morning cups of coffee. So, let's give them some processing time; we will go see what Julianna has been getting up to since last we saw her:

As Julianna scooted down her tunnel and back into her dungeon, she had begun to think about all that had taken place that night with the smugglers and the rumblings of an unhappy populace. At first, she'd been miffed that her first experience out hadn't gone as planned—she hadn't appreciated overhearing that troubling stuff from the guards, and it had been very scary lying to that smuggler. But, the more she thought about it, the more she realized she had nothing to complain about. She had wanted to see the real world, after all, and that was precisely what she'd seen. Reality was angry commoners, and reality was also some of those angry commoners going to extreme measures like smuggling and selling things on the black market and whatever else those criminals were up to. It was definitely uncomfortable for her to have bumped up against reality to that degree so soon after emerging from her protective little cocoon, but so what? That reality had been happening long before she had known about it and would keep on going now that she *had* experienced it.

The only difference was that now she had something new to think about.

Well, maybe not the *only* difference. Maybe she could actually do something to help, she thought suddenly and with a jolt of excitement. By the time Julianna had reached the bottom of the tunnel with a still silent and surly Dexter, her mind was running through a half dozen scenarios where she could figure out a way to make the people her father ruled more happy and less inclined to revolt. Maybe she could finally do something to make a positive change in the world! "Dexter," she whispered as she began to push the stone back into place at the bottom of her tunnel.

"What?"

"We are going back out tomorrow night. Out into the city. And the night after and the night after, and I am going to figure out how to make this country happy again," she said gleefully.

He stared at her, slack jawed. "*What?*"

"You heard me."

"Where did this come from? An hour ago, you were convinced you were never going to set foot outside the castle walls."

"I changed my mind. Obviously. I'm going to figure out what the populace wants, and I'm going to tell my father how to get things done."

"That is such an oversimplification of the issues that I don't even know how to begin to argue with you."

"Good. I don't need your cranky old pessimism bringing me down anyway."

"Don't be stupid. It's not pessimism; it's logic."

"Just be happy that we're going out into the city. That's what you wanted anyway, right?"

"Yeah…but not if you're going to be running off on some crazy, idealistic mission armed with only a bag full of stuff you scrounged together and my rusty 83-year-old knowledge of the city."

"Yeah? Well you don't have a choice," she said irritably. "You're coming."

He glared at her, sighed, and decided he was done with this fight. He floated off to find Curtis. If anyone could talk Julianna down, it was him.

But when Curtis found Julianna on her bed staring up at her ceiling with a faraway look in her eyes, she looked over at him and said before he could get a word in, "You're not convincing me of anything, so don't try."

He cleared his throat and said carefully, "Julianna, Dexter has told me that you have, after only *one night* out in the real world, decided you want to try to help your father sort out some kind of trouble with the populace? You want to go out and gather information? Do I have that right?"

She nodded.

"Don't you think you're being a tad overoptimistic about your abilities? Your father must have all sorts of spies who can bring him more information than you could *ever* hope to obtain."

Her face darkened. He made an unfortunately good point.

"Perhaps," Curtis said, seeing his remark had hit home, "he just doesn't care to fix things. Don't go endangering yourself on a pointless mission. If you leave the castle walls night after night, you are eventually going to get into trouble, and what if, when that trouble happens, you can't get to safety by sunrise?"

"Curtis, this is my Purpose," she said, the capital P very obvious. "I *am* doing this."

"How," he said with more than a little sarcasm, "is a sheltered princess with a few hours of experience outside the safety of her home going to carry out such a huge undertaking?"

Choosing to ignore his tone of voice, she answered calmly, "I think there's no way I *can* really plan, because, as you say, I don't know what's out there or where things will lead. So, I'm just going to—oh, I don't know—just jump right in and iron out the details as I go."

He started at her, appalled. "*Iron it out as you go?*"

She shrugged.

The other two ghosts had floated in a few minutes earlier to listen. They all looked at each other darkly. They knew there was nothing they could do to stop her.

Nothing, of course, but make her feel really, really guilty.

"Julianna," Montague said, "Please don't do this. For our sakes. And for your family. We will worry sick for you. Something *will* happen, and when it does, there won't even be anyone around to tell your family what has happened to you!"

"And," Curtis added, "On that day that you don't come back, do you realize what it will do to *me*? I was the one who told you where that tunnel was. And I don't have the luxury of eventually dying and not having to feel the guilt anymore. I'll be stuck floating around down here for eternity, always knowing that I got you killed."

"Geez," she muttered. "I'm not going to *die*. I'm not five years old. I'm nineteen. I can take care of myself."

Dexter snorted. "There are plenty five-year-olds out there in the city who have ten times more ability to get around alone on the streets than you do, Princess."

"But I won't be alone; I'll have you, Dexter!" she said with a grin, trying to lighten the mood. Then she looked silently at their worried faces for a few moments and said, more subdued, "I have always wished I could do something with my life. You *know* that. I want to make some sort of *difference*. Now that I have an opportunity, I think I would rather get into some danger trying to fix the country than sit around down here until I'm an old lady doing nothing and mattering to no one." A bit dramatic considering that she *did* have friends and family, but she was nineteen, so there you go.

"No one but us," Montague muttered, obviously hurt. It isn't only nineteen-year-olds who have a tendency toward the dramatic.

"Oh, Montague," she sighed. He had a passive-aggressive streak that drove her crazy sometimes.

He just gave her a gloomy look and floated away, muttering something about how unappreciated he was.

Their goal of making her feel guilty had succeeded, but she still wasn't guilty enough to change her plans.

"Please just think about it," Curtis suggested. "Talk to your parents and see if there's something you can do to make a difference from down here."

"What, stuff some women's rights bulletins for my mom? Respond to some angry letters?" she scoffed. "I've done that before."

"No... Nothing like that. Can't hurt to ask, is all I'm saying..." But Curtis knew this was not an argument he was going to win. She had that beady glint in her eyes that told him words were pointless. "Just be careful out there." And he floated off too.

Julianna looked at Dexter, bracing herself for another attack.

But he just said with a grin, "So I guess this means we're going to have some adventures!" He had done his due diligence, he felt, in getting the other ghosts to try to talk her out of her crazy plan, and, now that they had failed, he felt at liberty to get excited about the fun to come.

Ⓞ NCE CHARLES AND Myrtle had gotten over the shock of finding out that their daughter was being held captive by pirates, they were able to give Warren and his family some help in pointing them in the right direction in their quest to disappear into the city. Warren's parents' initial idea had been to find some old theater friends and see if he could stay with them, but Jane's parents had pointed out that exploring potential leads from their past was probably one of the first avenues Farland would travel down in his search.

They suggested instead that the family make use of Jane's parents' ties with the Women's Rights movement and the rebels; Charles and Myrtle were part of a group of citizens who had, in the old days, hidden suspected witches and moved them from house to house until they were able to sneak them out of the city and into the comparative safety of the countryside; but now that witch burnings were no longer en vogue thanks to the Queen's involvement in the cause, the families in this network and fallen into the general sphere of the revolutionaries who desired to hide people from the King's army for one reason or another. Jane's parents felt sure that their connections would be able to help Warren and his family disappear.

"But first," Myrtle had said, "I must tell you that there is an element of danger in this. These revolutionaries, they are, well... It's not like it used to be. There are so many people now, and they have so many causes. And we don't know everyone in the network anymore now that it has grown. So, we don't know, of course, whether this Farland is friendly with any of them."

"But," Charles had added, "We will try to make sure that you are only put in the homes of the Women's Rights people who we know and trust."

They also, after much emotion, decided that it would be best to divide up the family, Bernard and Emily going to one house, and Warren and Corrine going to another, and then after sneaking them through a series of a dozen or so households, steering them all to a farm in the north of the city that was owned by friends of Jane's parents. The whole process would take about a month, they figured, and the family was quite upset at the thought of being separated from each other for the first time. But they did see the logic in moving in pairs instead of in one group; Farland would be asking after a mother, father, sister, and brother, not an older couple and another separate younger couple.

So, after a bit more planning and some second guessing, they at last set out again after a nice early lunch of grilled cheese and tomato soup, to start the ball rolling.

The house where Bernard and Emily were to begin their journey was a large, grand place in a swanky part of town near the castle. Jane's parents led them around to the servants' entrance and asked that the maid who answered please take them to the butler. The maid led them wordlessly through a dark maze of cold basement hallways and into the butler's office. He was at a table, polishing the silver, how butlers do.

His wife, Fran, was the head cook, and had grown up with Jane's mom; they had gone to school together as kids before Conroy's father had decided to stop girls from going to school[9]. Myrtle's and Fran's parents had promptly formed an underground homeschool co-op and kept educating the kiddos.

The butler looked up from his reflection in the shiny spoon he was working on and said, "Charles! Myrtle! What a pleasant surprise!" And he was on his feet and rushing to them, embracing them with unbutlerly bear hugs.

"Hello, Alonzo," Myrtle said with a smile. "I hope Fran is well? It's been a while since I've heard from her."

"She's well, but very busy. Poor thing's been working night and day preparing for visitors. We're having some lords and ladies coming in from the countryside to stay here for the start of the King's hunting party."

"Hunting party?" Emily asked, more out of politeness than because she actually cared.

The butler nodded. "In about a week, King Conroy is having a big hunting shindig to mark Prince Conroy Jr.'s first hunt. A very big deal."

Jane's dad, Charles, added with a nod, "All the lords and rich folks and the best hunters across the land will be coming. I've heard it's going to be quite an event!"

Myrtle asked the butler, "You must be pretty busy as well?"

"Indeed, indeed. So many guests and meals ahead; haven't had so much silverware to polish since the coronation. And this is the fancy stuff with all the detaily doodads on the handles."

He held up a spoon for all to see.

It did, indeed, have many detaily doodads on the handle.

The butler elaborated, "Gotta get into all those darn little crevices."

"Have you tried using a toothpick with a handkerchief over the tip?" asked Myrtle.

"Ooh that's a good—"

Charles cut in. "We're not actually on a social call, Alonzo. These people are in need of some help." He indicated Warren and his family, who were standing awkwardly in the doorway. He briefly explained their circumstances (giving as few details as possible) and said, "Perhaps you could arrange with the Harrington's to take them in next?"

---

9   The smarter girls got, the tougher it got for guys who didn't want to compete for jobs or do their own cleaning and cooking.

"Yes. An excellent plan," Alonzo said, suddenly businesslike. "Yes."

"All right, then I think we had better get going," Myrtle said to Warren and Corrine.

Bernard and Emily hugged and kissed their kids goodbye and there was a whirlwind of, "It'll only be a few weeks," and, "I'm sure everything will turn out fine," and, "safe travels," and other such phrases loved ones say when parting ways. Then they hugged a bit more and walked off, all with tearful eyes, but all trying to appear brave for the sake of everyone else.

Chapter Thirteen

Warren trudged along behind Jane's parents, finding, now that he was separated from his parents, that things seemed a lot more serious. He didn't like it one bit. Yes, he was 21 and plenty old enough to take care of himself, but, all the same, this was the first time he'd been away from his parents before and he was feeling apprehensive about what was to come. At least he had Corrine, and though she was likely to roll her eyes at him and call him stupid more than a few times before their adventure was through, he was still glad to have her and her level head with him.

She looped an arm through his and said, "Mom and Dad will be fine, you know."

He nodded. "I know. They're not the ones that crazy wizard dude is after."

"Well, we'll be fine, too," she added, as they walked out onto the sidewalk. "This plan makes sense, don't you think?"

He nodded again. "Yeah, it does... But I just can't imagine it'll really work out that smoothly."

"You're only thinking that way because you're always reading those adventure books."

"How can you say that when you write plays and poetry for a living?"

"Making plays and reading plays are vastly different things."

"I doubt—"

"Ooh! I recognize this neighborhood!" Corrine cut in. As she'd been talking, she had been studying the area they were walking through with a rising certainty that she'd been there before. "Yes, this is the weaving district."

Warren perked up upon hearing this. "Isn't that where this Farland character lives?"

Corrine nodded enthusiastically, reading her brother's mind. "Let's go check out that harpsichord store!"

Charles and Myrtle turned around and stopped in their tracks. "What?" Charles asked.

"We'll just poke around a bit," Warren said. "I'm not saying let's break in or anything. Just peek through the windows and see if we can see anything that gives us a better idea of what is going on," he said lamely. Secretly, though, he wasn't discounting the possibility of breaking in. Where was the danger if Jane was keeping the wizard in a drugged state of unconsciousness on the pirate ship way out in the Bay of Fritillary?

"We really, really should get you two into hiding *as fast as we can*," Myrtle pointed out.

"I have to do this," Warren said. "We'll just pop over and peek around for a few minutes. It can't hurt. And it might even end up being helpful. If we can learn anything about this wizard, that is. We might find out something useful about the guy who's hunting me down."

"Hmph," Charles said, filling the sound with as much doubt as one syllable could possibly be filled with. In the end, the siblings wouldn't be swayed, and Charles and Myrtle decided that if time was going to be wasted either way, it was better wasted casing Farland's joint than arguing about how much time they were wasting.

Corrine led the way to Farland's place.

When Warren saw the building Farland was renting in, he had to admit he was a tad disappointed. He would have preferred his nemesis (for, pretentious though it was for him to fancy himself worthy of a genuine nemesis, he couldn't help but think of Farland as his nemesis) to have a more impressive base of operations. "What a lame place for an evil wizard," Warren muttered, eyeing the plain old nondescript building and the trio of pigeons bustling around busily in the muck at his feet. The sound of a baby crying could be heard through the open window of the upstairs rooms. The scene was downright humdrum.

Warren sighed and followed Corrine to Farland's door. Corrine had just noticed the harpsichord repair sign that had been hastily stuck on the door with poster putty was now lying face-down in the muck of the street. In the place where it had hung, she saw the much more official placard that it had been covering; it was made of polished wood and had swoopy gold lettering that read: "Farland Phelps. Evil Wizard for Hire." In smaller print below that was: "No job too unethical!" Warren and Corrine exchanged looks at this. Warren tried the doorknob. Locked. He gave it a shake just to be sure. Still locked.

"Let's peek through the front window," Corrine said. "It's really dirty, but we might be able to see *something*."

Just then, the door to the tailor's shop to the right of Farland's door opened, and a little old lady walked out. They took her for a tailor, for she had a tape measure tied loosely around her waist. Just as she was about to lock her door, she saw the siblings standing in front of the wizard's door and said, "Good day, children! I'm afraid the wizard is out. He hasn't been home for a day or two now."

"What a shame," Warren said with manufactured disappointment.

"Were you hoping to buy a spell?" she asked. "I could point you in the direction of a few other wizards who might be able to help you out. No one as good as dear Farland, of course, but if it's urgent...?" she inquired with obvious curiosity.

"Oh no, nothing like that," Corrine said. "You say Farland is a good wizard?"

"Oh yes, very good. He helped me out with a spot of trouble with someone who—" she stopped short and giggled. "Oh, I am always forgetting, I'm not supposed to talk about it! Word might get around about who was responsible for the 'accident'," she said, doing air quotes when she said *accident*, "and that's the last thing I want!"

Warren felt a sick feeling in the pit of his stomach. This seemingly nice old lady had had Farland do some sort of spell for her which had resulted in a nasty 'accident'[10].

"Wow, he sounds great," Corrine said, not too convincingly, but the old lady didn't seem to notice.

"Yes, he is. A great neighbor. Really a sweetheart. He even feeds my cat when I'm out of town, and in return I water his fern when he's traveling. Not often these days that you find a neighbor who will help you out like that."

"He sounds swell," Warren said, but he wasn't really listening anymore. If this old lady watered Farland's fern when he was traveling, did that mean she had a key to his apartment? He was pretty sure she hadn't locked her front door yet, and he wanted to make sure now that she didn't do it at all. So he could break into her house and steal the key, you see. He needed to distract her and make her forget to lock her door.

"Listen, are you going to the market?" Warren asked, hoping he hadn't changed subjects too fast. His guess of the market was fairly obvious, since she had an empty basket hanging over her arm.

"Yes, I am. Why do you ask, lad?"

"Well, since the wizard isn't here, there are a few things I need that I might as well pick up while I wait." He hoped Corrine would keep her mouth shut, but didn't dare send her any significant looks, since the old lady was looking right at him. "Would you like some company?"

"Why, thank you! That would be mighty kind, lad. The streets these past few days have been a bit crowded for one lonely old lady. And more hooligans are out than usual—everyone is so excited about the King's big hunting party." The old lady shifted her gaze from Warren to somewhere off down the street as she launched into a monologue about the impending hunt, and how kids these days weren't the same as they used to be, and neither were parents, and neither was society, and the whole of Fritillary was going down the tubes. Except Fritillary didn't have plumbing, so that expression didn't make sense. But the siblings weren't listening anyway, so they weren't confused.

---

10   People had been so much simpler before Farland had come into the picture; on the pirate ship Warren had known that (1) his family was nice, (2) the pirates were cutthroat mercenaries, and (3) the audiences who paid to see his family's performances had clapped and laughed when they were supposed to, so they were pretty good as a group. People on the mainland were tougher.

"Mmm," Warren said to the old lady, while meeting Corrine's eyes and trying hard to give his sister a look that said, "*Trust me.*"

Corrine looked confusedly at Warren, who was raising an eyebrow in a funny way and widening his eyes and obviously trying to tell her something without using words. Something that would explain why, when they were in a big hurry, he was, out of the blue, offering to walk a vaguely creepy old lady to the market. There was no way Corrine was in the mood to waste energy trying to decipher his expression, so she just waved a dismissive hand at him, and said, "You'd better get going to buy all that market stuff."

As Warren walked off with the tailor, Corrine gave Charles and Myrtle a shrug and came to join them where they had been waiting impatiently on a bench across the street from Farland's apartment. They all watched Warren and the old lady disappear around the corner at the end of the cul-de-sac, then Corrine sat down beside them to wait, since there was really nothing else that she could do. However, Corrine had no sooner started to explain to Charles and Myrtle that she was just as in the dark as they were, when Warren appeared again around the corner at the end of the road, alone this time and walking fast.

"Warren? What is up with you?" Corrine said as he joined them.

Warren explained as quickly as he could about the key, and he and his sister went over to the tailor's door while Charles and Myrtle remained on the bench, now taking on the role of lookouts in addition to that of impatient guides. Warren took a deep breath and tried the old lady's door. It swung open.

"Nice!" said Corrine, and rushed in. "Okay, so we're looking for a key." At a glance, she took in the shelves of fabric and the little drawers that Warren was already opening, which held all sorts of bobbins sporting threads of every color under the sun. She watched him ransack for a few moments while she thought strategy. Then she said, "Don't bother with those threads, Warren. People always have a drawer or a box or something where they put their random stuff. That's what we need to look for."

"Good sleuthing!" he said.

Then, he and Corrine began searching for the tailor's stash of randomness. Before too long, they found it in a woven basket on top of a bookshelf. Hiding beneath a cluster of paperclips all linked together, a pocketknife, and a slew of broken pencils, Warren found a heavy iron key with a skull on it. "This *has* to be it," he said with confidence. "I mean, look at this thing. It screams evil wizard. Just look at those tiny red stones in its angry little eyes."

"Quit speculating and try it out."

Warren put the basket back on the bookshelf and took the creepy key outside, then put it in Farland's lock, turned it, and heard a click. It worked. He felt a chill and a moment of hesitation—this had suddenly become pretty intense. Did evil wizards have apartments riddled with booby-traps? But he couldn't walk away now that he was this close.

Besides, his sister had already pushed the door open while he'd been standing there waffling, and no horrible fate had befallen her upon crossing the threshold, so he figured it was cool, and skittered inside.

After only a few minutes of nosing around, they discovered Farland's creepy skeleton-themed tapestry triptych rolled up in a wardrobe on top of his puzzle collection, his dark-wizard themed books, and his work station where he must whip up his spells and potions, all of which were weird but none of which were very illuminating. They also discovered that when they turned around the bottles of supposed harpsichord powders and oils, the true contents of the bottles could be seen on the labels.

"Wow, Corrine, this is so creepy. A guy who has bottles labeled 'Heart Stop Tonic' and 'Night Terrors Pomade' is after me. *Me.* I mean, he obviously has the wrong guy, but it's not like there's any convincing him of that..." He trailed off and went over to the window to peek out at Charles and Myrtle across the street. They looked pretty irate. He also noted that it was getting dark. They really did need to hurry.

As she examined the shelves with her back to him, Corrine said, "Yeah, yeah, Warren, this whole thing is crazy. All we can do for now is get as far away from him as possible. But you know, while we're here, if he has any of that orange stuff and some asparagus powder lying around, that might come in handy—"

Corrine kept talking, but Warren was no longer listening, so busy was he with jumping out of his skin with terror at the sound of the dry, croaky voice that suddenly filled his head and resonated through his body to the very marrow of his bones: *WARREN!*

Warren looked around wildly and was shocked to see that Corrine was still idly looking at all the creepy labels on the bottles and talking in a casual manner, as though a strange, harsh voice had not just reverberated through the room yelling his name. She picked up a jar of green powder and muttered something about asparagus.

It croaked again, *At last you have come!*

Warren's eyes darted frantically around. He tried to speak, but his mouth had gone dry. He swallowed, cleared his throat. "Corrine?" he whispered, his voice coming out in a hoarse rasp.

She turned around to look at him, and saw her brother looking around the room with frightened eyes.

"Dude, what the—"

WARREN! screeched the voice. It sounded like a crow, if crows could talk[11].

"AHH! Geez!! Stop it!!" he yelled at the voice, and on shaky legs backed into a corner, the better to see the whole room at one time and thus make sure no evil demon was swooping behind him.

"What?!" Corrine cried, catching his panic even though she wasn't hearing what he was. "What are you talking about? I'm not doing anything!"

"You don't hear that voice? It keeps saying my name! It sounds like a crow! I can't believe you don't hear—"

Not a crow! A raven! Honestly, bro, if I had a nickel for every time—

"Corrine! It happened again—it's still taking to me!" The absolute fear in his sister's eyes was doing even more to scare him than the voice itself. "Is it possible to lose your mind *this fast?*"

"Shut up! You're not crazy. It must be some spell," Corrine said, grasping at straws to come up with an explanation that didn't involve her little brother having gone suddenly insane. "Some sort of spell. Yeah. Something that makes you think you're hearing voices. Did you touch anything you shouldn't have? Spill something?"

The raven voice cut in again: *Warren! Take the top off the coffee table!* Then it added in a tone that might almost have sounded reassuring except that the voice itself was so darn creepy, *All will be made clear in a trice.*

---

11   Which they can't, even in Fritillary, though they *are* very smart (as birds go, anyway) and do have a language of sorts for communicating amongst themselves.

Warren wanted very badly for all to be made clear in a trice, so he nervously inched away from the safety of his corner and over to the only table in sight, a low one with a plaid tablecloth that displayed harpsichord music and magazines.

"*What is going on?* What are you hearing?" Corrine asked, watching him edge over to the table.

Warren had become certain that the voice was coming from within his head and not from anywhere in the room. Before seriously entertaining the thought that he was losing his mind, he needed to see if there was in, fact, anything under that table that could begin to explain this.

"*Answer me!*" Corrine whispered shrilly. "Warren, you're scaring me!"

Ignoring his sister, Warren put his hands on the edge of the table, took a deep breath, and gave a tentative push. It was loose—apparently not attached to the base of the table. He pushed it back slowly, revealing a big, gothic-looking stone basin full of a deep red, faintly shimmering liquid. Not at all what he had been expecting, which was a good sign as far as his sanity went.

Hi bro, croaked the voice. *I'm the magical pool of raven blood.*

"What on earth is that stuff?" asked Corrine, horrified. "That looks like blood."

"It is blood," Warren found himself saying. "Raven blood."

Chapter Fourteen

Julianna was so excited to get out of her dungeon that she drugged Delia earlier than usual and climbed up the tunnel before sunset. Her plan was to hang back in the shadows and have Dexter swoop out periodically and check to see if it was night yet. That way, she could exit the tunnel the moment the sun had set and maximize her time outside. In her bag, she had added to her supplies a bit more food and a necklace her parents had given her for her sixth birthday. The necklace was the proof she was going to give the smugglers to show that she could steal from the princess. The pendant on the necklace was absolutely encrusted with an utterly nonsensical number of jewels, and on the back was an engraving that read, "To our sweet Julianna on her sixth birthday. Love, Mom and Dad."

She stretched out on her back in the tunnel waiting for Dexter, running her fingers over the rough, bumpy surface of the huge pendant and thinking what a strange gift it had been for a six-year-old. She remembered how heavy it had felt around her neck that day her mom had given it to her. Julianna had not worn it again since, at first because it was just too big, and then later because her tastes ran more to jewelry that wasn't laughably excessive.

"Hey!" Dexter said, breaking into her reverie. "Sun's set, kid. Let's get moving."

Her heart leapt. She took a steadying breath, then stowed her necklace away along with all her other supplies and scooted to the top of the tunnel.

This time outside, she was so excited to get to the smugglers' tunnel and get on with her Purpose of making the world a better place that she wasted no time stargazing or enjoying the gardens. She was so focused on getting to the trapdoor that Dexter found himself having to warn her about approaching guards on more than one occasion, and she was twice almost discovered. "You've got to pay attention," Dexter lectured. "If you go blundering around like this in the city, you are going to get into trouble in about two minutes."

"Yeah, yeah. I know. I'll be careful once I'm outside the castle walls."

They walked through the orchard until they reached the castle wall, and then walked along it until, at last, she saw the orange star painted on the wall that indicated the trapdoor was near. She located it much easier this time around. She quickly opened it up and climbed in, then walked the length of the tunnel without stumbling once on the smooth, hard ground. Once she got to the trapdoor at the end, she took a deep breath, then gave it a cautious knock.

"Hector!" came a woman's voice from above. "Hector, someone's knocking!" There was a muffled response, and then the woman's voice said, "Come on up out of there!"

Julianna hesitated a moment, but the lady was clearly talking to her and not Hector, so she pushed up the trapdoor. She had been rather surprised that they hadn't asked for some proof or explanation or something before letting her up; their security didn't seem too great for a thriving smuggling operation. But once Julianna had climbed up, shut the trapdoor behind her, and stood up again, she saw that their security was actually pretty all right after all.

There was a lady standing before her, and in her hand was a plain but very functional sword (Julianna had made this deduction about the lady's weapon's functionality because the tip of it was resting against her throat, and it felt plenty sharp enough to do some substantial harm). Behind the lady were two burly guys, both of them watching her with knives or daggers or something at the ready[12], though they were sitting down at a table where they had apparently been playing cards before she had shown up, so they weren't as immediate a danger as the lady.

Julianna *eep*ed, which caused the blade at her throat to poke her a tad.

"Who in blazes are you, girlie?" the lady said with a glower.

"I'm—er—" Julianna was finding out the hard way that it was challenging for her to keep her lies from the previous night straight in her head when she was really, really scared.

"You're Jennifer. You're a maid in the castle," Dexter supplied, floating behind the lady and giving Julianna a reassuring smile. "She's not going to kill you, Princess. Unless you do something really dumb."

"I'm Jennifer. I'm a maid in the castle," she gasped. "I—I brought you something." She gave her bag a little shake. "Something that belonged to the Princess."

There were footsteps behind Julianna and she heard a man say, "Luann, put your sword down! This is just that kid I was telling you about from last night."

Luann said, "Oh? You said she wouldn't be coming back."

"I just assumed she'd chicken out. She was so jumpy when I was talking to her."

"Hey!" Julianna said. Never mind that she *had* been really jumpy, and also that she *had* very nearly chickened out and not come back. She still didn't appreciate him talking about her like that.

"She said she brought something that belonged to the Princess," Luann said.

The burly guards behind Luann appraised Julianna for a few more seconds, then put their weapons down on the table and began playing cards again, obviously deeming her threat level to be too low to be worthy of their concern.

Julianna felt strangely insulted.

"Seriously, Luann, put the sword down. Let's see what she's got in that bag."

Julianna gave a little sigh of relief when Luann at last took Hector's advice and lowered her weapon. Then Julianna opened the bag up with

---

12   Julianna was not clear on the difference between knives and daggers.

shaking fingers and drew out the necklace, placing the pendant in Luann's outstretched hand. Luann studied it intently and breathed some sort of curse that Julianna wasn't familiar with, but it must have been the sort that meant something positive, because when Luann looked up at last from the pendant, she was smiling a big, greedy smile that told Julianna quite clearly that she had picked the right item to bring. "Look at this thing!" Luann said, awestruck.

Hector joined her and they both examined it a bit more, *ooh*ing and *ahh*ing and muttering to each other. The burly guys playing cards looked up with only mild interest before going back to their game. They must be paid by the hour instead of by the haul.

Hector looked up at her and said, "If it is discovered that you took a thing of so much worth, you'll be in huge trouble. I'm inclined to think you must be rather stupid."

Julianna glared at him and said, "I'm certain the Princess hasn't looked at that thing in years. It's been sitting at the bottom of her jewelry box for ages. She doesn't wear jewelry."

"If you're sure…" he said hesitantly.

"Well, either way, we're taking it," said Luann. "So I hope for your sake that you're right."

Hector shot Luann a look but didn't disagree. "Anyway, this sure is proof that you work in the Princess's rooms, and that you are willing to steal for us. So, as far as I'm concerned, you're in." He looked at Luann, who shrugged.

After a moment, Luann peeled her eyes away from the pendant and said, "You know, she could actually get started tonight. At the inn. Sarah was going to do it, but he might know who she is. It'd be good to use someone new."

Hector thought a moment and said to Julianna, "Would you be interested in helping out?"

"Sure…" Julianna said, as Dexter nodded eagerly at her. "Uh, what is it you want me to do?"

"It should be right up your alley," Hector said. "We need someone to steal something from a guy who's staying at the inn up by the castle gates. We're not sure how many of our people he knows by sight, so a new person would be good."

Julianna paused, feeling nervous.

"Do it! Do it!" Dexter prodded.

"Okay," she said, trying not to look at the ghost. It was so annoying when he talked to her around other people.

"Great. He's staying at The Sign of the Dawdling Donkey. You know it?"

"Oh, yeah. Sure. The good ol' Dawdling Donkey," she lied, figuring it would be suspicious if a commoner working in the castle wasn't aware of a business by the castle's gates. "Why's stealing from a guy at this inn right up my alley?" she couldn't help but ask, since the logic was less than obvious.

"Well, you're a maid, and we need a maid. The plan we've worked out with the innkeeper is that you go into the guy's room in a maid uniform the innkeeper will supply, you clean up, and, while you're in there, find a small silver box with an orange star on it." He then explained, "It's always best with things like this to find someone who will be comfortable with the role. Hence getting a maid to do a maid's job."

She nodded. "Okay." It did sound pretty easy. A nice, straightforward way for her to dip her toes into this whole seedy underworld and begin to get an idea of what might be the best way to make the citizens happier.

"The guy is named Mortimer Perkins," Hector said. "I'm told he's leaving tomorrow morning for the north, so tonight is your only chance."

"Wow, so I guess I'd better get going now, then." How very sudden. Julianna's stomach churned.

Luann, who hadn't looked up from the pendant the whole time Hector and Julianna had been talking, interjected at that juncture, "Make hay while the sun shines."

Julianna bristled at the expression. It had never been one of her favorites, considering her curse. But she just said, "Okay, let's go!"

HECTOR LED HER up a dark, narrow flight of stairs and into a living area that, to Julianna, looked like the absolute epitome of poverty, but was actually pretty standard middle-class conditions.

"Quit staring!" Dexter said, as she stifled a gasp at the sight of laundry drying on a string over the kitchen counter. *Did people really live like this? What a nightmare!* She had never so much as *seen* laundry before (except her tunneling clothes), but she knew for a fact that there was an entire section of the castle devoted to cleaning, drying, ironing, and other laundry things. Julianna tried to quit staring, but no matter what she did, her eyes kept drifting from one evidence of privation to another. Why, these people had a living area, kitchen, dining area, and a bed, all in one room that could fit inside one of her walk-in closets.

Dexter had a good idea of what the source of her horrified expression was, and he said, "This is how people live when they aren't royalty, Princess. In fact, these people are doing pretty well for themselves, I'd guess," he added, looking around. "There are tons of people who live in much worse conditions than this. Seriously, you need to quit gaping."

She clamped her mouth shut and plastered a semi-normal expression on her face just in time. Hector turned around at the front door, and said, "The bartender is named Galt. Tell him I sent you. Once you have the box, bring it back here. Sound good[13]?"

"Yep," she said as he opened the door for her. Julianna then walked out into the dark city street and barely noticed the door slamming shut behind her, so absorbed was she with the scene before her. The moonlight was helpful, but still she had some trouble navigating the unlit, crowded street full of wagons and pedestrians bustling to and fro; some people had lanterns either in their hands or affixed to their wagons, but the majority seemed to be managing with whatever moonlight filtered through the haze of coal smoke that permeated the air. She was surprised to see so many people out and about past sunset.

"It's going to take you a while to get to the Dawdling Donkey. We're almost exactly halfway around the castle wall," Dexter pointed out. "You can gawk as you walk." He smiled a bit at his inadvertent rhyme and whispered it again to himself just to hear it again. "Gawk as you walk."

She strode down the steps and into the mucky, muddy road, and after

---

13   He secretly had no faith that this wimpy, pasty kid would be able to pull it off, but he was reserving judgment until he saw whether (1) she came back with the box, (2) came back without the box but with some lame story about how it was too hard or she got too scared, or (3) she got hauled off by soldiers to have a finger chopped off (the penalty for first-time thieving offenders.

only three steps, succeeded in slipping and falling[14]. She got up and brushed herself off as best she could, then continued, keeping just a bit behind her spectral companion so that he could lead the way. She tried not to get too sickened at the thought of what must be soaking through her soft-soled slippers. If it weren't for her preoccupation with the state of her feet, it would have been even harder to keep from staring at the conditions of the street than it had been for her to keep from staring at the home she'd been in. Everyone looked so tired and filthy, and their clothes were all so worn and shabby looking.

And then there were the buildings, all made of wood, and all in a general state of disrepair that clearly showed the residents didn't have enough money to keep up-to-date on maintenance. "No wonder everyone in this city is so unhappy!" she said with her hand over her mouth so no one would see her and think she was talking to herself.

"What do you mean?" Dexter asked, looking around happily at the city he had loved so much back when he was alive. It appeared pretty much the same as it had 83 years ago, except some buildings were gone and had been replaced by others; probably they had burned down and others had been put up in their places, but that was to be expected in a city whose buildings were made almost exclusively of wood. Some of the crooks he had known back in the day had taken advantage of the fact and set fire to the houses of their adversaries; while Dexter had been present at some of the fires, he had never actually set any of them—a guy had to draw the line somewhere, after all.

"What do you mean, what do I mean? This city is disgusting pit of grime," she muttered. "Really gross grime," she added as though there were varying degrees of griminess, which maybe there are.

"Princess. You are currently walking through one of those most affluent neighborhoods in the city." This was true. The closer they got to the gates of the castle, the nicer the buildings got. "You have no idea," he added derisively, "what a pampered existence you lead."

---

14   The citizens of the city had grown sure-footed as mountain goats due to constant practice, but newcomers tended to fall a lot until they adapted. You could always tell a first-time visitor to the city by the amount of muck covering their clothing. A few more stumbles, and Julianna was bound to be pegged as an easy mark for muggers or other hooligans. At least, since it was nighttime, the hooligans would have a harder time spotting her.

"Yes. I do," she responded tiredly. This conversation with Dexter was approximately as old as her ability to speak. "How could I not know, with you always reminding me and making me feel bad about it? As though I personally handpicked my parents or something." She had to admit, though, that she had never really known until this day just how very, very, very much better off she had it than the citizens of Fritillary. Hearing about it was one thing. Walking through it—and slipping and falling in it—was another thing utterly.

A few minutes later, Julianna was walking into the very nicest part of the city. It was the only part of the city that had streetlights, but to her it didn't look any better than the area she'd left behind. The only difference was that, due to the streetlights, she could now see all the grime better. These buildings were a story or two taller on average than the ones before, and they were almost all well-maintained, but to her eyes it was all still pretty much disgusting. It was only when they got within sight of the gates to the castle that the houses started to look remotely livable to Julianna. One even had a little fountain in its front yard; she felt very happy to see this purely ornamental, non-functional thing sitting there merrily spewing forth water—it was the first decorative thing she had seen since she'd left the castle walls, and it made her feel strangely comforted.

Dexter led her on closer and closer to the castle gates, and it was only when she saw the guards standing in front of them that it occurred to her to cover her face with the hood of her cape; odds were very, very slim that someone would recognize her, since besides her mom and dad and brother, there were only five people who would be likely to recognize her: Delia (who Julianna knew for a fact was in a drugged sleep down in the dungeon), the wizard Wendell, the gardener who tended her houseplants, the *real* maid who cleaned the dungeon, and the interior decorator. A few other people had seen her, of course, but not with any regularity. She was glad, for maybe the first time in her life, that her parents guarded her so closely in their quest to keep any potential connections between her and Farland to a minimum.

They took a left at the bustling intersection right in front of the huge, ornate iron gates, and though Julianna wanted to stop and stare at them, she didn't dare do so for fear of attracting attention. But, when Dexter finally guided her to the front door of the Dawdling Donkey, she did peek out from under her hood at the huge gates, and at the castle beyond them.

The gates themselves must have taken an army of blacksmiths to create; they were as tall as the wall encircling the castle grounds, and they were festooned with twists and curlicues, leaves and flowers, dragons and birds. From the distance she was observing from, it looked to her as though every single length of iron that went into the creation of the gate must have some sort of detail worked into it. It was opulent in the extreme. Complete overkill. But that was her family.

A few yards past the decorative gate was one that appeared much more functional; it was just as tall as the iron gate but was made of solid wood reinforced with iron beams. This was the gate that the soldiers would slam shut in the event of a riot. She looked up, and, sure enough, the archway above the wood gate sported a half dozen gigantic cauldrons to boil oil in—Crowd Dispersal 101. Julianna scrunched her nose in distaste.

The wooden gate was open, since it was the time of day when the first shift castle employees were leaving, and the second shifters were coming in. So, Julianna was able to look through past the gates and up to the castle. The city was built on a big hill, with the castle at its top. The castle was tall and made of white stone, with many a turret poking up into the sky. From the top of each turret flew a huge flag with puce and tan stripes[15].

Unlike the mud roads of the rest of the city, the road that led to the castle was made of stone[16]. It wound through the castle grounds, with big, lush hedgerows lining it all the way to the top of the hill. About halfway up the road was a cohort of soldiers practicing some drills. A bit further down was a gardener clipping the hedges.

Julianna let her gaze drift back down from her home to the iron gate, where the soldiers guarding the entrance were busy searching people going

---

15   Her family's official colors. The name of the person who first picked such an uninspiring duo of colors for the family crest had been lost to the ages, but somewhere along the line the royal folks had decided that, for the sake of tradition, they had better honor that dull person's color choices, rather than living it up a bit and going with some bold complimentary colors like, for instance, yellow and purple, which would have looked quite snappy when paired together on a flag flapping above the castle in the brisk ocean breeze.

16   Or maybe (as rumor had it) the city roads *were* made of stone, and the muck of ages had simply covered it up long ago.

both in and out of the castle grounds. It was no wonder, she thought, that a smuggling operation had evolved over the years, if the soldiers at the official entrance to the castle were so thorough in their examination of every person who passed through the gates in either direction. One soldier was turning the pockets of a man's jacket inside out, another soldier was sifting through a bag of what looked like rice that was in the back of a woman's wagon, and a third soldier was pouring the contents of a man's backpack onto the muddy ground. The guard who was emptying the backpack had that air about him of thoroughly enjoying the fact that his official position enabled him to pick on people without repercussion.

"Yo. You've been standing in front of this door for like five minutes," Dexter pointed out. "It's a wonder someone inside hasn't opened it and knocked you over."

She was pretty covered in muck by this point, but still didn't want to get a fresh coat of it. "Do I knock?" she asked Dexter, pivoting her gaze to the big wooden door.

"Just walk in," he sighed.

"Don't get cranky," she whispered. "I've never been to an *inn* before. How should *I* know the customs?"

"It isn't an inn-specific custom to not knock. You just don't knock on the doors of *any* places that you go to buy things. All you do is walk right in if it's during business hours, and if it isn't business hours you know you can't go in because the door is locked."

She stored away this helpful bit of information and opened the door.

CHAPTER FIFTEEN

The eyes of all the patrons of the Dawdling Donkey swiveled in Julianna's direction when the door creaked open. About half of them were at bar, and the other half were scattered around at the haphazardly placed tables that filled the rest of the room, which was itself made entirely of wood. Floor, ceiling, chairs, tables, barstools, walls. Even, by the looks of it, some of the plates and bowls. The effect was quite strange to Julianna, who had grown up surrounded by the stone of the dungeon walls, tiled ceilings and floors, marble and upholstery and iron and tapestries, and other such rich folk materials[17].

---

17   But for the commoners, it was wood all the way. Other materials were expensive, but due to the vast forest in Fritillary's wild North Country, wood was pretty cheap. On any given day, you could bet there was somewhere along the Fritillary River at least one shipment of logs floating downstream to the city. Logjams were a constant source of frustration to people who traveled by boat. Due to the fact that the whole city was essentially a big bonfire waiting to happen, the fire department was the one public works service that both Conroy and his ancestors before him had kept consistently funded. After all, it would be pretty rotten if a house fire spread too far and all of a sudden, BAM!, there you were the king of nothing but a big smoldering ash heap and a scattering of outlying little backwaters full of people too poor to contribute much in the way of taxes anyway. All you could do would be roast some marshmallows until the ashes cooled, and then try to figure out a new career path. One that actually involved *working*. And as much as Conroy loved a good s'more, he didn't want his city to burn to the ground and thus have to go get a job. So, he kept up

The bartender, Galt, kept watching Julianna long after the rest of the people in the room had gone back to their conversations, or in the case of the few who were there alone, their solitary, philosophical musings on the meaning of life as they stared into the amber depths of their ales.

Galt was of average height and weight, but by the looks in his eyes, Juliana guessed that he was above average in the anger department. Startled to see such a menacing glare directed at herself, she cautiously approached the bar. Once she was within range of a hissing whisper, he gave a hissed whisper, "You the new maid?"

"Yes, indeed," she said.

"Then why in tarnation," he growled, "didn't you come in through the servants' entrance? You want to attract attention?"

"I'm sorry," she said with surprise. It hadn't occurred to her that there would even *be* a servants' entrance at all on this building, when the owners of this inn most likely made less money per year than even the lowliest of servants she knew in the castle.

"Whatever. Just get in back and change." He gestured over his shoulder to a door behind the bar.

She was torn between her royal inclination to give him a piece of her mind for daring to speak so rudely to her and her feeling that as a maid she should be apologizing a bit more, but in the end she did neither of those things; she merely nodded to indicate she'd heard him, went behind the bar, and walked through the door, which, it turned out, was the entrance to the employee break room. Across from the door, there were five hooks hanging on the wall with labels above them that read, 'Hilda', 'Ellen', 'Galt', and 'Mary'. The fifth hook had no label. Both Hilda's and Ellen's hooks held a blue dress, a white, apron, and a white bonnet. The fifth hook looked like the place where extra uniforms were stored. Galt's and Mary's hooks were empty, leading Julianna to infer that the guy at the bar was indeed Galt, and that Mary was currently working somewhere in the inn. As she rifled through the spare uniforms on the unclaimed hook, she muttered to Dexter, "Why didn't you tell me about the servants' entrance?"

---

the family tradition of funding the fire department and left the s'more construction to the kitchen staff.

"Sorry. I wasn't thinking."

She just sighed and said, "Turn around." He did so, and she put on a blue dress that technically fit her, though she was horrified by the feel of the cheap fabric against her skin and the untailored fit of the thing. At least it was so long that it covered her feet, so no one would notice the state of them. The only things she retained from her previous outfit were her slippers and the anti-magic amulet she wore night and day as protective measure against Farland.

Next, she tied the apron around her waist, put the bonnet on her head, and thanked the heavens that there was no mirror to look in. Though she was considerably more grounded than her parents, she was still a princess, and was going to need a significant adjustment period before she became all right with things like looking how she looked. "What do you suppose I should do next?" she asked.

Dexter turned and stared, then stifled a laugh that told her just as effectively as a mirror would that she looked nothing like a princess anymore.

"Control yourself, man," she said disdainfully, even as her face began to turn red.

He managed to control himself after a bit more laughing, and said, "What did you ask?"

"I *asked*," she said, "What you think I should do next."

"Oh. Just wait for that guy to tell you, probably," he said unhelpfully. Then added, "Have a seat," as he nodded his head toward a table by the door. There were a few mismatched chairs grouped around it, and some books and magazines scattered on top of it along with a plate that held the remains of someone's dinner.

Julianna wandered over to the table and saw that the magazines were faded old copies with titles like *Innkeepers' Digest* and *Maids' Quarterly*. There was also a book entitled *Drink Mixing for Simpletons* and a newspaper that appeared to be at least fairly current. She grabbed up the newspaper and began to read. While she was not naïve enough to believe that journalists would dare write articles outright insulting the monarchy, she was hoping that, by reading between the lines, she might be able to get an idea about angry undercurrents. But no sooner had she begun to peruse a society piece about the upcoming hunting party her father was throwing for her little brother than the innkeeper burst into the room, still looking kind of mad.

"Listen, kid, I'm sorry I was so angry out there. It's just that the guy you're supposed to be stealing from is sitting out there at one of the tables, and he just saw you use the main entrance. You walk into the place all covered in street muck like someone who's never set foot in the city before; the last thing I need is him inferring that you don't know the ropes because you are not a real employee."

She considered him slightly paranoid. Surely that sort of thing didn't really matter? Not knowing what to say, she remained silent.

"Okay, well let's get moving. I'm going to take you down to the basement to show you where all the maid stuff is. On the way out of here, I want you to look at the table in the far corner. That's where the guy whose room you're going to search is sitting. Get a good look at him so you'll know to avoid him. But don't look *too* close or he'll get suspicious."

Julianna frowned. *Get a good look but don't look too close. Right. Whatever.* She followed him out of the door and toward another heavy wood door opposite the bar. On the way, she glanced at the guy sitting at the far table.

And their eyes met.

And she did more than glance.

She stopped in her tracks and stared.

Because there was something about him that was very worthy of a good stare. He wasn't earth-shatteringly handsome or anything, but there was something about this Mortimer Perkins that froze her to the spot.

In a good way.

Some exciting aura he somehow managed to exude (though all he was doing was sitting there gnawing at a turkey leg) that made her feel he must be a manly sort of fellow who swashbuckled and had devil-may-care adventures.

He caught her eye, smiled, and gave a little wave.

She found herself smiling back.

Dexter was saying something, but she was blocking him out.

It was only when Galt took her by the arm and physically yanked her through the door to the basement that she snapped out of it.

Down in the basement, she was too preoccupied to even pay much attention to the complaining of the bartender, or to give more than a slight nod when he introduced her to his wife, who they bumped into as she was leading a young man and woman in through the servants' door.

Galt stopped for a few minutes to ask his wife, Mary, who the young man and woman were and why she was bringing them into the inn. There was a note of suspicion in Galt's voice that Julianna would have found strange in a husband addressing his wife if she had been paying more than a shred of attention. But she was too busy reminiscing about the way Mortimer's blue eyes had sparkled at her to notice much else.

CHAPTER SIXTEEN

Even after Corrine and Warren had left Farland's place far behind and were well on the way to the inn that was the first stop on their journey out of the city, Warren was still reeling from the discovery of the magical pool of raven blood that spoke to him in his head. He looked down at the vial of red liquid he held in his hand, wondering whether it had been wise to follow the raven blood's advice and take a bit of the blood with him on his journey. But they'd been in a hurry, so he'd just taken a vial from Farland's workbench, scooped some blood out of the basin, and figured he'd weigh the pros and cons later.

"Warren, you shouldn't have taken that stuff," Corrine muttered at him, not wanting their guides to hear.

"I know. I've been thinking the same thing."

"Well then, get rid of it."

"Let me talk to it first," Warren stalled, for though he wasn't sure he trusted the magical pool of raven blood, he did think it had the potential to be a very convenient item to bring on this adventure. Back at Farland's place, the magical pool of raven blood had pointed out to Warren that if he took it along, it could inform Warren when Farland finally got back to his apartment. Warren just couldn't toss the blood aside on a whim when it was capable of giving him that sort of information.

"Okay. Whatever. Talk to the magic blood," Corrine muttered, not bothering to get in a fight with Warren about this, since she was planning to swipe the vial at her first opportunity and toss it into the street anyway.

"I'll see if it can present a compelling argument for why we should keep it," he said to Corrine, then thought at the magical vial of raven blood, *How do I know I can trust you?*

After a long, awkward pause, the raven blood finally said, *Are you thinking at me, bro? I can't read your mind, man. Just speak. You've got a mouth.*

"Oh. Uh, you can't—okay." He swallowed, cleared his throat, and said to the vial, "How do I know I can trust you?"

Unfortunately, you don't.

"Why are you offering to help me? You're *Farland's* magical pool of raven blood. Don't you want to help *him?*"

Dude, just because he created me, that doesn't mean I'm his. Like, do you belong to your parents just because they made you? No, you are your own person. And I am my own magical pool of raven blood, it squawked defiantly. *Farland is evil, man. I only help him when he does a future spell—the magic makes it so I have to answer him. And when he uses me as an ingredient, well, it's not like I can stop him doing that. But whenever I have a choice, I totally don't help him.*

Warren said apologetically, "While I do find that admirable, I can't help but think you might be lying. What's to stop you from telling Farland where we are?"

Keep me in your pocket and I won't hear a thing!

Warren doubted it was really that simple, but kept his mouth shut as the raven voice continued, *And if I steer you wrong, or you begin to doubt me, just drop me.*

"A valid point," Warren said, then caught sight of his sister watching him. She was not liking the one side she was hearing of this conversation. He shrugged at her and said, "I think we should keep it. For a bit at least."

Corrine was going to respond, but she caught a curious glance from Myrtle, and gave Warren a warning look that ended the conversation.

Corrine, Warren, Charles, and Myrtle walked on in silence, winding their way through the city streets to the Sign of the Dawdling Donkey, where the innkeeper's wife, Mary, was hopefully going to be able to give them a place to hide for a few nights.

Charles and Myrtle were impressed that these newcomers to the city were able to navigate the streets without slipping in the muck, but Corrine pointed out that after growing up walking on the uneven, slippery decks of various ships, the city roads were a piece of cake. Warren made a dumb joke about how that wasn't a piece of cake *he* would want to eat, ha ha ha. And then, there they were going down a dark alley and stopping at the servants' entrance to the inn.

Myrtle knocked, and Mary herself answered a few seconds later, exclaiming happily, "Myrtle! What a surprise!"

They exchanged a few more pleasantries, then Myrtle explained what they were doing there. Mary looked past Myrtle and Charles at the siblings. Then, she looked uneasily over her shoulder. "I will be able to take them in for a *few* nights," she told Myrtle. "But, er, Galt can't know who they are. I'll try to hide them in the basement out of the way, and hopefully they won't even cross paths with him. If they do, we'll just call them by different names. I'll move them on to the next place as soon as possible."

Getting a bad vibe, Myrtle wanted to ask if her friend was having trouble with her husband, but that wasn't the sort of question one could ask out of the blue and then hurry on one's way. Especially if the answer was in the affirmative. And they were in a hurry. So instead, she just said, "Let's get together for tea soon," and gave Mary's hand a chummy squeeze.

Myrtle found herself wondering whether she felt comfortable enough to leave the siblings there when there was apparently something fishy going on with Galt[18]. But in the end, she decided if a lady couldn't trust one of her oldest friends then who the heck could she trust? So, Charles and Myrtle said goodbye to Warren and Corrine, and they went on their way with only mild misgiving.

Myrtle should have paid more attention to that misgiving, but if she had heeded the warning bells in her head, then the story from here on out wouldn't have been as fun.

Mary quickly ushered the siblings in and was just shutting the door when she heard a voice down the dark hallway to their left. Mary cursed

---

18   Which didn't surprise Myrtle; she'd known Galt was bad news from the first time Mary had introduced her to him back when they were teenagers.

and tried to push them in the other direction, but then Galt rounded the corner. He was complaining to someone following him, asking, "How could you have been so stupid as to attract so much attention?", but stopped short when he saw Mary, Corrine, and Warren. "Who are these people?" he asked Mary suspiciously as he eyed Warren's banjo case. "We don't need any music here."

"This is nothing to do with you," Mary said shortly, since he'd happened upon her so quickly that she hadn't had time to formulate a lie about the siblings.

"Something to do with those women's rights pals of yours?" he sneered as though the idea of women and men being equal was laughable. If only Julianna, who was trailing behind him, had been paying attention instead of thinking about Mortimer and his dreamy blue eyes, she might have begun to form a different opinion about whether she should be helping Galt steal the box with the orange star. But she was in the beginning stages of her very first crush that wasn't on a character from a novel, so we shall forgive her for her preoccupation.

Corrine, however, was mentally fully present, and looked disdainfully right back at Galt, pegging him immediately as a pathetic loser who thought the key to retaining what little power he had over his life was picking on whoever else he could. She was an excellent judge of character.

Warren was thinking things much along the same lines as his sister but was in addition also pondering whether he should try to jump in and defend the honor of their kind hostess.

However, Mary, too tired of dealing with Galt to waste more breath on him, was already walking down the hallway. Corrine and Warren realized she'd gone, and they scampered to catch up, leaving Galt behind. Warren looked back, wishing he'd had the chance to impart some of the scathing comments he'd been formulating in his head; he saw Galt usher through a door the very pale, dark-haired girl who had been walking with him. Galt said something in a cranky tone of voice to her, slammed the door shut, and stormed off the way he'd come, grumbling.

When Warren caught back up with the ladies, Mary was in the midst of apologizing about her husband. "Sorry about him. His friends and mine don't really get along. It's driven a bit of a wedge between us over the years."

"That looked like more than a bit of a wedge," Corrine said, then continued with her skill for getting in other people's business by saying, "Why are you *with* that guy?"

Mary didn't seem annoyed by the question. She handed Warren the lantern she'd been holding and said as she unlocked a door at the very end of the long basement hallway, "I'm a part owner of the inn. It's my only source of income. And if I left, the place would fall apart. My daughters work here too, so it's not just me who's dependent on the money this place brings in." She pushed the door open and said, "Believe me, if I had a choice I'd be out of here."

Corrine gave Warren a warning look, because she knew he was probably trying to think up some way to help this lady. His desire to help everyone he crossed paths with had been all right back on the pirate ship where there weren't too many people, but in this city, you could barely take one step without crossing the path of a person who had a problem that needed to be solved. Already they had promised to help Jane get away from the pirates, and Corrine didn't want Warren making any more promises until that one was taken care of.

"Okay," Mary said as she showed them into the dark, windowless room. "Here's your room. I know it's kind of dreadful, but you'll only be here a few nights." Warren walked in, and the lantern he was holding shed light on a cramped little damp room furnished with two cots and not much else. "We only rent this room out as a last resort when the inn is really packed, or when someone is really desperate for a room but doesn't have much money. You're lucky you showed up before the King's hunting party, because once that's started even this room will be rented."

"We'll manage in here just fine," Warren said, setting the lantern down on the hard dirt floor. "Thank you so much for your help." His broken arm was starting to ache something fierce, and he was more than ready for a nap; he didn't care how gross the bed was, just as long as he could sleep on it.

But Mary wasn't quite finished talking yet. "Let me show you the one nice feature this room does have," she said with a sneaky smile, and walked over to the bed that was against the outer wall. She knelt down and indicated a big block of stone that was part of the wall. "This stone is loose. If you push it back, it leads to a secret room. We used it in the old days to hide women on the run from witch-burning mobs."

"Do you think we'll need to *use* that?" Warren asked, inclining his head toward the stone.

"Oh, no," she said. "No. But just in case. Can't hurt to have a hiding place on hand if you're on the run, I always say. If Galt hadn't seen you, I'd actually have suggested you stay in there right from the get-go. But now it would look odd to him if you up and disappeared completely."

"Should we be worried about your husband? He looked pretty suspicious about us." Warren didn't want to sound too suspicious himself when Mary had been kind enough to take them in, but he wanted to get a good handle on the situation. It was his life, after all, that was at stake.

Mary shook her head. "No, he's always mistrustful about my friends. It's nothing to do with you two personally. And he has no way of knowing who you are anyway." This last part was true enough. If Jane's calculations were correct, Farland would be unconscious for at least another half day, so he was currently in no position to start asking around in whatever evil circle of friends he might have to see if they had any leads on Warren.

"So why show us this secret room?" Warren persisted.

She shrugged. "Just walking you through all the amenities we have to offer. I'll bring some food down at dinner time. Bathroom's first door on the left down the hall. You'll want to stay out of sight as much as you can. And lock the door when I leave."

Corrine nodded. Warren, who was already lying down on one of the beds, said thank you to Mary as she walked out. Corrine locked the door behind her and turned to look at Warren, whose eyes were already shut. "I don't feel safe here."

"Me either," he said with his eyes still shut. "But I trust Jane to have a good idea of how long she can keep Farland unconscious. So I figure we don't have to start worrying for at least ten hours. Probably more. That's plenty of time to get some rest." He opened his eyes and gave her what he hoped was a reassuring smile. "We'll be fine. Take a nap."

She gave him a doubtful look, but in the end decided it was, indeed, sensible to sleep. She flopped down on the awful mattress.

ULIANNA STOOD WHERE Galt had left her in a closet full of cleaning supplies. He'd given her a lantern, which she was now holding up to examine the items on the shelf before her. While she had been right in saying she was good at cleaning, she had not known until this moment just how much specialized knowledge maids must have; so many products and tools! Big brooms, little brooms, mops, and scoopy things; yellow liquids, blue liquids, and green liquids; yellow powders, blue powders, and green powders. "Geez Louise," she muttered.

"Just fill up that bucket with some stuff and let's get moving," suggested Dexter. "You'll look authentic enough as long as you're holding a broom and a mop and a bucket."

"I guess. There's so much more to this maid thing than I would have thought," she said with irritation as she grabbed some bottles and jars at random and set them in the wooden bucket at her feet. She threw in a little broom and a scoopy thing for good measure, put the bucket over her elbow, then transferred the lantern to the bucket arm. She opened the door, then grabbed the broom and mop, already getting annoyed with how much work it was to carry all this stuff. As she proceeded awkwardly along the hallway, which seemed a lot narrower now that she was laden down with so much stuff, she hoped Mortimer Perkins's room was not too far. It was a good thing she had developed strong muscles through years of tunneling, otherwise all the supplies would have been even more of a problem for her.

As she bumped her way along the narrow staircase, she said, "I hope I get a chance to bump into that Mortimer fellow again before I swipe that box from his room. He's pretty gorgeous, don't you think?"

Dexter stared. "You're hoping to get a chance to flirt with the guy you're stealing from?"

"Again I say, he's *gorgeous*," she explained patiently. "I've never seen a real live gorgeous guy before."

"I thought you were in the city to mingle with commoners and try to solve all their problems or something. Are your lofty ideals so easily thrown by the wayside for the first halfway attractive guy you bump into?" he asked with a smirk.

"He *is* a commoner, Dexter," she said. At this point, she reached the top of the stairs, which meant her side of the conversation was at an end. She looked at the door before her and took a deep breath. Time to do some stealing.

Chapter Seventeen

As Julianna juggled mop, broom, and bucket while trying to open the door to the barroom, Dexter floated annoyingly right through the obstacle. When she finally opened the door to the bar and got all her cleaning goods through, she was horrified to see that Dexter had floated right over to Mortimer and was hovering in front of him. Mortimer, oblivious, was leaning over a newspaper that was spread out on the table before him. "He really isn't so great looking," Dexter hollered over the ruckus. "Is he?"

Well, Julianna thought, perhaps not *classically* good looking, but he had an air of excitement about him, and the rugged look of an adventurer. She sighed like a teenager staring at the lead singer of her favorite band. Or maybe the drummer of her favorite band. Yes, the drummer. Julianna wasn't a lead singer kind of girl. Lead singers were too polished and obvious, a lot like the nobles' sons she'd known.

Then Mortimer looked right up at her.

And he smiled.

And he waved.

And she smiled back.

And she waved back.

And she didn't even care that Dexter was floating above

him pretending to poke Mortimer in the eyes with his ghostly fingers, and then pretending to cut off his head by making chopping motions through Mortimer's neck with his hand, and then doing pretty much anything he could to make himself annoying.

Mortimer stood and began to weave through the tables scattered all around the room. The room had gotten a lot fuller since Julianna had been in there earlier, and most of the chairs were now occupied, so Mortimer had to do quite a bit of weaving, but she got the feeling that his general trajectory was in her direction.

And sure enough, at last his winding journey through the tables and chairs came to an end in front of her.

Dexter, growing tired of being annoying since he was not getting a response or making her flustered, floated off Mortimer's shoulders where his feet had been resting as he'd sat on Mortimer's head, and landed near Julianna.

"Hi," Mortimer said in a rather scratchy voice.

"Hi," Julianna responded, heart all of a flutter.

"This your first job day on the job?" he asked.

"Er, yes, how did you know?" she asked, hoping that Galt's worries weren't turning out to be well-founded after all.

"Your dress when you came in. It was covered in street sludge. A sure sign you're new in town."

"Er..." This was not how she had been hoping this conversation was going to shake out. Was he on to her?

He mistook her awkward silence for embarrassment. "Nothing to worry about," he said reassuringly. "You'll get your footing soon enough! Listen, the reason I'm asking if you're new in town is, I'm a union organizer."

"Pardon?" she asked. This was at least not what she'd been fearing.

"A union organizer. Specifically, coal miners' unions. But I have a friend whose thing is organizing unions for maids and other hospitality-type workers; I can give you her contact info. In my experience, people coming from the villages to work in the city don't usually know about unions. So I thought I'd bring it to your attention." He studied her for a moment, apparently trying to discern whether she'd understood him. His study of her face seemed to tell him that she didn't fully get it yet, so he persisted, "Some bosses take advantage of out-of-towners, you see. And, just from what I've seen of your new boss tonight, I imagine he might be the type."

"Oh, er, thanks. How nice of you." She tried not to be disappointed that he had approached her not because he fancied her but because he wanted to give her the contact information of a friend of his. She didn't know much about unions, but she had a notion they were something workers liked because it got them stuff. Or something. Hopefully Dexter would be able to fill her in.

Mortimer removed a pack that had been slung over his shoulder and said, "If you've got a minute, I think I have a few of my friend's business cards in here. Somewhere…" He set the bag down on a table behind him, apologizing to the man and woman who were sitting there. The lady glared at him and the guy said something about how some people have no common courtesy, but they let him keep his bag on the table as Mortimer began to rummage around, removing a leather-covered notebook, an extra pair of shoes, and a brown sack of maybe food, before finally saying with a grin, "Aha! Here we go!" And his hand emerged from the pack with a stack of business cards. He rifled through the stack and handed her one.

Julianna glanced at it and read the home address of a Gretel Merriman. "Thanks very much," she said as she realized it really *was* very nice of him to have flagged her down to help her out. Really, she thought, it was sort of better than him just coming over to partake in idle chitchat; his helpfulness told her that he was a considerate, kind sort of fella who had seen her and thought to give her some advice about her new job in the big city. "So, coal miners' union?" she asked, hoping to keep him talking for a bit. For one thing, she was liking the idea of getting to know a little bit more about this particular citizen.

But for another thing, when he had been rifling through his pack, she had caught a glimpse within it of what she was almost sure was a silver box with an orange star on it; if she was right, the thing she was supposed to steal was not in his room but in the bag that was now on his back.

"Yep," he said. "I'm a coal miner myself, so it's a lot easier for me to get other miners interested than it is for the guys who come in from the city for a day or two to get recruits and then go on their way." So that was why his voice was scratchy—he was a miner! Some sort of precursor to black lung was currently knocking about in his respiratory apparatus.

She found she didn't really know what to ask next since she felt woefully under-informed about unions and didn't want to look dumb. If only Dexter could tell her, but he was busy floating around the bar, eavesdropping on the customers. "I'd imagine so," she said. "How long have you been mining?"

"Since I was ten. So twelve years."

"Since you were *ten*? But mining is *dangerous!*" Right about then, Julianna noticed out of the corner of her eye that Galt was flapping his arms at her from behind the bar, behind Mortimer's back. She studiously ignored him and kept her eyes on Mortimer's handsome face, but she got the idea that Galt was pointing up toward the staircase, obviously wanting her to get on with searching Mortimer's room.

Oblivious, Mortimer talked on, "Well, yes...it's dangerous. But I was the oldest kid, and my dad was gone and I had six little brothers and sisters. So, really, I didn't have a choice. The only other job for a guy in the north is logging, and that wasn't an option because I was too little for most of the logging stuff. Besides," he said with a sigh, "logging is every bit as dangerous as coal mining, just in different ways."

"Wow." Julianna gave him an awestruck look. The whole time she'd been frittering away her life down in the dungeon pursuing her hobbies and eating tasty food and getting tutored by the best teachers in whatever field she cared to learn about, Mortimer and tons of others like him had been out risking their lives in order to keep their families from starving. This was an awful lot to think about, and it made her sad. Really, really sad. "That is really, really sad."

"And the saddest part is that it's such a common story for the people in the northern villages. They are trapped in a cycle of poverty and ignorance, and the cycle will not be broken until people in power begin to care." Those lines were taken pretty much verbatim from the usual speech he gave to prospective union members, so the words sounded slightly canned, but they were so applicable to the conversation that he just had to throw them in. He added, "Surely the same sort of stuff was happening where you're from?" He seemed suddenly curious as to why she appeared not to have known about this apparently common story.

"Oh. Yes, of course. But each new sad story just sort of... affects me anew, I guess," she improvised, summoning up some defensiveness. "Just because it's a common story doesn't mean I'm desensitized to it. I *do* have a heart."

"Sorry, I didn't mean to imply—"

"Of course you didn't."

"No, really. That was uncool of me."

"Forget it."

"Let me make it up to you," he said, flashing a swoon-worthy smile. "Let me get you a drink when you're done with work?" he asked, gesturing at her mop and cleaning stuff, which she had forgotten she'd been holding.

"That'd be nice," she said, smiling back. "Sure." *Yay!* Then she realized that, in order to keep up her pretense of being a maid, she had to now go do some cleaning even though the whole reason for her doing so was currently sitting in his pack. *Curses. What a bother.*

"Will you be done by three in the morning?" he asked. "I have to go out into the city and meet with a few people, but I should be back by then."

"Sounds perfect!" she said with a grin.

He nodded and smiled another lovely smile, then strode out the door.

Julianna began to gather her things, but then it occurred to her that she should probably be following him if she really wanted to steal that box. Maybe fate would present her with an opportunity to swipe it, thus proving to those smugglers that she was brave enough to be a part of their operation. For, if she didn't prove herself to them, they wouldn't let her use their house as a way in and out of the city, and she wouldn't be able to venture out of the castle walls anymore, and she would have no way to save the citizens from oppression and her family from rebellion.

Deciding she'd better get going fast, before she lost him out there in the city streets, she plunked her cleaning stuff all down by the door to the basement and scurried toward the front door, glancing at the bar long enough to wave a placating hand at Galt, who was staring at her in consternation.

Then Julianna ran out into the night, Dexter floating closely behind.

Julianna looked left, then right, and spotted Mortimer disappearing around the corner of a building right in front of the castle gates. Feeling quite sneaky like a spy from one of her novels, she flitted down the street after Mortimer, only slipping slightly in the muck before finding her footing.

"Why are we following this dude? Stalking is never the way to anyone's heart. Believe me," Dexter sagely doled out some hard-won advice.

"I'm not stalking him. He's got the box in his pack. I'm going to try to get it somehow." She gasped and flailed her arms wildly, catching her balance at the last moment.

"Oh, well that's different," he said. After a pause, he added doubtfully, "but how do you propose to do that?"

"How should I know?" she retorted. She was having a hard time staying upright on the slimy street as she tried to keep up with Mortimer's pace, and it was making her grumpy. It would be hard to explain if she showed up back at the bar at three o'clock covered in mud when she was supposed to have been cleaning the inn that whole time. "An opportunity may present itself, though, and save me from having to somehow steal the thing while sitting across from him in a well-lit bar."

"Want to hear my suggestion?" he asked.

"Sure."

"Wait until he's on an empty stretch of street and hit him over the head with my brick."

"I am *not* doing that," she said flatly.

"It's what *I'd* have done in your place back when I was alive."

"That doesn't surprise me in the least. You must have been a horrible thug when you were flesh-and-blood."

Dexter nodded his agreement.

Julianna saw her quarry stop in front of a heavily-bearded homeless man wearing a threadbare gray cape. Mortimer looked right and left in a casual, non-shifty manner, prompting Julianna to quickly swoop out of sight into the shadow of a parked wagon that she had been walking by. She was just congratulating herself on her artful maneuver when she noticed that Mortimer's gaze had flown to her hiding place, and he was searching its shadows. "Do you think he saw me?" she asked Dexter nervously.

"I don't think so. He probably just saw that silly dodge you did out of the corner of his eye, and the movement made him suspicious. Next time, just keep walking."

"Hmm. Good point." She assessed the situation for a moment. "Okay. Float on over there and eavesdrop, would you?"

Dexter obliged, and while Mortimer and the homeless fellow chatted, Julianna took a few moments to study her surroundings in more detail. She was still in the fancy part of town that had streetlights, so she could fairly easily see through the coal smoke. Across the street were three stores: a shoe repair place called the City Cobbler, an apparel place called Capes 'N' Caps, and a restaurant called Northwoods Buffet, which advertised "rustic peasant-inspired fare with a fun twist". Maybe the fun twist was that the serving sizes were actually adequate portions to fill a belly, unlike the fare on the plates of the peasants in the *real* Northwoods of Fritillary.

There weren't many people out on the streets anymore at this time of night, but still more than she would have expected. Everyone looked so faded and tired and troubled as they trudged about in the cold night doing whatever it was that commoners did with themselves. It was thoroughly depressing. After a few minutes of people-watching, Julianna became aware that there were voices conversing nearby. Two men. They were sitting on the bench of the wagon she was hiding behind, completely oblivious of her as she crouched in the shadows practically at their feet.

One was saying, "—can't wait until this hunting party is *finally* over."

"Clyde, so what if it means more trouble for us? It also means more money."

"Not saying I don't appreciate the money," Clyde grumbled. "I'm just so tired of this. We pack up the wagon, bring it to the gates, get searched like we're criminals planning to assassinate the Queen herself, go in and deliver our goods, get searched again on the way out as though we've kidnapped the Prince and are smuggling him out in one of our empty boxes, go home and start the whole process over again the next day."

"Yeah," his companion said, "but all I know is I got to buy my kids new coats and boots for the winter."

Clyde's response was lost in all the ruckus of the wagon starting, without warning, to creak and roll. Julianna's hiding place was now in motion. *Curses.* She scooted along with it for a few paces, crouching low, but quickly drew stares doing that, and decided it would be best just to hide in a nearby doorway instead. Sneaking was hard.

After a while, Mortimer walked on down the street and out of the section of the city that was lit by streetlights. As she followed him at a conservative distance, flitting from shadow to shadow, Dexter joined her to report about his eavesdropping. "Hey," he said. "Get this. He wasn't talking about unions. I think he's one of those rebels—he was saying some pretty bad stuff about your family."

"Hmm," Julianna mused. "That makes more sense. I was wondering why he was talking about unions with a homeless guy. Not like there are homeless unions."

"That's all you have to say? You're not put off by the fact that he hates you royal types? He was talking about overthrowing your dad."

She shrugged. As confusing as it was, she was actually kind of happy that he was a rebel. Trying not to think too much about that, she sneaked on after him.

DEAR READER, RIGHT about now you may be thinking that we've been hearing an awful lot about Juliana, but not much about Warren. This is true, but it's just because all he and Corrine are doing is sleeping, whereas Julianna is traipsing about the city spying on her crush.

But just in case you want an update:

Warren was fast asleep on his narrow little bed, cradling his banjo with his good arm, drooling a bit, and every so often muttering something about harpsichords. Across the room from him on her own narrow little bed, Corrine was sleeping as well, though not as soundly. She was restless, and every time she moved, her bed squeaked, making her toss and turn more and more, creating an irritating cycle of tossing and squeaking, tossing and squeaking, until finally she would wake up just a bit, lie still, and fall back asleep again. Only for the whole thing to start over a few minutes later.

A mouse scuttled across the floor and eyed Warren.

Warren drooled a bit more.

A floorboard creaked in the bar above, making him jump and mutter in his sleep.

Corrine thrashed about.

A bit of condensation dripped from the ceiling and onto the floor with a tiny splash.

There you go. Updated enough, I hope.

CHAPTER EIGHTEEN

Nearly two hours of following Mortimer through the city as he met with two more homeless people and visited three apartments, and Julianna was beginning to think that tracking him in hopes of getting an opportunity to steal the box in his backpack had been a mistake. The plain fact is that if you are following a person in a covert manner, you cannot get close enough to reach into their backpack, unless you are in a big, noisy crowd. No big noisy crowds being on hand, Julianna was almost ready to throw in the towel and get back to the inn.

But, luckily for her, and unluckily for Mortimer, there was apparently at least one person in this city who didn't share her belief that sneaking up on people from behind and hitting them over the head was wrong.

It happened when Julianna was waiting for Mortimer to leave an apartment building that he'd entered about fifteen minutes earlier. She was about a block away from the building, hiding in a shadowy doorway, having a whispered conversation with Dexter about unions. She had learned about them briefly from one of her tutors years ago, but her lessons had had a distinctly anti-union slant wherein all unions were horrible things that resulted in incompetent, lazy workers who wanted things like days off (thus producing fewer goods or services and decreasing the amount of money the Crown could make off of them through taxes) and excessive wages (money that the Crown could otherwise have claimed from the employers).

Dexter's lessons had a distinctly pro-union slant wherein all unions were the best things ever, keeping The Man from inhumanly working his employees to the bone for as little money as possible, all while in the worst imaginable conditions. While she knew the truth was somewhere in between, she still figured it was worthwhile to listen to Dexter's propaganda, since it was probably the same opinion held by the majority of the populace.

"So, you see, unions are the only way to keep *your* dratted family from working the citizens of this country into the ground until they're doing nothing but slaving away until they day they finally collapse under the tyrannical iron fi—"

"Shh!" Julianna cut in, though of course she really didn't need to shush a ghost.

The door of the building Mortimer had entered a bit ago had opened. Mortimer walked out. He turned around to say a few final words to whoever had walked him to the door, and then he started back down the street in her direction, probably now heading back toward the Dawdling Donkey after a long night of meeting with either union contacts, or rebels, or whatever.

She slid further back into the shadows and watched him approach. Then she saw someone sneaking out of another shadowy doorway and swooping quickly and silently up behind him. This person obviously intended to do more than follow Mortimer—the person was approaching too fast and was raising their hand in the air over Mortimer's head—Julianna caught a glimpse of something glinting in the person's hand. Just before they brought the weapon down on Mortimer's head, Julianna forgot all about how she was supposed to be sneaking, and she cried out, "Mortimer! Behind you!"

Mortimer startled at the sound of his name, then whirled around, but it was too late. There was a sickening thud, and he collapsed at his attacker's feet.

"Idiot!" Dexter spat. "That person's going to come after *you* now!"

Erg. She hadn't thought of that. She hadn't thought at all. Julianna stared in horror at the person, waiting to see what would happen next. She couldn't run, so her best chance was to just stay in the shadows and hope that they didn't know where her voice had originated from. She held her breath and didn't move a muscle.

But the person only gave a quick glance in her direction, leaned down over Mortimer, reached into the lining of his coat, grabbed something out of his pocket, and scampered off. It all happened in the space of a few seconds.

She waited just a few seconds more to make sure the person wasn't coming back, then she rushed over to Mortimer's side and put a hand to his wrist. He had a pulse, and it seemed strong. But he was out cold.

"He alive?" Dexter asked.

She nodded distractedly, trying to think what to do next. She thought she saw blood matting his hair.

"Grab the box and get moving," Dexter said.

Trying not to feel too guilty, she tugged Mortimer's pack out from under him and rummaged around until she found the box. Sure enough, it was silver with an orange star. She transferred it to her bag, studying his handsome face the whole time, ready to dart away the moment he showed signs of waking.

"Okay, now let's go," Dexter said.

"I'm not leaving him here in the middle of the road. A wagon could come along and run him over." She stood, took him by the hands, and dragged him through the muck to the side of the road, glad for the second time that night that her tunneling project had earned her some respectable muscles. He groaned a bit, but his eyes were still shut.

"All right, *now* let's go," Dexter snapped.

But instead of walking in the direction of the Dawdling Donkey, Julianna rushed over to the building Mortimer had just left. She knocked on the door, then pulled her hood close around her face.

The door opened a crack and an old lady peered out at her.

"Do you know the man who was just here?" Julianna asked without preamble.

The lady started to shut the door, a distrustful look on her face. Of course she wasn't going to answer a question like that from a hooded stranger knocking on her door in the middle of the night.

Just before the door slammed in her face, Julianna said, "He was attacked in the road just now. He's unconscious. He needs help."

The old lady halted the door's progress and peered out past Julianna and into the dark street, obviously concerned.

"Over there." Julianna pointed toward where she'd dragged Mortimer.

"Who are you? How do you know him?" the old lady asked, then called into the building, "Reynolds!"

Julianna was about to respond, but Dexter said, "You've told her all she needs to know. Get moving."

He was right. She couldn't stay and talk. Mortimer could wake up at any moment. She had to go back to the inn.

"Move!" Dexter said again.

Julianna began to walk away.

"Hold on, you!" the old lady said.

Julianna picked up the pace.

"Girl! Stop!"

Julianna would have broken into a run if she had had any faith that she would be able to keep her feet under her at a sprint.

She heard the lady talking to a man, and then he called out to her too, but Julianna just kept on moving, heart hammering. She was too afraid to look behind her. "Are they following me?"

"No," Dexter answered. "They're looking for your boyfriend. Oh—they found him."

"Good," she breathed. "And don't call him that. Don't joke with me right now. I feel awful." Just then, a wagon came into view ahead of her, and she moved to the side of the road to make room for it. It barreled past her and on into the night.

"Why do you feel awful?"

"I just stole from him after he'd been knocked unconscious and mugged!"

"Kid, it's a good thing he *did* get mugged, because there was no way you were going to get that box any other way. Instead of feeling guilty, feel happy you saved his life. That wagon that just went by would have run him over if you hadn't decided to follow him."

This was true. She sighed. "I just hope he'll be ok."

"He'll be fine. People who mug folks know what they're doing; thievery's a profession like any other, and thieves know their jobs. If they want their victims dead, they just kill them, not hit them over the head," he said as though he were pointing out the most obvious thing in the world. "If you kill someone, the authorities take it a lot more serious than if you knock someone out and take their stuff. Muggers don't want to go to jail, so they make sure not to kill anyone."

"Pfft. Thievery is *not* a profession like any other."

"Is so. Granted, it shouldn't be, and if this country was run by a king who cared about his citizens, citizens wouldn't have to resort to such things in order to get food—"

"There is always another way, Dexter. Hitting people over the head and stealing from them is never the answer."

"You don't get to make that call," he said. "You've never wanted for anything in your entire life. You don't know what it's like out in the real world."

"Don't be an idiot. If there really was no alternative to mugging, then everyone in this city would be out at night breaking down each other's doors and smacking each other over the head and stealing each other's stuff. Muggers just aren't creative enough."

"You're the idiot. You have no clue. You know nothing about their circumstances, their struggles, their education—"

"You will never convince me that mugging people is okay."

"You do realize you're a hypocrite, right? You who have, since you were eight years old, used my knowledge I picked up as a criminal to drug your nurse into unconsciousness while you tunneled out of your home. Why is it okay for you to knock people unconscious to get what you want for your life, but other people can't?"

"I'm not using a *brick* to do it! I can't believe we're even having this argument!" She walked by a homeless woman who looked up at her nervously, which made Julianna realize just how crazy she herself must look, walking down the road in the middle of the night in a filthy dress, yelling at a ghost. "I must look insane," she muttered.

"Yes, you do look insane. And it's probably the only thing that has kept you from getting mugged just like ol' Mortimer back there. There have been two people I've seen, and probably more that I haven't, who have followed you tonight only to walk away when they heard you start yelling at me."

"You've been making me yell at you on purpose?" she asked.

"People tend not to mug raving lunatics. They assume crazy, filthy folks wandering the streets in the middle of the night don't have much money."

"Well, thanks," she said. "For making me look crazy."

"Any time."

She was very happy to see the glow of the first streetlights up ahead of them.

B ACK IN THE Dawdling Donkey, Julianna quickly changed into a fresh maid uniform in the break room and got to work cleaning. It was good she had something to distract her from her thoughts, but even with all the scrubbing and polishing and getting used to using real cleaning tools and supplies, she still couldn't keep her worries about Mortimer out of her head. She kept telling herself that the fact that he'd been moaning in pain instead of completely unconscious when she'd left was a good sign.

Julianna had started out by cleaning the vacant upstairs rooms, but then found herself gravitating toward the barroom where she could keep an eye on the front door and see when Mortimer walked in. She was so preoccupied with her worry that she didn't care that Galt was behind the bar radiating bad vibes. Once she'd returned from stalking and stealing from Mortimer, Galt had interrogated her about why she'd run off. In order to shut him up, she had shown him the box to prove she'd gotten the job done. He had demanded she hand it over to him. She, however, had refused, pointing out that she barely knew Galt and had no reason to trust him. Julianna had then slipped the box into the pocket of her apron with a "so there!" look on her face and walked away.

Galt had since been glowering madly at her every chance he got.

She was scrubbing a table clean with a rag when the door flew open, helped by a gust of wind.

Julianna looked up.

In walked Mortimer.

It could have been her imagination, but he looked a little unsteady on his feet. He had a preoccupied look on his face, and she wondered if he already knew the box was stolen—but the preoccupation could merely have been because he'd been smacked over the head and robbed. She was very happy to see him conscious and walking around but tried to play it cool. "Hi," she said and put the rag down. "You okay?"

He looked up at her and blinked in a disoriented sort of way, then said, "Sort of. I was just mugged."

"What!?" she cried and was happy to hear how authentically shocked she sounded. She scurried over to him. "For goodness sake, sit down!" She pulled out a chair at the table.

He flopped down into it with an *oof* and brought his hand gingerly to his head.

"You got hit on the head?" she asked.

"Yep. Whoever it was, he knocked me right out. Then he apparently dragged me to the side of the road." He gave a bleak sort of laugh. "I guess I should be happy that he didn't kill me or leave me to be run over. But right now, I'm just mad—he stole something very important. Oh, and my wallet."

Julianna pushed away the guilt that was bubbling up within her; she *needed* that box; it was the only way she could keep escaping out into the city. She could not give it to him, no matter how much her conscience was badgering her. "That's awful! But yes, at least you are alive." She studied his face for a few moments. He really did look pretty beat up. "Shouldn't you go up to your room and rest?"

"Eh, probably, but I'm not tired," he said with sigh. "Adrenaline still pumping, I guess." He then flashed her a smile that was still quite winning even though there was a slight wince of pain that went along with it, and said, "Might as well have that drink, eh[19]?"

"Sure," she said with a smile. "What do you want? I'll get it. You rest here."

"I can get it," he said and made to stand up, but she put a hand on his shoulder and shook her head.

"Stay put. I'll get your drink."

"Aw come on, if this is a date, then *I'm* supposed to go get the stuff and bring it back to *you*," he countered. "And besides, I managed to walk a mile through the city at night with a head injury; I can handle walking up to the

---

19   People in the Land of Fritillary didn't know you're not supposed to consume alcohol after a concussion.

bar and back again."

"Okay, fine. If you insist," she said, while thinking to herself: *A date! Gasp and swoon!* "You can go get your own drink. But I'm going to get mine myself. You seem like a nice guy, but I don't know you. You might be some crazy dude who intends to slip me something."

But though she said it playfully, she knew very well that it could be true. That sort of thing *did* happen, which she knew all too well since she'd been slipping sleeping potions into Delia's tea on an almost nightly basis for more than half her life. If Delia considered Julianna to be trustworthy when she obviously wasn't, then it logically followed that Julianna couldn't assume anyone, especially a stranger, was trustworthy.

"Smart lady," Mortimer said with approval, as he carefully stood.

They both moseyed to the bar where a surly Galt took their orders. Mortimer ordered a pint of ale and Julianna ordered a Bitsy McGovern[20].

They brought their drinks back to their table and had a jolly old time chatting and getting to know each other.

Mortimer was thinking what a shame it was that he had to leave in just a few hours to go back home, so regrettably he wouldn't be able to get together again with this delightful lady.

Julianna was thinking what a shame it was that, after that night, she would be done being Jennifer, the maid at the Dawdling Donkey, so regrettably even if Mortimer stayed there again in future, she still wouldn't be able to see this delightful guy again.

Her first date of her life was going swell.

Until it wasn't.

It was when she stood to get a refill of her Bitsy McGovern that the silver box fell out of the hole in the bottom of her apron pocket.

It crashed to the floor with a thud.

---

20   A nonalcoholic drink named after a precocious and adorable young theater star who had taken the city by storm with her charm, bouncy curls, and song-and-dance numbers.

CHAPTER NINETEEN

Julianna stared at the box.

Mortimer looked down, first casually just to see what she was gaping at, but then he did a double-take and his eyes widened in astonishment. He looked up at her, his expression the picture of shock and anger.

Neither of them moved or spoke for a few moments. Mortimer was too shocked to move, and Julianna was too scared.

Then she broke the spell by swooping down and grabbing up the box. She darted backward just in time to avoid him as he reached out to grab her by the wrist.

It was probably only because he was still disoriented from his blow to the head that she was able to scamper away from him, through the maze of tables and chairs, and across the room. She turned around to assess the situation and saw that he was not chasing her but standing in front of the door to the street. "You!" he yelled when she turned around. "*You* are one of *them*?" The disappointment in his voice made her feel like trash. If only he'd sounded mad, she wouldn't have felt so guilty.

A few of the patrons looked up at the hubbub the two were causing, but not as many as you might think. This sort of thing was always happening at the Dawdling Donkey.

"I'm sorry!" she cried. "It really isn't what you think!"

Mortimer took a few steps toward her, and she looked around wildly for an escape route.

"Oh no?" asked Galt from his place behind the bar. "I'm pretty sure it is exactly what he thinks."

Julianna spat at Galt, "Shut up!"

"Give me the box!" Mortimer roared and took another step toward her, not wanting to get too far from the door since he didn't want her escaping out into the city. Then a thought seemed to occur to him. "*You're* the one who mugged me?"

Julianna stared in horror. "No! Oh gosh, no, I didn't mug you!"

But he didn't believe her. She saw it in his eyes.

"Yes, I stole the box, but it was only after someone else hit you over the head! I think it was just some regular mugger, because they only took your wallet!"

"You think I'm an idiot? That's the stupidest—" Then he put his hand suddenly to his head and stumbled a bit.

She took that opportunity to dart toward the door to the basement. She flung it open and ran down the stairs. His footsteps pounded behind her.

Julianna stumbled down the dark basement hallway and ran right into Corrine, who'd been in the bathroom and was now making her way back to the room at the end of the hall. "Hey!" Corrine snapped. "Watch where you're going!"

"I'm sorry," Julianna gasped. "I'm just—"

"Stop!" yelled Mortimer from the stairs. "Get back here!"

Corrine assessed the situation. A frantic female running from an angry male in a bar at three in the morning. She made the logical but erroneous assumption that Julianna was the one in need of help and Mortimer was the villain. Corrine said firmly, "Come with me," and took Julianna by the arm and hurried her down the hallway to the room she and Warren were staying in.

"But what—who—" Julianna gasped, glancing over her shoulder and seeing a faint silhouette of Mortimer cursing and bumbling along down the hall behind them.

"Hold on. I'll explain once we're behind a locked door," Corrine said and rushed Julianna to their room. She opened the door and shoved Julianna through, then followed and locked it. And not a moment too soon. Just a few seconds after Corrine slid the bolt into place, Mortimer was there pounding on the door and yelling.

"What in tarnation—" came a voice from behind them, and Julianna whirled around to see Warren sitting bolt upright in bed and looking around wildly, as he tried to make sense of all the commotion that had woken him.

By the light of the lantern, Julianna locked eyes with the guy who met all the criteria for breaking the curse.

She felt an earthshattering bolt of—

Nothing much.

The feeling was apparently mutual; Warren gave her a confused, slightly annoyed look, and then looked at Corrine. "What the heck?"

"That dude pounding on the door was chasing her—and yelling at her," Corrine gasped as she double-checked the lock.

Warren assessed the situation as quickly as his sleepy brain would allow and leapt to the same erroneous conclusion as his sister had. "One moment, miss. We'll hide you," he whispered so that Mortimer wouldn't hear, though Mortimer was still pounding and yelling, so chances of his overhearing were slim.

"Thanks but, where?" asked Julianna, nervously looking at the door that Mortimer was at that moment threatening to break down. In answer to her question, Warren pulled his bed back from the wall and began to push the stones at the base of the wall, not quite sure which was the one that led to the hidden room. Julianna was confused about his actions for a few moments, but when he finally found the right one and it slid backward, she understood.

As Warren gestured silently for her to climb through the hole, he yelled over Mortimer's curses and hollering, "What in blazes do you mean by this, waking us in the middle of the night and subjecting us to your drunken raving?"

The pounding stopped. Mortimer yelled, "I am neither drunk nor raving. That lady in there stole something from me. I need it back!"

"The only lady in here is my sister, sir, and she has been here the whole night. Except a quick bathroom break, anyway. But she wasn't gone nearly long enough to go steal whatever from you."

"I demand to talk to her."

"Sure, sure. Hold your horses. And, may I add, I take offense at you accusing my sister of thievery."

Both siblings had been, the whole time, gesturing insistently at Julianna to go through the hole in the wall, but she was feeling nervous. You'd think after her tunnel she'd be used to this sort of thing, but not all secret passageways are created equal, and unfortunately there is never any knowing where a secret passage sits on the quality spectrum until you are in the thing.

However, after a few moments, she sighed and crawled through, trying not to think about rats and cockroaches and mold. Once through, she pushed the stone back into place and stood carefully, not knowing how big the space was. Then she put her ear to the wall to see if she could hear what was happening in the other room. Nothing but muffled voices. "Go through the wall and listen to them," she said to Dexter. "I can't hear a thing."

"As you wish," he grumbled and floated through the wall. Almost as soon as he had gone, she wished he hadn't. It was pitch black, and she was hesitant to feel around for fear of what she might find. At least she didn't hear any scurrying sounds or feel cobwebs.

On the other side of the wall, Warren had waited until the stone was back in place, then he had unlocked the door and flung it open with a look of utmost perturbation upon his visage. "What gives, man?" he inquired of the angry silhouette in the hallway. Corrine joined her brother, bringing the lantern along with her in order to shed a little light on the situation.

Mortimer looked at Corrine with confusion. "But—" he spluttered. "You're not her—" and then he peered beyond them into the sparse little room. He pushed Warren aside and walked right in, spinning around in a slow circle to take in everything. "Where is she?"

"Where is who?" Warren asked with fake but convincing confusion.

"I followed her down here. I followed her to this room," Mortimer insisted, though he found himself becoming steadily less sure by the second. Corrine and Warren were pretty good actors (they had been members of a traveling theater troupe since they'd been in diapers, after all), and their looks of confusion seemed mighty real.

"No... You followed *me*," Corrine said. "I was just coming back here from the bathroom when you came slamming down the stairs, yelling like a crazy person. I assure you, you were following me, not someone else."

"Well, yes," Mortimer spluttered. "Yes, I followed you. But you were with *her*. I saw her bump into someone halfway down the hall. You. And you brought her here." He looked around confusedly. "I *know* what I saw."

"Well then, where is this mystery lady?" Warren asked, gesturing at the empty room.

Mortimer looked angrily from Corrine to Warren and back again. "Okay. So you must be in cahoots with that moron innkeeper as well. Which means you aren't going to tell me anything." Then he went and plunked himself right down on Warren's bed. "So I'm just going to wait right here."

"You can't do that!" Corrine exclaimed. "It's the middle of the night. We need to *sleep*! We have nothing to do with whatever it is you're blathering about!"

"I don't believe you."

"Come on. You mistook what you saw out there in the hallway," Warren said. "It was dark. You thought you saw a lady come in here with my sister, but she probably just went into some other doorway. You should be out there searching the basement," he said pointing toward the hallway.

"I know what I saw. I'm a *miner*. I'm used to seeing in poor light." Mortimer glared at them. "She ran into this room. She is hiding somewhere." He felt a bit like an idiot being so insistent that Julianna was here when she clearly wasn't. He began to worry that more damage had been done during that mugging than he'd originally thought. "Oh!" he cried, making Warren and Corrine jump. "An invisibility potion! She must have used one!"

While they watched Mortimer stretch out his arms and feel all around the room for an invisible person, the siblings exchanged silent looks of amusement.

"You're loony, man," Warren said. "My sister and I have nothing to do with whatever you are a part of. And we need to sleep."

"Yeah," Corrine said. "And I can't sleep with some strange man in my room."

Warren nodded. "Yeah. Like, her reputation and stuff."

"Maidenly honor," Corrine elaborated. "Gotta keep that intact."

Mortimer snorted as he reached under one of the beds. "Uh huh. Right.

This dude here—your brother?—he'll protect you, right?"

"Well sure," Warren conceded. "But people will talk. And we can't have that. Maidenly honor is important."

Corrine nodded. "I'll never land a man if you stay in here."

Warren went on, "And she needs to land a man."

Mortimer shook his head and glared at them while feeling around under the other bed. "I'm not going anywhere. Besides us three, the only person who knows I'm in here is that other lady, and I'm guessing she won't be gossiping about you since you're all working together."

They kept up the argument for a good long while. Corrine and Warren insisted that Mortimer had lost track of his mystery lady in the dark hallway, and Mortimer insisted that they were hiding her somewhere. As with most heated arguments, in the end no one's mind was changed, and if anything, Mortimer was more convinced than ever that he was right and that these two were stonewalling him. Somehow, though, by the end of the argument they had decided that if Mortimer was indeed going to stake out their room, and Warren and Corrine were indeed not going to get any more sleep that night, they might as well have a little fun instead of continuing with a pointless argument.

So, Warren pulled out a stack of cards. "You know Crazy 8's?" he asked Mortimer, who nodded and flexed his fingers. They sat down on the ground and began to play.

"*O*HEY'RE DOING *WHAT*?" Julianna whispered to Dexter when he floated through the wall to report.

"Playing Crazy 8's. I think you're going to be in here a while."

She sighed and leaned against the wall. "I wonder what time it is. I can't have more than two hours left to get back."

"Well at least if you get stuck here after sunrise, you're in a dark place."

She gasped, "*If I get stuck here after sunrise?*" It had never even occurred to her that this might happen. But yes, if Mortimer had really decided to plant himself down in that room, then she couldn't leave her hiding place. And if he stayed there for even a few more hours, then she would indeed be stuck in this room until the following night. Delia would wake and find her missing. Her family and ghost friends would go crazy with worry. "Oh no," she breathed. "Dexter, what if I get *stuck* here? How long can Mortimer *possibly* stay?"

"Whatever will be will be," Dexter said calmly. "At least you won't die. Not that there's anything wrong with that."

Since there was nothing for her to but sit down on the floor and worry and wait, that's what she did. After a while, Dexter got tired of her whining and decided to float off and see how much of the inn he could explore before reaching the end of his spectral tether.

○○

MEANWHILE, BACK ON the high seas, Jane and Captain Maximus McManlyman were hauling an unconscious Farland Phelps up the stairs and onto the deck of the pirate ship. When Jane had asked McManlyman to help her out, he had taken it all in stride, not even thinking to ask who Farland was or why they were dragging an unconscious guy out of the infirmary and onto the deck in the wee hours of the morning.

It was only when she asked him to help her stuff Farland into a barrel that he asked, "Now *what's* going on here?"

"The barrel's so he won't drown when we throw him overboard."

"Um…"

"Look, we don't have much time. I'll explain later. Right now, all you need to know is that he's a bad guy and I've been keeping him unconscious for Warren and his family. I can't keep him unconscious any longer, though, because the drugs have run out. But he's a wizard, so I don't want him around me when he wakes up and realizes what I've done. So, I'm just tossing him overboard instead," she explained. "He'll wake up and magic himself back onto land," she added as though McManlyman might actually be concerned for Farland's safety.

McManlyman pondered a moment. "Wait. Why do you want him to magic himself onto land? He's a bad guy, right?" He pulled out his cutlass and asked, "Wouldn't killing him solve things?"

"Captain, if I thought killing bad guys was the way to solve problems, I could have poisoned you and your pirates about ten times over and made my escape."

McManlyman frowned, feeling a bit hurt by her words. He had thought that, while they hadn't exactly started out on the best foot, they had bonded over the past few days. They'd had dinner two nights in a row in his quarters and had had some good heart-to-hearts.

Or so he'd thought.

To find that she still considered him a bad guy who could theoretically be neutralized through poisoning made him feel quite depressed. It had been a while since McManlyman had been in a relationship. He was starting to daydream about the possibilities with Jane.

That very morning, he had been scanning through one of his very favorite romance novels—one that featured a lovely lady who had been taken captive by pirates, but in a great plot twist she actually ended up falling in love with the dashing, misunderstood pirate captain who was really quite a sensitive guy on the inside and just needed the love of a good woman to sort him out. A first-rate book in his opinion.

Clearly, her thoughts were not running in the same direction as McManlyman's.

"Put away your sword," she said with obvious annoyance. Violence and Hippocratic oaths just didn't mix as far as she was concerned. "Warren and I talked it through, and the plan is that I stick this guy in a barrel."

"My way is better," McManlyman grumbled. But he didn't want to make her mad, so he refrained from slitting Farland's throat, and instead sheathed his cutlass with a sigh. "You 'good guys' make things so much harder for yourselves when you take murder off the table."

She stared at him incredulously for a few moments and looked like she was about to say something, but instead clamped her mouth shut and rolled over the empty barrel she'd brought up from the galley. Together they stuffed Farland in and sealed the top up good and snug. Then they rolled it over the edge of the ship and stood side by side, watching it bobbing off into the ocean and toward the sun which was just starting to rise over the horizon. McManlyman toyed with the idea of mentioning how romantic he found sunrises to be, but he looked down and saw Jane had already walked away.

Without even so much as a thank you.

CHAPTER TWENTY

Julianna had, at long last, managed to fall asleep as she sat against the wall of the hidden room. She woke only when the sound of the stone rubbing against its neighbors pierced the silence. "You can come out," came Warren's voice. "He's gone."

Dexter had already informed her that there were no windows in their room, so Julianna crawled through the hole in the wall with no fear of sunlight. Warren extended a hand to help her to her feet.

No magical curse-breaking sparks flew upon contact.

"Hi," he said, "I hope things weren't too uncomfortable for you in there last night."

"Better than getting caught by that guy who was chasing me," she said, brushing off her dress. "Are you sure he's gone?"

"Yeah. My sister even followed him for a few blocks to make sure he wasn't going to circle back. I think he would have stayed indefinitely, but there was apparently something important going on back in his village, and he had to start his journey this morning to make it in time."

"Lucky for me," she sighed, thinking guiltily of Mortimer. But then she pushed away the guilt because there was currently no fixing it. She said, "Thank you so much for your help. Really.

If I hadn't run into you guys, I'd have been in big trouble." Warren had no way of knowing what an exaggeration that was; really, it wouldn't have been too bad if Mortimer had caught her. He would have just taken back the box that belonged to him anyway, given her a disappointed look because up until the box fiasco things had been going swimmingly between them as regarded potential future romance, and gone on his way; she would have had to go back to the smugglers with no box, but that wouldn't have been the end of the world. Just the end of her adventures.

"Happy to help," Warren said with a smile. "You know, I gotta say, that Mortimer didn't seem too bad. A little lecturey about workers' rights, and a bit too good at Crazy 8's if you're playing for money, but I tell you if I hadn't seen with my own two eyes that he chased you down that hallway, and if I hadn't heard him threatening to break down the door, I'd never have believed it of him. Pretty cool dude."

"Oh yeah?" Julianna asked and sat down uninvited on one of the beds. It had been an uncomfortable night, and even the lumpy old musty mattresses were looking mighty welcoming. She was very aware that Mortimer was a pretty cool dude; aware that he was the good guy and she was the bad guy. But she felt that in order to keep up her façade as the damsel in distress, she had better malign Mortimer's character, pronto. "Well, he seemed like a big jerk to me." Not the best maligning, but all she could muster up, considering how bad she felt and how much she still liked Mortimer even after all the yelling and chasing and misunderstanding.

"Naturally. And I'm sure he really *is* a big jerk. Just saying he's good at faking niceness." Warren changed the subject then. "My name's Warren." He held out his hand.

"Jennifer," Julianna said. She took his hand in hers and gave it a shake.

Still no magical curse-breaking sparks upon contact.

At that point, there was a knock on the door, and Corrine announced from the other side, "It's me."

Warren went to get the door, but Julianna screeched, "Are there any windows in the hallway?"

Warren stopped short and looked at her confusedly with his hand on the doorknob. "Um."

"It's *very* important," Julianna insisted. "Don't open the door until I know whether there's any sunlight. *Any sunlight at all.*" As she talked, she got up and walked to the corner behind the door so it would act as a shield if needed.

"Er, Corrine, are there any windows in the hallway? Any sunlight at all?" he asked as he looked questioningly at Julianna.

"I'm allergic. Very allergic," Julianna said by way of explanation.

"Nope, no windows," said Corrine. "No sunlight."

Julianna nodded, and Warren opened the door. In walked Corrine, who saw Julianna and said, "So, you're out! Hi, I'm Corrine."

"Jennifer," said Julianna again. "Thanks for helping me out."

"No trouble. Hey, did you really steal something from that guy? He was super mad."

"Nope," Julianna lied. "I don't know what that was all about."

"He was pretty certain you stole something," Corrine insisted.

"I'm guessing someone else in the bar last night stole whatever it was, and he just assumed it was me for some reason," Julianna said with a shrug.

"I just don't see why—"

"Geez, Corrine, don't interrogate her. Why are you acting so suspicious?"

"I dunno. It just seems like someone like her could quite plausibly be the thief he accused her of being. It isn't much of a stretch."

"Whatever do you mean by *that*? A person like me?" asked Julianna, so annoyed at Corrine's implications that she found herself talking in her haughty, princess voice.

"I *mean*, a person who doesn't even have the money for shoes might be inclined to steal. Obviously, you're pretty strapped for cash."

"Oh!" Julianna said, looking down at her destroyed slippers. "I can *so* afford shoes. It's just…I'm new in town and I haven't had a chance…It's hard…" She found herself struggling to explain why she didn't have shoes when probably everyone but the poorest people around (or cursed princesses who never set foot outside) had them.

"Being allergic to sunlight and all, it must be hard to get to a shoe store during business hours," Warren commented.

"Exactly," Julianna said, thankful that he'd supplied her with a somewhat believable reason.

"Hey, listen, Corrine and I are going out for a bit," Warren said; they had decided to risk a bit of early morning shopping since there were some provisions they needed, and the earlier they went out the less the chance that some Farland-related hijinks would come up. "Obviously you can't come, but if we can get your shoe size, we could pick up something for you. It's only a matter of time before you step on something sharp and germy with those slippers, and then you'll get an infection."

Julianna was impressed that he was among the minority of the population who thought infections came from germs and not spells cast by angry wizards. "That'd be swell!" she said excitedly, because he was right: walking around in her slippers was dangerous, since the discovery of antibiotics in Fritillary was at least a few decades down the road, she could well end up dead, or with an amputated foot, if she stepped on the wrong thing. "But I don't know my shoe size." The Royal Cobbler had never shared that intelligence with her.

"Here, we're about the same height, let's compare feet," he suggested, and they soon ascertained that she needed a pair of shoes a little smaller than the size Warren wore.

Corrine watched the exchange from her bed without comment; Julianna felt strongly that Corrine was busy judging her and forming some fairly negative conclusions. However, once Julianna had handed over her pouch of money ("See!" she said with a glare at Corrine. "I have plenty money.") in order for them to pay for her footwear and Warren had put his shoes back on in preparation for departure, Corrine said in a friendly enough manner, "Take a nap on my bed if you want. Make sure you lock the door. The innkeeper's a creep. But you probably already know that."

"Tell me about it," Julianna muttered.

After they left, she laid down, staring at the ceiling and smiling a bit; those had been some friendly folks! Or at least the brother had been.

If Dexter had been with her, he'd have been telling her not to hand her money over to strangers; he'd have said she was too trusting, and she didn't know anything about the world. But Dexter couldn't lecture her because he was somewhere upstairs floating around. So, she had no advice to listen to but the voice of her instinct, which told her that they seemed trustworthy enough.

UTSIDE THE NEAREST cobbler's store, Warren peeked into the pouch of money Julianna (or Jennifer) had given him; not for stealing reasons, but so that he could have an idea of how nice a pair of shoes he could get before going into the store and being harassed by the sales clerk.

His jaw dropped.

He blinked and peeked into the bag again.

A hoarse sort of gurgle escaped his mouth, and his eyes bugged out.

"Are you having a stroke?" Corrine inquired from where she stood looking at shoes in the window.

"Garg!" he spluttered and shook the purse in her direction. He cleared his throat and said, "Look in here!"

She walked over, glanced in the purse, and gasped, "What the *what?*"

"Right?"

"There's gotta be—I don't know how much!"

"Those are some *huge* monetary denominations in there," Warren said dazedly.

It occurred to them both at the same moment that if they kept on gaping and exclaiming while staring into a heavy money pouch, they were going to end up getting mugged, thus leaving them with no money, no new shoes, and maybe no life if the mugger wasn't good at his job.

They simultaneously began to try to play it cool.

Warren leaned nonchalantly against the wall of the store, Corrine leaned nonchalantly against a lamppost, and they both tried to think of something nonchalant to say.

But they couldn't get that vast quantity of money out of their heads.

Julianna had had no idea that she was carrying around an insane amount of money—more than enough to keep an entire city block fed for a year. Warren and Corrine were both having trouble processing things, but after a few moments even honest and honorable Warren was considering taking the money and running.

He met his sister's eyes and whispered, "*We can't.*"

"Can't what?" she asked all fake-innocent, her eyes on the pouch in his hand.

"We can't steal it. I know that's what you're thinking." He decided it was okay to risk talking about the money as long as they didn't do anything to make themselves look weird or suspicious. If they just acted natural no one would have a reason to eavesdrop.

"I was thinking no such thing," Corrine lied.

"Were too."

"Well, so what if I was? You must have been too," she whispered.

"Of course I was thinking of stealing it," he whispered back. "But that doesn't mean I think we *should*. Morality aside, it would be dumb simply because a person with that much money must have connections galore. Connections that could easily track us down and kill us or land us in the Forest of Looming Death[21]."

"You think she really has connections?" Corrine asked. "She's a *maid*."

"You still think she's really a maid? Why on earth would she need to work cleaning rooms at an inn if she's got this kind of money?" he asked, shaking the purse at Corrine.

"Maybe she's a nobleman's daughter who likes mingling with the rabble in order to remain grounded?" Corrine suggested.

"Hmph," he answered, unimpressed with her theory. "I'm going to go buy her some shoes. How about you go pick up the provisions and meet me back here in an hour?"

She sighed and said, "All right. But you know, if we just took one of those coins, I bet she wouldn't even notice it was missing. Think about it."

"No, Corrine, we're *not* stealing from her," he said and, without another word, turned and walked into the cobbler's shop, thinking what a good thing it was that they'd cut ties with the pirates, because his sister was starting to think in rather piratical terms.

The bell above the door jingled when Warren walked in, and immediately the shopkeeper swooped over. He was just getting started on his sales pitch when suddenly there was a trumpeting sound from the road outside. Then, the sound of a slew of horses approaching at a fast clip, shortly followed by

---

21   After Julianna's birth had necessitated a repurposing of the dungeon, Conroy had decided that instead of building another dungeon (which would cost tons of money that he figured would be better used buying dogs and horses for hunting, and for building a new, state-of-the-art croquet field) they could instead send *all* the criminals to The Forest of Looming Death, and if The Forest got too full they could just start executing folks.

the sound of someone announcing something that they couldn't hear. It all sounded quite official and royalty-related, so Warren and the shopkeeper hurried to the door and peered down the road in the direction of the hubbub. Sure enough, there were a cluster of horses and riders all wearing the royal colors of puce and tan.

At the head of the group was a fellow who was just taking a deep breath in preparation for conveying again the message that he had been hollering all morning as they made the rounds through the city streets. "Every citizen will gather, NOW, at the nearest fountain for a very important message from the King and Queen." This was the usual way that official information was conveyed to the population. Everyone gathered at the nearest watering hole and listened as one of the King's soldiers imparted the message.

Behind the horses, a crowd of people was scurrying along.

Warren and the shopkeeper gave each other puzzled looks and, once the horses had passed, they joined the throng. After a few minutes, they reached the local fountain and everyone gathered around, jostling and bumping shoulders and pushing for a good spot. Announcements like this were quite rare, and usually conveyed bad news, so naturally everyone wanted to hear. Was the King dead? Was there some unfriendly army approaching from a neighboring kingdom? Were they going to have to donate another kid to the Crown?

The guy at the head of the soldiers dismounted his horse and hopped up on the edge of the fountain.

"Can you all hear me?" he asked. Everyone stopped jostling and got very quiet. "The Princess has been taken!" he said without preamble.

Gasps and murmurs.

"Soldiers will be searching every building. Make sure that every door, cupboard, or space of any nature at all that could fit a person is unlocked and open when the soldiers come through so that we can streamline the process." He paused here and looked around at them all with a stony sort of expression. When he was sure they were all looking at him, he said, "Argue or resist in any way and we kill you."

More gasps and murmurs.

"No log will remain unturned. Any person who has any knowledge of the Princess and does not convey it to a soldier ASAP will be thoroughly and completely killed. As a reminder to any potential kidnapper who may have forgotten, the Princess is cursed, and if sunlight touches her, she will die. If you have anything to do with her kidnapping, be aware that if she dies through exposure to sunlight, or of course through any other means, you will die as well. Slowly and unpleasantly."

Warren had known that the Princess was cursed since it was common knowledge throughout the land, but he had never known the particulars since he had been at sea his whole life and hadn't kept up with the court drama the way that the citizens of the city did. So, when he heard the bit about not being able to be touched by sunlight, he gave a hearty gasp as the puzzle pieces fell in place: an insanely rich girl who couldn't be exposed to sunlight. A maid who obviously wasn't really a maid but someone with a big secret.

The girl Warren was buying shoes for was the Princess.

She had to be.

CHAPTER TWENTY-ONE

So, Jennifer was really the Princess Julianna. And the King and Queen thought she had been kidnapped.

But she certainly didn't appear to Warren to have been kidnapped, which led him to assume she must have left of her own accord. It was a good thing that the soldier had stopped talking, because Warren was already stumbling backward through the crowd, anxious to get back to the cobbler's shop in order to meet up with Corrine and talk to her. After about a minute of walking down the street listening to his own clamoring thoughts in his head, he realized the shopkeeper was still at his side and was talking. "—believe that? It just isn't possible! I mean to say, how could kidnappers have gotten all the way down there to that dungeon and then escaped again with her? It just doesn't make sense! Maybe that wizard Farland found a way? But Wendell has that castle packed with anti-magic stuff..."

"Mmm," Warren said, still deep in thought. "But all the same, they say she's gone, so she must be gone."

"True enough. I pity whatever poor souls are in any way involved with this. They're going to end up deader than dead when they're found out."

Deader than dead. Aw, man. Were he and Corrine going to get dragged into this? He needed to talk to his sister. He looked up to

211

see that they were back at the cobbler's shop. And the cobbler was holding the door open for him, now talking about shoes instead of the Princess thing. "Were you coming in, sir?" he asked.

"Oh, er, yes," Warren said. He supposed he still had to buy the shoes, even though it felt really weird to do so now that he knew he was buying them for a runaway princess.

"What kind are you looking for? Fancy? Casual? Boots? Tap shoes? We've got everything. You've come to the right place."

"Er, they're not for me. They're for a friend. A lady. I guess some boots or something?"

"Size?" the shopkeeper asked.

"A little smaller than mine," Warren said. "Need me to take one off so you can compare?"

The shopkeeper nodded and held out a hand. Warren untied his boot and handed it over, then limped around waiting while the shopkeeper rustled around in the back room. Warren was looking at a shiny pair of boots covetously (his boots were about ten years old) when the door opened and Corrine swept in, staring at him with a wild look in her eyes that showed him that she'd also heard the news about the Princess and had drawn the same conclusions that he had. Warren shook his head sharply at her when she opened her mouth to speak, and he pointed at the back room.

She nodded and said in a strained voice, "Hi Warren! Buying shoes, I see?"

He answered, "Yes, for my friend, Jennifer."

"Yes. How nice. That will be nice for her. To have new shoes."

Warren winced at her stilted delivery.

She saw the wince and nodded her understanding, then made a motion which indicated she was zipping her lips. They browsed the showroom for a bit, and the guy came out with a few pairs. Warren bought the most princessey looking ones, and the siblings set off to interrogate their new acquaintance.

MEANWHILE, IN A barrel bobbing along in the Bay of Fritillary, a very angry Farland was waking up feeling cramped, damp, confused, and quite groggy from the few days he had passed in a medically-induced coma.

"What in blazes...?" he grumbled as he felt around his barrel. "Not cool," he concluded after he had deduced what was going on; he knew he was in a barrel (a grog barrel by the smell of it) and could guess by the rocking motion that he was in the ocean.

He was so disoriented from the drugs that it took him a few tries to magic himself back to his evil lair, but at last he finally managed it, and a few moments later appeared in his living room. His cape was wrinkled, his hair needed a reapplication of pomade, and he needed a change of clothing like nobody's business if you know what I'm saying. He was very glad that the only witness to his current state of filthiness was the magical pool of raven blood, which was shimmering away in its stone basin.

It took Farland a moment to realize that the board he'd put over the top of the basin in order to create a makeshift table had been removed and was now leaning against the wall.

"Cripes!" he exclaimed and looked around wildly at his ransacked abode. "What happened here?" he asked the magical pool of raven blood.

A voice cawed in his head, *I dunno. I was sleeping.*

Farland eyed the pool suspiciously, not doubting for a moment that it was lying; the magical pool of raven blood had never liked him, and its favorite pastime was lecturing Farland about how he was too mean and that he should give peace, love, and understanding a try for a change. "You were not sleeping."

Was so. I sleep like the dead.

"Come on," Farland whined. "I need to know who was here! I know you had to have been awake, at least for *part* of this ransacking. You couldn't have slept through the board being taken off your basin."

Okay, fine, I was awake. But I am not telling you who was here.

Farland sighed. "Whatever." There was no convincing the magical pool of raven blood to do anything it didn't want to do once it had put its metaphorical foot down. Another thought occurred to Farland and he gasped, "Can you tell me what the date is?" While the revenge plot he was working on regarding Warren and Julianna was something he could take care of at his leisure, the other revenge plot he had brewing with Mirabella was time-sensitive, and he had to make sure he hadn't slept too long.

It's November 2, the magical pool of raven blood told him, since it saw no harm in informing Farland of something that he could just as easily have gotten the answer to by asking anyone out in the street, or by consulting his day planner.

"Good," Farland sighed. "I haven't missed the hunt." There were still a few days left before he and Mirabella carried out their plan on that front. And that meant he had a few days still to sort out this thing with Warren.

But first thing was first. A new pair of trousers, a fresh cape, and a bit of time in front of the mirror to spiff himself up. Then, he could start asking his friends in the city's smuggling and thievery circles about any leads on Warren and his family.

WARREN AND CORRINE had made it back to the inn, and were walking down the basement hallway, both very nervous because they had never addressed royalty before or accused royalty of posing as a maid.

But they both agreed they had to do something. They couldn't just hand the runaway princess her new shoes and then go on their way; the unanswered questions they would have had to deal with would have plagued them for the rest of their days.

Warren eyed the door at the end of the hallway; he felt jittery and couldn't shake the feeling that the winds of change were blowing pretty fierce, twirling into a hurricane that was going to be shortly blowing his life seriously off course.

Corrine felt no such apprehension, because she wasn't nearly intuitive enough in that way, so while Warren hung back and second-guessed, she plowed ahead and knocked on the door. "It's us!" she announced.

A few moments later, Julianna opened the door and they walked in. Julianna looked at them curiously as they stared at her. Corrine looked suspicious, and Warren looked overwhelmed, and Julianna felt a little shiver; something was going on here, and it was nothing good. She, too, felt those winds of change that Warren had just noticed.

"So, do we call you Your Highness, Your Majesty, or what? I'm not clear on the protocol," Corrine asked.

Julianna squeaked and backed up a few paces, staring at Corrine with horror. *Oh no! Were they going to kidnap her? How had they found out?* She glanced at Dexter, who was hovering behind the siblings.

Dexter shrugged. "Maybe try denying it?"

"I don't know what you're talking about," Julianna gasped, but her reaction to Corrine's words had already convinced the siblings they were right.

"Piffle. Let's cut to the chase here. We know you're the Princess. One: you gave us a downright dizzying amount of money for the purposes of buying a pair of *shoes*. Two: you are 'allergic'," Corrine said, doing air quotes, "to sunlight. Granted, those two things wouldn't have made us suspicious on their own, but then we went out and discovered number three: the Princess went missing last night. She is nowhere to be found in the entire castle."

Julianna stared at her, unable to make a sound.

Dexter said, "Just hear them out. Remember, you've got tons of money on you. You could buy their silence, easy."

"Imagine that!" Corrine went on. "The very night that the Princess disappears from the castle, we bump into a super-rich girl who can't go out in the sunlight."

Warren had been standing by the doorway, watching the two of them. Jennifer, or rather Julianna, looked like she was going to cry; he jumped in and said, "Corrine, don't be so mean."

"Why not? I'm mad! She has endangered us by associating with us and keeping such a secret. There are soldiers swarming through the city right now searching for her," she said, jabbing a finger in Julianna's direction. "Soldiers who will kill anyone who has anything to do with hiding her. *And we hid her!*"

"She didn't know any of that was going on," Warren reasoned.

"Yeah," Julianna said, recovering a bit from the shock of this verbal attack, "and, by the way, I owed you no explanation. I had no reason to trust you. Kidnappers are a very real danger for a person like me."

"Well, all the same—"

They all stopped short and froze. From the room above, they heard the sound of many heavy footsteps pounding about and lots of harsh male voices.

"Soldiers!" Julianna breathed.

"They're searching the inn!" Warren whispered.

"Let's turn her in," Corrine said, eyeing Warren.

"No!" Warren and Julianna gasped.

"Why would you want to do that?" Warren asked his sibling, staring at her with confusion.

"So they don't get mad at us and kill us when they find us with her, idiot! Do you think they'll believe us when we say we didn't know anything about it? Heck, do you think they'll even bother asking us for our side of the story before killing us?"

Warren was busily pushing back the stone in the wall that led to the secret room. He then grabbed the lantern and pushed it through the opening. He was too mad at Corrine even to answer. How could she be so cowardly?

"I wouldn't let them kill you!" Julianna gasped.

Warren gestured urgently for Julianna to move through to the hidden room.

Julianna gave Corrine an anxious look, and said, "How do I know she won't tell them I'm hiding in there?"

"Easy. We'll be in there with you, so she won't be able to tell them anything. I don't feel up to lying to a bunch of soldiers at the moment, and," he said with a glare at Corrine, "I don't really trust my sister all that much either right now, so I think we'd better all just hide and sort this all out later." He then pushed their bags and his banjo case through the hole.

"Well then, I want her to go in first," Julianna said.

"Sounds good to me," Warren agreed and they both looked at Corrine, while Dexter floated through the wall and into the hidden room.

Corrine was starting to feel self-conscious about her cowardly reaction in the face of adversity, and also was pretty distressed to see Warren's obvious disappointment in her. "Okay, okay," she said with a sigh. Perhaps she had been wrong to opt for self-preservation over honor, but she wasn't too sure.

They heard the pounding of armored boots running down the stairs.

Corrine gasped, and scurried through the hole in the wall.

Julianna followed.

Warren had almost made it through when he remembered the door was locked. Once the soldiers broke down the door and saw that the room had no windows or other doors, they would know for sure that there must be a hiding spot somewhere. So, though footsteps were fast approaching from the other side of the door, he jumped up and unlocked the door.

He scampered back, tripping in his haste, and crawled through the hole with only seconds to spare.

Julianna and Corrine were waiting with their hands on the stone, ready to push it back into place the moment Warren was through.

He rolled out of their way.

They pushed the stone into place, then all hurried to the wall to see if they could make out any sounds. Had any of the soldiers seen the stone moving? Or had they closed it in time? Corrine dimmed the lantern so no light could be seen through the cracks around the stone.

They all held their breaths and waited. Seconds ticked by and became minutes. "If they'd seen the stone moving, they'd have tried to push on it by now, right?" asked Julianna.

"Probably," Warren said cautiously.

After a while, they agreed that since they hadn't heard any sounds from the adjoining room for ten minutes or so they would be safe to turn the lantern on low. Shedding a little light on the situation revealed a hammock hanging in the corner, a chamber pot, two spindly chairs, and some random boxes and bags all lined up against the walls. Corrine and Julianna took the chairs, Warren stretched out on the hammock since he was the invalid with the broken arm, and they began a whispered chat about what the heck they were going to do next. Dexter watched from a corner, not bothering to say anything since Julianna would only ignore him anyway.

It was while Corrine and Julianna talked about what to do come sunset that Warren's head was suddenly filled with the raven's voice. *Hey bro*, it said, *just a quick FYI that Farland just left his apartment about ten minutes ago. He's on the hunt for you.*

Warren gasped, "Corrine!"

"What?" she asked sharply, hearing the panic in his voice.

"It's starting. He's back."

"Did that raven thing tell you—" she started, then they both looked at Julianna uneasily. There was no conceivable way to explain the magical pool of raven blood to her.

Julianna was watching them with curiosity. It was clear to her that something was up. She gave a fraction of a glance at Dexter, but all he did was shrug again.

"Should we tell her?" Corrine asked.

"Er, um, it can't hurt, right?" Warren said.

Julianna asked, "Is something wrong?"

Warren looked from his sister to Julianna and said, "So, we're sort of... on the run."

"On the run? Who from?"

"There's this wizard guy," he said. "We don't know what it's even about, really. We think it's a case of mistaken identity or something. See, this dude shows up on our ship out of the blue a few days ago and says he's been looking for me for years and he wants to kill me."

"And you'd never seen him before that?"

"Nope. I guess maybe *he* saw *me* before if he was in the crowd at one of our performances, but I know *I* never met *him* before. It was really weird. He just said something about—" and here Warren froze, for he had just remembered that, when Farland had been explaining why he had come to the ship, he had mentioned something about a curse and the King's firstborn child. Warren couldn't for the life of him remember the particulars, because at the time he'd just written it all off as the raving of a lunatic, but he was almost certain that Farland had referred to him, Warren, as a... counter-curse... whatever that was. For the King's firstborn child.

And here he was, talking to the King's firstborn child.

Warren's mouth had gone dry, so he swallowed, cleared his throat, and said, "Have you ever heard of a wizard named Farland Phelps?"

Julianna stared at him with mounting confusion, and whispered, "He's the one who cursed me."

CHAPTER TWENTY-TWO

The journey to the Northwoods of Fritillary was not, ideally, to be attempted alone. However, Mortimer Perkins was in a hurry, and so he did not have the luxury of waiting around the city gates in hopes of finding a party going his direction who was willing to let him join their group. He instead figured it would be best just to get moving and hopefully meet up with a group on the road.

So, he set out on his own at first light. At least, though it was dumb to travel alone, first light was statistically the best time to do it—the criminal element was mostly all in bed, exhausted from a long night of mugging and thieving and sneaking and other such activities that worked best with the least possible sunlight.

Mortimer wished he was in bed too, for he was drained from a sleepless night of getting hit over the head, having a date with a thieving maid named Jennifer, and then having a Crazy 8's marathon with a brother and sister who he was still sure had helped Jennifer escape. Mortimer gritted his teeth and cursed at the thought of her, the young lady who had stolen his box and, in so doing, singlehandedly set back his plans by at least a month.

Mortimer was nearly always a pretty great judge of character and had been so sure that Jennifer couldn't be working with Galt and all his short-sighted, greedy, self-serving, idiot friends. He still couldn't quite believe how wrong he'd been about her. Jennifer, if that was even her real name, had to be one devious lady.

He gave a stone in the road a savage kick and watched it soar through the air and hit the dirt. Then he looked behind him at the city, pleasantly surprise to see how much distance he'd already covered. If the weather and the criminals both cooperated, he'd make it all the way to his planned halfway point before nightfall. Once there, the plan was to meet up with some friends who were waiting for him. Then they'd all travel north to their village the next day.

Not that he was all that eager to get home, since once he was there, he'd have to break it to everyone that he'd gone and let the box get stolen. But he had two days ahead of him to try to think of a way to explain it that might cushion the blow.

GALT WAS STARVING. Just as he had been sitting down to his usual breakfast of ale with a side of ale, soldiers had burst through the door saying something about the Princess. He had no clue what they were talking about, and his head was too muddled to sort it out, but it hardly mattered because it wasn't as though he could have stopped their search of the inn even if he'd wanted to. So, he just let them go about their business. But every time he tried to start in on his breakfast, some soldier or other came up and complained about a locked door or stuck cupboard that needed his attention.

Finally, the soldiers had departed with no Princess (as Galt could have told them from the beginning and saved them some time) and he was at last sitting down to partake, when there was a loud popping sound, and a column of smoke appeared right in front of the fireplace.

Galt nearly fell out of his chair.

His old friend, Farland Phelps, stepped out of the dissipating column. He brushed aside the smoke and starting to talk before Galt had even fully comprehended what was going on.

Having no capacity to do anything else, Galt just sat and listened as Farland said in a rush, "Galt. I am making the rounds to all my contacts." He waved his address book at Galt. "I started with the A's and now I'm at the G's. If my calculations are correct, I'll reach all my contacts in two more hours, as long as I'm not waylaid. I have no time to waste, so don't interrupt."

Galt had the sense to nod mutely and try to muster up some focus. This looked pretty serious.

"I'm tracking down a family. A mother, a father, a sister, a brother. Mother and father in their 40s, kids in their late teens or young 20s. They're running from me, so they'll probably be in hiding. Send word if you hear of any leads. Spread the word among your contacts."

Galt nodded. Farland was just about to disappear when something occurred to Galt and he said, "Hey, hold on!"

Farland paused with a look of perturbation on his visage. "*Yes?*"

"My wife's hiding two kids down in the basement. Not a family, but maybe they separated so they wouldn't look so much like the group you're looking for?"

Farland narrowed his eyes and considered this. Yes, breaking up the family would be one of the first things they'd do if they really wanted to hide well. Which apparently, they were attempting to do. If this was them. If Galt's wife was hiding them, that meant they had even somehow weaseled their way into the sphere of the bleeding-heart liberals who ran the old Underground Railroad for witches (though Fritillary had no railroads, above or below ground). Farland knew that the group still functioned to some degree, and that Galt's wife was among their number.

Yes, Galt might be right. The kid might be hiding in this very building. "Lead the way," Farland sleazed.

"**O**FARLAND SAID WHAT?" Julianna gasped.

"I'm almost certain he called me a counter-curse. For the King's firstborn child. But I have no clue what that's about. No clue at all." Warren was as confused as she was, and his lowered eyebrows and frown testified to the fact.

She stared at the wall behind him, thinking hard. "Well, I *am* certainly cursed. But if there is a way to break the curse, I never heard about it."

Warren shrugged. "It's weird though, that's for sure. I mean, what are the odds of us bumping into each other? This is super strange."

Corrine cut in, "And it's not really the most pressing issue currently, is it? Shouldn't we be caring a little less about how you two may be connected, and caring a little more about how to keep Warren alive and away from this crazy wizard?" (The crazy wizard who was, with Galt, at that very moment, on the other side of the wall they were hiding behind).

"That's true," Julianna said. "I'm sorry. I—"

Dexter floated through the wall at this point and looked around. "Hey kid, get this: I was just up in the bar and *Farland Phelps* materialized. He's looking for those two," he said and nodded toward the siblings. "Or more accurately, the brother. He's in the other room *right now*, so shut your traps and turn off the light."

Corrine and Warren watched as Julianna stopped talking mid-sentence and stared in horror at someone who wasn't there.

Julianna said, "What—are you sure?" to nothing, and turned to them and whispered sharply, "Quiet! Turn off the light!" Then she hurried to listen at the wall.

Corrine and Warren exchanged puzzled looks.

Corrine dimmed the light.

Warren followed Julianna and stood beside her, also listening. No sound at all. "Wha—"

"Shh!!!"

"But—"

"SHH!!!"

Five minutes elapsed.

Since the siblings couldn't see or hear Dexter, they were extremely confused. Occasionally, Corrine or Warren would try again to ask Julianna what was going on, but she just shushed them and kept listening at the wall.

At last, Dexter floated through and said, "All clear, Princess. But you should stay in here anyway. Farland seemed suspicious, but I don't know why. There was no trace of any of you in that room. Must be some wizard sense telling him you guys are nearby."

"You can turn the lantern on again. Low," Julianna said.

Corrine complied.

"What was that all about? You heard something out there? Because I didn't," Warren said.

"You wouldn't believe me," Julianna said.

"Probably not," agreed Corrine. "I can't imagine a reason for all that crazy, unless your explanation is that you're insane. Or that you can see ghosts."

Julianna looked at her hopefully. "Do you believe in ghosts?" It hadn't been a question asked out of idle curiosity, and the siblings didn't take it as such. They had heard the hopefulness in her voice.

"You don't mean that *is* your explanation?" Corrine said with astonishment. "*Ghosts?*" She laughed and looked at Warren, expecting him to laugh along with her.

He didn't.

"Just one," Julianna said weakly, wondering even as she spoke why she was admitting this to these people. But so what if they thought she was crazy?

Dexter shook his head wearily at her.

"His name is Dexter. He told me Farland was in the other room."

"That's crazy," Corrine said. "*You're* crazy."

Julianna shrugged; Farland *was* out there, and because Julianna could see Dexter, she had saved them. That was all that mattered.

"Why would Farland be here?" Warren asked, but not in the accusatory manner of his sister.

Julianna looked at Dexter, who supplied the answer that Julianna then told Warren, "He was going through his address book A to Z checking with all his evil contacts to see if they'd heard of you guys. I'm sure the way he can disappear and reappear at will, he could visit a lot of people in a short amount of time. That's how he found you so fast."

"Except he didn't find us," Warren said with a smile. "Thanks to your ghost."

Corrine sighed and sat down. "Seriously, Warren?"

Warren said apologetically to Julianna, "Is there any way you could prove this ghost thing?"

Julianna looked at Dexter for help. Dexter asked, "Have any of you looked in these boxes and bags along the wall?"

Julianna shook her head.

Dexter went over to one of the bigger boxes and stuck his head right in. "If you tell them the contents of a box they know you haven't looked into, that should convince them, eh?"

Julianna shrugged and waited expectantly, very aware of how the siblings were watching her watch someone they couldn't see.

Dexter took his head out of the box. "Tell them this is full of books. Some women's rights thing called *Five Easy Steps to get your Man to Stop Spending all the Money on Booze Instead of Household Necessities.* Cumbersome title."

Cumbersome indeed and depressing to learn that there were so many women in Fritillary who needed advice on this issue that a book had been published on the subject. Julianna stored that knowledge away to talk over with her mom[22].

Julianna said, "Okay, here's some proof. Dexter just looked in that box over there, and it is full of books called *Five Easy Steps to get your Man to Stop Spending*—" here she had to pause for Dexter to remind her because she'd forgotten the rest of it, "*all the Money on Booze Instead of Household Necessities.*"

Corrine went over to the box and, with some trouble, pried the top off. She reached in and held up a book for Warren to see.

Warren and Corrine exchanged a look.

----

22   Though Lillian served mostly just as a figurehead for the Women's Rights movement and didn't do much in the way of planning or hard thinking on the subject, she *was* married to the king and thus was, in theory, in a position to influence policy. The main problem was that Conroy could so rarely be bothered to get the ball rolling, because he didn't want to annoy the male citizens; males were, after all, the ones who tended to take to the streets and form mobs with the ol' proverbial pitchforks and torches when sufficiently riled up. Conroy was all for wars with *other* countries, but *civil* wars were different because they were harder and had more consequences; with wars with other countries, you just brought your army and horses and weapons and ran around being manly; with civil wars, things just fell apart, and once you'd finally subdued the tax base, you had to smooth down their ruffled feathers, worry about rebels holding grudges, waste money rebuilding stuff, and apologize about those makeshift hospitals you'd 'accidentally' burned down. Conroy was certain that there was nothing that was more likely to incite civil war than the King telling all the dudes that they had to listen to their wives' opinions and start treating them like people. Yes, he figured equality of the sexes was better left as an organic process that would evolve over the centuries as mankind advanced and became more enlightened as regarded the chicks. No need for an official proclamation that would endanger his comfort and chip away at his treasury.

"Wow," Corrine whispered. She put the book down and looked around warily. She was still doubtful, but how else could Julianna have known the title? Unless she had second sight, which was yet another thing Corrine didn't believe in. Julianna had been in this room alone for a few hours, but there had been no lantern, and thus no way for her to read the title of the book. Plus, she probably couldn't have pried the top off the box and then stuck it back on.

Warren shrugged and said lightly, "So I have a magical vial of raven blood that only I can hear, and she had a ghost that only she can see. You're in the minority here, Corrine."

"You have a *what*?" Julianna asked.

"A magical vial of raven blood that talks to me. Farland has a big cauldron of the stuff, and we took some when we broke into his place. You know, I don't know why he needs that much because this little vial seems to work fine." Warren thought for a moment. "Probably he just likes the ambiance of a big cauldron full… or maybe the big amount keeps it from coagulating…" he muttered, getting sidetracked as he pondered why on earth Farland required so much raven blood, and how many ravens' worth of blood it was. He shook his head and said, "Anyway, Corrine can't hear it, and apparently you can't either, but I sure can. It's bizarre, but it's been helpful."

Julianna nodded as though she understood, even though she didn't.

There were all quiet for a while, feeling funny about the information they'd just revealed to each other; after all, they'd only just met, and seeing ghosts and hearing magic talking vials of raven blood are the sorts of secrets that one doesn't usually divulge to people until they've been pals at least a few months and have built a good foundation of normalness.

"Okay then," Corrine said at length. She was able to brush the weirdness off easier because she wasn't seeing or hearing things that others weren't. "What are we going to do?"

"Well I've been thinking about it, and, I mean, assuming we want to stick together—?" Julianna asked and looked at them nervously. They technically had no ties to her, and might very well want to go on their way and leave her behind; that weird thing Farland had said about Warren being a counter-curse was certainly something that would be nice to get to the bottom of, but if they didn't want to come along, then she couldn't force them. Or, anyway, she didn't *want* to; she technically *could* pull royal rank on them and make them do whatever she wanted, but that sort of thing didn't sit right with her.

Corrine looked at Warren, and he said, "Well, I for one would like to stick together. But, uh, Your Majesty, it seems like the quickest solution to your problem is for you to just to go back to the castle. Unless you've run away or something? In which case, maybe we could help you out. You could just stick with us because we're on the run too."

"Oh no, I haven't run away," she said, brushing aside the notion with a swish of her hand. "I just got stuck here at the inn when Mortimer wouldn't leave until after sunrise. You see, I dug a tunnel out of my dungeon so that I could get out at night and see the world a bit. And I was hoping that I would be able to keep sneaking out indefinitely, but," she sighed, "I've only been sneaking out for two nights now, and already I've messed it all up."

They both looked at her with surprise.

"You...tunneled out of the castle?" Warren asked.

Julianna nodded. "My only hope is that they may not have found the entrance to my tunnel. It would be a shame for me to have been digging it for more than half my life only to have to stop using it after two days..."

"Wow," Warren said, impressed. "You know, I think they think you've been kidnapped. So maybe that means they haven't discovered your tunnel?"

"Hopefully," she said. "Anyway, so in that I have *not* run away, I was thinking you guys could just come home with me. The castle is absolutely packed with anti-magic amulets and talismans and such for warding off Farland. Wendell, the royal wizard, makes them. Or his interns do anyway. It's got to be a full-time job to keep them fresh. But anyway, if you're in my dungeon, you are totally safe from Farland."

"That sounds perfect!" Warren exclaimed, his eyes lighting up. "Would that really be okay? I mean, are we going to get killed or anything for walking through the front gates with you?"

"Hmm..." she pondered that one for a bit. She didn't want to make any rash decisions where their lives were concerned. "Well, how's this: I just go up to the gate first, and you guys stay back so it doesn't look like you're with me. Then I tell a guard who I am—they might not believe me at first, not many people know what I look like—and then once I've convinced them,

I'll tell them you guys are with me. As long as they believe I'm who I am, they won't dare argue with me about you two." Of that she was sure, at least. "From there, if we run into any issues, we can just iron them out when we talk to my parents."

"What do you think, Corrine?" Warren asked.

Corrine shrugged. "I do love the thought of you being surrounded by all those amulets and things. Those are really to keep Farland away?" she asked, looking at Julianna.

"Yep. He became blood brothers with my father back before I was even born, and that means that, since my dad's blood is in his veins, Farland has access to my dad's blood whenever he wants it for a spell. And that also means he has power over my brother and me because we're blood relatives. But Wendell says it's a watered-down power because we're just relatives of my dad and so our blood is only *similar* and not identical."

"Dang. How does the King ever leave the castle?" Warren asked. Even having lived at sea his whole life, he had heard that the king loved to hunt, and that was something he sure couldn't do in the castle.

"Oh, he's wears a few amulets when he goes out, and when he isn't in the castle he's always surrounded by his very best soldiers; Farland has a lot of power, but he has to be physically near my dad in order to cast a spell. He wouldn't risk appearing near all those soldiers. He isn't as dangerous as all that."

"That's for sure," Warren said, thinking back to when they were on the ship and how Farland had tried to use the asparagus/tangerine potion and it had fizzled, and then Jane had vanquished him by simply smacking him unconscious with Warren's banjo case.

"But that doesn't mean he's harmless. He really is pretty dangerous if you aren't heavily guarded, or if you have no magical abilities. It's just that at the castle he's not a problem because it's so fortified against him." She looked at Warren with concern, afraid she might have downplayed the danger Farland presented him. "He *could* kill you, easy as pie. Easier than pie, in fact. While we're out here, anyway. So, don't let your guard down."

CHAPTER TWENTY-THREE

Farland was perturbed. No one had been in the room that the innkeeper, Galt, had told him his wife had been hiding the two kids in. But Farland just couldn't shake the feeling that there was a presence in the room.

He assumed this feeling meant that the two kids Galt had seen had very recently left. While this was indeed true, Farland was actually just sensing the presence of Dexter, who was hovering at his side, eavesdropping.

It was Farland's inclination to stick around and see whether they would come back, but, on the off chance he was mistaken about the identity of these two kids, he really did need to finish up doing the rounds to all his other contacts.

"Galt," he had said with a sleazy little sigh, "I must go, but if I don't get any other leads, I'll be back this evening in order to case the joint. It's possible that they were here and left at sunrise to do some sightseeing."

"Sightseeing?" Galt asked. "What's that[23]?"

---

23   Tourism was a fairly new concept in the city because technological innovations in farming and factory production had only recently reached the levels that allowed for workers to have any amount of free time to waste on such pursuits. Also, the mass layoffs that went along with the technological advancements meant there were more unemployed people than ever; people who

"It's when people from out-of-town come to a place and look at landmarks and stuff. You know, like the castle gates, the bazaar, the gallows. Like that."

"Hmm," Galt said, unimpressed. *Sounded like a waste of time but could be good for business.*

"Anyway," Farland sleazed briskly, "I'll be back. If they are out sightseeing or shopping, they'll be back by sunset, so I'll try to get back here a bit before dark and see if we can catch them."

"Right," Galt said. "Happy to help." He wasn't really. Farland was one of those friends who demanded a lot but never gave anything in return. Galt was stuck, though, because Farland was an evil wizard, and (as I hope you do not know from personal experience) when you have fallen into an association with an evil wizard, the best you can do is to do what they say and hope they aren't reading your mind as you mentally curse them out.

WARREN, JULIANNA, AND Corrine had decided that as soon as sunset came, they'd set out for the castle. Once Dexter had given the all clear after floating out to make sure that it was dark, Julianna opened up the servants' door and peeked cautiously out into the alley.

She peeked right. No one.

She peeked left. Still no one.

She didn't think to peek upward to see if anyone was looking out of any of the inn's windows, which was unfortunate since Galt was right up there in a window above the door they were walking out of.

And he was on the lookout.

Farland had not stumbled on any new leads, except for a few that were even weaker than his lead at the inn, so he was back at the Dawdling Donkey. Farland had installed himself at the front window that faced the main street, hoping that his prey would come back to the inn via the front door. Galt's wife, who was tending the bar, was bestowing many an angry

---

had to use their free time *somehow* (picking pockets and breaking into houses to steal food from the cupboards was by no means a fulltime job), and some of the unemployed masses figured this tourism thing they'd been hearing about was worth a shot since as of yet no one had thought to charge admission.

glare upon the wizard but didn't dare say a word because Farland was such a jerk; there was no predicting what someone of his combined temperament and abilities could do when angered.

Julianna, Warren, and Corrine crept up the alley toward the main road.

The only reason Galt hadn't seen them was that he was expecting his quarry to appear at the alley entrance and walk toward the inn, not the other way around. It was only when Julianna got so close to the main road that the glow of a streetlight fell on her that Galt jolted upright in his seat, squinted his eyes to see better through the darkness, and yelled, "Farland! Three people in the alley! Moving toward the road!"

It was stupid of him to yell because Julianna, Warren, and Corrine all heard it.

They whipped their heads toward the sound of his voice, and Warren saw Galt through the window standing up and darting out of sight.

"Run!" they all yelled at each other.

They flew out of the alley.

Julianna was first out onto the street. She looked to the left in time to see Farland and Galt leap out the front door of the Dawdling Donkey.

She and Farland locked eyes.

She felt a chill shoot down her spine. Though she'd never seen him before, she knew this had to be the evil wizard who'd messed her life up so thoroughly.

She froze.

Hovering by Julianna, Dexter watched the proceedings with interest. This trip into the city was seriously exceeding his expectations. "Run!" he yelled, snapping her out of her paralysis.

"They're coming!" she yelled to Warren and Corrine. They all darted down the street toward the castle gates, their plan completely abandoned in their need to get to safety. "Guards!" Julianna yelled. "Guards!"

The guards at the gate up ahead had been searching a wagon that was leaving the castle, but when they heard her yelling, they stopped and looked up.

"I'm the Princess!" she panted, as behind her Farland roared angrily and began rummaging through the satchel at his side. "I'm Julianna! Help!"

Just then, Farland flung some sort of magical whats-it their way, and a blue spark hit the ground at her feet. Some of the sparks hit her in the leg, making it go numb where she'd been hit, and causing her to stumble.

Warren and Corrine were close behind. Corrine had been trying to reach into her bag for the vials of asparagus and tangerine, but gave up, cursing herself for not having thought to do it before they had set out.

They were almost to the gate.

Farland threw a few more of the blue sparky things, missing Warren by a hair. His hitting Julianna had been an accident. It was very hard to run on the mucky ground while trying to aim properly in the near-dark.

The guards took in the scene at glance. Most of them recognized that Julianna was, indeed, the Princess, because when she'd gone missing Conroy had had her portrait hauled down from the wall of the castle's private portrait gallery where it hung along with all the other portraits of royalty old and new, and he had ordered a hoard of artists to make copies to distribute to all the guards and soldiers so they'd know what she looked like[24]. So, recognize her they did.

They saw the missing Princess sprinting toward them, yelling for help and being chased by a young man with one arm in a sling who was nearly close enough to grab her with his good arm, a young woman who was a bit further behind, a paunchy old bald dude, and none other than the evil wizard Farland Phelps. And the evil wizard was tossing spells at the Princess.

They sprang into action and ran toward Julianna with swords drawn. At that same moment, Corrine turned and saw Farland halt in his tracks and mutter something, then raise his hand with a look of deadly focus on his face; he was going to throw one more spell at Warren, and this time it looked as though he was not going to miss. Corrine waited until he had thrown the thing, and then (being the good big sister she was) she flung herself in front of Warren.

The spell hit her square in the back. She cried out in shock as her body went numb, then collapsed. Her frozen hands released her bag. It fell to the ground at her side.

Warren turned, saw her, and ran back.

Farland grinned and began to stride toward Warren. He hadn't hit his

---

24   A time-consuming process that had made Conroy regret for the first time ever that he had had all the known printing presses in the land rounded up and tossed in a big, inky bonfire.

intended target, but things seemed to be working out fine anyway.

"Run!" Corrine yelled at Warren, getting a mouthful of muck in the process. "Take my bag and run!"

"No!" Warren gasped, frantically looking up and seeing Farland approaching at a trot with a malicious glint in his eyes. "Ahh!" Warren yelled in frustration. He couldn't leave his sister, but now he was going to get captured by Farland.

Listen to her, cawed the raven's voice in his head. *Seriously, bro. Pointless heroics is just stupidity in disguise.*

"Go!" Corrine yelled. "He'll kill you if you don't run!"

Fortunately for Warren, the decision was made for him. Right around the time Farland had hit Corrine with the spell, the guards had reached Julianna. They'd swiftly surrounded her in a protective circle. One of them caught sight of the young man who had been chasing the Princess. He stepped forward with a zealous, "Gotcha!" and hit Warren over the head with the hilt of his sword.

Warren collapsed unconscious beside his sister. The soldier advanced on him, sword raised as though he had every intention of running Warren through.

"STOP!" Julianna screeched.

The soldier froze and looked back at her with confusion. "But Your Highness, he was—"

She spluttered, "The wizard! Shoot the wizard!" as she pointed frantically at Farland, who had almost reached Warren.

The guards responded to her command instantly and began to get their bows and arrows ready. In those few seconds it took for the confused guards to prepare to fire, Farland registered what was going on; he wasn't close enough to Warren to reach him, but he *was* close enough to Corrine, and that was better than nothing since she was Warren's sister and could thus be used as leverage.

He reached down, took her by the wrist, and disappeared in a poof of smoke.

Chapter Twenty-Four

Captain Maximus McManlyman had never been much for brooding (being a man of action and all) but then he'd never before been in love with a lady who didn't love him back. The broads were usually crazy for him, but Doctor Jane wouldn't give him the time of day. So, he was sitting in his quarters brooding like crazy. It was irksome in the extreme to find that, while unrequited love was great to read about in a work of fiction, it was downright lame in real life.

That morning, Jane had met with him in order to address some concerns regarding a recent pillaging she'd witnessed. McManlyman had assured her his pirates had quite efficiently pulled off a perfect pillaging and that there was nothing to worry about, but she had said something about frightful carnage and abominable cruelty. The meeting had gotten nothing but worse after that, culminating with her storming out of his quarters in a rage, proclaiming him a scoundrel and a monster.

In the books he read, the broad only called the guy a scoundrel before falling helpless into the guy's arms, so when she'd called him a scoundrel, he had scooted closer, arms at the ready.

But then she'd just walked out.

McManlyman was quite shaken. He glared at the books on the shelf across from his desk. They had lied to him. They'd taught him that women like Jane called guys like him scoundrel and rapscallion and cad, but deep down all they wanted was to fix guys like him. Jane should be wanting to mend him, then marry him. But gosh darn it all if that was not how life really worked, at least with Jane. It seemed glaringly obvious to him that when Jane called him a scoundrel it was not code for, "If only I could love you, you poor, broken soul."

If it was code for anything, it was code for, "I find you repulsive."

McManlyman knew he shouldn't be so surprised. He had known from their first conversation that she was a goody-goody doctor with a bit too strict an observance of the Hippocratic Oath. And then only a few days after she had unwillingly joined his pirate crew as a doctor, McManlyman had also learned, through reading between the lines in their conversations, that Jane was also one of those revolutionaries he'd been hearing about more and more in recent years. As things deteriorated in Fritillary, more and more citizens were apparently thinking about shaking up the status quo. They wanted big changes. Some wanted war, some wanted peaceful resistance, but all wanted the monarchy to fall. Jane was one of the peaceful types.

McManlyman sighed and stood, then moseyed over to his door and threw it open to drink in the sight of the dark clouds and the steely, rolling sea, which suited his mood to a T. It thoroughly depressed him to find that he was in love with someone with such intense moral convictions, since he himself really *was* the thieving, mercenary meanie she accused him of being and he really *didn't* want to change; intense moral convictions were exhausting and rarely made people wealthy. But on the other hand, one thing he really *did* want was to have his reckless, bloodthirsty, bruised, and battered heart mended by the love of a good woman. That'd be pretty awesome, the love of a good woman.

He studied the steely, gray waves a few moments more, then hollered, "Biggby!" at his first mate who was scampering industriously about the deck, making sure the pirates were all doing their jobs.

Biggby halted and looked up at him.

McManlyman gestured him over and then stalked back to his desk, leaving the door to his quarters open.

Biggby strode in a few seconds later, shut the door behind him, stood before McManlyman's desk, and asked, "Yes, Captain?"

"Have a seat, man," McManlyman gestured at a spindly, wooden chair beside the first mate.

Biggby sat down, hesitantly, with a glance over his shoulder. "There's a lot of stuff that needs doing on deck, Captain."

"It can wait," McManlyman said with a wave of his hand. "I have a problem that needs working through. A problem of the heart."

Biggby's eyes widened. He'd figured the Captain had been off his game because of that lady doctor, but he had never expected the Captain to actually come out and admit it.

Then Captain Maximus McManlyman asked, "What do you think is the best way that we pirates could aid the revolutionaries in Fritillary?"

WARREN HAD A splitting headache. It hurt so much that all he wanted to do was be unconscious again. But his consciousness was having none of that, so Warren gave in to his body's desire to wake up. Grudgingly, he attempted to open his eyes. His surroundings were blurry and bright, he was warm, and he was lying on something soft and comfortable.

And that didn't seem right...he had been somewhere else...what had been going on? His thoughts were jumbled from the abuse his cranium had sustained, so it took him a few moments, but then it all came rushing back. He sat bolt upright and yelled frantically, "Corrine!"

The quick movement, the yell, and the acute stress were too much for him in his fragile state. He passed out again. But only for a few seconds— just enough time for Julianna to hear, come running, and be at his side once he woke up again.

She had been in her library with her parents having an epic argument. She was very glad to hear his yell, because it gave her a legitimate excuse to take a break from all the yelling with her parents. She pleaded with them not to follow, because the last thing a concussed patient needed was to be surrounded by loud arguing. They had readily agreed, because her absence would give them time to strategize and strive to present a united front once she returned.

Julianna ran into her bedroom, and stood at the foot of her bed, looking apprehensively at Warren. "You awake?" she whispered.

He moaned and opened his eyes a bit. "Blarggg."

Julianna waited expectantly a few moments more but got no further response.

She was tiptoeing out again to find Delia and tell her to get the doctor, but then Warren said, "Corrine?"

She went back to the foot of the bed. "No, it's Julianna."

"Where's Corrine?" His words were slightly jumbled, and his eyes were shut tight against the light.

She hesitated, "Maybe we could talk about that a little later?"

He may have been pretty out of it, but he was at least aware enough to know that a response like that could not mean anything good. If Corrine was okay, Julianna would have said, "Hold tight while I get her!" or something to that effect. "Where is she?" he repeated through teeth gritted in pain and stress.

"I'd rather not—"

"Where is she?!" he yelled, then took a few calming breaths, because that yell had been super painful. He needed to remain calm if he wanted to remain conscious.

"Here's the thing..." Julianna stalled, "Hey wait, are you hungry? Thirsty? You look thirsty. Let me just go and..."

He gave a pathetic sort of moaning growl but said nothing.

She sighed. Of course he was not going to be sidetracked until he knew where Corrine was. "Okay. Farland sort of, um, kind of...took her."

"What? No." Thankfully for his head, the truth was so dreadful that part of him didn't want to believe it. So the shock of it didn't hit him all at once.

"Yes," she answered. "And let me add before we go any further with this conversation that Farland sent us a message saying that she is alive. Said he'd be in touch about ransom."

He just blinked and stared at the ceiling, processing the horrible information and trying not to pass out.

"We sent some soldiers to his apartment, of course, to check things out. But no one was there," Julianna said.

"The raven blood," Warren muttered, "Where's my vial of raven blood? It might have some information for me."

"Your clothes are being washed right now. I can have someone check the pockets."

"What am I wearing now?" he asked.

"Something from the hospital ward, I'd guess. You're under some blankets right now, so I can't see," she answered. "I'll have Delia go see about your raven blood. Unless the vial was in your sister's bag? Because I picked that up."

"No, the vial was in my pocket."

"I'll have someone go check on it then. Try to get some rest." She rushed out of the room and bumped right into her parents, who had been standing just outside the door, snooping. "Hey!" Julianna exclaimed. "What are you doing? Were you eavesdropping?"

"Who is this *Corrine?*" asked Lillian suspiciously. While Warren had been unconscious, Julianna had told her parents what Farland had said about Warren being a counter-curse for the spell. Lillian was consequently very annoyed to hear that the boy who might free her daughter from her curse was talking agitatedly about another woman.

"She's his *sister*, mom," Julianna sighed, still mad at her mom about the fight. The whole reason for their fight had been that her parents had told her about the particulars of the counter-curse. Julianna had become enraged that they had never told her before that there was hope of her curse being lifted.

Julianna was also infuriated that, almost as soon as Lillian had heard the news, she had sent for the Royal Wedding Planner. Her parents had explained all the criteria of the counter-curse, and Julianna understood that Warren was an exact match, but she thought sending for the Royal Wedding Planner was a bit premature. Because she had no feelings for Warren. At least, no romantic feelings. And she was pretty sure that it wasn't just because her crush on Mortimer Perkins, the dreamy miner and union organizer, was clouding her vision. Also, she was fairly certain that Warren was not harboring any romantic feelings toward her, either. Heck, 24 hours earlier, they hadn't even known each other.

Lillian's ecstatic chatter about planning a quick little sickbed ceremony that could be carried out as soon as Warren was lucid enough to say "I do" was causing Julianna no end of stress.

Julianna wanted some time to think about things. And, of course, some time to talk to Warren about it. But Lillian wanted to get them married, and pronto, because she was convinced that it was the marriage ceremony itself that would break the spell. Julianna thought it was insane that Lillian had started to plan a wedding ceremony for them while the groom-to-be was still suffering a concussion and had no idea what was going on, but Lillian just steamrolled on. There was no use trying to win an argument with a queen.

"You're sure this *Corrine* is his sister?" Lillian asked with a frown.

"Why on earth would they lie about that?" Julianna swept past her parents. She found Delia and sent her on a mission to find the vial of raven blood. It was a mark of how good she was at following orders that Delia didn't question the request.

Then Julianna turned to face her parents again, addressing her dad since, through the whole fight, he had remained pretty quiet, only speaking up when Lillian directly addressed him and asked him to agree with her. "Dad, this is crazy. We need some time. You *can't* make me marry him."

Conroy sighed and looked at his wife nervously. "My love, what's the rush?"

Lillian stared at him in disbelief. "What's the *rush*? What do you *mean*? Your daughter's curse is going to be *lifted*!"

"We don't know that for sure, dear. I don't recall the particular words Farland used when he was telling me about the curse all those years ago, but I *believe* I remember him saying that, in addition to all the other criteria the boy must meet, the two must love each other." He took a deep breath and braced himself, "Marriage doesn't necessarily equal love, my love." He took advantage of Lillian's stunned silence and added, "How about this: let's just put it off until after Conroy Jr.'s hunting party. All the lords and ladies from out-of-town will have packed for hunting, anyway, not a wedding. We need to give them time to prepare for a royal wedding—get the right clothes, the right presents. Things like that."

Julianna stared at her father. He was actually defending her against his wife and showing some capacity for logic[25].

Lillian relented. "Well I suppose we could put it off for a bit. It *would*

---

25   His motives for postponing the wedding were actually not at all to do with the question of love, or of the risk of inconveniencing party guests. His motives were altogether different, but he couldn't tell them about it. Suffice to say that Conroy did not want this wedding to proceed. Not at all.

be nice if the wedding wasn't happening at the same time as the hunt…That way the kids' special days won't overshadow each other…"

Julianna gritted her teeth. *Special day? Bah!* But she remained silent. At least it looked as though she wasn't going to be forced immediately into a rushed wedding to a semi-conscious Warren.

"That's the spirit, darling," Conroy said. "We don't want to rush things. A royal wedding should be fancy!"

"Yes, a royal wedding *should* be fancy!" Lillian agreed. "Yes. We'll just use this extra time to pull together the fanciest darned wedding this city has ever seen!"

Julianna collapsed onto a couch and put her head in her hands. Her ghost friends settled beside her, murmuring reassuring things to her, but she barely heard, so preoccupied was she with the thought that her life was over.

"AND WHAT DO you propose I *do* with her?" Mirabella asked Farland irately, looking at Corrine with icy annoyance. "I have things to do. I can't babysit this girl."

Corrine was lying awkwardly on the floor of Mirabella's cave in the Forest of Looming Death. She was still paralyzed from Farland's spell and, when they'd materialized in the cave, Farland had not thought to make her comfortable.

"I'm really sorry, Mirabella," Farland said. "I don't know where else to bring her. My place isn't an option, I don't trust my city friends, and I can't just leave her somewhere in the Forest, because the wild animals might get her. I need her alive."

Mirabella gave a martyred sigh and muttered, "All right. Tie her up and put her out of the way somewhere. It's good you've come, because there are some things we need to discuss."

Farland dragged Corrine back to the cave and tied her up, which was a relief to Corrine because, if he was tying her up, it meant that this paralysis thing was only temporary.

Corrine watched as Farland walked to the front of the cave and joined Mirabella. "So? Is there trouble with the plan?"

"The only thing that isn't in place is the bait. I can't figure out how to draw him into the trap."

"Are you talking about my brother?" Corrine yelled from across the cave.

Farland looked back at her with eyes narrowed. "No, this is something else. Mind your own business."

"What other evil stuff are you in the middle of?" Corrine asked incredulously. "You really have something *else* on the backburner in addition to trying to kill my little brother?"

Farland gave a derisive laugh. "You think your brother is on the *front* burner on the stovetop of my evil kitchen? Ha! The plan with your brother is a mere side dish that has been left to warm in the oven, while the burners are occupied with more important matters. Main course matters." At this point, he ditched the stove metaphor since it was falling apart, "There are plans set in place for this kingdom that your puny mind cannot comprehend."

CHAPTER TWENTY-FIVE

The magical vial of raven blood was on the floor of the castle laundry room, feeling absolutely rotten. Alone, confused, and worried about Warren.

A few hours earlier, the magical vial of raven blood had thought everything had been going swimmingly. Warren, Corrine, and the Princess had been on their way to the castle, where they would be safe from the threat posed by Farland. They'd been almost to the castle gates. Then, the world had been turned upside down as a flurry of shouts and screams filled the night. Warren had suddenly fallen like a rock and squelched into the filth of the city street, landing on top of the vial and thus muffling all sound to the point where the magical vial of raven blood could barely hear a thing.

All it knew for sure was that it had heard the Princess yell, "The wizard! Shoot the wizard!" And, of course, that had to mean Farland, because what other wizard would she be shouting about?

For a few more moments, it had been just more muffled voices as a worryingly-still Warren laid on top of the vial. Then, Warren's body had been jerked suddenly upward, and the magical vial of raven blood had been able to hear clearly again. The Princess hollered, "Get him to the doctor! As fast as possible! Go!"

Bro? the magical vial of raven blood had asked worriedly. *Hey, bro?*

No answer.

The jostling of Warren's body as the soldiers ran him up to the castle had been near enough to shake the vial out of Warren's pocket, but to the vial's relief, it made it all the way to the presumable hospital wing without falling out. The vial was just doing a glass container of blood's equivalent of a sigh of relief, when it heard a voice say, "Get those putrid garments off him and get him into a hospital gown. Stat!" *Stat.* Must be a doctor.

There had been some more jostling about, and the magical vial of raven blood had found itself in a laundry basket in the folds of Warren's filth-caked clothing.

"Get that to the laundry room!" barked the doctor.

Dude! Warren! the magical vial of raven blood had squawked anxiously as the basket had been picked up. *Dude! Wake up! Wake up and get me out of here!*

But it had been no use. The magical vial of raven blood had been whisked away from its unconscious friend and out of the hospital wing. Then down into the labyrinth of hallways that snaked through the servants' wing.

To the laundry room.

The magical vial of raven blood had done a glass container of blood's equivalent of quaking in fear as it had imagined what would likely be its fate: Warren's pants would be shaken about, and the vial would fly from the pocket and be dashed to bloody pieces on the floor. It would seep into the grout or dirt or whatever and be stuck listening to the prattle of washerwomen for the rest of its days.

But luck, it turned out, had been on the magical vial of raven blood's side. The pants had indeed been removed from the laundry basket and shaken about, but when the vial had flown from the pocket it had, mercifully, fallen not onto the brick floor, but instead onto a pile of blankets. Next, the momentum had sent it rolling off the blankets and into a dark corner.

Which was where the magical vial of raven blood was now, fretting about Warren and feeling utterly helpless and desolate.

S HE KNEW IT was cowardly of her, but Julianna did not at first tell Warren about their impending nuptials. She did, however, inform him that the vial of raven blood had gone missing.

"It probably fell out of your pocket in the street after the guard smacked you on the head," she commented. With every word, she felt guilty, knowing that she should be telling him instead that he was about to become a prince.

He cursed and then said, "Hey, could you get someone to get more at Farland's apartment?"

"Good idea," she said and set off to make it happen.

She then avoided him as long as possible.

First, she pretended to read, then she picked at some food, then she did some embroidery and a few scales on her clarinet. But after a while she sighed, owned up to the fact that her guilt was going nowhere, set aside the clarinet, and steeled herself for an unpleasant conversation.

Julianna walked into her room to see Warren propped up against a pile of fluffy pillows with a tray of food on his lap. "Ah, I see you're up," she said. She'd been hoping he would be sleeping so she could put off all talk of marriage and of his missing sister until later. She was emotionally exhausted and not in the mood for such weighty topics. But ignoring the conversation was exhausting too, so she figured if she was going to be stressed either way she'd might as well just get on with it.

Warren cut her off before she could even start. "Did you get some more raven blood?" he asked, by way of a greeting. She didn't take offense at the abruptness because, of course, his mind was on his sister's safety, and he was convinced this raven blood thing was his only chance of getting some information about Corrine.

"Not yet. But I'm sure the soldiers will be able to get you a new vial of blood."

He sighed but said not a word. He just looked down at the lobster on his lunch tray.

At that moment, Lillian bustled into the room. She gave her future son-in-law a radiant grin and spoke over her shoulder to someone in the hallway, "He's awake! Come on in!"

In strode one of the most immaculate, shiny, powdered, and painted ladies Warren had seen in his life. And he ran in theater circles, so that was saying a lot. "Hello, young man, my name is Serena. I'll be handling all the details. Don't you worry. I'm the best of the best. Your big day is in good hands." She grinned down at Warren, who stared up at her in utter confusion.

"Pardon?" he managed. "Handling all *what* details?"

Julianna spluttered a few incomprehensible words, but no one was paying any attention to her.

Serena reached down and gave Warren a patronizing pat on the hand. "Typical groom," she trilled. "No clue how much attention to detail goes into an event such as this."

"Typical *what?*" he choked, meeting Julianna's eyes. A sudden spike in blood pressure sent a horrible jolt of pain through his head, and he winced.

"Out!" Julianna spluttered. "Mom, Serena, out! *He doesn't know yet!*" she hissed. Then she herded them out of the room and slammed the door. She turned and faced him. "Ha! I bet you want an explanation about all that, huh?" More nervous laughter.

"Yes. Yes. I would very much like an explanation about all that."

"Okay, here's the deal," she said and cleared her throat. "So, apparently, and I had no idea about this until today either, that stuff Farland was saying about a counter-curse is true. And the counter-curse *is* you, as we suspected. I think." She met his gaze and almost lost her nerve but took a deep breath and soldiered on. "Farland told my dad that the spell could be broken by a guy whose parents were part of a traveling theater troupe, who had lived at sea his whole life, who played banjo, accordion, and harpsichord, and who is allergic to asparagus. That's you, right?"

He just stared.

"But there's one more thing. My dad's pretty sure we also need to be in love. And nothing personal, but I don't feel that way about you."

"The feeling's mutual," he said bluntly, then realized that, in his shock, he might have come across as insulting so he elaborated, "Probably if I'd thought it was an option my mind might have gone there, but you're the *Princess.* It never occurred to me. You must be engaged to some prince somewhere."

"Nope. My parents never pushed marriage. And now I know why. They were waiting to find *you.*"

"I can't even wrap my head around this," he muttered, staring into the eyes of the dead lobster on his plate.

"I know. I'm sorry," she said and sat down in a pink, puffy chair by the bed. She watched him for a few moments, wondering how much more

Warren could take. Then she said reluctantly, "And there's more. My mom has gotten it into her head that by 'love' Farland meant that it just had to be made official. Hence the wedding planner. They intend to make us get married after my little brother's big hunting party."

Silence.

"No, no, no. No." Warren shook his head blankly. "No. I can't do that. Marry into royalty? That's more than just being your husband. I have no interest in governance or public policy or the rest of that stuff. Whatever you people do when you're not having parties and whatnot. I want to be an *actor*."

Julianna winced. "I don't want this either, but I don't know how to get out of it," she said. "My mom's heart is set on this, so my dad will never say no. And there are guards down here now. They're afraid I'm going to sneak off again. There are two outside your door and two by the stairs." She'd thought of drugging the lot of them, but it would be too risky for her to get tea for everyone and spike all the cups and hope they all passed out before noticing anyone else had done so first.

They sat in bleak silence for a good long while.

Then Warren had an idea. He beckoned her closer and whispered, "Do you think they know about that tunnel of yours?"

She shook her head and whispered back, "I led them to believe I had somehow snuck up the stairs when I escaped."

He grinned. Excellent. "And you have my sister's bag?"

"Yes... So?" she whispered curiously. "The guards will see us."

He beckoned her closer still, and whispered, "She's got some vials of asparagus powder and tangerine juice in there. When they're combined, they make this big cloud of smoke that makes everyone who breathes it in pass out for a while. We can just use the asparagus and tangerine stuff, and I can escape back out of that tunnel of yours."

She contemplated him for a few moments while she thought it through, then broke into a grin and nodded. It wasn't the most well thought through plan, but what the heck? They'd gotten this far with rotten planning, so why not push their luck a bit more?

CHAPTER TWENTY-SIX

For the rest of the morning, Julianna dealt with her mom and the wedding planner by herself; Warren had played the concussion card and was being left alone in Julianna's bedroom, where he was ostensibly resting, but really just panicking about being pretty much forced to become royalty.

Julianna was busy pretending to pay attention to fabric samples for her wedding dress, when a soldier came down the stairs with a new vial of raven blood he had obtained from Farland's place. When Julianna saw the vial in his hand, she unceremoniously shoved the fabric at Serena, then rushed over to the guard and grabbed the vial. She flew into her bedroom, without even knocking, and found Warren doing pretty much the same thing he'd been doing when she'd left the room hours earlier: lying, shell shocked, flat on his back amongst her frilly pillows and blankets, staring vacantly at the ceiling. Poor guy. At least she had a bit of good news for him.

He slowly turned his head her way and said, monotone, "Hi."

"Hey," she said, then held up the vial.

His eyes lit up and he said, "Ooh, give it to me!" He extended a hand from beneath the folds of her pink, lacy duvet.

She walked over and plopped the vial into his hand.

A familiar voice squawked in his head: *Warren? Oh, bro, I am so glad you're okay! I was worried, man!*

"Er. Um. Thanks for the concern," Warren said. The raven

blood sure was getting buddy-buddy. "I've got a question—"

Dude, you would not believe the day I have had, cut in the magical vial of raven blood. *I'm lying on the floor of the laundry room right now, man—the other vial of me, that is. I've been kicked three times, and it's only a matter of time until I break and seep into the floor. I don't suppose you could come and get me?*

"No way, man. I've got a concussion. I feel almost back to normal, but the doctor told me I can't get up."

Tough break, dude. Concussion. I figured it was something like that. Seriously, though, it would be awesome if someone could just come down to the laundry—"

"You know where my sister is?" Warren cut in.

She's in the Forest of Looming Death. In the cave that belongs to the Queen's sister.

"Oh!" Warren hadn't been expecting it to be that easy to find out.

Farland stopped back at his place on the way out of town. He and your sister were yelling at each other. He told her where he was taking her, and I overheard.

Warren pondered for a moment how difficult it must be for the magical vial of raven blood to be in three places at once. Here in the dungeon, back in the basin at Farland's apartment, and apparently also in the laundry room. "Okay, well, uh, thanks. Glad to have you back. Uh, bro…"

No prob. Happy to help.

Warren set the vial carefully down on the duvet and asked Julianna, "Do you, perchance, have an aunt who lives in a cave in the Forest of Looming Death?"

Julianna raised her eyebrows. "That vial of blood just told you that?" Well, at least that proved he was sane, and that she wasn't going to be forced to marry a lunatic.

"So you do?"

"Yes, I do. She's my mom's soulless evil twin. Mom doesn't like to talk about her, so I don't know much, but I *do* know she lives in a cave in the Forest of Looming Death. Dad banished her there the same day that Farland cursed me, in fact."

"How far away is this forest?" Warren asked, a plan taking form in his brain.

She shrugged. "I don't know."

Montague, the guard ghost, who had been floating around aimlessly listening, informed her, "It's about three days walk north of the city."

"Three days north," Julianna said.

Warren looked at her confusedly. "But you just said—"

"A ghost told me just now."

"Of course. The ghost."

"*One* of the ghosts. This one is Montague. The one from before is Dexter. Dexter's in the other room catching up with Curtis. Curtis is the third ghost."

He shook his head. "Sorry, this ghost thing is still weird to me." He looked around as though hoping to see a shimmery shape in the air. "Anyway, I want to give you a heads up about my plan. Once I'm well enough to walk, I'm going to go rescue my sister."

She waited a moment to hear the rest of the plan, but then he didn't say anything else. "*That's* your plan? She asked incredulously. "Warren, you can't go on a solo three-day trip with a broken arm and recent concussion, to a forest full of murderers to rescue your sister from my soulless aunt and one of the most powerful wizards in the land. You just can't. It's *dumb*."

"Well, when you put it that way..." Warren pondered.

"Just wait a bit, and maybe I could talk to my parents—"

At that point the doctor barged in, thus necessitating a halt in the conversation. Julianna left. Not wanting to rejoin the wedding planning party that was happing in the main room, she whiled away some time in the hallway outside her bedroom, getting the ghosts all up to date on what had been going on with her since she had been in the dungeon last.

At last, the doctor left, and Julianna swooped back in. She was happy to see that Warren was now sitting up. "So, how's your concussion?"

"The doctor said I'm okay to walk," he said with a smile. "Which means I can leave as early as tonight! To rescue Corrine. And to stop this wedding by my absence."

She was sorry to hear he was still on the rescue plan but did agree with the last point at least. "Stopping the wedding *is* the one good thing about your stupid idea."

He ignored that. "Okay, so I guess I leave tonight. To go to the Forest of Looming Death."

Julianna felt a little shudder as she tossed all caution to the wind, and heard herself say, "We set out at sunset?"

"*We?*" he repeated. "All we need to stop this wedding is for *one* of us to be gone."

She bit her lip and looked him in the eyes. "I know that, but I was hoping I could come along anyway. I'm so fed up with my parents, I'm not staying either way. If I stay, they'll just imprison me and hound me about marriage and interrogate me about where I think you might have gone. So, if you sneak out, then I'm sneaking out too. And if you don't want my company, then I'll go my own way, but I was hoping we could stick together. Also, since Corrine has only been captured by Farland because of me, I really would like to help you out."

"It's not your fault he took her," Warren pointed out.

"Well, my family's fault anyway. If my dad hadn't been such a jerk, Farland wouldn't have cursed him."

"True, but it's not even really your dad's fault. No one is to blame for all this but Farland."

"Details, details. All I'm really saying here is that if you are going to go to the Forest of Looming Death, I would like to go with you."

He gave her a long look while he thought. Rationally, he knew it was dumb (not to mention pretty much certain death) to go alone into the Forest of Looming Death in his condition. And he was no use to Corrine dead. And Julianna *was* freely offering to help. *And* if he said no, she'd just go off on her own somewhere and probably get into trouble, because she had next to no experience dealing with real world stuff. Finally, he nodded and said, "Okay, so we go at sunset?"

"Actually, a little before sunset," she said with a grin. "We'll knock them all out about fifteen minutes before. It'll take a little while to get up to the top of the tunnel, especially with two of us."

JULIANNA AND WARREN whiled away the remaining hours of the day sleeping in preparation for their escape, and pretending to be excited about the wedding, since that was easier than fighting about it. Besides, Warren had no option but to play along. He was not in a position to fight with the King and Queen about anything. As he looked at flower arrangements and color swatches, it was a great consolation for him that he'd soon be knocking everyone unconscious and getting the heck out of there.

Though, he had to admit, he would miss the food when he was gone.

They were sitting around the dining room table looking at pictures of ice sculptures, when a dozen or so maids descended the stairs, each carrying a tray of food. Warren stared eagerly at the approaching trays. He was particularly entranced by the dizzying array of fresh fruits and vegetables; a life lived at sea meant that growing up, the only fruit he had seen on a regular basis was the shriveled old limes they sucked to ward off scurvy. As for vegetables, the pirates scoffed at the very notion of them, calling them 'rabbit food' and saying that any dude who ate one was a sissy. Potatoes were the only exception to the rule, since they could be deep-fried, and were a good base for things like butter and bacon and all sorts of other man-safe ingredients.

In addition to the trays of fruits and veggies, there was fresh seafood; fancy breads and cheeses; three different kinds of asparagus dishes; pies; cakes; and, of course, a whole roasted pig with an apple in its mouth, because this was an opulent feast and they were in a Medieval-esque castle.

Before Julianna or Serena had even picked up their plates, Warren had grabbed his and was filling it with a little bit of everything he could reach, except, of course, the asparagus, since he was allergic.

Serena stared, horrified, at the sight of Warren shoveling food into his mouth.

He ignored her, having no reason to impress her with fancy manners. And more to the point: if there was food to eat, he was darned well going to eat as much of it as he could, since, after today, it was back to the usual stale bread and questionable cuts of meat that were the usual fare for the commoners of Fritillary.

At this point, Conroy and Lillian descended the stairs to check on the progress of the wedding planning, forcing Warren to reign in his appetite. He stood up and began to bow, but Lillian stopped him almost before he started. "Oh, dear boy, no need for that. You're nearly family!" she trilled.

He righted himself and nodded awkwardly. He had no idea what to say to the Queen. Not only was she the Queen, but also, he was shortly going to be magicking her into unconsciousness.

Lillian and Conroy sat down, and then Lillian said, "Conroy Jr. will be down, too, once his lessons are done."

"Oh good!" Julianna said. It had been ages since she'd seen the kid, and it might be ages before she'd see him again. He was a sweet little boy, and she felt he might have a fair shot at being a halfway-decent king, despite their father's influence.

While Conroy Jr. was part Conroy, he was also part Lillian, and, consequently, he had a kind and gentle side to his personality that his war tutor just couldn't seem to stamp out no matter how he tried to explain that, in a war, the lives of the enemies just weren't as important as the lives of the people on the *right* side. Conroy Jr. resisted all such logic and clung to the pesky, sentimental line of reasoning that the enemies were just as much people and that their wives and children were just as likely to end up starving on the streets in the absence of their husbands/fathers as the people fighting for Fritillary were[26].

Warren frowned. The whole Royal Family would be down here. Before Go Time came, he'd have to ask Julianna if knocking out her family was a hanging offense.

---

26   This was a great source of worry for Conroy. A Prince (especially a firstborn one destined to be King) should be bloodthirsty and ruthless in war and shouldn't clutter his head with too much thinking. All thinking did was take your gut reaction and throw it into question. Conroy was a firm believer that going with your gut and letting other people sort out the consequences was a very important trait in the leader of a country. After all, as a ruler, there were absolute oodles of decisions to make every single day, and, if you devoted too much time to any one of those decisions, you had no time left for any fun.

Chapter Twenty-Seven

Mortimer passed through the crumbling gates of Coal Harbor and looked around with dread; during his two-day trip from the city to his home, he had racked is brains for a way to explain the loss of the silver box in a way that wouldn't make everyone mad at him.

But no bright ideas had come to him.

And now, here he was with Eugene and Ray, his traveling companions he'd met up with halfway through his journey, and they were itching to hear an update. He had told Eugene and Ray that he didn't want to talk about the box until he was back home, since it was so top secret and all. They'd bought his excuse easily enough. But now that he was home, it was only a matter of time until he would have to confess the truth. Mortimer braced himself for an ugly scene and looked around the village.

The gate they'd walked through led to the main square, which was a largeish open area lined with dilapidated one- and two-story buildings. There was a fountain with chronic water pressure issues dripping away in the center of the square. A few roads branched off the square and led to small, rundown homes with pathetic little dusty gardens.

Standing where Mortimer was at the gate, he could look straight past the fountain and down the street across from him, out to the one pretty thing about Coal Harbor: the ocean. The view raised his spirits just a touch. No matter how drearily pathetic a village on shore happened to be, there was no way to make that village's ocean view drearily pathetic. Oceans could be many things ranging from placid to churning to sparkling to terrifying and everything in between, but they could never be drearily pathetic.

It was early evening, so most of the guys were down in the mines, most of the ladies were cooking dinner or washing stuff or doing whatever ladies did in their houses when the guys were mining, a few kids too young or sickly to be mining were running around in the dusty square, and some elderly guys were sitting by the fountain chatting and coughing and watching the kids.

Eugene smacked Mortimer on the arm to get his attention. "Hey, I'm going to head home. I wanna have Cora look at this cut. Meet you at the inn once the guys are off work?"

Mortimer nodded and watched Eugene hurry off home to have his wife tend to his wound. They had, of course, been attacked on the road. And they had not emerged from the scuffle unscathed. Eugene had been cut across his left arm, Ray had a black eye and a twisted ankle from when he'd tried to run away from the scuffle, and Mortimer had a broken, bloody nose and two black eyes, the result of a particularly powerful punch from a gigantic troll of a dude who had then stolen his wallet as Mortimer lay moaning on the ground, in too much pain to care that the troll was digging through his pockets. With Fritillary's countryside in the state it was, travelers pretty much had to figure being attacked into their itinerary.

That had been the second wallet he'd lost in the space of just a few days. Yet another indicator that things in Fritillary were getting out of hand.

Mortimer wanted nothing more than to trudge home, clean up his bloody face, and curl up in bed until it was time to go face his friends that evening. But one of the old men by the fountain spotted the travelers and motioned them over. Ray and Mortimer walked wordlessly toward the three old men.

"So you're back, eh?" asked a grizzled guy with a short, gray beard.

"Indeed we are, Dominic," Mortimer sighed, and leaned wearily against the fountain's edge.

"And how did the trip go?" Dominic inquired. It was a mark of how common violence on the road was that the old man didn't even mention

Mortimer's or Ray's injuries.

"About as expected," Mortimer responded.

"You get the you-know-what?"

"I'm going to wait until tonight to talk about it. We're meeting at the inn," Mortimer responded and stared at the dusty ground, feeling more and more disappointed in himself with each passing moment. *Why had he let the box get stolen? He should never have trusted that accursed maid.* "Anything new in the village since I left?"

"Nope. Same old, same old," Dominic replied, and then began to cough as only an elderly man who has worked in a coal mine since he was eight can cough.

The guys all milled around a moment to see whether the hacking would stop, but, when it devolved into a full-on coughing fit, it became clear to everyone that the conversation was at an end. Ray gave them a wave and wandered off home.

Mortimer asked Dominic, "Need help getting home?" even though he knew Dominic would refuse his offer.

Dominic waved a hand dismissively at Mortimer and coughed on.

"Okay, then, see you around," Mortimer said. He nodded to the other two old men, and headed home. It could have been merely the power of suggestion, but Mortimer could swear his lungs felt a bit funny. He glanced over the rooftops at the headframe of the coalmine and sighed. As badly as his trip had gone, at least he had had a break from going down into the dark, dangerous, sweltering mine. On his trip to get the box, the fresh air of the countryside (and even the city air full of coal smoke) had done wonders for his own newly-developing chronic cough. He was glad that he was the village's designated box-retriever, because he was pretty sure that his vacations away from the mine were the only thing keeping the sickness from becoming fully entrenched in his lungs.

But there was no need to worry about health issues when he had plenty more immediate concerns to deal with. The revolution was coming, which he would probably get killed in long before he got a chance to die in old age of black lung.

Dying in the revolution. Now *that* was something to worry about.

*A*FTER HE'D CLEANED the blood off his face and taken a good nap, Mortimer felt tons better. He woke with a bit of time to spare before the meeting at the inn, so he took about ten minutes just to stretch out in bed and relax. It felt like a luxury to him to just lie there—he was always *doing* something. Every moment of his waking life was consumed by mining, union organizing, revolution organizing, and taking care of his siblings (who, though now all grown and with lives of their own, still looked to him to fix their problems).

After a bit, Mortimer took a deep breath and sat up. He looked around the tiny, sparsely furnished attic room he called home, and was pleasantly surprised to see a few slices of bread and some dried asparagus on a plate on his table by the room's one window. His sister, whose house he lived in the attic of, must have brought it up while he'd slept. He walked over and ate the food standing, looking out the little window down to the street below. It was nearly dark, but he could make out a few people walking in the direction of the inn. In most towns and villages, the revolutionaries were in the minority and had to sneak around to get to their meetings, but in Coal Harbor, pretty much every citizen wanted the King overthrown, and those who didn't had the sense to just shut up and let everyone else do their thing.

Mortimer shoved an asparagus into his mouth, grabbed the last piece of bread, and strode to the door. Time to face the music.

*T*HE INN, THE Piebald Goat, was packed. Mortimer swung the door open and was hit by a wave of ruckus. He took a step back and breathed a steadying breath as he looked in at the cozy pub packed with villagers, most of whom were friends and family. Friends and family who wouldn't hesitate to scream and yell at him and make him feel horribly guilty once they heard what he had to say. He just hoped, if anyone punched him, they'd keep away from his head since he'd had enough of that lately to last him a while.

"Mortimer!" someone yelled. "Come on in!"

His cousin, Bertrand, who was standing near the door, realized Mortimer was there and pulled him inside. In a matter of moments, everyone was greeting him and asking him about his trip and telling him he looked like a wreck. And, pushing him in the direction of the stage, which was usually reserved for the local bluegrass band The Hullabaloo, but was sometimes used for speeches and such.

Someone pushed him up the steps. He nearly lost his balance but found his footing and turned to face the expectant faces of the villagers.

A few of them kept up their conversations, but most shut their traps and waited.

Mortimer gave a smile that felt more like a grimace. It looked ghastly paired with his black eyes and broken nose.

"Well?" hollered someone from the back. "Where's the box?"

Mortimer saw the other two leaders of the revolutionaries, Rex and Hughey, making their way up to the stage. This was the way these meetings always went. Mortimer, Rex, and Hughey would all get up on the stage in front of everyone, Mortimer would take out the most recently collected box, Rex would put a key into one of the keyholes on the box's side, Hughey would put his key into the other side, and they'd unlock it. Mortimer would then open the box and read to everyone present the note that was written on the paper inside, thus ensuring that everyone was on the same page and that there were no secrets. The notes in the boxes always contained two things: one, information about where to find supplies that would aid the revolutionaries, and, two, where and when to find the next box.

You are asking, dear reader, what is up with the mysterious boxes? Well, Mortimer had received the first box from a mysterious stranger at a union meeting two years earlier. It had been the end of the meeting, and everyone had been milling around the refreshments table, wolfing down punch and doughnuts, when suddenly Mortimer had noticed an intense fellow with a scar across his chin watching him.

Mortimer had said, through a mouthful of doughnut, "Hey."

In response, the guy had swooped up to him and said in a rush, "I have a friend who wants to help you and your cause. A powerful friend. A friend with access to things you need. He wants you to have this." And he had held up a plain, black bag, offering it to Mortimer.

Mortimer had ignored the bag, and said, "Your friend wants to help me organize a miners' union? What's in that bag that could help me organize a union?"

The mysterious stranger had sighed. "No, not *this* cause. Your *other* cause."

Mortimer had clammed up then, since one didn't share with a stranger information about plans to overthrow the King. Especially if that stranger was super intense and had a scar across his chin.

The guy had said, in response to Mortimer's silence, "Whatever. Here's the bag if you want it." Then the guy had said something that Mortimer hadn't understood at the time: "The only catch is, for all future boxes, you are the only one who can collect them. Come alone. Each time." He'd plunked the bag down on the refreshments table between a tray of doughnuts and a plate of devilled eggs and had swooped out.

Once Mortimer was sure the guy wasn't coming back, he had dropped his play-it-cool charade and grabbed up the bag. He had opened it and dumped the contents out. A little silver box and two keys. On both the box and the keys, there was painted an orange star. He'd easily figured out how to unlock it, and, since Fritillary didn't have bombs or germ warfare or anything like that, he'd seen no danger in opening it up then and there. He'd read the note and had been shocked to read in it information on where he could find a big stash of weapons. It had also told him where and when he could expect to find the second box.

Mortimer had consulted Rex and Hughey, and they had decided that, though it seemed super suspicious, they should probably check it out. Being young adult males, they'd leapt in with a spirit of invincibility and fearlessness that its usually a bad idea, but, in this particular case, worked out pretty well. As far as they could tell, it had not been a trap, and they had acquired weapons! Score!

Mortimer had been hesitant to go to collect the next box, especially since he had to do it alone, but he'd thrown caution to the wind and had gone for it. That box had contained a note that had directed them to a cave in the King's nearby wildlife refuge. In the cave, they had found food and medicine.

As time had gone on and the mysterious benefactor had kept helping them (with apparently no ulterior motives), they had begun to fear a trap less and less, until finally it had just become another part of their lives. Sometimes, when Mortimer went on his solo excursions to collect a box, he would catch a glimpse of someone lurking in the shadows, but whoever it was, they didn't bother him, so he assumed it was just someone making sure he was really coming alone.

He and the villagers had worked out their current system wherein the box was opened, and the note was read only in front of all the villagers, in order to keep things on the up-and-up.

But now, because of Mortimer's carelessness—letting his guard down in order to flirt with a lady—the box was gone. So, not only were they not going to be able to get whatever supplies their benefactor had planned on providing them, but they also had no way of knowing where the next box was going to be hidden.

No more boxes, no more supplies for the revolution.

It was over.

All over.

Rex and Hughey joined Mortimer on the stage, and they looked at him expectantly, keys at the ready.

Mortimer gave a bleak sort of laugh, and nervously blurted out, "I lost the box."

He could swear he felt an icy wind sweep through the room, but that was probably just a physical manifestation of the fear he felt as he saw the eyes of every villager stare at him with something that started out shocked confusion but turned quickly to rage.

He put his hands up before himself defensively. "Now wait! Wait! Let me explain!"

But, no, the explanation would only make them angrier.

So far, they were all still too stunned to say anything, so Mortimer quickly added, "Come on guys, it was only a matter of time, anyway, right? I mean, with all the hoodlums running around the countryside, it's a wonder a box wasn't stolen sooner. At least the other chapters of the Order of the Orange Star are still getting their boxes, eh?"

The air was filled with a menacing rumble of people murmuring angrily to their neighbors.

"Right, guys?" Mortimer asked, and laughed weakly.

Then the yelling began.

Chapter Twenty-Eight

As the maids served up food for the King and Queen, Lillian looked over at her daughter earnestly, and said, "My darling, I've been thinking."

Uh oh, thought Conroy; he listened nervously as he spun his cursed BFF ring around his finger.

"I understand why you are reluctant to marry. I do. You're afraid that even if you do, the curse won't be broken. And then you'll be married to someone who you say you don't love." She looked apologetically at Warren and said, "I don't mean to insult you, my boy."

"No offense taken, Your Majesty," he said nervously through a mouthful of watermelon.

Conroy perked up his ears and listened intently. It was starting to sound like Lillian was perhaps changing her mind about the wedding.

Julianna was guardedly optimistic. "Exactly, Mom. That is exactly it."

"Yes. Well. I just want to give you some advice." Lillian studied her daughter a moment, then set down her golden fork beside her golden plate in order to give Julianna her full attention. "I have heard it said that arranged marriages have just as much chance at long-term love as do marriages that begin with love. So, you two have a good chance of growing to love each other in the future."

Serena cleared her throat significantly, indicating she had something to add.

"Yes?" asked Lillian.

"That is, indeed, true," Serena said, with all the authority of a wedding planner. If anyone knew statistics about marriage success, it was her.

"Well there you have it!" Lillian pronounced triumphantly as though that settled everything and her daughter's trouble was now solved. "You will in all likelihood grow to love each other!"

Julianna frowned.

Conroy frowned.

Warren chewed on some carrot cake, barely registering their conversation since his plans to blow this Popsicle stand remained the same no matter what anyone said.

Lillian looked at her daughter's downcast face. Her pep talk hadn't gone as well as she'd hoped.

Everyone ate silently for a few minutes.

"Hey!" Julianna tried to change the subject. "So, Warren's sister. Farland has her. Dad, you'll send an army out to try to find her, right?"

"Why would I do that?" Conroy asked, surprised. "The soldiers are all busy with preparing for Conroy Jr.'s first hunt, dear. They're practicing some really neat marching stuff for the parade. They can't go traipsing about the country looking for one commoner." He then actually had the decency to realize that what he'd said might be hurtful to Warren. He looked at his future son-in-law. "Sorry about that. But we have *so* much to do, you see. After the hunt we'll send out some soldiers."

Warren stared at him, fighting an inner battle. He was not a violent dude, but he wanted to punch the King in his stupid face. "Perfectly understandable," he heard his voice say. "The hunt is very important."

Conroy nodded. "It's going to be quite an event."

"Dad!" Julianna exploded, "How can you be so heartless?"

Conroy turned to her, and said angrily, "You've gotten quite uppity since your little adventure, miss. I am the King. No one argues with me. Besides, they're *commoners*, dear. They're *used* to hardship. It's not as big a deal to them if something happens to a family member, because they're always dying in droves. Mining accidents, angry wizards, logging accidents," he further explained, trying to appease his horrified daughter as he waved a fork in Warren's direction. "Gang stuff, bar fights, ships sinking, diseases, factory mishaps, starvation, filthy drinking water. And that's only the tip of the iceberg, eh my boy?" he asked Warren.

Warren gaped at Conroy, wondering whether the King was really asking him to confirm that he didn't really care all that much about Corrine because commoners didn't get too bothered when their family members died.

It was into this scene that Conroy Jr. bounced down the stairs.

"Hi, Julianna!" he yelled when he saw her.

"Hi, CJ!" she called, her voice ringing with the false happiness of a grownup who is trying to hide a fight from a kid.

The kid scampered over to the table and sat down. Maids swarmed around to fill him a plate.

"Excited about the hunt? Three days away, huh?" Julianna asked her brother, casting apologetic look toward Warren, who was still looking pretty shaken by Conroy's words.

"Oh, yes, sure," said Conroy Jr. with a glance at his dad. Julianna was pretty sure CJ was not really into hunting, but just played along for their dad. She was also pretty sure he didn't want to be King, either, but there was no getting out of that one. A firstborn son was, after all, a firstborn son.

"I hear it's been very good for the economy of the city, anyway. All the businesses making extra stuff for the big event," Julianna said.

"Oh. That's good," her brother said politely.

Silence for a bit.

"Who's that?" Conroy Jr. asked at length, pointing an asparagus spear at Warren.

"Oh, this is Warren," Julianna explained. "He's a friend of mine."

"You met him when you ran away?"

"I didn't run away, CJ. I just wanted to get out and see the city a bit, and things got messy. But yes, I met Warren when I was out in the city."

"And," Lillian interjected, "he is going to marry your sister! You just wait, you two men will be great pals!"

Warren gave Conroy Jr. a weak smile. "Hi!" His upbringing was such that he had never talked to a child before.

"You're a commoner?" asked Conroy Jr.

"Yes, I am," Warren said, then thought to add, "Your Majesty," after a moment.

"Then we must talk," Conroy Jr. said in a tone very official for a child of his age. "I've never spoken to a commoner before. I'd like to hear what you think about the state of the kingdom."

Julianna smiled fondly at him. Yes, he did indeed have a decent shot of being an all right king, even if he didn't want to be one.

Conroy cut in and said, "Now, now, son. No need for things like that! Just shut your mouth and eat your dinner."

Conroy Jr. frowned.

"Er," Warren said, "I've lived at sea my whole life up until a few days ago. With pirates. So I don't think I could give you any practical information." He was happy he had a good reason for not being able to give Conroy Jr. any useful intelligence, since the King obviously didn't like the idea.

Conroy Jr. nodded with a look of disappointment.

Julianna said helpfully, "But we've met a few commoners we can introduce you to."

Conroy Jr. smiled.

"Quiet!" Conroy barked. "This country has been run for generations without asking commoners—of all people!—for input, and it will run for generations more on the same policy!"

"So sure of that, are you?" Julianna snapped. "After just two nights out there in the city I have learned a lot that you might be—"

Warren sharply coughed and caught Julianna's eye. She looked at him with annoyance; she didn't like to be interrupted mid-rant. He glanced at a clock that was hanging from the wall.

It was time to go.

"Hey, Julianna, where's the bathroom?" Warren asked.

"Oh! Yes, of course. Let me show you," she said, taking her napkin off her lap and putting it by her plate.

"Sit down, dear. One of the maids can show him," Lillian said.

"No, no, I insist," Julianna said awkwardly. "I *want* to show him the bathroom."

They scampered off to Julianna's room to get Corrine's bag, leaving

Lillian and Conroy exchanging flummoxed looks.

While Warren got the vials ready, Julianna got her own bag from where she had stowed it under her bed. She dumped all the jewelry from her jewelry box into it, figuring the necklaces and whatnot would be good to have on hand. "Do you still have my money?" she asked Warren over her shoulder.

"Yep, it's here in Corrine's bag."

"Good. Okay. All set?"

"Yes. But hey, will I get in trouble for this? I mean the King and Queen are out there and we're about to knock them out. Not to mention your brother."

"Don't worry, I'll just tell them I did it. Better yet, I *will* do it. You just take care of the guards, and I'll take care of my family."

"Good enough for me," he said recklessly, though inside he was petrified. But no way was he getting married and becoming a prince, so that meant he had to get out while the getting was good. He handed her one vial of asparagus powder and one of tangerine and said, "Now watch closely."

She watched as he emptied the asparagus powder from one of his vials into the tangerine juice and then quickly capped the vial with his thumb. "You see?" he asked. "When you're ready, give it a shake and take your thumb off. And of course, hold your breath." He watched as she combined her powder and juice, then he said, "Great. I'll meet you at the entrance to the tunnel."

"Good luck," she said, and they walked out of her room, hearts hammering.

As SOON AS Julianna rendered her family and her wedding planner unconscious, she ran to her room to throw on the maid dress from the Dawdling Donkey. Then, she put a hastily scrawled note (*We don't want to get married, so we're leaving. Don't worry, we'll only travel at night, and we'll stop in plenty of time to find good sun-proof shelter. I'll send word in a few days. XOXO Julianna*) in front of her mom at the dining table, then ran to her tunnel and began to pull the loose stone out of the way.

There was a heart-stopping moment when she heard one of the guards yell something that sounded like the beginning of an alert, but it was followed a second later by silence and the thud of a body hitting the floor.

"Do you think that was Warren? Or a guard?" Julianna asked Dexter, ready to spring to her feet and run toward the sound of the commotion.

"If it was the guard, he'd be yelling," Dexter pointed out.

"Right. Good point."

A few moments later, Dexter was proven right when Warren came jogging her way, shoving a few oranges into Corrine's bag as he ran. He joined her and helped her with the stone; neither of them said anything because both were preoccupied with what they'd just done. Even though they hadn't harmed their victims, having that sort of control over people who had no idea what kind of magical power you were wielding was still not cool. And they both knew it. But forcing people to get married when they didn't want to was also not cool, so that about evened things out on the morality scoreboard. Except for the collateral damage in the form of the guards, Conroy Jr., and Serena.

But whatever.

What was done was done.

Corrine needed to be rescued, and they needed to not be married, so what alternative did they have?

Off they went. Warren, Julianna, and Dexter all scooted into the tunnel, then the two corporeal members of the party pulled the stone back in place through means of a rope that Julianna had attached to it before sneaking out the first time.

Julianna then explained to Warren how to use the wheeled board to bring him to the top. "Don't climb out of the top of the tunnel until I get there," she said. "It's tricky."

"Right-o." And off he went.

She waited with Dexter and said, "They're going to be really mad when they wake up."

"An understatement," he said. "I'm very impressed. A few days ago, I'd never have thought you capable of what you did back there."

"I'm not *proud* of it, Dexter. I know you think that sort of thing is justified, but I'm feeling very, very bad right now." She sighed gloomily and was glad Dexter didn't respond.

The board came rolling back down the tunnel, and Julianna hopped on, then pulled herself to the top, where she joined Warren. "Okay, we have to get to the wall as fast as we can," she said. "We can't be sure how long that stuff is going to keep everyone unconscious. That dungeon has some high ceilings, so the fumes will disperse pretty quickly."

He nodded. "Lead the way."

Chapter Twenty-Nine

A mere fifteen minutes later, Julianna was kicking leaves and dirt off the trap door to the smugglers' tunnel. Once Warren realized what she was doing, he joined in, and soon they were opening the trap door and slipping down into the passageway under the castle wall.

"You have more of that stuff, right?" Julianna asked. It had only just occurred to her that, if things went badly with the smugglers, the asparagus and tangerine concoction would be an easy solution.

"Yes," Warren said. "One more vial of each. You think we could stop by Farland's and steal some more on the way out of town?"

"No way. As soon as they wake up, they're going to have soldiers looking for us. We have to get as far away as we can as fast as we can." She paused a few moments to second-guess herself. No, they couldn't get any more of that oh-so-helpful concoction. It would be too dangerous to waste time. "Be ready to use those vials. I don't trust the people at the end of this tunnel."

"Then why are we going this way?" he asked, eyeing the darkness before them distrustfully.

"There's no other way. We can't very well go through the front gate." As they talked, they walked carefully down the tunnel.

He sighed and got ready to grab the vials. Mixing the potions wasn't exactly something you could do sneakily or at the drop of a hat. You had to uncork and mix them, then re-cork, theoretically giving the people you were trying to use the potion on quite a bit of notice that something was up. "Ready." Then an idea occurred to him. "Hey, hold on a second. How about I wait down here for a bit and see how things go for you? If you need help, I'll pop up with the potion all mixed and ready to go, and if things go fine you can just tell them you had a friend coming close behind you or something."

"Hmm. Yeah. I like that."

"Okay, good." He felt a lot better.

"Here I go then," she breathed and pushed open the trapdoor. She peered around at as much of the room as she could see. No feet. No sounds. Julianna looked questioningly up at Dexter, who had floated on ahead of her.

"All clear," Dexter said.

She climbed out but had no sooner given Warren the thumbs up and shut the trap door than someone walked through the doorway behind her. She spun around to see one of the two goons who had been playing cards when she had come before. The goon halted in his tracks. "I wouldn't have thought we would be seeing *you* again!" he said, then swooped forward and grabbed her by the wrist. "Luann!" he called over his shoulder. "You'll never guess who's here!"

There was some muttering from the other room, then Luann bustled in with a surly look on her face. The surliness turned to a creepy sort of glee when she saw Julianna. "Well, well, well. My, my, my. Lookie who we have here. *Jennifer*, the maid from the castle." Something about the italicizey way she'd said 'Jennifer' made Julianna certain that they knew who she really was.

It must have been that moron Galt from the Dawdling Donkey. He must have told them.

"*Jennifer*," Luann said unpleasantly, "You'll never guess the rumors that are flying around about you!"

"Do tell," Julianna said nervously, trying to plot out her next move. The last time she'd been there, there had been four people. The two goons, Luann, and Hector. If they were all on the job tonight as well (which was likely since there was no such thing as a day off in Fritillary) then Warren using the potion now would only take care of half of their problem. The other half might well be out in the other room.

Luann continued, "Well, Galt told us that he saw you running up to the castle gates and yelling to the guards that you were the Princess!"

"Why, fancy that!" she said tensely. "Of all the darndest things! I do declare!"

"My thoughts exactly," Luann sneered. "Hector!"

"What?"

"Come on in here!"

Julianna took a calming breath. If Hector was coming into the room, then that was 75% of their adversaries, leaving just one goon to go. Also, as she recalled, Hector had seemed a lot nicer than Luann. Maybe he would talk her into letting Julianna go, and then they wouldn't have to use their last bit of potion.

Hector walked in and halted in his tracks upon seeing what all the hubbub was about. "No way!" he breathed, then smiled at Luann. "We are going to make a *fortune!*"

Julianna frowned. So much for Hector talking some sense into Luann.

"Let's take her to Headquarters. Fast," he said. "If castle guards aren't searching for her yet, they will be soon."

The goon started pulling her toward the door. Okay, so there was no chance of waiting until all four smugglers were in the same room. It was now or never. Julianna turned, and was about to yell for Warren, but then she saw that he was already leaping out of the tunnel with the potion at the ready.

They locked eyes and took deep breaths.

Warren took his thumb off the vial, and smoke began to pour out the top of it. He rolled the vial across the floor toward Julianna. She felt the hand holding her arm loosen, and turned in time to see the goon, Luann, and Hector all collapse simultaneously to the floor like so many sacks of potatoes.

Warren and Julianna scampered out of the room and shut the door behind them.

"What are you two doing?" said a deep, goonish voice.

They spun around, still holding their breaths. But if the goon who stood before them had not passed out, then that must mean the fumes were not in this room, or at least not in great enough levels. They began to breathe again.

They had no idea what to say, though.

Julianna saw in the goon's eyes that he was beginning to recognize her. Puzzle pieces were falling into place in his head.

"Just run!" Dexter said.

Julianna darted to the left, Warren followed her lead and darted to the right.

But of course, that didn't work.

The goon just reached out and grabbed each of them by an arm. "Hold it. What's going on?" he asked.

"You'd better go in there!" Warren gasped, jerking his head toward the door they'd just slammed shut. "I think they might need some help."

"Yeah right, like I'm going to go into a room that you two just scurried out of like the Hounds of Hell[27] were nipping at your heels. I have brains *as well as* brawn, for your information. Now what in tarnation are you two doing here?"

Julianna sighed. They were wasting valuable time. "OK. Look, will you let us go if we give you some money?" Julianna asked, thinking back to when she'd first seen him and the other thug playing cards; they'd shown no interest in the pendant she'd brought for Luann and Hector, leading her to believe that they must be by-the-hour employees who were probably not paid too well.

The guy paused and pondered. "You know, I know who you are. How about I just kidnap you and ask your parents for some ransom instead?"

Julianna tried not to panic. "No, my way is better. You won't get as much from me as you would from my parents, that's for sure, but even what I could give you is more than you could otherwise make in your lifetime."

The thug looked at her squintily, far from convinced.

"And most importantly, you wouldn't have to steal it from me or bribe me in order to get it; it would be yours fair and square, and thus no one from

---

27   Conroy's ancestors had long ago squashed formal religion (as far as his spies knew anyway) since totalitarian regimes are pretty adamant that their people only worship the kings and queens. Thus there was no understanding of Hell in a religious sense. 'Hell' in Fritillary was merely the name of a seedy pub founded by a fellow named Augustus Hell; it was in a very bad neighborhood and had been frequently broken into before the owners had begun to keep a trio of ferocious hounds on site to guard the place after closing time.

my family would send soldiers searching for you. You could just take it. Then you go your way, we go our way, and you won't have to live your life looking over your shoulder. Whatcha think?"

The goon thought hard. You could tell because his eyebrows were all scrunched up and he was scratching his chin. "And if I just take this money from you, and *then* kidnap you and thus *still* get all that money from your parents?"

"Then you would anger my parents, and they would use all their resources and their bottomless pit of money to track you down. It might not be today or tomorrow, but eventually they'd find you. Take what I'm offering you, and you can live a peaceful life; steal from me and kidnap me, and you'll always be looking over your shoulder, and you *will* be caught, eventually."

The guy pondered for a bit more. "How much you got?"

Warren rummaged about in Corrine's bag, and found the coin purse. He handed it over to Julianna. She opened it up, took a handful of coins out, and plopped them into the guy's hand.

His eyes widened in shock at the weight of it alone; when he took a moment to calculate, he stumbled as though his legs had nearly lost their ability to hold him up. "Whoa!" he breathed. "And you'll really just let me take this if I let you go?"

Julianna nodded energetically.

"A life of peace does appeal, you know. I've been in the thug business for so long I hardly know anything else, but there was a time I dreamed of being a writer..." he said dreamily.

"Ooh!" Julianna said. "What kind of stuff would you write?"

"True crime. The experts say to write what you know, after all, and I come from a long line of criminals. I've always dreamed of something more, but it's the cycle of poverty, you know. Parents poor and uneducated, kids don't know anything different, it takes an awful lot of luck and resourcefulness to—"

"I hate to interrupt," Warren said. "But we are in a big hurry. We need to get out of the city before the King and Queen realize we're gone."

"Which direction you headed?" the thug asked.

"North," Julianna said.

The guy was silent for a moment, thinking something through. "Need a lift?" he finally asked.

"What?" Warren asked in disbelief.

"My mom lives northwest of the city," the goon explained. "If I take this money and run, Luann and Hector and all their friends will be on the lookout for me in the city. So I really should head to the country. And it's been ages since I've visited my mom, so that's where I'd go. Since we're both heading the same general direction, and since I owe you one for changing my life, how about you hitch a ride on my wagon?"

It was thus that Warren and Julianna found themselves in the back of the thug's wagon on their way out of the city, hiding under a stack of empty burlap bags.

CHAPTER THIRTY

The magical vial of raven blood had thought things couldn't get any worse when it had found itself all alone in a dark, dusty corner of the castle laundry room. But that was before it had been swept up, along with some lint and bits of thread, and tossed into a bin; thankfully, since it *was* the laundry room, the bin had been full of old clothes and linens. If the magical vial of raven blood had been in a dark, dusty corner of the blacksmith shop, for instance, it'd have been shattered for sure. But that was small comfort to the poor vial of blood as it was wheeled off by a brusque maid who was quietly complaining to a companion about how she hadn't been given the time off she'd requested to care for a sick grandchild.

The magical vial of raven blood did have some pity for the poor, sick grandchild and the overworked grandmother, but it was too preoccupied with its miserable circumstances to care very much. After all, it was off to the dump, for goodness sake! The *dump*! Of all places for a quality magical ingredient such as itself to end up! It contemplated breaking its way into the maid's mind in an attempt to see if she might be able to get it out of this predicament.

But this maid was not the best candidate; she had to work late, and then go take care of her grandchild, so she'd have no time to help the vial of blood. It took a gamble, and decided to bide its time, in hopes of finding a more helpful candidate.

A few minutes later, the bin was being wheeled outside, and dumped into the back of a waiting wagon. "Here's all the stuff from the laundry!" the maid announced. "You headed out now?"

"No," answered the driver of the trash wagon. "I'm waiting on the maintenance guy."

The wagon driver and the maid joked around for a bit about the lazy maintenance guy who was always running late, then the maid said, "See you later, Tony!" and wheeled the bin back into the castle.

The magical vial of raven blood whiled away some time listening to the driver sing a song under his breath about how lame unrequited love was. But the driver had a horrible singing voice, and the subject matter was beyond cliché, and soon the magical vial of raven blood was daydreaming, its mind wandering through the magical mists to see what Warren was up to.

It was hard to hear anything from within the vial in Warren's pocket since it was a bit muffled, but it sounded as though Warren was on a wagon, too. And, the Princess was with him, talking to someone the vial of blood was fairly sure it had never heard before. It did not hear Corrine's voice, and this was odd since Corrine always seemed to be inflicting her opinions on people. Had something happened to her? The magical vial of raven blood tried to get Warren's attention. *Bro*, it squawked into Warren's head.

No answer.

Hey, Warren! The vial of blood tried again.

It figured Warren must be sleeping. The magical vial of raven blood tried to hear what Julianna was saying to the mystery man, but no luck. Okay, not much was going on with Warren then. It shifted its consciousness briefly to the basin of blood in Farland's evil lair, but no one was home. So, it went back to where the action apparently was: the wagon full of trash.

The wagon driver was now talking to someone who was presumably the maintenance man. "Dude, try to stick to the schedule next time! I want to get to the dump by midnight."

"Take a chill pill, Tony," the guy answered. "There's more to life than work, man."

"I think that logic only applies when you're not *at work*, Luther," Tony countered.

Luther grumbled something.

"What was that?" Tony asked.

"You need to learn to have a little fun," Luther responded.

"Oh, I do, do I?" Tony asked. "I know what kind of *fun* you're talking about. The kind of fun where you plot against the very people who are paying your salary and putting a roof over your head."

"Shut *up*, man!" Luther hissed nervously. "You want to get me banished to the Forest?"

"Not particularly, but then I might end up with a more punctual coworker. That'd be pretty nice."

The magical vial of raven blood listened intently. This Luther character sounded pretty interesting. More interesting than Tony, anyway. Tony's implication that Luther was plotting against the King might very well mean that Luther had some ties to Farland. And the raven blood could use that to his advantage when trying to convince Luther to help. But how to get Luther to pick him up? It couldn't just pop into Luther's head and tell him to go rifling through the old laundry.

Instead, it broke into Luther's mind long enough to say, *Hey Luther! Watch this! I'm going to scare the daylights out of Tony!*

Luther gave a sort of yelp but didn't say anything. Silent panic was a fairly normal response, in the magical vial of raven blood's experience.

Then the magical vial of raven blood went out of Luther's head and into Tony's. *TONY!* It squawked as scarily as it could, all low and crackly and ominous. Poor Tony. But the vial of blood needed to get Tony out of the picture long enough to talk to Luther in private.

Tony gave an alarmed yell. "What the heck!" Tony was apparently not the silent panic type.

TONY! It croaked again. It couldn't think of anything to add for a moment, so there was an awkward pause, but then it finally came up with, *Beware the, um—beware the drive to the dump! Yeah. I am the voice of the future! And I say unto you, if you drive this wagon to the dump right now, you will be attacked by a hoard of thugs!*

"What—what—Luther, what are you doing? How are you doing that?" a frantic Tony cried. A sudden creaking of the wagon indicated that Tony might be on his feet, hopping about.

Luther's not doing anything, man. Look at him. He's just as confused as you are, the magical vial of raven blood pointed out, making the safe assumption that Luther was probably gaping up at Tony in consternation.

"But if Luther's not—I mean—what—?" Tony spluttered.

Don't worry. You're not going crazy or anything, man. Just don't drive to the dump right now, because if you do it'll totally be the death of you. For real. Go into the break room and lay down for about fifteen minutes. That should do it. By then, the thugs will have moved on.

Tony spluttered a bit more but didn't say anything. Probably he was realizing just how crazy he must look to Luther.

Seriously, man, go lay down or something, the magical vial of raven blood nagged.

Tony finally said shakily, "I'm going to go to the break room. Um, I'm not feeling well." There was a big creak and a thud. He'd jumped off the wagon.

"You okay, Tony?" asked Luther.

"Headache," Tony responded distractedly. "I've got a headache." He shuffled off, and moments later the raven blood heard a door open and then slam shut.

It let go of Tony's mind and swooped back into Luther's. This was getting exhausting. *Hi Luther,* it squawked.

"What is going on?" Luther hissed.

I just popped into Tony's head to scare him away from the wagon for a few minutes. I need your help.

"Am I losing my mind?" Luther mumbled.

Nope. I would have thought seeing Tony go all crazy and start talking to a voice in his head would have shown you that you're not the only one hearing things. This was always the toughest part of getting into a person's mind for the first time. There was no way of knowing how long it would take the subject to figure out they weren't crazy. The key was speaking calmly and presenting a logical argument.

"Um. True, but still—I mean, this is still really weird," Luther whispered.

Sorry I had to pop into your brain like this. Look, if you need further proof I'm real and not in your imagination, just dig through the trash from the laundry room. If you search around, you'll find a vial of blood. That's way too random to be anything your brain would have come up with out on its own, right?

"I guess…"

Okay, well then dig around! Carefully. But be quick. I need you to find it before Tony comes back.

The magical vial of raven blood heard some rustling. As Luther rummaged, he said, "Look, voice, I don't like this. At all. You've got no right—"

Suddenly, the towel the vial of blood was nestled in was tugged out of the wagon, and the vial flew out of the towel's folds and landed on a pillowcase. *Careful!* the magical vial of raven blood cawed.

Luther looked down at the vial. "Oh!" He picked it up gingerly. "Well, that's a relief. I'm not crazy."

See, I told you, said the magical vial of raven blood. *I'm the vial, by way, in case you're still confused. I'm a magical ingredient. Raven blood that has been enchanted.*

"Okay…" Big pause. "Why are you talking to me?"

I was hoping to find a person who could take me out of the castle. And I got the impression from overhearing your conversation with Tony that you're plotting to overthrow the King. Right?

"If I was, would I admit it to a disembodied voice?"

Okay, okay. Well, listen. I can help you if you want to overthrow the King. Farland Phelps created me. I know things. Its hope was that if it dropped Farland's name, Luther would think the vial of blood was on his side.

"The wizard?" asked Luther with shock. "The *evil* wizard?"

Yeah… the magical vial of raven blood answered. It didn't like Luther's tone.

"Well, if you're in cahoots with that guy, I'm gonna chuck you back in the trash," Luther responded.

What? But I thought—you're part of the group that wants to overthrow— It was the magical vial of raven blood's turn to stutter incoherently.

"My friends and I have nothing to do with that guy! He's bad!" Luther said. "It's not as though there's just one group of people who want to overthrow the King, vial of blood."

That was a good point. Why had the vial of blood been so silly as to assume anyone who wanted Conroy off the throne must be in cahoots with

Farland? Conroy was a bad enough ruler to have made just about every possible group of people in the kingdom mad at him. So, Luther was part of some *other* revolutionary group. One that didn't like Farland. Interesting. Were there good revolutionaries too, then? *Please don't throw me away. Please! I promise I'm not evil. Yes, I admit Farland made me. But that doesn't mean I agree with what he does. And even if I was evil, I can't do anything to you. All I can do on my own is talk. I can't do anything bad unless a wizard uses me in a bad potion!*

Luther scoffed. "Whatever. You *would* say that." Then he tossed the magical vial of raven blood back in the wagon.

Wait! it squawked. *Wait! Do you have a wizard among your number?*

A pause. "And if we do?"

If you do have a wizard, then give me to him! He'd know I'm not a threat! I could even help you! Please, please, please give me a chance.

There was silence. But the magical vial of raven blood was pretty sure Luther hadn't walked away.

Aw, come on! Give me a chance! I'm a really rare ingredient. Very hard to make. Your wizard would be so happy to get his hands on me!

There was a sigh, then the vial of blood was picked up once more. "Just don't talk to me anymore, you creepy thing," Luther said.

No problem, bro, the magical vial of raven blood agreed happily.

"Seriously. One more word and I smash you against the nearest wall. I don't care how great a magic ingredient you are."

The magical vial of raven blood kept its peace and hoped that the wizard it was being taken to wasn't a loser.

Chapter Thirty-One

About ten minutes outside of the city's walls (which were both a lot less impressive and a lot less protective than the castle walls), the thug said, "Okay, I think you guys are probably safe to come out of there now."

Warren had fallen asleep, but Julianna popped out, and joined the thug on the wagon's bench. "Thanks again for helping us out."

"Thanks again to you for all the money," he responded.

They lapsed into silence but for the clip-clop of the horses' hooves. Julianna looked around at what the light of the moons and stars allowed her to see of the outlying area of the city. Houses were more spread out, and some had gardens, but the houses themselves were even more ramshackle than the ones in the city. Suburbia in Fritillary was not where the rich folks moved to get away from the bustle of the city; it was where the poor folks lived because they didn't have enough money to pay for pricey city living. Another strike against living in the Fritillary suburbs, or suburbs of cities in general, was, of course, that unfriendly armies on the way to attack castles reached the outlying areas first, so the country and suburbs were the first to be pillaged.

"So, what's your name?" Julianna asked by way of a conversation starter.

He gave her a distrustful glance.

"Aww come on. You know *my* name already. It's only fair," she wheedled.

He gave a sigh. "Copernicus."

She didn't push for a last name. Instead she asked, "But your friends call you Copper?"

"You guessed it," he said, staring straight ahead at the road over the heads of his two black horses. He was deep in thought, imagining the new life that was unfolding before him. He wasn't in the mood to chat, but he couldn't very well ask the Princess to shut up.

After a long pause, she asked, "May *I* call you Copper?"

"No," he said distractedly, and then looked at her. "Am I allowed to say no? And also, should I be calling you Your Highness or something like that?"

"Just call me Jennifer. It's easier that way." More silence. "We're going to the Forest of Looming Death, by the way. You surely have a better idea of the geography, so you'll know better than I when would be a sensible time for us to part ways."

"What on *earth* are you going to the Forest of Looming Death for?" he asked; her words had finally gained his full attention.

"We need to rescue someone."

"You've got armies to do that for you, right?"

"The person we want to rescue is a commoner, and my dad doesn't want to send soldiers for her; he'd prefer they keep practicing their drills for the upcoming parade," she grumbled.

"But the guards at the Forest will be able to help you, yes?" Copernicus asked.

"Not a chance. They can't know we're there. Since Warren and I snuck out of the castle, my parents will be sending word all over the countryside to all their soldiers and guards and whatnot."

"Hmm." Copernicus lapsed into silence, weighing whether he wanted to get involved in this or not. He'd been looking forward to getting started on his life of peace and leisure and writing true crime novels, but he kept thinking of his brother and cousins who lived in the Forest; they might be able to help these two out.

After a while, there was a rustling from the back of the wagon that indicated Warren was waking up. Sure enough, a moment later, he popped his head out of the burlap sacks and said, "Where are we?"

"A bit outside the city walls. Soon we'll be in the countryside," Copernicus said.

"Cool."

Copernicus glanced at his passengers, and said to Warren in a fake casual voice, "So, hey, Jennifer tells me you two are going to the Forest of Looming Death." He felt much more comfortable talking to Warren than Julianna since Warren was, to the best of Copernicus's knowledge, an Average Joe like him.

"Yes, indeed."

"You know the Forest is jam packed with criminals?"

"Yep."

"You have any friends in there to help you?" Most citizens of Fritillary had at least one friend, relative, coworker, or neighbor who had been banished to The Forest.

"Nope."

"Okay. And also, the place is surrounded by a bunch of guards who you're hoping to avoid."

"We know."

"So…why are you even bothering with trying to rescue this person? You're going to fail."

"She's my sister. I have to try. Preferably succeed of course, but at the very least try."

Copernicus sighed again. He really, really didn't want to get involved. But they really, really needed help. They were downright pathetic. "Jennifer," he asked, "May I ask how you got mixed up in this, considering who you *really* are?"

"Well, Copernicus," Julianna answered, "I feel I owe Warren some help due to some past issues that I won't get into. And also," she said, staring off into the distance and getting all philosophical, "Recently, I've been gaining an understanding that the life I've lived thus far has been quite an empty life, see. Lately it has been occurring to me that what I really need in order to feel like my life has any meaning at all it to be of some use to someone."

"But what if you die?" Copernicus asked. "Because, from where I'm sitting, it sure looks like you're going to die."

"Well, that would be no good. Can't say it'd make me happy. But taking a risk in order to finally be *doing* something, now that is something I can say does make me happy. And besides, people die all the time. If I wasn't doing this, I might very well choke on my breakfast sausage tomorrow morning or crack my head on the edge of my bathtub, or something."

"But logically speaking," Copernicus carefully pointed out, "I think you'll find the odds are perhaps maybe less great of you dying eating breakfast or taking a bath than if you walk unprotected into a forest swarming with angry murderers."

"Copernicus," she said firmly, "My mind is made up. But thank you or your concern."

He shook his head disbelievingly. "May I just reiterate that you two are going to die?"

"You certainly may."

"You two are going to die."

Yet another uncomfortable silence descended. They all looked around at their surroundings. Houses were few and far between now, and the trees were beginning to get thicker. Not much was going on because it was the middle of the night. An owl flew by close overhead. A deer trotted out from the forest edge and gave them a blank stare. A trio of bandits hiding behind a fallen tree readied themselves to spring to the attack, only to change their minds when the moonlight shone on the symbol painted on the side of the wagon: an orange star inside an orange circle[28].

---

28   This symbol, which I had better explain to you since it keeps showing up in this tale, was the mark of the loose collective of smugglers and thieves and such that had formed as an outshoot of the general group of citizens who were resisting the Crown in one way or another. In early days, the symbol had been just an orange star, and it had been used mainly by rebel-type people who were against things like witch burning, excessive taxation, oppression, and soldiers breaking into homes at all hours of the day and night and taking whatever they fancied. The symbol just as an orange star with no circle still was used by those strait-laced types (for instance, the orange star on the key that Warren's mom had found at Jane's house, or the orange star on the box that Julianna had stolen from Mortimer). But then the more radicalized and increasingly violent offshoot had arisen and split from the main group, so in order to cut down on confusion they had all agreed that the goody-goodies would keep the orange star, while the ones who liked their rebellion violent added the circle on to the symbol. Thus ended a bunch of awkward situations where, for instance, people seeing an orange star on a door showed up at what they thought was a meeting about nonviolent resistance only to find themselves instead sitting in on a planning session for blowing up a bridge and raiding a caravan that was shipping weapons for soldiers.

Julianna heard a rustling from a nearby fallen tree and looked over at it but saw nothing. "Hey, Copernicus," she said. An idea had just occurred to her.

"Yeah?"

"Could Warren and I crash at your mom's place tomorrow? That is, if it isn't too far? I need to make sure I have some shelter before sunrise."

"Uh, sure. But it's kinda out of your way."

"I'm okay with that as long as she's got some place where no sunlight can reach me through the day."

Copernicus nodded. He knew what she was talking about because, like most citizens of Fritillary, he knew about her curse. "Ma does have a root cellar that's good and dark."

"That'd be perfect," Julianna said, feeling a lot more at ease now that she had a safe place on the horizon, and wouldn't have to spend the day huddled under the thick blanket she had packed in her bag. "So how far is she from here?"

"Fourish hours."

Julianna decided that this fourish hours was a perfect amount time to drill a genuine citizen about his ideas about how the country was being run, what was being done well, what was being done badly, etc. Copernicus grudgingly answered her questions, but Warren stayed out of the conversation because he was too busy worrying. Of course he was worried about Corrine, but now, in addition to that, he was also worried that Julianna was going to be spending the entirety of the coming day trapped in a root cellar at the home of the mother of a man who had, until a few hours earlier, been a member of the criminal element. What if Copernicus reverted to his old ways once he had been given a bit of time to think things through? Copernicus could very easily decide that taking Julianna for ransom was worth the risk after all. Being a criminal for his whole life, Copernicus's mind had to be pretty good at rationalizing the taking of stupid risks.

M EANWHILE BACK AT the cave, Corrine was busy pretending to be unconscious. Farland had initially tied her up and left her at the back of the cave, then gone to do some plotting with Mirabella. But Corrine had kept cutting in and asking questions and generally driving them crazy with all the interruptions. So, Farland had taken some sleeping potion out of his pack and tried his hardest to force her to swallow it; Corrine had pretended to drink it and pass out, but as soon as Farland had walked off she had spat out the majority of the potion onto the floor of the cave. A bit of it had made it down her throat, though, so she did genuinely lose consciousness for a bit, but after only about a half hour she was awake again, and intently eavesdropping on their plans.

Mirabella was saying, "So once we kidnap the Prince from his hunting party, we'll bring him back here, and I just watch the brat until you've found more permanent accommodations for him."

"Yep."

"The closer this plan comes to completion, the more annoyed I get about the fact that I'm going to have a child living here with me."

"I promise it won't be too bad," Farland responded. "It won't take me long to find a new place. There are some nice remote rental properties along the south shore. And as soon as I've found a good, solid fortress, I'll just pop back over here and take him with me. Then I'll get on with the brainwashing and the turning him against his family."

"Good. The sooner the better. How am I supposed to entertain a child? Even when I *was* a child, I found children irritating."

"Crafts, songs, puzzles, board games..." Farland suggested.

"More like B-O-R-E-D games," Mirabella muttered. "And there's no way I'm singing. I guess I could do some crafts with him...teach him to make paper or something."

Farland added, "And if he gets too annoying, we can always keep him knocked out with a spell like with this chick."

"Now that sounds like a good plan."

They continued to blather on about their plan for a while.

Corrine listened with horror. So this was the other plan that Farland was cooking up on his stovetop of revenge. He was going to kidnap Julianna's brother and brainwash him. Brainwash the future King. Corrine began to try to think of a way she might be able to escape and alert someone about this plot. But she was all tied up. Literally.

"It's going to be so nice to be the Royal Wizard again," Farland said with a sigh. "I wonder if my old evil lair is still as I left it."

"You make sure that once the Prince gives you back your position, you don't get so wrapped up with all your plans that you forget to un-banish me," Mirabella huffed. "I've spent more than enough of my life in this cave."

"Oh, fear not, Mirabella," Farland reassured her. "Getting you un-banished will be my first order of business." And he meant it. He was still crushing on her pretty severely and was hoping that she'd be so grateful to him for getting her out of the Forest of Looming Death that she might consent to go on a date with him. He gazed at her sappily and gave a sigh.

Mirabella saw, and narrowed her eyes. She had a good idea of what he was thinking and had no intention of playing along; if getting out of the Forest was in any way contingent on going along with his silly infatuation with her, she would sooner live the rest of her life in the cave.

"Okay, so that's that for *that* plan," she said briskly. "What about the other one? The one with that boy. And more precisely, when is this girl going to be out of my cave?"

Farland sighed and said, "I don't know. I was hoping to get to that after the Prince thing since that's the time-sensitive one. This one with the Princess's curse can *technically* wait if you can put up with the girl lying around here for a few more days."

"I guess I can wait," Mirabella growled. "It's just all the potty breaks. They're so time-consuming, and they require more logistical planning than you'd think."

"Just remind her how many murderers are roaming these woods. She'd be a moron to run away."

Listening in the shadows, Corrine had to agree he had a point. But then again, she'd *also* be a moron to stay in the cave. Which meant what? She had no clue. What that boiled down to was that she had to do some pretty intense brainstorming now because, if she was going to listen to the promptings of her conscience, she had to get out of this cave, and get word to someone about the fact that the Prince was in danger.

CHAPTER Thirty-two

Four-ish hours later, Copernicus, Julianna, and Warren pulled up in front of a little cottage on a hillside surrounded by pine trees. A dog that had been sleeping on the front porch heard the wagon and woke. It began to bark like crazy. Copernicus cried out happily, "Helio! I can't believe he's still alive!"

The dog ran up to the wagon and, as soon as it heard Copernicus say its name, its barks turned from fierce to jolly. Copernicus stopped the wagon and hopped down, kneeling in front of the dog and petting it while it slobbered all over his face in a way quite disgusting unless you are a dog person. Copernicus must have been a dog person.

The front door of the cottage opened, and an old lady hollered, "Who are you and what in the name of tarnation are you doing on my land in the middle of the night?"

"Ma!" said Copernicus, "It's me!"

"It's who?" she asked suspiciously. She had quite a few sons, and there were a handful of them who she would be less than thrilled to have pay her a visit in the middle of the night when she was home alone with nothing for protection but her kitchen knives and sassy retorts.

"Copernicus," he clarified, as he stood and walked over to her with Helio trotting along at his side.

She gave a relieved sigh, and said, "Oh, good. I'd heard rumors your brother Martin was in the neighborhood. Thought you might be him."

"Nope. Nor did I cross paths with him on the way here," he said, and hugged her hello.

"Copper, dear. It's been ages!" she exclaimed. "What have you been up to? Whatever it is, the pay's been good."

"Probably best if I don't tell you," he responded.

She nodded knowingly and gave him another hug[29]. He'd always been one of her favorites[30].

When she had raised her sons, she had tried hard to steer them away from mining and logging because they were both such dangerous professions. But unfortunately, since the family was poor, they had had no access to good schools; the school they attended was horrible; the teachers were too busy keeping students from knifing each other, starting bonfires with the tables and chairs, and rolling cigars with the textbook papers to do too much actual educating. So, with no options or education, the unforeseen consequence of steering her sons away from logging and mining was that they all fell into crime instead. But, as she told herself when she began to question her parenting decisions, at least her sons were all alive, which was more than most peasant parents in her circumstances could say of their kids who had chosen more conventional, legal channels to obtain their daily asparagus.

Warren and Julianna walked up beside Copernicus then, and Copernicus said in response to his mom's questioning look, "Ma, these are my friends, Warren and Jennifer. Warren and Jennifer, this is my Ma. Can they stay here

---

29   When Copernicus had taken a career assessment test in school and the results had come back (1) Criminal, (2) Club bouncer, and (3) Bodyguard, she had been unsurprised; when he had gone off to the big city in search of work, and had started mailing back hefty chunks of money, she had assumed he must have gone for option (1), but had never inquired via the mail, because one didn't put things like that in writing unless one wanted one's permanent mailing address to change to The Forest of Looming Death, or worse yet to The Graveyard. Not that you get mail when you're dead

30   She was the type of mom who had favorites, which generally is a cold and unnatural thing for one who is a practitioner of the Maternal Arts, but in her case, it was at least a tad forgivable considering that some of her kids were murderers.)

for the day? They'll leave at sunset."

"Fine by me," she said with a shrug as she surveyed them neutrally—until, that is, she caught sight of Warren's banjo case. "What's that you've got there?" she asked with interest.

"My banjo. You like music?" he asked enthusiastically.

"I sure do! Haven't had any music since a dance at the community center a few months back."

"I'll play for you if you like," Warren said.

"Looks like you've got a sling on that there arm, lad," she pointed out.

"Oh, yeah, it'll be okay. The doctor said I should do a bit of playing to keep the muscles all working right. High time I heeded her advice."

Copernicus's mom smiled, and said, "Come on in and let me get you all something to eat."

The travelers hadn't realized how hungry they were until she mentioned food. They walked into the little cottage and sat down at the table. As Copernicus's mom bustled around by the fireplace at the wall opposite the door, Julianna looked around with interest at what must be a fairly good representation of an abode of a country-dwelling commoner. It was one room with a little bed, a table, a spinning wheel, some clothes drying on a line across the ceiling, and a few chairs. There were plants and hunks of meat hanging from the ceiling. The whole place was lit only by the fireplace.

Julianna didn't know if she'd ever grow accustomed to observing the homes of poor people. She tried not to stare too blatantly, but when Copernicus's mom slapped some stale grayish bread, floppy asparagus, and mugs of smelly tea in front of them, Julianna couldn't control her gasp, or her look of shock.

"Well, Miss Citified Fancypants, if you don't like my food, you don't have to eat it," Copernicus's mom snapped.

Julianna cringed. "I'm sorry," she said, not knowing how to explain herself.

"Jennifer worked at the inn near the castle, Ma," Copernicus said. "The fanciest inn in the city. I'm sure she means no offence; she's never been outside the city until today."

Copernicus's mom just gave her a glare and stalked over to the fire. It was obvious no amount of talking would make the situation better. Julianna met Warren's eyes; he gave her a shrug and a half smile that somehow made her feel a little better.

Warren snapped open his banjo case and pulled it out, lovingly running his good hand along its strings before getting down to the business of tuning it.

Julianna fixed her eyes down on her plate, ate the stale bread and asparagus, and choked down the icky tea; she was very glad that shortly she would be excusing herself to go hide away in the root cellar. Hopefully the old lady wouldn't get too inquisitive about why Julianna had to be down there.

Everyone was very glad when Warren cut the awkward mood by starting in on a rollicking folk tune.

BY THE TIME the sun rose, Julianna was tucked safely away underground, taking a nap amongst Copernicus's mom's carrots, turnips, squashes, cabbages, potatoes, and a few dozen jars of what the labels informed Julianna was some prize-winning spiced peach preserves.

Warren would have loved to be sleeping as well, but he felt like he had to keep an eye on Copernicus and keep him talking so that Copernicus didn't change his mind about not kidnapping Julianna. So, Warren was helping Copernicus slop the hogs, who lived in a pen in the back yard behind a huge vegetable garden that was currently not producing too much because it was nearing winter. All that was growing was cauliflower and broccoli and kale and such—all those gross veggies that people only eat because of the antioxidants[31].

"So, um, Copernicus," Warren said carefully, eyeing his silent and thoughtful-looking companion. "Whatcha thinking about, buddy?" He winced at the word 'buddy' as soon as it was out of his mouth, but there was no helping it.

Copernicus wrinkled up his nose. "Buddy?"

"Er, sorry."

"Look, don't try to be my pal, okay? I don't want to get involved in whatever you guys are up to. As far as I'm concerned, once *Jennifer* is out of that root cellar and you two are on your way, I don't owe you anything else

---

31   In Fritillary they didn't know about antioxidants, but they still did eat things from the broccoli family because they were among the only plants that produced in cold weather.

and I can get on with my life. Dig it?"

"Yeah, sure, I dig it."

They slopped in silence for some time, then Copernicus said reluctantly, "You two really have no plan at all?" Try as he might, he just couldn't stop being concerned about them. "*Please* tell me you have some sort of plan and you just don't want to tell me about it."

"Nope. No plan."

"And this is all to rescue your sister?"

"Yes."

More silence.

"What's she like?" Copernicus inquired.

Warren looked suspiciously at Copernicus. "Why do you ask?"

Copernicus shrugged. It had just occurred to him that if she sounded like a nice, single sort of lady he might be more inclined to join in on this adventure. Up until this point in his life, he had not been moving in social circles that were conducive to finding a soul mate. "No reason. Just shooting the breeze. Chewing the fat."

Warren wasn't fooled, but it occurred to him that telling Copernicus about Corrine could be helpful; if he described her in a positive light and made Copernicus feel bad for her and her plight, he might be more inclined to keep his word and let them go on their way without any trouble. Guys were suckers for distressed damsels, after all. "She's a first-rate lady. Always there when I need her. I know I can count on her to help me whenever I need it." He got all broody for a few seconds, and said, "Actually it's that trait of hers that got her captured. The guy who took her had intended to take me instead, but then she pushed me out of the way of the guy's spell, and it got her instead of me."

"That was nice of her," Copernicus said.

"Yeah. That's the kind of person she is."

"Nice."

"Yep."

"She single?"

Warren bristled. But then he remembered his quest to make Corrine human to Copernicus. "Yeah, she's single. There was something going on a while back with the first mate of the pirate ship we lived on, but that ended badly. I'm sure she's done with him."

"Pirate, eh? So she's not adverse to dating guys on the wrong side of the law?"

"She's not too bothered about that sort of thing. Not a big respecter of authority. Though I'm sure she'd draw the line at murderers. To her, the most important thing for a long-lasting relationship is that the guy's kind and respectful."

Copernicus pondered. He'd never murdered anyone before. That was where *he* drew the line as well! What were the odds?! And he was kind and respectful. To ladies, anyway. And to dudes who didn't make him mad. "Pretty?"

"Oh, sure. She's plenty pretty. She's related to me, after all, and look at how dreamy I am."

Copernicus contemplated Warren's visage for a few moments and imagined him as a lady. "Yeah, I bet she is pretty."

Warren flashed him a smile, and said, "You know, she's a writer as well. Published writer." Ah ha! Yes, this would ensure that Copernicus would let them go. "You said that was your dream? I should introduce you to her once I've freed her. She does poetry and plays, not novels, but I'm sure she could give you some pointers and introduce you to some people in the biz."

Copernicus stared. "For real?"

"Oh yeah, Corrine's got connections in the literary world. She's a great playwright. And poet."

"Anything I might know?"

"Well her most famous play is *The Lady Who Tamed the Roguish Pirate*. And she's got a book of poems called *Wistful Musings from a Crow's Nest*."

Copernicus froze mid hog slop and stared at Warren in disbelief. He'd never heard of the play, but he had found *Wistful Musings from a Crow's Nest* in a suitcase in a carriage he'd once robbed. That night back in his team's hideout, he had curled up by the fireplace and read it from cover to cover while his friends had divided the spoils and partied around him. He'd barely even registered their mocking jokes when they'd realized he was reading poems. And, since that day, not a day had gone by that he hadn't cracked open the book and read a poem or two.

Copernicus wordlessly reached into his pocket, drew out his much-worn copy, and showed it to Warren.

Warren grinned at the sight of the book. *Perfect.* "I bet she'd sign that for you," was all he said.

Copernicus was in no state to respond. He was too busy thinking about the fact that, if all went well, he'd soon be meeting the lady who wrote those poems. *Those* poems. All revolving around the same general topic: she wanted to find love. True love. With the man of her dreams. Could he, Copernicus, a lowly ex-criminal and budding true crime author, begin to hope that he could be the man of her dreams? Heart all of a flutter, Copernicus grabbed the slop pail and walked back to the house, with Warren trailing a few steps behind, oblivious to the can of worms he'd just cracked open in Copernicus's heart.

CHAPTER THIRTY-THREE

Julianna was woken from a deep sleep by the sound of someone knocking on the door to the root cellar. She cleared her throat and yelled, "Yeah?"

"The sun's set!" Warren hollered down. "I'm going to open the doors, if that's cool with you."

"Go for it," she said and stood up, stretching. He opened the root cellar, and Julianna clambered out, and took a breath of the cold night air, which was quite refreshing after a day spent in a small dirt-walled underground room full of aging vegetables. "Let's get moving," she said without preamble. Wanting to cover as much ground as she could before sunrise, she was in no mood to fritter away what time they had with small talk about how their respective days had gone. "Did Copernicus tell you what direction we should be heading?"

"He's doing better than telling us; he's showing us."

"What's that now?"

"Copper said he'd take us. I guess he's even got some pals and relatives in the Forest who might be able to help us if he can get in touch with them."

"Wonderful!" she enthused. "And are we taking his wagon then?"

"Yes. He said we'll get there tonight easy as pie. Maybe in

just three hours or so."

"Awesome!" she said, though the closer they got to the Forest, the more nervous she got. But she didn't want to mention that to Warren and risk making him get worried too. She followed Warren from the root cellar behind the house to the front of the house where Copernicus was busily loading the wagon. "*Copper*, eh?" she then asked Warren a bit jealously.

"Yeah. We bonded today talking about Corrine. Apparently, he is a fan of her poetry. He's excited to meet her. That's why he's helping us out, actually."

"I didn't realize Corrine was a poet," she said with interest. "Anything I'd have heard of?"

"Probably, if you like poetry. Her compilation was a big deal about two years back. She made a ton of money. It was pretty awesome."

"What's the book called?"

By now they were at the wagon, and Copernicus supplied the answer eagerly, "*Wistful Musings from a Crow's Nest*. It's the best ever! I have a copy on me if you want to read it."

"Oh! I actually have read that!" she said with surprise. She'd gotten it as a gift from the son of some lord or other a while back and did not mention to either of the guys that she had found the poems to be way too sentimental and sappy, and some were, in her opinion, rather anti-feminist (not that she was judging; to each her own); she had not even been able to finish it. Julianna was surprised that Corrine, who could be so cranky and rude in person, had been the writer of those syrupy verses. Perhaps the poems were an attempt at irony that hadn't quite hit the mark? Or maybe Corrine had a super emotional side hidden deep, deep down?

"Good stuff, huh?" Copernicus asked.

"Oh, yeah, it sure was good," Julianna lied. She didn't want to insult the guy who was supplying them with a wagon for their journey. She was saved from elaborating on what specifically it was about the poems that was so great by the arrival of Copernicus's mom, who came out of the house to see them off.

Copernicus hopped down from the back of the wagon, where he'd been arranging boxes and barrels. "Thanks again, Ma."

"It was nice to see you again, dear," she said fondly. "Do you think you'll be coming back my way?"

"Oh sure. Once I'm done helping these two out, I was planning on coming back and visiting with you for a while."

"Lovely," she said with a smile, then handed him a basket of food. "Just some veggies and bread and some of my prize-winning spiced peach preserves," she said.

"Super. Thanks, Ma."

"Send Phil my love, will you? And your cousins."

"Will do." He took the basket, gave her a hug, and hopped up into the driver's seat. "Ready, guys?" he asked his passengers. He was no good at farewells and wanted to leave before his eyes got all teary. They nodded, and Copernicus took the reins and started the horses up.

"Who's Phil?" asked Warren.

Copper frowned and cleared his throat. "My brother."

Copper's frown told Warren quite clearly that this Phil was not a topic of conversation that Copper would like to chat about, but all the same, Warren couldn't hold back a few questions. "Is he one of your brothers?"

Copper gave a short nod.

"He's a prisoner in the Forest?"

Another short nod.

"Is he—"

Copper turned and gave Warren a glare.

"You don't want to talk about Phil."

"Clever lad."

Warren bit his lip and looked at Julianna, who was sitting in the back of the wagon, having opted to keep a bit of distance from the ex-thug who still wouldn't let her call him by his nickname.

She shrugged and rolled her eyes.

Warren decided to leave Copper to his brooding. He hopped off the front bench and went back to sit by Julianna. Within minutes, they were ensconced in a game of Twenty Questions.

THE FURTHER THEY went, the more nervous they all got. Consequently, they (even Copper!) got pretty chatty, since talking took their minds off what they were about to do. Warren and Julianna found themselves telling Copernicus all about Julianna's curse, and how Warren was supposed to be the guy who would break the spell. "Except," Julianna said, "I think something must be wrong with the spell."

"Why's that?" asked Copernicus.

"Well," Warren said, "For one thing, some sort of smoke or sparks always seems to accompany spells, and when we met there wasn't any of that stuff. Also, it seems like if the spell was working right, we would have fallen in love, or at least felt *something*, by now. But I haven't."

"And nor have I," Julianna agreed. "I'm starting to wonder whether maybe Farland was lying about the curse. Or he messed it up. But the only way of testing that theory is to put my life at risk. So that's not happening."

"Maybe you two just need to get to know each other a bit better," Copernicus said, trying to be helpful. "Talk about your hopes, your dreams, your fears, the deepest longings of your hearts. Relationship stuff."

Julianna and Warren exchanged skeptical glances.

"Yeah," Julianna said, "My mom said the same thing."

"Maybe it'll happen eventually? My Ma always told me you can't hurry love," Copernicus said sagely. "Nope, you just have to wait. It don't come easy."

"Again, my mother gave the same general advice," said Julianna. "But I maintain that Warren and I are not meant to be. We would have felt some connection by now. Feeling a connection with someone *can* happen pretty quick." The image of Mortimer floated into her mind then, and she sighed wistfully.

Warren nodded and said, "And there's no way I'm going to marry into royalty. No way."

Copernicus asked, "Why not? Seems like it'd be pretty cool."

"But you'd have to act all proper and learn about public policy and go to lots of meetings. And worry about how the decisions you make impact the entire population. And weigh the pros and cons of wars, and then *carry out* the actual wars when they became necessary and have all the deaths weighing on you. And do all sorts of other stuff that people who are born into that lifestyle are taught from day one."

"I guess…" Copernicus said doubtfully. He, like King Conroy, thought of being royal more in terms of having lots of money and power, and being able to do whatever you wanted without fear of consequences.

As Copernicus and Warren began to discuss politics, Julianna got quiet. An inconvenient thought had just occurred to her. In explaining why he didn't want to be royal, Warren had just made a good argument for why he might actually be good at it; his views about what royalty should be were spot on. Someone with those sorts of views was the kind of person who *should* be running things. Was she, in a way, being as selfish as her father? She was a princess after all, so shouldn't she be thinking about marriage in terms of what was best for the country, not what was best for her heart?

But, she reminded herself with relief, it wasn't as if the decision was hers alone, and Warren was even less inclined to get married than she was. This line of thinking was too troubling for her since she was already plenty troubled about their impending romp into a forest full of murderers, so she stuffed it away to the back of her brain for later. With a sigh, she directed her attention back to her traveling companions, for they were now talking about what to do once they got to the Forest.

"—no clue what we're going to do when we get there," Copernicus was saying unhelpfully.

"Yeah, I've got nothing either," was Warren's input.

"The only thing I can think of is that I need a disguise, so the guards don't recognize me," Julianna said. "But, aside from that, I don't think there's really much that we can plan. Corrine's got to be rescued, so we've got to try, but that doesn't mean we can plan for the unknowable."

"I guess so..." said Copernicus. "Anyway, as long as we've got money, getting in won't be too tough."

"It won't be tough as long as they don't look too close at me when we go in, that is," Julianna said.

"Which brings us back to finding a disguise for you," Warren said, grasping eagerly onto the only practical thing that they could accomplish at this point. "I learned a lot about applying theater makeup for the plays I did with my family, but I don't have a makeup kit on me. Um..." he said and looked around vaguely as though he expected to see something helpful hanging off a tree branch.

"We could do the ol' Disguise Her as a Dude trick; you might think it's a bit cliché, but it's only the disguises that work that stick long enough to *become* clichés," said the career criminal, who knew his business when it came to disguises.

Julianna shrugged. "Sounds good. All we need is some guy clothes."

Neither Warren nor Copernicus had packed a spare, because in those days travelers weren't as particular about having a fresh outfit for every day they were on the road. For one thing, clothes were expensive, and harder to come by in Fritillary than they were for you and me, because their garment industry was a long way from developing big factories with huge machines operated by grossly underpaid, overworked employees, thus supplying cheap and disposable clothing for the masses. For another thing, it was best in Fritillary to travel in dirty old clothes because it made you look like less of a target for highwaymen.

"We could steal something off a clothesline," Copernicus suggested.

Julianna didn't much like the sound of that, but it didn't seem there was any other option, so every time they passed a house, they kept their eyes peeled for a clothesline.

I T WAS THUS that, about an hour later, a wagon carrying what looked like three dudes approached the Forest of Looming Death. But it wasn't really three dudes at all, but two dudes and Julianna. They rode across the wide, treeless expanse that ran around the perimeter of the Forest; the treeless space was there so the guards could easily spot any prisoners running away.

Pretty quickly they attracted the attention of the guards, who stood in pairs at regular intervals around the Forest. Little bonfires and folding chairs marked their stations. There was a flurry of excited talking amongst them at the sight of the wagon; their job was exceptionally boring for the most part, since prisoners so rarely tried to escape, and even when they *did* try they never did it in groups[32]. While it was important for the guards to be there, their mere presence meant that there was nothing to do, so for the most part they just killed time doing target practice and bird watching (and often both at the same time); they also played some epic games of Telephone that

---

32   No one in The Forest trusted anyone much since about ten percent of the prisoner population was really spies planted there by the army in order to watch out for uprisings and deal with them before they became a problem.

stretched around the entire perimeter of the Forest[33].

"Ooh, it looks like the wagon's coming toward *us*!" a guard named Murray said to his partner Clive.

"I think you're right! Awesome!" said Clive excitedly, pocketing his bird identification booklet and watching the wagon as it rolled toward them. "What do you think they want?"

Too excited to wait to find out, Murray started to trot out to meet the wagon.

"Why's that guard running at us?" Julianna whispered, gripping Warren's wrist.

"I dunno. Don't panic," said Warren, looking down at her hand.

"Hey!" yelled Murray as he trotted up to them.

Copernicus halted the horses and looked down at the guard.

"What brings you to the Forest of Looming Death?" asked Murray. "Do you have any news from the Capital?"

"If it's all the same to you, we'd rather keep the particulars of our business to ourselves. And no, we don't have any news. Not much going on in the Capital except that the Royal Family and all the lords and ladies are getting all excited about the Prince's first hunt."

"You guys haven't gotten news in a while?" asked Warren casually. They might not even know yet that Julianna had run off.

"Nope. No one really bothers with us out here unless they've got a prisoner to deliver. Or if, in theory, we send a signal for help via yon signal beacon," he said, waving a hand toward what looked like a big torch sitting out in the middle of the treeless expanse. "I'm not sure how to use it, but I think you can send a message to folks on the outside, letting them know what kind of help we need if we run up against some trouble."

"You don't know how to use your signal beacon?" Warren asked, eyebrows raised. "That doesn't seem safe."

"Oh I'm sure *someone* here knows how," Murray said with a shrug. "And there's a manual for it too, back at HQ. They showed us how it worked in training, and as I recall, it wasn't too tough." It had been so long since the

---

33   Though of course they didn't call it Telephone. They called it Pass the Phrase Along and See How Messed Up It Gets.

signal beacon had been needed that most of the current guards had only used it for training exercises when they first started the job.

Julianna listened with displeasure. The guys who were in charge of containing the land's worst criminals seemed kind of incompetent. She would have said something to Murray about it, but her fake guy voice was pretty awful, and she didn't want to speak with it unless she had to.

"Hop on up," Copernicus said then to Murray. "We can chat as we drive."

"Thanks," Murry said and hopped onto the seat beside Copernicus. "So you three are going into the Forest?"

"Yep," said Copernicus.

"Dangerous business, lads."

"We know."

"You may die."

"Yeah."

"Even if you survive, you'll have a tough time getting out again. Even if you come out my way again, I can't guarantee I'll recognize you." There were no photo IDs or other surefire ways of identifying people in Fritillary. The guards hated the headache of trying to ascertain whether the beaten and bloodied people leaving the Forest were really the neat and tidy visitors they'd let in, or whether they were criminals with stolen visitor passes.

"Is that an oblique request for a bribe?" asked Copernicus.

"Nope. It's the truth. People get beat up in there; they get messy. You very well may look unrecognizable coming out of the Forest. However, on the subject of bribes, I do definitely accept them. Pay up and we'll let you in without any trouble. Pay a bit more and we can send you in with a sack lunch."

"Hmm. How much for a bribe and three sack lunches?" asked Warren. Julianna needed to find a dark hiding place fairly soon, so they couldn't waste time haggling. Plus, every minute his sister was imprisoned was one minute too long.

"*Three* bribes and three sack lunches, you mean. One bribe for each of you," Murray said apologetically. They reached the edge of the Forest and halted by Clive, who was waiting expectantly to see what was going on. Clive had been joined by two other guards, one from the guard station to their left, and one from the guard station to their right.

"Could we work out a package deal?" Copernicus asked.

"What do you think, Clive?" Murray asked. "Can we give them a three-for-the-price-of-two?"

"Eh, sure, what the heck," Clive said. "But they pay for all three lunches." There were murmurs and nods of agreement from the other guards.

"You lads know your odds of getting out of there alive are about 50/50, right?" asked one of the guards, an old guy with a long, matted beard.

"Unfortunately, we've got no choice," Warren said. "Or at least, *I* have no choice." Which reminded him that this was the part of the journey where he was obligated to ask his companions whether they wanted to change their minds about going into the Forest. He looked at Julianna and Copernicus. "You guys know you don't have to come with me, right? No hard feelings if you're having second thoughts." He held his breath then, hoping like crazy that they wouldn't chicken out.

"I'm going with you," Copernicus said. He was too starstruck about Corrine, and too excited at the thought of being part of her rescue party, to even contemplate not going. "You need me; I have a brother and some cousins and friends in there."

"I'm in," Julianna said shortly.

"Oh good," Warren sighed with relief. "Because that place looks scary." He glanced into the dark trees and wondered how many criminals were at this very moment watching and listening to them.

CHAPTER THIRTY-FOUR

Julianna paid up for two bribes and three sack lunches, and the old guard with the matted beard scampered off to get the lunches from their HQ. Initially, our heroes hadn't wanted to waste time waiting for their lunches to be brought to them, but the guards had told them there was some essential information they needed to impart to them.

"Where are you headed in there?" asked Murray as they waited.

"Our end goal is the cave where Mirabella the Traitor lives," said Warren.

"Whoa!" Clive said, then gave a low whistle. "She's one of our most famous prisoners! How'd you get mixed up with her?"

"Again," Copernicus said, "I must say we'd rather keep that information to ourselves."

"Sure. If *she's* involved, I probably don't want to know the particulars anyway," Clive said. "You know how to find her?"

"Nope. Could you point us in the right direction?"

"Well we've never actually been *in* there, but I believe it's pretty much in the center of the Forest. Right?" He looked at Murray for confirmation.

"Yeah. I think so. You said you had family in the Forest?" Murray then asked Copernicus.

"Yup. My brother Phil. Phil Barton. And some cousins and friends."

Murray made the three travelers jump when, without warning, he barked into the trees, "Hey! Art! You in there?" He then squinted into the shades of the Forest, waiting. Everyone else stared in the same general direction. Murray explained, "There's always someone hiding in there spying on us. This time of night it's usually Art."

After a few moments, a scrawny guy with filthy clothes ambled out from behind a big tree trunk and said with annoyance, "Yeah, what you want?"

"These guys are looking for a Phil Barton. You know him?"

"Maybe."

"Oh, of course," Murray said. "Money." He looked at Julianna, since she was the one who'd paid the bribe. "Have any money for him?"

She nodded and reached into her bag, then pulled out a silver coin and showed it to Art, whose eyes widened in amazement.

"You bring Phil back here and you can have it," Copernicus said. "Do it fast and you can have more."

Art scampered off without a word.

Clive turned to them then, and said, "You guys have a lot of money? That's the number one most important thing for going into the Forest. The best advice I can give you is to have tons of money."

"I think we're pretty well prepared in that regard," Warren said cautiously, not wanting to admit to having tons of money and fancy jewelry.

"Good. That'll be helpful. Most of the guys in there have come to the realization that if they kill a visitor and take all his money, that will just make them a huge target for all the other prisoners. As long as you have enough money to appease anyone who crosses paths with you, you might manage all right. You'll get attacked plenty, but not killed as long as you pay them off."

Warren tried to appear brave as he asked, "Any other concerns?"

"The crazy prisoners are a bit of a problem. They'll attack you for nothing. And there's gang stuff. You're going to need a guide in there, and the prisoners are all in some gang or other, so you'll probably end up in a few fights with your guide's rival gangs." He looked at Murray. "Anything else?"

"Just stumbling into traps and getting lost. But, if you have a good guide, that shouldn't be too much of a problem."

At this point, the old guard came trotting back with three sack lunches. "Here you lads go."

"Great. Thanks," Warren said and grabbed the lunches and some visitor passes from the old guard with the matted beard. "And thanks for the advice."

"No problem," said Clive. "Best of luck in there."

"Can we leave the wagon here?" asked Copernicus. "I've got some supplies I wanted to leave with my relatives."

"Sure thing. Take care of your business in there, and then if you manage to come out alive, we'll help you get the supplies dispersed," said Murray.

A few minutes later, Art appeared with a guy who must be Phil, because the guy's eyes lit up and he cried, "Copper! What are you doing here?"

Copernicus looked at the ground. "We can explain as we walk."

Art extended his hand expectantly, and Julianna gave him the silver coin and another smaller one, muttering a quick thank you. Art grabbed the money and disappeared into the trees without a word.

They watched him go and then, without further ado, the travelers squashed down their fears and stepped into the Forest of Looming Death.

The guards watched them until they disappeared into the black shadows. "Should we have told that lady how bad her disguise was?" Murray asked with concern as he turned to poke at the fire.

"Naw, they'll probably figure it out soon enough. If we told them, they'd just fret," Clive said with a wave of his hand as he sat down in one of the folding chairs and pulled his bird ID book out of his pocket, starting to read by the light of the fire.

THE FIRST ORDER of business was, of course, telling Phil that they needed a place where no sunlight could get in. Sunrise was only an hour off.

Phil was, of course, curious about this, but Copernicus just told him not to ask questions.

Phil, who also seemed a little confused about his brother's cold behavior, didn't push the issue, and merely said, "Well my gang's got a lot of traps dug in the ground. We cover them up with branches and leaves and stuff. It'll be pretty dark under them. Especially since the forest canopy is already blocking so much sunlight."

Copernicus looked questioningly at Julianna. She nodded, and he said to Phil, "Sounds good. Lead the way."

Warren looked from Copper to Phil. There was a thick cloud of awkwardness hovering around the two brothers. Obviously, there was some unresolved issue between them. Warren cleared his throat and said, "So, um, Phil?"

"Yeah?" Phil asked, looking back at Warren.

"Can you take us to the cave where Mirabella the Traitor lives?"

Phil raised his eyebrows, looking every bit as impressed as Clive had been. "Yeah I can take you there. But there's no way I'm going near that lady." Then he asked Copernicus, "How'd you get mixed up with Mirabella?"

"I didn't," Copernicus said. "They did. I'm just helping them out."

"Then how'd *you guys* get mixed up with her?" Phil asked, directing his question toward Warren since the lady disguised badly as a guy didn't seem too inclined to speak.

"I'm not too sure, actually," Warren said. "My sister got kidnapped by an evil wizard, and he apparently brought her to Mirabella's cave. No idea why. The wizard and Mirabella must be pals."

Warren kept Phil engaged in small talk for a while because he didn't like the uncomfortable cloud that descended on them when everything was quiet; the air was thick with things that the brothers wanted to say to each other but were keeping bottled up.

After about a half hour, just when Julianna was starting to get pretty anxious about sunrise, Phil informed them that they'd reached the pit in the ground where she was going to be spending the day. "Careful there. Don't walk past that big branch or you'll fall right in," he warned.

They all looked at the ground with amazement. They couldn't see anything; it looked just like the ground all around it.

"You ready to go down there?" Phil asked Julianna.

She muttered, "Just a minute." She reached into her bag and gave Warren her money, since he would likely need it more than her. Then she whispered to him, "What are your plans while I'm down there?"

"Just spy a bit at the cave and see if I can manage to formulate a plan once I've actually seen the place. After that, I plan to sleep if I can. Then once the sun sets, we rescue Corrine. I don't know how we'll do it yet, but by tonight I'll have an idea."

She nodded. "Good luck."

"Thanks. We'll make sure one of us is always watching your hiding place through the day." He gave her a weak smile; he was feeling nervous and didn't like the idea of being separated from her in this forest. "Watch my banjo for me?"

She nodded again, and whispered, "It'll all turn out fine. Don't worry." She didn't know if she really believed that, but she felt it was the right thing to say, even though he probably didn't believe it either. Then she took the banjo and signaled to Phil that she was ready to hide. He moved aside a few branches, revealing a dark hole in the ground. Then he went to a nearby tree, reached into a hole near its base, and pulled out a rope which he then tossed over the edge of the pit.

"It's not too deep, but you'll definitely need the rope," he explained to Julianna. Wordlessly, she climbed down, hoping that this would be the last time on this journey that circumstances would necessitate her going into a creepy, dark space. If she'd known when she'd ventured out of her tunnel for the first time that she'd end up in just a few days' time hiding in a hole in the ground in a forest full of murderers, and would soon be helping someone rescue his sister from Farland and her aunt Mirabella, she might very well have just stayed put in the castle. Maybe.

"So," Julianna whispered to Dexter. "What do you think of all this?" She pulled out her thick blanket to hide under just in case sunlight did seep through the top of the trap.

"Oh, I see you're talking to me now?" he huffed.

She sighed, "You *know* I can't talk to you around living people."

"I know, I know. It's just been so stressful seeing you do so much dangerous stuff and not be able to talk to you about it."

"Well, talk to me now," she said as she gingerly felt around in the dirt for a place that felt safe to sit down. "I've got nothing to do for the rest of the day, and I'm not tired yet."

As they chatted, she got out Mortimer's silver box with the orange star and ran her fingers over it as she daydreamed about its owner.

C OPERNICUS WAS MORE than happy to stay back and hang out by Julianna's hiding place, because that meant he didn't have to be near his brother. He'd been afraid seeing Phil again would be awkward, and his worst fears had been exceeded, mostly thanks to his own unease. But what else can you expect when, after a decade, you come face-to-face with the brother who has taken the blame (and been imprisoned) for a crime you were accused of?

Yes, back when Copernicus was just a little thirteen-year-old thug-in-training, one of his rivals had framed him for murder. Phil had found out, and had done the brotherly thing: he had said he, Phil, had committed the crime, his rationale being that Copernicus had dreams of becoming a great writer, while he himself had no dreams at all to speak of, except his aspiration to pick twenty pockets in a single night. At the trial, he had pulled a tearful Copernicus aside before being hauled off to the Forest of Looming Death and had given him a very moving speech about how Copernicus had to follow his dreams and become the brother who made something of himself.

Afterwards, Copernicus had been super inspired for about a week, but then he had run out of money for paper and quills and ink, and he'd fallen back on making money the only way he knew how—crime. He told himself that staying submerged in the life o' crime was good research for his true crime novels he intended to write, but eventually he got so busy with work that he found himself writing less and less until one day it hit him that he hadn't picked up a quill for two months straight.

And now that he was in the Forest with Phil, Phil was sooner or later going to ask about how the writing was going. And Copernicus was going to have to break it to Phil that he'd sacrificed his freedom for jack squat.

Copernicus leaned dejectedly against a tree and sighed, then did what he usually did when he was feeling blue: pulled out his book of poetry.

Chapter Thirty-Five

Phil and Warren had been walking about twenty minutes before they got attacked the first time. Warren was pushing aside a big fern that was in his way, when a guy jumped down from a tree branch above his head and punched him in the nose before Warren even had a chance to react. Warren stumbled back a few paces, cursing. How were his dreams of being an actor ever going to be realized if some ruffian damaged his face? Dudes didn't get lead roles unless their faces were symmetrical. Secondarily, he was also mad because the punch had hurt like crazy. Warren tasted blood in his mouth. "Not cool!" he yelled and dodged away just in time to miss an elbow to the throat. He backed up a few more paces to buy himself some time to feel his nose; yes, it seemed as symmetrical as ever.

To his left, he caught a glimpse of Phil knocking a second ruffian to the ground with a solid kick to the stomach. Phil, at least, seemed to know what he was doing; all Warren knew about fighting was stage fighting with cardboard swords and choreographed punches and dodges.

Warren was just psyching himself up to try a bit of real fighting (and wishing he'd taken Captain McManlyman up on his offer to teach Warren personal defense) when he saw his opponent pull a rusty-looking knife from a sheath at his side. "Oh *heck* no!"

Warren said in disbelief. This thing was getting way too real, way too fast. First fists, now knives! He screeched, "Put that thing *away!*" Tetanus is never a laughing matter, but it was especially not a laughing matter in Fritillary where tetanus shots did not exist.

The guy looked at him quizzically for a few moments—he had never in all his time in the Forest run up against such a wimp. Then he lunged at Warren with his rusty blade, and Warren dodged to the side again, crying out in fear and frustration at these irrational savages who stabbed first and asked questions later, which is a silly order of operations indeed.

"Hey!" Warren yelled. "Seriously, cut it out! We've got money!"

The guy wavered in his assault. "How much?"

"Six gold pieces. Three for each of you." Warren looked from one of the criminals to the other and let himself relax a little since they were no longer actively attacking. "Why the heck don't you guys ask about money *before* attacking? It makes more sense that way."

"We'd lose the element of surprise," pointed out his opponent, then he added, "Four gold pieces for each of us and we'll let you go on your way."

"Sure, it's a deal," Warren agreed. He then paid them off and said, "There. Now you can buy yourself a shiny new dagger and get rid of that rusty old thing."

The guy wasn't listening to Warren's advice though. He was peering into the pouch of money that Warren was holding and hadn't quite shut all the way after paying them. He caught a glimpse of gold, silver, and even some jewels, before Warren realized he was staring and pulled the drawstring closed.

The guy's greedy eyes clearly showed he wanted to snatch the pouch of money. But the thing about the Forest was that there were always spies lurking, and there was a good chance that, if he took that pouch of money, word would spread very fast; then he'd just end up dead with all his newfound wealth dispersed amongst his killers. No, it was best in the Forest of Looming Death if you just took your fair share from the visitors and let them go on their way to be mugged by the next band of criminals in line[34].

---

34   A neat thing that sometimes happens when a small population lives in a confined area cut off from the population at large is that they work out an equilibrium that works best for all the residents a lot faster than big populations in unconfined spaces do. That's in

Phil brushed himself off and nodded to Warren. "Not much of a fighter, eh?"

"Nope. I have some pacifistic leanings, but mostly I just hate getting hurt."

"Fair enough. Hopefully your money will hold out long enough that that won't be a problem for you."

"You said it," Warren agreed. They walked on toward the cave. "So, are you Copper's older or younger brother?"

"Older by two years," Phil said as he stopped to look around and get his bearings. They needed to wade across the Brook of Dashed Hopes, and he wanted to make sure they did it in a shallow, rocky place, otherwise they were going to get their feet all wet, which is big no-no for those who live outdoors.

"And you haven't seen each other in how many years?" Warren asked. He wanted to get to the bottom of the awkwardness between the brothers but didn't want to inquire too directly since it might make Phil mad.

"Ten years," Phil said, and began to walk again, shifting course slightly and going a bit more north.

"Nice to see him again after all this time?"

"Yeah. Sure," Phil responded. It sounded like he was starting to get a little cranky about the questioning. Warren was ready to lay off, but then, after about a minute, Phil said with a sigh, "At least I would have *thought* it'd be nice to see him again. But—" he said and paused for a long time, lost in thought. "But Copper's acting weird. And I don't know why."

Warren thought for a bit. "Did you guys part on good terms?"

"I thought so, but I guess something must have happened between now and then. Someone must have told him something about me that made him mad, or something?" Phil was glad that at this point they got to the Brook of Dashed Hopes and had to give all their attention to navigating the slippery

---

part why so many small island populations are so peaceful; they figured out how to live in harmony ages ago because they had to, whereas mainland folks still haven't worked it out over the entire span of human existence. When you've got nowhere to run to, you are nicer to your neighbors. Thus it was that, shut off from the rest of Fritillary, even the criminals in The Forest of Looming Death could manage to live without killing each other off. And thus it also was that visitors managed sometimes to go into The Forest, have a visit, and depart un-murdered (though much, much poorer).

rocks without twisting their ankles or falling into the water. Part of him felt he needed to talk about this thing with Copernicus, but most of him was not into talking about feelings; he'd never in his life been one to acknowledge emotions as legitimate things, and a decade in the Forest of Looming Death had done nothing to get him more in touch with his softer side, since even his closest murderer pals weren't the types to have heart-to-hearts[35].

It was when Warren and Phil were halfway across the Brook of Dashed Hopes that they were attacked for the second time. This time, some guys on either side of the brook hopped out from behind trees and started pelting them with rocks. Unfortunately, their aim was pretty good. Weapons were in short supply in the Forest, so some of the residents had to resort to sticks and stones in order to break folks' bones. Since there weren't many ways to entertain yourself in the Forest, those whose weapon of choice was rocks killed a lot of time (and targets) doing target practice.

Before Warren even knew what was going on, Phil began dodging the rocks and moving toward one of the assailants.

In no time flat, Warren had caught a projectile to the back of the head, slipped on a wet rock, and fallen flat into the brook. Everything went black for a flash, but in a few seconds, he was awake again, on his side, gasping and spluttering, his head nearly submerged in the rushing water. Also, he was still being pelted by rocks. He brought his arms protectively around his head and tried to notify the aggressors that he had more than enough coin with which to pacify them, but he was so busy coughing that words wouldn't come.

Fortunately, in addition to dodging, leaping, warding off flying rocks, and fighting, Phil was also explaining to the attackers that Warren was strapped with cash and willing to pay them off. So, after just a few more seconds of coughing and slipping about in the brook and bumbling blindly around in a pointless quest to avoid being hit by rocks, Warren became

---

35   The general thought the criminals had about such things can be summed up in this equation: Heart-to-hearts = weakness = someone who isn't man enough to be a reliable cog in the workings of a worthwhile gang. And if you weren't in one of the worthwhile gangs, you were a sitting duck. Or, rather, Sitting Duck; The Sitting Ducks was the unofficial name that the cool criminals had for the group of losers who no one wanted in their gangs. The outcasts were all forced, out of necessity, to band together into one pathetic gang full of weaklings, half-wits, and guys who talked too much about emotions.

aware that the assault had ceased, and that Phil was speaking. "Come on over here, Warren," Phil said, "and pay these guys off."

Warren cautiously lowered his arms and looked around. When he saw all the hoodlums gathered around Phil looking at him expectantly, he grinned and said, "Thanks, Phil!" Then he made his way carefully to the shore and reached into his bag to obtain the money pouch with one hand while examining a painful head wound with the other hand. Once again, he was happy no harm had come to his face.

"No problem, Warren," Phil said as he watched his pitiful companion picking his way across the brook. When Warren joined him, Phil told the attackers, "We gave the last guys four gold pieces each. So that's what we're giving you."

After some obligatory squabbling so none of them would feel like they'd come off as pushovers, they all settled on four gold pieces per attacker since no one wanted word getting around that Warren was being inconstant in his payoffs; things could get ugly pretty quick for both the givers and receivers if Warren gave more to some and less to others.

Warren helped them pick up a few of their rocks, then he and Phil went on their way.

After a few silent minutes, Warren asked, "Hey, is this bleeding like crazy? Like, should I be concerned?" He indicated the wound on the back of his head; it was so bad he could feel the blood oozing down his neck.

Phil just gave it a glance. "Eh, head wounds always bleed tons. Let me know if you start to get dizzy."

Warren bit his lip; he didn't care for Phil's offhand manner when the back of his head was being soaked in blood. But even though he already did feel dizzy, he was hesitant to mention it since Phil already obviously considered him a coward. Warren wanted Phil to retain what little good opinion he might have of him.

On they trudged for a while. They got attacked a few times, but it was just more of the same so we needn't clutter up the story by detailing more little squabbles.

The next landmark on the way to Mirabella's cave was the Bridge of Misery, where they, of course, had to pay an exorbitant toll to a big, burly bridge keeper. To add injury to insult, once they had gotten across the bridge they were yet again attacked by more thugs. But eventually, after about two hours of toiling through the Forest, they found themselves crouching behind a raspberry bush at the edge of the clearing that surrounded the cave Mirabella called home.

Upon finding himself this close, Warren was finding it difficult to refrain from running right up and trying to free his sister then and there. But that was stupid. So, they cased the joint. Which meant they stared and stared at the cave, waiting for something to happen.

Eventually, it got so boring that they decided they'd take turns, one person casing the joint while the other person got to daydream and stare about idly and eat raspberries. It was Warren's turn to stare at the cave when something finally happened; he was looking at the ghastly scarecrow that graced the center of her vegetable garden when Mirabella herself walked out of the cave, then said something over her shoulder to someone in the cave, and began to weed the garden. (Warren knew it was Mirabella because she looked pretty much exactly like her twin sister The Queen).

Warren said, "Psst!" to Phil, and elbowed him in the ribs.

"I'm already looking!" Phil snapped.

"It's her! Mirabella!"

"I know, Captain Obvious," muttered Phil.

Warren gave Phil a sidelong glance. He made a mental note to try not to be too much of a bother to his guide, but there was no helping the fact that he and this hardened thug just weren't going to connect. "Sorry," Warren said. "You're the pro. What do you think we should do?"

"Just wait and watch," Phil said. "And if we don't observe anything helpful after a while, we'll just come back tonight with lots of weapons and hope for the best. Maybe some of the fellas from my gang will want to come along—it's been pretty boring around here lately."

Warren was taken aback. "Oh. You don't have to—I'm not expecting—"

"Nonsense," Phil said. "All I do day in and day out is risk my life. This is no different from any other day."

"But—"

"Seriously. It's fine."

"But—"

"Shut up. Watch." Phil nodded his head toward Mirabella.

Warren nodded. They could talk about this later. He held the sleeve of his good arm to the wound on the back of his head and applied pressure as he watched Mirabella.

Mirabella puttered around in the garden for a looooong time, then suddenly she sighed, stood up, and yelled into the cave, "*What* do you *want?*"

Some incomprehensible words echoed from the cave, too quiet and jumbled to be understood, but Warren knew it was Corrine.

"Hold on!" Mirabella yelled. "Just hold *on* a second!" Then she tossed a handful of weeds back onto the ground and stalked back to the cave, grumbling under her breath. A minute later, she came back out again leading Corrine, who appeared to have her hands bound in front of her and did not look happy. Nor did Mirabella. It was impossible to tell which woman was angrier as they glared at each other with loathing.

Warren jolted forward as though he was about to rush out into the clearing, but Phil put a hand on his arm and stopped him.

Mirabella said, "Go on. Be back in four minutes. If you run away, I will find you. And, yes, Farland wants you in one piece and unharmed, but frankly I don't much care—if you give me trouble, I won't be bothered about adhering to my promises to him as regards your wellbeing."

Corrine said, "Whatever. I just have to pee. Why would I go running off into a forest full of criminals? I'm not an idiot."

Mirabella made scoffing sound that indicated her disagreement, then she waved a hand toward the trees and said, "Time's a'wastin'."

Corrine jogged off toward the trees. Phil stood quickly and, crouching low, followed her from the tree line. Once Warren realized what was going on, he followed too. They caught up to her just as she had walked a few paces into the trees. Her eyes hadn't adjusted yet to the shade, so she wasn't aware of Warren and Phil hiding behind two trees a few feet away from her. "Corrine!" Warren whispered.

She jumped at the sound and looked like she was about to dart back to the cave, but then she froze and squinted into the dark in Warren's direction. "Warren?" she asked, eyes wide.

"Yup, it's me," Warren whispered. He stepped out from behind the tree and hurried over to her.

She flew at him, wrapped her arms around him.

At the impact, Warren felt a jolt of pain, but he suppressed a gasp since he didn't want to worry her.

Corrine whispered, "I was afraid you were dead! They wouldn't tell me—"

Phil popped out from behind his tree and said without any explanation or introduction, "We don't have time for chitchat, kids. Look, we're here to rescue you. We're coming back tonight. Two hours past sunset. Tell Mirabella you need to leave the cave again. Go to the tree line to the left of the cave. We'll be waiting."

Corrine stared at him for a few moments then asked, "Who are you?"

"Explanations later," Phil said. "Warren, let's move."

Warren reluctantly let go of his sister. The last thing he wanted to do was leave her now that he'd found her, but night was a much better time for an escape mission. "I hate letting you go back in there," he said to Corrine. "Will you be ok?"

"Oh, sure," she said in an amazingly offhand manner considering that she was a hostage to a soulless villain. "She's pretty angry she has to watch me for Farland, and she wants me gone as soon as possible, but she's not going to do anything to me."

"Unless you're not back there in about a minute," Phil reminded her.

"Right," she said. "And I have to pee. So you guys go away." She was pretty stunned to find her brother in the Forest of Looming Death, but when a person has to pee a person has to pee, so she waved him on his way, and he and Phil scuttled off.

After a few minutes of running, Warren asked Phil, "So *that's* the plan? We just go meet up with Corrine two hours after sunset and we run? With a measly little four-minute start?"

"Essentially," Phil conceded as he jogged along.

Warren sighed and stumbled along in silence. He supposed it had been silly to hope that somehow an actual *good* plan might materialize, but still he didn't like how lame this particular plan was. However, it wasn't like he had a better idea, so Phil's would have to do.

They ran on at a good clip, only stopping to be attacked by groups of greedy prisoners who had heard through the grapevine that there was a wealthy visitor to the Forest running around and paying quite well for people to leave him alone.

When they finally reached the hole in the ground where Julianna was hiding, Warren was quite relieved; he was exhausted, his head was throbbing where the rock had hit him, and he was really dizzy. He needed some sleep like nobody's business if he was going to have a hope of pulling off a midnight escape out of the Forest of Looming Death while being tracked by the evil Mirabella.

CHAPTER THIRTY-SIX

It was the middle of the night. A swell time for clandestine meetings. Throughout the city, there were probably at least a half-dozen scheduled for one thing or another. The castle maintenance guy, Luther, was walking through the grimy streets on the way to one of these meetings. In his pocket was the magical vial of raven blood, who had had a tough time keeping quiet when it had so many questions it would have loved to have asked. But it didn't want to be dashed to pieces against the nearest wall, so it kept all its questions bottled up. Hopefully it could get some good eavesdropping in at this meeting, then report some information to Warren.

Luther was talking to himself, but so quietly that the magical vial of raven blood couldn't hear anything. Occasionally, a wagon would drive past, or a group of merrymakers would cavort by, but other than that it was quiet.

Earlier, the magical vial of raven blood had heard Luther talking with his wife about the Prince's upcoming hunt. The citizens were getting so excited about it, and about all the parties that went along with it. The commoners were even allowed to attend some of the planned events. That day, there had been a hunting-themed festival in the city center, and the next day there was going to be a parade with deer-shaped floats, hunting dogs demonstrating tricks, and marching bands playing hunting songs.

It all sounded pretty awesome. The magical vial of raven blood wished it could see. When it had been ravens, those ravens could have soared above the crowds and taken it all in.

After a while, Luther's mumbled speech became clear, and another voice started responding to him. He must have met up with a friend. Sounded like a lady. "You know what this meeting's about?" asked Luther.

"Steph mentioned something about pirates," commented the lady.

"Pirates? Sounds suspicious."

"I know. Hardly in line with our pacifistic stance," she agreed with a sniff.

"Yeah. Well, I'm sure Steph has her reasons. She's never steered us wrong before." A pause. "Or, she hasn't *often* steered us wrong."

The lady responded too quietly for the magical vial of raven blood to hear, but whatever she said made Luther laugh and say, "Tell me about it. But nobody's perfect."

They laughed a bit more, then walked on quietly for a few more minutes. The magical vial of raven blood then felt Luther stop walking and heard knocking.

Hinges creaked and someone said, "Password?"

"Seriously, Dustin?" asked Luther.

"Password," Dustin repeated firmly. "The rules are the rules, Luther."

"Whatever. Commune," Luther said.

"That was last week's," Dustin said.

"Oh, thanks. Um…" Luther thought.

The lady Luther had met up with said, "Equality."

"Right-o," Dustin said. "Come on in. Steph is just about to get started."

And into the meeting they went. It sounded like this Steph character was already being introduced. "—straight from a strategy meeting with our comrades in Masonville, one of the best revolution strategists in the kingdom: our own Stephanie Collins!"

Roars and cheers!

Hoots and hollers!

Once the ruckus died down a bit, a strident voice cut through what remained of the talking, "Friends! Silence!"

All promptly complied.

"Thank you, members of Chapter 8 of the Orange Star, for gathering on such short notice! The news I have was so important it couldn't wait until your usual Thursday evening potluck. By now, you've probably heard rumors—"

Here someone cut in, "Pirates! Someone said it was something about pirates!"

"Yep," Steph answered. "And please don't interrupt, Shaunn. Who's behind the podium? You? Or me?"

"You are," mumbled a contrite Shaunn.

"Right you are. Now shut your trap and listen up. Yes, pirates. You may know the name of Captain Maximus McManlyman—"

There were gasps and a few comments that Steph didn't bother silencing because the name of the pirate captain was a fairly intense bit of information to spring on them.

So, the crowd did its hubbub for a bit, and when she felt they'd done all the gasping and gossiping that the situation warranted, she continued, "Right, right. The evil Captain Maximus McManlyman. You're wondering how pacifists such as ourselves could be considering any sort of association with him. Well, you remember how Jane disappeared? And how her parents said she'd been kidnapped by pirates?"

She paused to let them murmur and whisper some more.

"Well, I just got a note from Jane. I brought it along in case those of you who are literate want to give it a look-see. But for now, let me sum up: she's been captured by McManlyman. While being held prisoner, she's been talking to him about the revolution, and apparently her words have gotten through to him. You know how eloquent our Jane can be."

Steph paused again for everyone to murmur to their neighbors about what a great lady Jane was and how they were glad that, though she was a captive on a pirate ship, at least she was doing well enough that the Captain was allowing her to send letters.

"So anyways," Steph said at length. "Jane said in her letter that the Captain wants to help us out. Which is pretty cool because, up until this point, the revolution hasn't been able to get control of any ships, since the King seems to think it necessary to have a few soldiers on board every vessel capable of traveling any appreciable distance." She paused and said, "Hey, could I get a cup of water?"

While someone rustled up some water for their prestigious visitor all the way from distant Masonville, the magical vial of raven blood heard Luther ask someone, "Hey, is Ross here?"

"The wizard? Yeah, I think I saw him around somewhere."

Luther spun around, presumably scanning the place for Ross the Wizard, then began to walk. Steph started talking again, but the magical vial of raven blood couldn't hear what she said because Luther started to talk too. "Hey Ross. Stick around after the meeting, would ya? I've got something that may be of interest to you."

"Sure. What's going on?" Ross whispered.

"Quiet!" Steph barked. "Seriously, guys. This is important."

"Sorry!" Ross and Luther chorused.

Steph continued, "So, yes, McManlyman is not to be trusted. He's a pirate, after all. But, still, I agree with Jane that it is worth a try. He told her he wants to help. And if she's willing to take the risk—which she says she is—then why not give it a whirl? Her plan is essentially this: the pirates sail north, and Jane seeks the help of our neighbors in Apamea."

"Why Apamea?" asked a lady. "They're so far away! What about Inachis?"

Steph sighed, "Shannon. Inachis is closer, yes, but they're jerks—and a monarchy. If they decided to help us, it would only be so that they could take over once King Conroy was overthrown. Apameans are much nicer. And since they only overthrew their king a few years back, they're not likely to want to take over Fritillary since they still have their hands full rearranging their whole government. Make sense?"

Shannon must have made some sort of non-verbal response, because after a pause the magical vial of raven blood heard Steph talk on:

"So, if Apamea is willing to help us on the road to the same sort of government they're trying out, then we may have a chance. Our mysterious benefactor with the silver boxes has been supplying our chapters with a lot of stuff, but not enough for a full-on revolution. Yet. But, with Apamea on board, we could be ready to go in as little as a year!"

Stunned silence. Perhaps not everyone in the room was prepared to have their lives upended quite so soon.

"Can I get a 'huzzah'?" Steph persisted.

Once they'd had a few moments to let this development soak in, there were a few hearty huzzahs from the braver members. Soon their enthusiasm spread about the room until even the wimpier members of the Order of the Orange Star were giving a hoot or two.

"That's more like it," Steph yelled energetically. "But now simmer down!"

They did.

"I'll write Jane back and tell her to go for it. From there, we wait for word from her. Any questions?"

Someone asked something, but Ross the Wizard said to Luther, "Wanna step out into the street and talk?"

"Yeah. Sure," Luther agreed and began to walk.

There was the sound of a creaking door. It slammed shut a moment later, silencing the chatter from the meeting place. The city at that time of night was relatively quiet, so the magical vial of raven blood had no trouble hearing when Luther said, "So, I've got some raven blood. It says it's a good ingredient."

There was a big pause. "It *said* it's a good ingredient?" Ross responded excitedly.

"Yeah…" Luther answered.

"*Talking* raven blood?"

"Yeah…"

"Wow! No way! Where'd you—how—"

"I found it in the trash. Or it found me, I guess."

"Sweet! No way!"

"It told me to give it to you."

"Awesome! Can I see it?"

The magical vial of raven blood was grabbed out of Luther's pocket and handed over to the wizard.

"Ooh!" Ross breathed. "Wendell—you know, the Royal Wizard—he has some of this stuff." Then he grumbled, "But he won't let me touch it yet. Says it's not for interns. Too powerful."

"Well, you've got some now," Luther said.

"Yeah. Yeah, I sure do. You said it talks?"

"Yep. I don't know how to make it work, though."

The magical vial of raven blood felt itself being shaken. "Umm. I wonder—do I need a spell?"

"Nope. If you did, I wouldn't have been able to make it talk," Luther pointed out.

The magical vial of raven blood would have rolled its eyes if only it had eyes to roll. And if ravens did things like roll their eyes. Seriously, an *intern wizard?* Ah well, it was better than nothing. And, if Ross was one of Wendell's interns, that meant he had to be pretty good. Tired of being shaken and examined, the magical vial of raven blood finally entered Ross's mind and squawked, *Hey bro.*

Ross gasped, then said gleefully, "Hi, vial of raven blood!"

Hi.

"So, um, thanks for having Luther give you to me! This is *so* cool."

Yes, son, I am a good ingredient. And I'd like to help you. All of you. You revolutionaries.

"For real?"

Totally.

"Why?"

Farland Phelps created me, the raven blood admitted. *I want to help fight the evil he did using me as an ingredient.*

"Cool, man. That's totally honorable and stuff. Steph's going to be so happy!"

O N THE BAY of Fritillary, Dr. Jane was leaning against the rail of the pirate ship, staring out at the little dots of light of the distant city. Somewhere out there, her parents were fretting about her, Warren and his family were running from a crazy wizard, and her friends were—maybe that very moment—meeting and discussing the whole McManlyman thing.

Jane felt conflicted about accepting his help, since he had clearly only offered because he had a crush on her. But an offer for help was, after all, an offer for help, and she'd be silly to turn down something that could potentially be a very good thing for the resistance. It wasn't as though she'd agreed to go on a date with him in return or anything like that. The attached strings were all in the subtext, which meant she could pretend she hadn't noticed. It was a low and tacky move, but if a heart was going to be broken in the name of the greater good, at least it was a murderous, greedy, vain heart. The revolutionaries needed help, McManlyman was offering help, end of story. All they needed was to get the okay from her friends in the Order of the Orange Star, and then the pirates would be setting out on their first philanthropic voyage of their entire career.

Jane looked down, watched some waves sloshing about for a bit, and then redirected her gaze to the lights of the city. She hoped she'd see it again. Soon.

Suddenly, from behind her, heavy, piratical footsteps sounded on the deck. She didn't even bother turning to see who it was. It had to be the Captain. None of the other pirates ever bothered talking to her, except her assistant, Brock. But Brock was currently keeping watch over some pirates who'd been slashed up while raiding a cruise ship that morning.

The captain joined her at the railing, standing a bit closer than she was comfortable with.

She kept staring at the city, not giving him a smile or a greeting. Ever since she'd become aware that he liked her, she'd been hyper-conscious about not doing anything that could come across as flirty. The result was lots of awkward silences.

"Hi, Doctor," he said uncertainly, wondering whether he'd done something to make her mad. She had barely spoken to him all day long, except when she'd met with him and his first mate, Biggby, to discuss how he wanted to help out the revolutionaries. "Having a nice night?"

"Just taking in a last look at the city," she responded.

"Mmm. Yeah," he said, staring out at lights, trying to think of something to say. "Looks a lot better at night, eh? Can't tell it's a huge mess of falling apart buildings. Can't see all the coal smoke either."

"True enough, I guess. But that's my home," she said, though she wasn't able to summon up too much defensiveness. If not for her parents, she'd have left ages ago. She conceded, "The fresh air out here on the ocean is a nice change."

"Why aren't you asleep?" he asked.

"Not tired. I'm too anxious. I can't sleep until I get word from my friends about Apamea."

"Same here. I'm anxious too," he answered, then cleared his throat. "Perhaps we could—er—keep each other company this evening. To keep our minds off our anxieties."

Jane shot him a look. "What do you mean?"

McManlyman chickened out and changed directions. "You know, checkers, cards, backgammon. Or we could see if anyone wants to play some blind-man's-bluff or charades or something."

"Oh," she said, exhaling a relieved breath. That had sounded perilously close to a come-on. She was living in constant (though low-grade) fear that he might do something stereotypically piratical that would force her to attempt to use the sharp and shiny dagger she had strapped to her ankle. "Um, I guess so. How about backgammon? I'd hate to wake up a bunch of pirates just so we can play a parlor game in the middle of the night."

"Great. I'll have Biggby fetch it from the games closet," McManlyman said and strode off to awaken his first mate. "Meet you in the galley?" he asked over his shoulder.

"Sure," Jane said and watched him, feeling guilty. He had sounded so happy when she'd consented to play a game with him. Poor guy. There was no chance of anything between them. Not even friendship. But, still, she had to be nice to him, otherwise he might get disheartened and decide that helping out the revolutionaries in order to impress her wasn't worth the bother.

So off Jane went to play some backgammon with Captain McManlyman.

Chapter Thirty-Seven

Julianna, Warren, Copernicus, and Phil were all creeping through the dark forest on their way back to the cave.

After waking up from his nap, Warren had felt not better but about ten times worse—his voice was now slightly slurred, and he kept getting confused about very basic things. (Sleeping after an untreated concussion is a bad idea.)

They were trotting along with Phil in front of them and Copernicus behind them. Trailing behind Copernicus were four pals of Phil's from his gang. They'd been interested enough in the story to come along but had made no promises about sticking with them if things got tough. They were pretty scared of Mirabella. Most dudes in the Forest were. Since she was a woman who didn't adhere to Fritillary's notions of what a woman should be, the guys thought she was a witch.

Julianna, who had been filled in on the events of the day by Phil and Copernicus while Warren slept, said to Warren, "Are you sure you're okay? Your hair is positively caked with blood. And so's your sleeve and the back of your shirt."

"I'm fine," he mumbled.

Julianna persisted, "Can you go?"

Warren glanced at their guides and said quietly, as though he didn't want them to overhear, "What choice do I have?"

"Well hopefully we'll get there in time for you to get a bit of a rest," Julianna said, then sighed when she saw yet another hoard of attackers looming on the path up ahead of them. These accursed attackers were wasting their time.

The threatening silhouettes advanced.

Dexter floated up to Julianna and said, "Reason with them."

She whispered with annoyance, "I *know!*" to him, causing her companions who weren't in-the-know about the ghosts to exchange confused looks. "Come on, guys," Julianna called in her fake guy voice to the menacing forms. "We're in a hurry. Just come on over and we'll give you the gold. Please, please don't take up our time by attacking us."

The silhouettes halted and conversed for a few moments, then began moving toward them again, but this time with a bit less menace. The two groups converged, and the spokesman for the bad guys stepped forward and said, "So, uh, what's the hurry? These fights are sort of standard protocol, you know."

"We need to rescue my sister," Warren slurred distractedly and stumbled a bit, then brought his hand to the back of his head.

Julianna watched him with mounting concern.

"It's a time-sensitive mission," Phil explained, "so we'd appreciate it if you'd just let us go."

One of the thugs tapped his cudgel restlessly against the palm of his hand, while the group all waited for their leader to come to a decision as to whether they were going to dole out some beatings or not.

Warren had more than enough time to survey the group and begin to get nervous, because they were more well-equipped than most of the groups he'd run up against, and there were seven of them; Warren had the uneasy feeling that he was just one more blow to the head away from a world of trouble.

The guy with the cudgel met Warren's eyes and gave him an evil smile.

Warren swallowed heavily and looked down at his boots.

The long pause finally was broken by the leader saying, "Okay, we'll let you go without a fight for six gold coins for each of us."

Julianna readily agreed and grabbed the coin purse from Warren, then doled out the gold to the greedy hands that presented themselves before her.

One of the thugs even said politely, "Thanks, Miss."

It was only after they'd been walking for a few more minutes that Julianna realized she'd been called 'Miss'. "Hey, that guy knew I'm a lady!" she said.

Phil responded, "That's because your disguise is rotten."

"Why didn't you tell me?" she growled.

Phil shrugged. "It didn't occur to me, I guess."

Julianna looked at Copernicus next.

"I thought it was so transparent to me because I already knew you're a lady," he explained.

She shot Copernicus a glare and then looked at Warren but didn't demand an explanation of him because he looked so pathetic as he trudged on, staring blankly into the trees with his eyes all unfocused and concussed.

She sighed, put aside her annoyance about finding she'd been traipsing about the Forest in a horrible disguise, and fell into step beside Warren. She said, "Corrine's lucky to have you. Not every sibling would go to so much trouble and put themselves in so much danger."

He waved a hand dismissively, which was enough to make him stumble. She grabbed his arm to steady him and he mumbled his thanks, then slurred, "You'd do the same for Conroy Jr. if he was in danger."

"Sure, in theory," Julianna said. "But he's got armies to take care of him."

Warren was quiet for a few moments, his eyes narrowed as though pondering something weighty. Then he cleared his throat and said, "What were we talking about?"

Julianna winced, but merely said, "Nothing important." She glanced back at Copernicus and met his eyes; he'd obviously been listening to their conversation, because he looked pretty worried too.

At last, our ragtag band of travelers reached the place where they were going to meet up with Corrine. They had made good time since there were fewer menacing hoards out at night, so they found themselves with an hour to kill before Corrine joined them.

"Make him comfy over there by that log," Phil directed Copernicus and Julianna, pointing to an old fallen tree covered in moss. "But don't let him sleep anymore. He might not wake up. I'll watch for his sister. Be ready to run when I say so."

"Might not wake up!?" Julianna hissed at Phil, her blood running cold.

He shrugged. "The kid's doing pretty bad."

Julianna stared from Phil to Warren, feeling shaky and sick.

Phil pointed to his four gang pals who were hovering around in the shadows, and he conveyed with some sort of sign language something that must have been meaningful to them, because they all nodded upon seeing the gestures, then dispersed out into the trees at regular intervals.

Phil positioned himself behind a tree and stood motionless, his eyes trained on the cave.

Julianna and Copernicus busied themselves trying to keep Warren engaged in conversation.

Warren tried in vain to fall asleep.

Copernicus kept finding himself staring at his brother's back. He had to tell Phil that he had not become a writer but had stayed with the life of crime. Phil needed to know the truth. Copernicus might not get another chance to come clean. "You got this?" he asked Julianna, gesturing toward Warren.

She nodded and watched him walk over to his brother. They began what turned quickly into a very quiet, but very heated, argument. She looked back at Warren, then and said in a falsely jolly voice, "Boy, will it be good to be out of this forest!"

"Mmm hmm," he agreed and added in a nearly incomprehensible slur, "Need to find a wizard or a doctor or something soon. Think I might have a concussion."

She blinked at him with surprise, took his hands in hers, and said, "Um, Warren, you *do* have a concussion. No question."

He looked surprised. "No way. Seriously?"

"Yeah," she said uneasily. "You're all dizzy and out of it, and your speech is really slurred."

"Shoot," he said and stared vacantly ahead of him for a bit. "That's not good, right?"

"No," she said, opting for honesty. "No, it's not good." She decided to let the conversation die out, but to watch him like a hawk to make sure he didn't doze off.

Time passed.

Phil and Copernicus fought some more.

Julianna worried and watched.

Warren sat there feeling confused and in pain and vaguely uneasy.

An owl hooted.

The four gang members stood around shuffling their feet and cleaning out their fingernails and stuff like that.

Suddenly Phil put up a hand to silence them all, though he and his brother were the only ones talking. "Up!" he whispered sharply. "Get ready to run!"

Copernicus darted over and helped Julianna get Warren to his feet. They all waited for Corrine. Just a few seconds later, she ran from the clearing and into their midst.

As soon as she was there, Phil cut the rope around her wrists, and they all began to run. Phil took Corrine by the arm to guide her until her eyes adjusted to the darkness of the Forest. Running as fast as you can run while concurrently trying to be as silent as you can be, all while racing with eight other people around trees and over logs in the middle of the night is no easy feat.

Actually, it's impossible.

So, it didn't take Phil too long to realize that they might have a little more luck if he sent his four pals off in another direction to confuse Mirabella.

He told them to scram, and off they went, leaving Julianna, Corrine, Warren, Copernicus, and Phil racing for the border of the Forest of Looming Death.

Once Corrine's eyes had adjusted to the dark, it didn't take her long to notice that Warren was stumbling along with Julianna on one side of him and some big thug on the other side. She couldn't stop and she couldn't speak, so she couldn't figure out what was wrong with him. All she could do was worry and cast anxious glances his way.

It wasn't long before they began to hear signs of pursuit. Or, not so much signs as blatant announcements. "Corrine!" they heard Mirabella yelling from somewhere behind them.

It hadn't even been four minutes.

"*Really?* Are you *seriously* trying to run away?" Mirabella roared. She sounded ornery. And close. But then, she wasn't being slowed by either an invalid or by a need for silence. And she had the advantage of being able to hear her quarry as they blundered on ahead of her.

"Oh forget about trying to be quiet," Phil grumbled as he looked behind him and began to pick up the pace. "She's on our trail and she's not going to lose it." He stopped a moment to get his bearings, and Corrine nearly ran into him. "Let's try to get her caught in a trap."

He shifted direction, and the rest of them followed.

Julianna, who was holding Warren's right arm, felt him slowing and tried to urge him on while at the same time feeling horrible because she knew that he was really tired and that his head was probably throbbing with each jarring step. Rest was, of course, out of the question since Warren was the one that Mirabella and Farland *really* had wanted in the first place. Plus, the faster they went, the sooner Warren would be out of the Forest—and surely there was a doctor or a wizard among the guards.

Now that they were no longer bothering with being quiet, Corrine was able to ask, "What's wrong with Warren?" She trotted up beside Julianna and peeked at her brother.

"He got hit on the head. He's got a concussion," Julianna panted.

"Here's one of our traps," Phil said suddenly. "Careful not to fall in." He pointed to the area in question on the ground and led the group carefully around the edge that only he knew the perimeter of. Once they were safely around it, they all began to run again.

About a minute later, they heard a muffled crash and a roar of rage from behind them.

"Did it actually work?" Julianna asked. "Did she really fall in?"

They all halted for a moment and listened intently.

"I don't hear anyone following us…" Phil said uncertainly.

"Should we go back and check?" asked Corrine.

"No," Phil said. "It could be a trick." He began to jog.

"That seemed way too easy," Copernicus said.

"Yeah. Well she doesn't know too much about the Forest. She sticks pretty much to her cave. So she doesn't know where the traps are," Phil pointed out. "And anyway, we're not in the clear. She'll be out of that trap soon and following us again."

"You think she'll be able to climb out?" Copernicus asked.

"She'll get help. All she needs to do is holler, and someone will hear. She'll bribe them with vegetables from her garden—we're all pretty starved for veggies out here—and then she'll be after us again."

"Do you think we have time to give Warren a rest?" asked Corrine.

"He needs to get out of here more than he needs a rest," Phil snapped, and trotted on.

Corrine shot him a glare.

Julianna whispered, "He's right. Warren's going to keep getting worse until he gets help."

As they ran on, both women looked at Warren.

He looked back at them and slurred, "My head hurts." Then he tripped. Copernicus and Julianna righted him.

Copernicus said reassuringly, "We've got to be nearly there. Right Phil?"

"Yup," he answered.

"Why haven't we been attacked?" Julianna asked.

"It's nighttime," Phil said over his shoulder while inwardly thinking how annoying it was that he had to keep on pointing out the obvious to these people. "Most everyone's asleep. There are a few groups who work nights, but not too many. And only groups of five or six would bother messing with a group of our size."

Everyone was just thinking how nice that was, when one of those groups of 3rd shift prisoners materialized before them. Our ragtag band of intrepid underdog heroes halted in their tracks and braced themselves for whatever was about to happen.

A quick appraisal of the situation told them that they were surrounded by seven big, tough-looking silhouettes. Moonlight glinted off a few sharp-looking blades.

CHAPTER THIRTY-EIGHT

Hoping to stop the fight before it started, Julianna took a step toward the biggest, toughest looking silhouette and said, "How much do you want? We've still got plenty of gold."

"We don't want your money; we want that lady," came a grumbly voice that sounded like it belonged to a talking bear. "Er, wait, is *that* the lady we want? I didn't realize there were two ladies in this group...or are you a dude?"

"I'm a lady too," sighed Julianna and decided it was high time to remove her newsboy cap and rub off the goatee and moustache Warren had painted on with mud; the goatee was mostly all flaked off anyway. As she rubbed at the mud smeared on her face, she said, "And you aren't taking her. We came here to rescue her, and that's what we're going to do." In this pronouncement she used her best Royal Person Voice, and the thugs found themselves momentarily second-guessing their mission.

"Yeah!" said Copernicus in a pointless, confrontational way that added nothing to the dialogue, but ratcheted up the hostility a few notches.

Corrine listened anxiously, surprised that Mirabella had gotten word to these thugs so fast. But they didn't have an invalid in tow. And speaking of the invalid, how was she going to make sure that Warren didn't get hurt in this fight? She needed to stop them before they started, or Warren was going to get hit in the head. And she needed, preferably, to stop the fight in a way that didn't involve her going along with these thugs back to Mirabella's cave. But the last thing Warren needed was another knock to the head, so if she had to, she'd just agree to go back with them to the cave.

While Corrine was pondering all this, the lead thug was coming to the conclusion that he'd better get this thing going. Without preamble, he tossed a dagger at Phil. Phil dodged it, of course, because he had fancy reflexes; the dagger thunked harmlessly into a tree trunk, but even though no harm had come to Phil, that dagger toss signaled the beginning of a big squabble. Phil did what he could to fight the attackers off singlehandedly, but even though he was awesome he was only one and they were seven.

Copernicus watched, and realized that he had to leave protecting Warren to the chicks; his skills as a thug were best used punching these people, not being a bodyguard.

Julianna briefly considered joining the fight. After all, she had gotten some personal defense training in the dungeon. But now was simply not the time for her first real-world test of her skills. Warren needed protection.

It became clear quickly that this fight was going to end badly for the good guys; the attackers were getting closer and closer to Warren, Corrine, and Julianna.

Corrine looked at Julianna and said, "I'm going to run for it. Which way is the border of the Forest?"

"Um, that way I think," Julianna pointed in the direction they'd been heading. "But you can't run off alone!"

"If I can sneak away and get far enough, then I can yell at them and they'll chase me. Since the only reason they're here is because they want me," Corrine explained hurriedly. "As soon as they follow me, you guys all run."

"But Corrine—"

"You get Warren out of here!" Corrine hissed. "This is his only chance! I will not let my little brother die. Do you understand me?"

Julianna swallowed, and nodded.

"Good. I am entrusting his safety to you," Corrine growled.

Julianna gave another nod.

Corrine watched the fight for a few moments and sprinted away as soon as it looked like the majority of the attackers were pretty distracted by Phil and Copernicus.

"What? What's going on?" Warren asked anxiously, staring after his sister.

Julianna watched with horror as Corrine leapt away, but to her relief Corrine actually managed to cover some good ground without being noticed.

Corrine turned once she was nearly hidden in the shadows of the trees and yelled, "Hey! I'm over here!"

They were all too busy fighting to notice.

"Hey!" Corrine yelled again.

No reaction. The guys just kept punching and slashing at each other.

"Guys!" Julianna joined in. "Look! She's gone!"

One of the attackers looked over at her questioningly.

Julianna explained, "The lady you're supposed to be getting. She's gone. Over there." She pointed to Corrine.

Corrine waved energetically. "Hi!"

"Arg!" yelled the guy.

Corrine ran.

The guy ran after her, notifying his comrades of this turn of events as he went. His pals stopped what they were doing and stared after him for a few moments (time enough for Copernicus to land a punch to the side of one of their heads and for Phil to flip one to the ground) then, those who were able ran after their friend, who was running after Corrine, who was running for the edge of the Forest.

"What's she doing!?" Copernicus roared.

"She's giving us a chance to get Warren out safely!" Julianna said quickly. "Let's go!"

"But we're supposed to rescue *her*!" Copernicus fumed, staring at the trees where she'd disappeared.

"She'll be fine," Julianna said apprehensively. "She's heading in the right direction, right Phil?"

Phil looked around at the trees for a few moments and then nodded. He said uncertainly, "She's nearly out. She'll be all right." He didn't add that she'd be all right only if the guards didn't shoot her on sight thinking she was a prisoner making a run for it.

Copernicus sighed and said, "Right, let's move." It had occurred to him that if they all managed to get out of this forest, Corrine would be very grateful to those who had gotten her little brother to safety. He glanced one more time at the direction she'd run and thought about what a brave lady she was. Then he took Warren's arm, and he and an impatient Julianna started to run again, at a different angle from the one Corrine had run, with Warren bumping along between them. Phil took up the rear, watching intently over his shoulder for Mirabella, who he was expecting at any moment to come tearing through the trees with some thugs at her heels.

However, after just a smidgen more running, they were amazed to see the clearing through the trees ahead of them.

"Yay!" Julianna cried. "Look!"

"Okay," Phil said, "You guys be careful on the edge. You don't want the guards to get overexcited and run you through before you have a chance to explain yourselves." He was glad this was almost over—he was exhausted and didn't think he had the energy to do much more than trudge back to his lean-to and collapse on his pile of leaves.

Copernicus halted and looked sadly at his brother. He'd forgotten that he'd have to leave Phil behind. "Phil—" he spluttered. "Phil, I'm so sorry— I'm sorry I didn't become a writer. I'm sorry I didn't change my ways…"

Phil clapped him on the shoulder. "No use dwelling on the past, Copper. Just promise me that from here on out you'll try to follow your dreams and—" This heartfelt, brotherly exchange was interrupted by a holler from behind him.

"Stop right there!" came the harsh voice of Mirabella. "You guys have been making me *soooo* angry. You think I like traipsing about the—"

"GO!!" Phil yelled at them.

They went.

Phil turned to face Mirabella and the three big thugs who were trailing in her wake. He gritted his teeth, squared his shoulders, and positioned himself between our heroes and the villains.

The last thing Copernicus saw as he glanced over his shoulder was Mirabella advancing toward Phil, looking positively livid.

"Guards!" Julianna yelled, thinking it best to give some warning of their impending exit from The Forest. "Guards! Don't attack us!"

And without further ado, Julianna and Copernicus dragged Warren out of the Forest of Looming Death and into safety.

Chapter Thirty-Nine

For the second time in the past few days, Warren woke up in a strange place after having been concussed. He blinked into the semi-darkness of the room and tried to figure out where he was. Remembering well from his previous concussion that it would be unwise to sit up quickly, he cleared his throat carefully and called out, "Hello?" in the direction of what appeared to be the room's only door; there was light shining through the cracks around it.

No answer.

"Hello!?" he tried a bit louder and winced. But it didn't seem to hurt as badly as when he'd woken up from his other concussion.

There was shuffling from behind the door, and a few seconds later Copernicus came in. He smiled, and whispered, "Hi. How are you feeling?"

"What happened?" Warren asked. "I don't remember getting here."

"You were pretty out of it toward the end. We got out of The Forest and—"

Warren cut in suddenly, "Corrine! Did we get her?"

Copernicus nodded and smiled. "Yes. It took her a while because she had to hide for a bit from the people chasing her, but she got out too. She saved you, you know. Quite a lady."

Warren raised an eyebrow at Copernicus's obvious admiration. "Is she here? And where are we?"

"We're at the guards' headquarters. And yes, she's here. She's been with you the whole time—just left a few minutes ago to get the wizard when you started to stir."

"A wizard? Not a doctor?" Warren asked with a frown. He was a progressive guy in this regard and would have preferred a doctor. But since he was not currently dead or in a coma, Warren supposed he had to admit the wizard must have been competent enough. It was scary to think about what weird potions the wizard might have used, though.

"Yes. A wizard. He seemed to know his stuff—"

The door swung open and Corrine walked in, followed by none other than the wizard himself. Since Warren's only experience of wizards up to this point was Farland and fictional wizards with capes and pointy hats, he at first didn't think the man accompanying Corrine could be one. However, when the little guy strode up to him and sprinkled green glittery powder over Warren's head, Warren figured a wizard he must be, even though he was short and skinny and young and wearing just regular old clothes that didn't fit well: worn old brown pants, a worn old yellow shirt, and worn old leather boots.

When the wizard spoke, his voice was not a deep boom that resonated with a confidence born of a sure knowledge of his mastery of the supernatural world. He just sounded regular. "Hey, how ya feeling?"

"Er. Okay. My head hurts a bit, but actually not as bad as when I woke up from my *last* concussion," Warren said, as he realized with cautious optimism that he *was* really feeling pretty good.

"I bet you had a doctor treat you last time," the wizard guessed.

Warren narrowed his eyes, and said, "Well, yes, it was a doctor who treated me."

"Well, that explains it," the wizard said smugly. "I bet you had to recover for a long time, too, huh?"

"Yeah, I guess. Few days."

"Well, you will be up and walking in a few hours' time with *my* spells and *my* magic," said the wizard with a proud smirk.

"Er, thanks," said Warren.

"No thanks necessary," said the wizard. "Payment is the only thanks I need."

Warren raised an eyebrow. "Jennifer's got all the gold, I think."

The wizard peeked into Warren's eyes, felt his head, sprinkled more powder on him, and said, "Well then, I'll go find her. You'll be fine by nighttime."

Warren and Corrine watched the wizard go, and then Corrine sat down on the bed and said, "Warren, I am so glad you are okay! I was so scared for you back there!"

"Thanks for saving me," he said with a smile. "I'm glad you're safe too."

"Thank *you* for saving *me*," she said. "Warren, if you hadn't come when you did—" and here Corrine looked around cautiously even though they were the only two people in the room, "If you hadn't come, I wouldn't have been able to get word out in time—it may already be too late—I overheard Mirabella and Farland talking about another plot they're working on. They're going to kidnap the Prince and brainwash him so that Farland and Mirabella can go live at the castle; Farland wants to be rich and powerful like he used to be before the King kicked him out."

"They're plotting *what?*" Warren said and a flash of pain stabbed through his head. "*When?*"

"When the Prince is out on his hunting party. I guess the guards are always on the lookout for Farland, so he can't swoop in and take the kid without risking being killed, but Farland's going to magic Mirabella out of the Forest, and he's going to take her to where they're hunting, and she's going to pose as the Queen and take the Prince. She's going to sneak him somewhere away from the guards, get the kid's anti-magic amulets off him, and then Farland's going to take him."

Warren stared in horror. "Did you tell the guards?"

"Yeah. They're trying to get the signal beacon working, but no one here seems to know how to use it. And they've misplaced the manual," Corrine said with frustration.

Warren sighed. Based on what he'd seen of the guards before they'd gone into The Forest, he wasn't surprised. "But they're sending messengers?"

"They sent out two guys. It's all they could spare. They're stretched pretty thin here. They need two guys per watch station all around the perimeter of the Forest, and they need enough on reserve so they can rotate."

Well two messengers were better than nothing. "Does Julianna know?"

"No. Copper and I figured it was best not to tell her until after sunset. She'd go crazy worrying all day about her brother, and there's nothing she could do anyway." She sighed and said, "But once the sun sets, we're going to set out to find the hunting party, and we're going to make sure the King knows. I don't trust that the messengers will do their job. As I learned when I was a prisoner in the cave, the Forest of Looming Death is positively *crawling* with spies. Some of the prisoners are working for the guards, some of the guards are working for the prisoners. A lot of intrigue going on."

Warren stared at the blankets, trying to organize his bruised brain. Fortunately, it looked like while he'd been lying there unconscious, Copernicus and Corrine had worked out the plan already anyway, so all he needed to do was what they told him to.

I T WAS A good thing that with two moons there was always at least some degree of light at nighttime, because otherwise our intrepid travelers would not have been able to be racing at an irresponsible speed through the forest on their way to the nearest inn, where they hoped to hear word of the Prince's hunting party, which had started the previous day.

Innkeepers were always in the know about social whatnot, so our heroes figured an inn was probably the best place to start on their quest to save Conroy Jr. A Forest guard had directed them to the nearest inn, and as soon as the sun had set, they had collected a confused Julianna from where she'd been whiling away the day in the barracks basement sleeping on a spare cot and messing with the guards' pool table. Then they were on their way, dashing off on Copernicus's wagon past the frantic group of guards blundering around trying to figure out the signal beacon.

Julianna was thrilled to see that Warren was doing much better; the last she'd seen of him before going down into the barracks basement to hide from the sunlight, he'd been blathering incomprehensibly and staggering around. Now he was sitting on the jostling wagon with focused eyes and barely a wince at even the biggest bumps in the road. "That wizard sure knows his business," she commented.

"Yep," Warren said from where he sat across from her. "He does. I didn't dare ask what he did to me, but I sure feel better." He gave her a sidelong glance and said, "How are *you* doing?"

When they had explained to her all about the threat to her little brother, she had seemed to handle it pretty well—or at least she hadn't flipped out and panicked. She'd stayed pretty quiet and listened intently to the plan Corrine and Copernicus had worked out, then she'd darted out to help ready the wagon. Once they'd finally set out, she had pretty much just sat in the back of the wagon staring ahead into the darkness, occasionally urging Copernicus to speed things along.

But Warren was pretty sure she must be scared even though she wasn't acting like it.

"I'm fine," she answered shortly, in a way that clearly meant she was not fine but also was not in the mood to talk about it.

"All right," he said lightly, deciding to respect her desire not to talk. He instead opened up his banjo case, took the instrument out, and started playing some scales, which was somewhat difficult due to the sling and the motion of the wagon, but he was in the mood to play.

They both looked up at Copernicus and Corrine, who were sitting side by side on the bench and seemed to be deep in conversation.

"Nice of him to help us with this next leg of the journey," Julianna said, nodding to Copernicus.

"I think he has ulterior motives," Warren whispered with a significant eyebrow wiggle and a look from Copernicus to Corrine. The banjo went from scales to a romantic tune for a few moments.

Julianna grinned and nodded. She'd thought she had noticed something going on between them.

Warren smiled to see her thinking of something other than Conroy Jr.

They looked idly around the dark forest and listened to Copernicus and Corrine as they talked about the publishing industry in Fritillary; Copernicus seemed all fired up to begin his first true crime novel once he was done with this adventure, and Corrine was more than willing to give him pointers.

Before too long, they saw the inn up ahead. It was a small two-story building sitting right at a crossroads between the north/south road they were on and another road that was running (you guessed it!) east/west. Over the door, the inn had the usual wooden sign hanging from an iron rod sticking out at a ninety degree angle from the building; the sign was flapping gently, and sporting an intricately carved blob that must have been supposed to be a guy with an axe, because above the blob were words that read: The Lonely Woodsman.

Copernicus parked the wagon, and Julianna and Warren hopped down and went into the inn to see if they could get some intel on the hunting party. The Lonely Woodsman was a sad little establishment with just two lonely patrons bellied up to the bar and one lonely barkeeper bellied up to the other side. The two lonely patrons didn't even look up when our heroes walked in, which was odd because usually when one walks into a backwoodsy bar, the locals all turn and stare, and someone says something confrontational that causes a fight.

The barkeeper asked them what they wanted, and they both ordered Bitsy McGoverns because they needed their wits about them. They leaned against the bar, and Julianna asked, "Any news from the Capital?"

Sure enough, the hunting party was the hot topic out in this far flung little establishment, just like it was in the city. The barkeeper said, "The talk's all about that hunting thing with the Prince. They rode past going east yesterday. Big, fancy group they were."

"Oh?" asked Julianna.

"Indeed. Yesterday evening. They're headed toward that wildlife refuge up past the coal mines[36]."

Warren and Julianna exchanged significant looks and engaged in a bit more small talk with the barkeeper while they finished their drinks, then they moseyed out.

"Lucky they're hunting so near us," Warren commented as they hopped back into the wagon. And while it *was* lucky that the wildlife refuge was pretty close to them, it wasn't actually so much to do with luck as it was to

---

36   In a rare instance of foresight, the royal family had, a few generations back, realized that if logging progressed at the rate it was going, then, in the not too distant future, there'd be nowhere good left to do their hunting. So, they'd come up with a national wildlife refuge system. The one past the eastern coal mine was the biggest and wildest, so it was the most logical place for the big hunting shindig.

do with the fact that Fritillary was only about 200 square miles in size. So, with a wagon and a good pair of horses, nothing in Fritillary was really all that much of a trek.

"Head east. They're at the refuge past the coal mines," Julianna told Copernicus.

They trotted off.

Julianna would have been quite interested to know that the mining town they rode through a few hours later (Coal Harbor) was the very one where Mortimer Perkins lived. They actually trotted right past his front door. He was inside leading a secret revolution meeting.

Warren checked in with the magical pool of raven blood to see if it had an update.

It didn't have much to say that was relevant to their current situation, but it did let him know about the situation with Jane and McManlyman.

Not much of consequence happened for the next few hours. So how about if we just skip ahead to when stuff happens again? Onward to the national wildlife refuge!

CHAPTER FORTY

The hunting party was camping just past the big sign that read King Moltar National Wildlife Refuge. Lots of big, white tents were scattered about. Lots of maids and servants were busy bustling around, trying to create a nice outdoorsy experience that made the rich folks feel as though they were roughing it.

Meat and asparagus were cooking over fire pits, lake water was being boiled, s'mores were being assembled, some annoying ladies were pretending to be scared of the wildlife so that they could get some easy attention from the guys they had crushes on, some annoying guys were taking advantage of this fact in order to appear more woodsy and capable than they really were.

Farland and Mirabella were peeking through some trees beyond the outer circle of soldiers who were keeping an apparently very ineffective watch over the party. "So, you're sure my sister's there?" asked Mirabella.

"Yeah. She's in the big tent in the middle. Sneaking in there will be the tough bit, but once you've tied her up and disguised yourself as her, its smooth sailing! Get the anti-magic amulet off the kid, get him to our prearranged meet up location, and BAM! we're out of here and the brainwashing begins," Farland sleazed.

Mirabella glared at him; just because he was able to sum up

the plan succinctly, that hardly meant it would really be smooth sailing. She was further irritated because, while she was going to be doing all the work, he was just going to be lazing around their meet-up location and waiting.

"All right," she said abruptly. "Let's do this thing." She reached into her bag for some vials that Farland had given her. They couldn't use the ol' asparagus/tangerine mix because (1) they were outside so it would disperse too quickly to be of much good, and (2) if she knocked out the whole crowd, it would be a dead giveaway that something was up. Since stealth was the order of the day, she had a few vials of some brown concoction that she would just shove under the nose of anyone who got in her way. A few passed out people was nothing that would draw attention, especially the way they were partying down there at the camp.

She thought it was hardly the right example to be setting for the young Prince, but perhaps he was already sleeping. Mirabella then froze and gave a sort of gasp; had she really just felt concern about the example that was being set for her nephew? It was an odd feeling. But it passed quickly. She stood abruptly and shook her head to clear it.

Farland stood when Mirabella did, and they both got to work. The one thing Farland had to do besides magic Conroy Jr. out of the refuge was distract the nearby soldiers so that Mirabella could sneak through their ranks to get to the tents. He scampered off to a hollow tree they'd found earlier and yelled, "Yes! I think the camp's over here! Let's just scout it out and then we can come back with the other guys and all the weapons!"

Sure enough, this attracted the attention of the soldiers.

"What was that?" one yelled.

"Was some guy just yelling about attacking the camp?" asked another soldier incredulously.

In moments, half a dozen soldiers were darting off in the direction of Farland's voice. Farland watched from behind the hollow tree as, behind their backs, Mirabella snuck through their ranks.

Once he was sure she had gotten far enough toward the camp, he simply bent down, crept into the hollow tree, and disappeared; the smoke that accompanied his disappearing spell stayed contained in the tree trunk, so no one even noticed.

Eventually the soldiers gave up their search and went back to their stations, but not before notifying their captain, who summoned all the extra soldiers from the camp to reinforce the outer ring, handily making things easier for Mirabella once she reached the camp.

ⓘNSIDE HER TENT, Queen Lillian was humming tunelessly as she brushed her hair before her little golden fold-up camping mirror. She was glad she'd decided to accompany Conroy Jr. on this trip. At first, she had not wanted to go because hunting dear woodland creatures made her sad, but she knew that she had to shove aside her disapproval of hunting and stand by him for this rite of passage. Never mind that she considered it a silly, pointless rite of passage. Conroy had been so excited about it that she hadn't had the heart to point out that Conroy Jr. really didn't seem that into it. Also, she figured going along on this little adventure would help her to keep her mind off the fact that her daughter had run away again and that there had been no sign of her.

So, here they were.

And here also, she saw through the reflection in her mirror, was Mirabella.

Lillian whirled with a gasp and managed a hoarse cry that was too weak to be heard over all the carousing going on outside the tent. "Mirabella! How did you escape?" she gasped, looking around wildly.

She and her evil twin sister were alone.

Mirabella didn't waste her breath saying a word in response. Her sister didn't need to know that because of Farland's magic, she was able to leave the Forest of Looming Death whenever she felt like it. Instead of speaking, she just swooped in with a vial at the ready and held it under her sister's nose. Before Lillian had a chance to get it together and manage a respectable scream for help, she hit the dirt, sprawled out in an ungainly pile of unconscious queen. Mirabella wasted no time and was quickly switching clothes with her sister and letting her hair down, then giving it a hearty brushing so that it looked all glossy and wavy like Lillian's was. Next, she stuffed her unconscious sister into a nearby trunk that contained a few forest green and camo patterned gowns, propped the vial up amongst the folds of the dresses so that the fumes would keep floating out, and then she slammed the trunk shut.

Before exiting the tent to find her nephew, she glanced in the mirror with a look of surprise; she really did look indistinguishable from the Queen (except for her empty eyes). In the dark of the camp it shouldn't be too difficult to pretend to be Lillian as long as no one engaged her in conversation—she imagined she wouldn't be able to manage talking like her insipid, soppy twin for too long.

With all the confidence of a person who doesn't care about anyone but herself, she swooped out into the midst of all the partying and realized that this was going to be even easier than she'd thought it would be. Because of course, upon seeing her, everyone present collapsed into a bow or a curtsy, and they didn't rise until she told them to.

So, she just didn't tell them to.

She merely said in as pleasant a tone as she could manage, "Has anyone seen my son?" and swooped through the midst of all the lords and ladies who had come to the hunt.

Someone said from behind her, "He's in his tent, Your Majesty."

"Summon him. Tell him I must speak to him," she said in what she hoped was a flighty sort of voice. "Please." Then she added after scanning the camp, "I'll be over there by those tables." There was a group of picnic tables on the edge of the camp. From there, she would hopefully be able to sneak off with the child into the forest without too much trouble.

She then told everyone to stop bowing, and walked off to the picnic tables to wait for Conroy Jr.

JULIANNA, WARREN, CORRINE, and Copernicus were making good time, but they had a bit of distance yet to cover before they arrived at the King Moltar Wildlife Refuge.

"We're nearly there," Copernicus announced. They had just passed an intersection that had one of those posts with a slew of arrows pointing down the roads saying how far it was to this or that village; one of the arrows had proclaimed that the refuge was two miles away. Julianna was glad they were near the end of their journey, because sunrise was only about two hours off. They had just enough time to notify people of Conroy Jr.'s danger and then backtrack to a little inn a few miles back where she could hole up for the day.

"Okay, so when we get there, you guys just go and tell some soldiers, right?" Warren asked Corrine. She and Copernicus were going to go to the campsite to get word to the King and Queen while Warren and Julianna were going to hop off near the refuge and wait. They didn't want to be spotted, trapped, and forced to get married.

"That's the plan," Corrine said uncertainly. "But what if they don't take us seriously?"

"Then you come get me," Julianna said. "They'll believe if I tell them. But I'd rather try with you guys first. Once my parents see me, they're not going to let me out of their sight again."

They covered the last few miles in pretty good time, and right about the same time Mirabella was settling down at the picnic tables to wait for Conroy Jr., Copernicus stopped the wagon so that Julianna and Warren could hop off and hide about a quarter mile from the edge of the refuge. From that distance they could make out the glow of the fires from the hunting party and even hear a bit of the carousing.

Julianna and Warren watched the wagon roll off, then sat down on a nearby log and waited. Though they were so close and she knew that soldiers would be telling her parents in a matter of minutes, she still couldn't keep from fidgeting.

"He'll be fine," Warren said, patting her arm.

"I know," she said, then added, "I should just have gone and told them myself."

"No," he said firmly. "No, there's no reason for you to go risking your freedom to deliver the same message that Corrine and Copernicus can deliver just as well. Plus, if they see you, they may well assume I must be nearby. They'd track me down and then I'd be trapped too, and then before we know what's up, we'd be married. You'd be Mrs. Warren Kensington," he joked as he packed away his banjo.

"I think you'd actually be Mr. Julianna Fritillary," she corrected him, then lapsed into a thoughtful silence. "Which reminds me...I've been having some inconvenient thoughts lately. What if we *should* get married?"

He somehow managed to choke and splutter even though he hadn't even been eating or drinking anything. "*What now?*" he managed. She had just taken a simple little playful comment of his and turned it around in a manner most alarming. This was not where he'd been expecting the conversation to go.

She patted him on the back like people do when someone's coughing even though it does no good, and then she said apologetically, "Well, I've been thinking a lot about this. That you'd be pretty good at it. Being royal, I mean. Not being my husband."

He hacked a bit more, and then managed, "No, I most certainly would not. To either."

"You would, though. You care about people. You would consider the populace, not how decisions you make might inconvenience you."

"So what? With you and Conroy Jr. at the castle there'll be plenty of reasonable folks running the show before too long. You don't need *me* there as well."

"And what if it really does break my curse if we get married?" she asked then, bringing up the selfish aspect of her line of reasoning.

"But it won't!" he said nervously. "We're not in love!" He then looked at her with apprehension; had she somehow fallen for him during the course of this adventure? He wouldn't have thought it would be possible, the way he'd been lumbering about all out of his element and constantly getting injured. But then there was no way of knowing what she might like in a guy.

He was quite relieved when she said, "True. But what if my mom's right? What if we were to fall in love later? I mean, you're a nice guy. There's nothing about you that I *don't* like."

He scoffed and said, "The longer we were married the more you'd realize that that's just because you don't know me too well right now."

"Warren, are you even giving this any thought at all? *Try* to think of it not from a personal perspective but from the perspective of someone making a decision for the good of the Kingdom."

"You're a princess. You can think better in those terms. I'm a commoner, and when I think of marriage I think of love."

"Don't you feel some sort of... fondness or something though?"

"I think that just means we're friends."

She sighed and pushed at the ground with her foot. Friends was nice; she'd never had a live one of those before. "Okay, okay. I didn't really think you'd think it was a good idea. But I had to mention it anyway."

He was quiet for a few moments, watching her kick at the dirt. "Once all this is over—once your brother is safe and Farland's not trying to kill me—we could always just sort of see what happens? There's no rush. You never know."

She cast a glance his way and said, "But you don't want to marry into royalty."

"True. But, I mean, let's just keep being friends. Not leap into marriage right away hoping for a quick fix. That's a huge gamble. But I guess it is possible we might fall in love later. Right?"

"Sure, I guess. It's not like I've got some other guy waiting in the wings. And you're single, yes?"

"Yep. The pirates were all dudes, and I'm not into dudes. I've actually never been in a relationship."

"Thanks, Warren. This is really weird. Thanks for offering."

He shrugged. "No problem. Can't hurt."

"I guess." Then she said abruptly, "Let's talk about something else."

He gave a relieved laugh, and said, "So we're done with that for now?"

"Yes, we're—" she said and then trailed off, staring with sudden fear toward the refuge.

Warren followed her gaze, and saw a wagon heading toward them. Fast. It was Copernicus and Corrine, and they were in a big hurry.

Julianna stood up and began to run toward them.

Warren followed a few paces behind.

Copernicus stopped the wagon and said urgently, "Get on. Your brother's already gone. He was there a few minutes ago, but now no one can find him. Some soldiers said he went for a walk with the Queen."

Chapter Forty-One

"**M**irabella," Julianna breathed and hopped onto the wagon. "It must have been my aunt disguised as my mom." That brought up the question of what had happened to her mother, but she could only worry about one family member at a time.

Once they were all on the wagon, Copernicus turned around and headed back for the refuge.

"We'll help search," Corrine said. "Mirabella might not have met up with Farland yet. Our best chance is to somehow find Farland before Mirabella gets to him."

Copernicus drove the wagon to the edge of the refuge and then turned off the road and drove as fast as he could over the field in the direction that the soldiers had indicated Mirabella had disappeared with Conroy Jr.

As Copernicus drove, Warren pulled out the vial of magical raven blood and asked, "Do you have any ideas?"

The vial was silent.

"Any ideas would be very helpful right now," Warren yelled at the vial.

You talking to me, bro? squawked the voice in Warren's head.

"Yes. Yes, I am," Warren snapped.

Dude, how was I supposed to know?

"Sorry. Geez. Do you have any ideas that might help us right now?"

I don't even know what's going on. It's all muffled and rustley in your pocket.

Warren quickly got the vial of magical raven blood up to speed.

Oh, wow. Tough break, it croaked. *Um. Um. Hmm... Let me think here...*

Warren sighed and tapped his foot, staring at the vial.

Okay. I think I remember something. Farland was always walking around talking to himself about his plots and plans. I think I remember him saying something about meeting up with Mirabella by the water after she got the kid. Unless that was some other plot. I lose track. There are so many.

"By the water?" Warren asked. "That's vague."

That's what I've got. Sorry I can't be more help, the magical pool of raven blood squawked.

Warren shoved the vial into his pocket and looked up at his pals. "Here's the deal. Mirabella might be meeting Farland by some water. Maybe."

Julianna looked like she wanted to cry.

"I know. I'm sorry," he said apologetically, reaching out and patting her hand. "It's not much."

Warren then asked Julianna and Copper, "Have either of you ever been to this refuge before?" He had a pretty good guess that the answer was no, but it would be nice if someone in the group had some sort of idea of the lay of the land. Lakes, rivers, ponds, etc.

Julianna said shortly, "Of course not. I'm cursed."

Copernicus shook his head. "We couldn't afford vacations."

"Okay," Warren said, and took a deep breath. "Well. Um. We're going downhill right now; that has to be a good sign, yeah?"

"Probably," Julianna agreed. It did seem logical that bodies of water might be more inclined to be in lower elevations. "So, let's keep going downhill for a bit and then get out and go into the refuge and see if we can find water?"

They all sort of nodded their heads in agreement while still trying to think of something better, but no other bright ideas surfaced in their little impromptu brainstorming session, so that's what they did.

At the bottom of the hill, they got out and divided into two groups, Corrine and Copernicus going north, Warren and Julianna going south. They raced through the trees, looking wildly around for a body of water, not because they had any real hope that they'd find Farland this way, but because it was the only hope they had.

Julianna and Warren sprinted about, looking through the woods all around them for any break in the trees that might mean a body of water. Initially it was difficult to see well enough to look around very efficiently, but it got steadily easier and easier. At one point, they crossed a hiking path, and Warren happened to notice that just a few paces down from them there was a box nailed to a tree with a sign over it that read, "Trail maps supplied by the Friends of the King Moltar Wildlife Refuge Association".

Warren leapt over to the box, threw the lid open, swatted away a few sleepy wasps who had taken up residence inside, and grabbed a map. Warren and Julianna peered at it intently. "We're maybe about here?" Julianna asked, jabbing he finger at a point south of the main entrance and a little bit into the refuge.

Warren nodded. That looked about right.

"Water. Where's some water?" Julianna mumbled, looking at the map with the help of the increasingly good lighting. "There!" she pointed to a patch of water that looked like a small pond. It was not too far.

"Let's check there first," Warren said, and pocketed the map.

They were both so worried and distracted that at first it did not occur to either of them why it was becoming so easy to see. But at the same moment they both stopped in their tracks and stared at each other.

"Sunrise!" Warren gasped.

Julianna couldn't believe she'd been so dumb. She reached immediately for her bag and rummaged through it for the thick blanket she had packed for just such an emergency. "I have this," she said, waving it in the air. "I can hide under it just before sunrise. We still have some time."

"Julianna," he panted, "You need to hide *now*."

"Just a few more minutes, Warren. The sun's not up yet." She threw the blanket over herself though, just in case, as she ran. She left just a slit for her eyes.

"Julianna—"

"Water!" she gasped. For a moment he thought she was really thirsty, but then he looked ahead and saw the unmistakable glimmer of sparkling blue through the trees.

They raced to the tree line and scanned the shore of the big pond they had found. In the tree above them, a raven croaked. Warren looked up at the raven and was startled to see how clearly he could see it. It was too bright.

"Cover up," he said urgently. She must have agreed on the necessity, because she didn't resist when he guided her over to a patch of bushes and said, "Sit down here. I'll come back once I've figured out what's going on."

She nodded and covered her face up. She was suddenly feeling very scared now that she had before her the prospect of sitting all alone in the woods for who knew how long worrying about her little brother, all with only a bit of blanket separating her from life and death. She felt like saying, "Good luck," would be too empty and inadequate, so she said nothing instead.

Satisfied that Julianna was as safe as possible for the moment, Warren stood and scanned around the perimeter of the pond. "The sun's up," he whispered when he saw it pop up over the treetops a few seconds later.

"Okay," she said miserably.

Then, Warren saw Farland.

The wizard had just stepped out from behind a tree on the opposite side of the pond, eagerly looking around. Warren couldn't believe it. They'd found him. Farland looked up at the sun and then back around as though expecting someone. Was sunrise their designated meeting time, then?

Warren hoped against hope Farland had not seen them. They had not, after all, actually gone out onto the shore of the pond, so there was a chance he had not noticed their presence. "Farland's here," he breathed. "On the opposite side of this pond."

"Do something!" Julianna hissed. "Go over there!"

But Warren was already creeping as fast as he could go through the woods. It was pretty slow creeping because he had to stay absolutely quiet. He was about halfway there when Mirabella burst through the trees not far from Farland with the (presumably unconscious) form of Conroy Jr. in her arms. She said something to Farland and then began to walk toward him.

Abandoning all caution, Warren ran like lightning. There was no point in being quiet anymore. He'd never get there in time sneaking. But if he ran, he might be able to manage it. Especially since Mirabella, though closer to Farland, looked exhausted, and was carrying the dead weight of the Prince.

Warren sprinted like he'd never sprinted before. Panting, he skidded to a halt in front of Farland. Mirabella was still a few paces away.

Farland stared at Warren in astonishment. "*You?*" he sleazed. "What in blazes?" he asked, then looked over to Mirabella questioningly as though she might have some clue as to what Warren was doing in the middle of the King Moltar Wildlife Refuge just in time to attempt to thwart their evil plan.

Mirabella merely shrugged and put her nephew none too gently down on the ground at her feet. She stretched her arms a bit and said, "I have no idea. But it hardly matters. Just kill him and let's go."

"But the *other* plan!" Farland pointed out. "I need him as a pawn in my *other* plan!"

"Farland, for goodness sake! Just let that plan *go*. You can always come up with something else to get back at Conroy. I don't want your fixation on that old plan to get in the way of *this* one after I've devoted so much time and energy to it."

Warren hovered there indecisively, listening to them bicker. If they'd attacked him, at least he'd have known what to do (or at least what to *try* to do), but here they were debating whether or not to kill him in a very casual, matter of fact manner that was seriously throwing him off.

"I've been planning that one near my whole life!" Farland whined.

"Okay then, fine, *don't* kill him. Just knock him out or something. The point here is that we have to *go!* The woods are swarming with soldiers."

"Yes," Farland finally agreed, and was about to turn on Warren to give him yet another concussion (though this one of a magical instead of a physical nature) but Warren had seen it coming, and he flew at the wizard, punching and kicking in a very unskilled and thus unpredictable manner that left Farland momentarily defenseless.

Warren knew his only chance was to somehow keep Farland from using his hands. Also, ideally, he would like to stop Farland from speaking, because he might be able to do some damage with his voice alone.

Farland was not much of a fighter either (in skirmishes, he usually relied on spells and his ability to disappear, but if he disappeared now he might lose his chance to get the Prince, so he was disinclined to resort to that just yet), so Warren was actually able to wrestle Farland to the ground and manage to sort of pin one of his arms behind his back while kneeling on the other arm and trying to shove his face into the dirt so that he couldn't speak to say a spell. Warren's broken arm protested heartily, but he persisted.

Up until this point, Mirabella had not deemed it worth her while to get involved, but just then she heard men yelling and a few hunting dogs barking through the forest. She sighed, unfolded her arms, leaned down, pulled a long, evil-looking dagger out from its hilt at her ankle, walked over to where the guys were thrashing about on the ground, and stabbed Warren.

Chapter Forty-Two

Mirabella had been aiming for Warren's heart, but as she lunged, Farland jerked to the side, bringing Warren with him, and Mirabella's knife only managed to imbed itself in Warren's shoulder.

Warren screamed and looked down; the hilt of Mirabella's knife was sticking out of his shoulder, which meant the rest of the knife was lodged deep in his body. Which meant he was in serious trouble.

"You stabbed me!" he gasped, gaping in horror at Mirabella as the pain shot through him.

She gave another shrug and looked over his head, scanning the forest again for soldiers. Then her empty gaze snapped back to him, straight into his eyes. She pulled the dagger slowly out, watching him with a cold curiosity as he cried out again in pain.

Farland seized the moment and knocked Warren off him and into the dirt. Then he lunged toward Conroy Jr., intending to magic him out of the woods and back to Mirabella's cave.

AFTER JUST ABOUT two minutes of waiting, Julianna couldn't take it any longer. She figured the blanket covering her was plenty big enough that she could walk with it covering her as long as she was careful. All she had to worry about was her hands and face because the rest of her was covered in fabric or shoes.

"Dexter," she breathed. "I'm going to walk around the pond. You guide me? Don't let me trip or hit a tree—"

"You sure?"

"Yes."

"What on earth can you do stuck under a blanket?"

"Nothing. So what? I'd rather be doing nothing over there than over here."

Dexter knew that tone of voice; if he didn't help her, she'd just try to do it without his help, and then she'd trip over a root or slam into a branch and lose her blanket. There had been a time at the start of this adventure that he would have tried to talk her out of it, would have told her how stupid she was being. But now he merely said resignedly, "Okay. Stand up. Let's go."

Slowly but surely, Dexter guided her over logs and roots, under branches, and around trees; she was nearly there when she heard voices raised in an argument. Dexter steered her to a stop behind a tree so close that if Mirabella and Farland hadn't been so distracted by Warren they might have seen her. She stood silently, listening with mounting fear as the argument turned into a physical altercation.

Julianna heard the soldiers and dogs at the same time as Mirabella did, and felt relief wash over her. The soldiers would see them. Everything would be fine.

Then she heard Warren cry, "You stabbed me!"

"Dexter!" she cried. "What's happening? This stupid curse!" Warren had been stabbed, and Mirabella and Farland were about to take her little brother, and there was nothing she could do, though she was standing mere feet away from them.

"Warren's stabbed. Farland's going to take your brother!" Dexter said with dismay.

Julianna lurched forward in the general direction of where their voices had been, her only thought of her little brother who was going to be kidnapped in a matter of moments. Her little brother who, despite their father's constant nagging and disapproval, really *did* have a good chance at turning into a good king who could help the people of Fritillary.

In a flash, she realized she had to do something. If Farland and

Mirabella succeeded in taking Conroy Jr. and brainwashing him and turning him into a horrible monster for their own benefit, she would feel guilty for the rest of her life for having done nothing. There she'd be, sitting down in her dungeon while Farland and Mirabella drove the country into the ground, and she'd have to live with the knowledge that she could have tried to stop them.

Which was no way to live.

So she gave a wild scream to notify the soldiers of her location, threw off the blanket, and flung herself at Farland, who was just about to close his hand around her brother's wrist and disappear. She figured if she was fast enough, she'd be able to knock Farland off Conroy Jr. before the sunlight got her. Hopefully that would give the soldiers enough time. Or, if Warren was alive, she'd give him enough time for him to do something.

But once she'd slammed into the wizard and knocked him to the ground and crashed down on top of him, she was surprised to find that she was still alive. She froze, bracing herself. Maybe the sunlight had to soak in a bit before it killed her?

Farland stared up at her with bewilderment. "Wha—?" Then he gasped and started to writhe about in what looked like severe pain.

"Julianna! NO!" cried Warren from where he knelt in his steadily-growing puddle of blood a few paces off.

"*Julianna?*" Farland gasped though his pain. "The *Princess?*"

"Why am I not dead?" she asked frantically, conveniently finding herself at this moment face to face with the only person who might have the answer to that question. "I don't love him," she nodded toward Warren. "So the spell shouldn't be broken!"

Farland fought to get her off him, but she held on tight. She didn't understand why he appeared to be in so much pain, but it was working to her advantage, that was for sure.

"You've got an anti-magic amulet?" he gasped.

"Of course. Everyone in my family wears them, in case we run into *you!*"

"Take it off! It hurts!"

"No way," she answered. "Give me some answers! Why am I alive?!"

"I don't know!" he cried. "You should be dead! The sunlight—"

"Was the curse fake?" she prodded. "Was it a lie?"

"No!" he yelled. "No! I didn't make any mistakes! I was so careful—It should have—"

"Farland!" Mirabella cut in sharply. She had been frozen with shock at this turn of events, but, being soulless, she didn't have many emotions to slog through, so she snapped out of it pretty fast. "Farland! We have to go!"

The soldiers were getting closer. If they hadn't seen them yet, they would soon.

Farland was galvanized into motion by Mirabella's sharp reminder. He summoned up some strength, tossed the befuddled Julianna off him, and lunged once more for Conroy Jr.

This snapped Julianna out of her shock at being not dead, and she lunged after him, grabbing him by the leg and sending him crashing to the ground with a thud and a roar of rage. He tried to crawl forward to get a hold on Conroy Jr.'s unconscious form, but Julianna kept pulling him back.

Mirabella gave an exasperated curse and was about to kick Julianna off of him, but she was stopped by Warren, who had managed to stagger to his feet and stumble over to them, slipping a bit on his blood, but somehow managing to stay upright. With all his might, he tried to stay on his feet long enough to help Julianna. He reached them just in time to slam into Mirabella so that her kick missed Julianna. She staggered to the side before gaining her balance.

Mirabella shot Warren a venomous glare; she had every intention of flying at him then and there and putting her knife where she'd originally intended, but just then soldiers burst through the trees. "Farland! Now!" she yelled and rushed toward him.

Farland looked up and saw the swarming soldiers. Mirabella reached him. He grabbed onto her wrist.

Julianna realized what was going to happen just in time to let go of him and scramble away.

Farland and Mirabella disappeared in a big puff of smelly, dark smoke.

ONCE THE SMOKE had dissipated, Julianna looked wildly around until she saw her brother still lying on the ground. He was already surrounded by soldiers who were industriously trying to wake him up. She felt a rush of relief. He was safe.

Then she whirled around to look for Warren. He was kneeling in the mud where he'd fallen after knocking Mirabella away from Julianna. He was staring vacantly at her as blood rapidly soaked his already blood-and-grime crusted shirt. Not a single soldier was paying any attention to him.

"Warren!" she cried and ran over to him. "Soldiers! Get over here!" She knelt in front of him and looked intently into his unfocused eyes.

"You're alive," he observed, and coughed weakly.

She nodded. "Yes. I am. Let's make sure you stay that way too."

He nodded.

It occurred to her then that no soldiers had responded to her. She whirled around and yelled, "Soldiers! Anyone with any medical knowledge!"

"Or magic knowledge," Warren added too quietly to be heard.

A few of them looked at her disdainfully, and then turned their attention back to Conroy Jr.

They didn't know who she was. Of course they didn't. She was filthy and dressed in old maid clothes, in the middle of a wildlife refuge, and in the sunlight to boot. "Hold on a second," she said to Warren, and stalked over to the soldiers.

"Look at me!" she barked at one of the soldiers in her Royal Person Voice.

He glanced at her and muttered something about not having time for a crazy backwoods yokel, then looked back with concern at the Prince. But he had seen her imperious gaze, and though it took a moment for him to sort it out, he did look back at her with confusion. "Are you…?"

"Yes," she said angrily. "I am Princess Julianna."

"But—the sunlight—" he spluttered.

"I know. I know. I don't get it either. But that's not the most pressing issue at hand. I need some soldier with medical knowledge to see to that man over there." She pointed to Warren just in time to see him collapse from his knees to his side in a puff of dust. "He helped save the Prince's life, and you are all ignoring him while he is bleeding from a severe stab wound."

"But—I'm sorry—but we didn't know—"

"Don't waste time with excuses!" she exploded. "Take care of him! Construct some stretchers and get these two back to camp!"

They all began to rush about, doing as they were ordered.

"If that man dies, I will have you all stationed at the Forest of Looming Death for the rest of your lives!" she roared for good measure.

$\mathcal{B}$ACK AT THE camp, Julianna accompanied Warren to the wizard's tent in order to make sure he was well taken care of. She stalked right up to Wendell the wizard and, ignoring Wendell's amazement that she was out in the sunlight and not dead, snapped at him that if Warren died Wendell would never work in the kingdom again. Not a cool move, but she was stressed, so we'll forgive her.

It was then that she looked up and saw that Warren and Conroy Jr. were not the only patients in the tent. There was also an unconscious Lillian, who was still suffering from the aftereffects of her run-in with Mirabella. King Conroy was sitting at her bedside, holding Lillian's hand and staring at Julianna, not with amazement (like everyone else that morning who had seen her out and about in the sunlight) but with a sort of dread.

"Julianna!" Conroy stuttered. "Hey, will you look at that! You're alive!"

"Yes. I'm alive," she said, looked at him through narrowed eyes.

"What a stroke of fortune!" He wiped a bit of sweat off his forehead.

"Dad," she said warily. She left Warren's side and walked over to the King. "What's up?" She studied his face. "You're not surprised."

Behind her back, Wendell and some wizard interns converged on Warren and began to work.

"I am *so* surprised!" Conroy said defensively.

"No. You are not surprised to see me out in the sunlight." She looked at him suspiciously. "But *why* not?"

He gave a nervous smile that looked more like a wince. "Okay, so I'm not surprised." He looked at her beseechingly, as though begging her mutely not to press the issue. But when all she did was stare stonily at him, he continued. "I, um, well I just always had a pretty good idea that Farland was lying about cursing you. Because that must be the reason, right? He either messed up the curse or he was lying about it the whole time. So that's why you are okay." He laughed nervously and looked down at his unconscious wife. Had Julianna imagined it, or did Conroy look relieved to see that his wife's eyes were still shut?

Julianna looked from Conroy to Lillian and back again. "Dad…" she whispered as something clicked into place in her head. She looked over her shoulder. Wendell and the interns were gone (they'd worked very quickly because they did not want to be eavesdropping on this action), and Warren was lying peacefully, apparently asleep. She turned back and asked Conroy, "Am I your firstborn child?"

Conroy spluttered and his eyes bugged out. Sweat was pouring down his face. But when he spoke, he said, "You know you're our first child!" Unable to hold her angry gaze, Conroy looked down at his cursed ring and twirled it around.

"Dad! I didn't ask whether I was *both of your* first child; I asked if I was *your* first child."

"Honey, don't go jumping to crazy conclusions," he said pleadingly. "Farland just lied about the curse!" He gave another nervous giggle.

"Dad, I happened to be staring right into Farland's face when I jumped out into the sunlight. I saw his face the moment he realized that the sunlight hadn't killed me." She locked eyes with her father and said, "Farland was *surprised*. He was more than surprised. He was *confused*. I asked him why I was alive, and he was sure he hadn't messed the spell up. He said he'd been careful and hadn't made mistakes."

Conroy waved a dismissive hand. "Well everyone makes mistakes, dearest. He just added the wrong ingredients or something. Some of those spells have tons of ingredients. I remember watching him whip up some at the castle back from when we were pals."

"Dad," she said, deciding to take this in a different direction. "If you have another kid out there somewhere stuck in some dungeon or basement or wherever, and you have her counter-curse right there," she pointed with her thumb over her shoulder in Warren's direction, "How can you in good conscience deny your kid the chance to get the curse broken? Just because—I assume—you don't want mom to find out that you had an affair."

"It wasn't an affair!" Conroy finally sighed and looked at Julianna with big, sad eyes. He gave a huge sigh. "I had a girlfriend before your mom. Margaret. Then I met your mom and I dumped Margaret. I never knew about the baby until she was about to be born! By then, I was married to your mom and I just couldn't tell her about Margaret! She'd have been *devastated!*"

Julianna gaped at him. "I've been living my *whole life* in a *dungeon* because you couldn't admit to mom that you had a kid with someone else? Before you even *knew* mom?"

"Well, when you put it that way it sounds so bad–"

"That's because it *is* bad!" Julianna roared. "I could have been out doing things! I could have—argh! There are so many things I could have done with my life that I can't even think of an example right now! I've lived my life thinking I was cursed, all because you made a mistake in your youth? You were a *prince,* for goodness sake! Isn't that sort of thing *expected?*"

Conroy frowned. "Dearest, I'm sorry." He managed to meet her eyes for a moment, then suddenly a fake look of surprise popped up on his face and he said, cupping a hand to his ear, "Oh, whatever is that? I think I hear someone calling for me. You hear that?" He pointed in the direction of the pretend sound that wasn't fooling anybody, then shot to his feet and said, "I'd better go. Could be some important kingly thing that needs doing."

Without objection, Julianna let him scuttle off. Fuming, she turned and watched as he ran away from her. Then she glanced down at Warren, who was lying on the bed nearest the exit.

He was awake and staring at her with wide eyes. "Whoa," he breathed.

"Yeah," she said crabbily. "Whoa." She stalked over to Warren's bed and sat down on the edge. There was a lot of silence for a long time while they both thought about what they'd just heard.

She shook her head as though to clear it. "You all right?" she asked at last, looking at his shoulder. The wound was covered in some bright blue paste. Warren was very pale from all the blood loss but seemed pretty okay otherwise.

"Yeah. Those wizards are good at magic. Barely hurts at all."

"Good. Hey, thanks for all your help back there," she said.

"No problem. Likewise."

"No problem."

They were quiet for a bit longer.

"So, you've got a lady in a cellar somewhere waiting for you, huh?" Julianna said finally.

"Yeah. I guess I do," Warren said. "And you've got some life to live."

"Yeah. I guess I do," she agreed with a smile.

EPILOGUE

ulianna was lying in the grass, soaking up the sun's glorious rays. Sunlight sure was awesome, so much so that she felt like saying it out loud.

"Sunlight sure is awesome," she commented.

The banjo music that had been wafting through the castle garden paused for a moment, and Warren said, "Yeah. Nice and warm. But you're totally going to get a sunburn."

"I don't care."

"You will care once you've got a sunburn."

Julianna sat up with a sigh, then picked up her parasol from where she'd tossed it in the grass beside her. She opened it up and held it over her head. "So that's what the city looks like in daylight," she mused as she looked down the gently sloping lawn, out over the castle walls, and at the sprawling city below. "It really is ugly."

"Yup," Warren agreed over the folksy tune he was playing. How he managed playing with a sling on one arm and a recent stab-wound on the opposite shoulder was beyond Julianna.

"I mean, seriously. What a dump. Look, over there," she said and pointed. "Is that a fire? Like, an actual burning building?"

Warren glanced up. "Looks like."

"Man, this city is messed up," she muttered as she watched the distant smoke and flames, and down by the harbor the tiny little firefighters, presumably setting up one of their pumps that would bring water to the fire.

"This whole *country's* messed up," Warren said.

"True," she agreed as she shifted her gaze from the fire to where Conroy Jr. was playing tag on the lawn with his two best friends: the son of the Royal Gardener and the son of the Royal Silversmith. "I'm glad Conroy Jr. seems to have recovered from his ordeal."

"Resilient little dude," Warren agreed. "I'm sure he'll—" He stopped abruptly, and his music halted with a discordant twang.

Julianna looked quizzically in his direction and saw her friend staring past her toward castle's front doors. She turned to see what had spooked Warren.

There was her father, striding toward them with a set to his jaw that clearly indicated a man on a mission. Behind him trailed two servants, one laboring under the weight of a heavy chair, and one holding a mug.

Conroy had been trying to have a conversation with his daughter ever since they'd gotten back from the hunting party. But she'd been evading him.

Julianna hopped to her feet and said, "Come on, Warren, let's get out of here."

He remained seated, his eyes still following the progress of the angry King. It felt beyond inappropriate to stand up, turn his back, and walk away from the supreme ruler of the kingdom. Even if he was just following the lead of the Princess. "Um," he said uncomfortably, "He's going to keep trying to talk to you. Shouldn't you just let him before he gets any madder?"

She glared down at him and twirled her parasol while she thought. "I guess." Then she flounced back onto the ground in a puff of lacy purple gown, with her back to her father.

Warren set down his banjo and stood, bowing low to the King.

Conroy ignored him completely and stopped in front of Julianna. "Dearest. We need to talk."

"Well, then, talk," she grumbled.

Conroy flicked a finger at the servant with the chair, then said, "There," pointing at the ground by Julianna.

The servant set the chair on the ground.

Conroy sat. "Tea," he barked. The other servant put the mug in his hand.

Julianna watched the spectacle with disdain.

Conroy waved a hand at the servants, and they scurried off. "Julianna. I have been trying to talk with you for five days. It's important. If you keep running off with this commoner every time I approach, I will simply kick him out of the castle."

"Dad, *this commoner* is the only reason I'm listening to you at all. He suggested I stay and hear you out. And it would be stupid to kick him out; he's the counter-curse for your mysterious firstborn daughter. And, please, he has a name, so stop calling him 'this commoner'." She glared at Conroy a bit, and then something else occurred to her. "Oh, and also, if it weren't for Warren, Conroy Jr. would have been kidnapped! So, seriously, you should be treating him a lot better than you are." She looked behind her at where Warren stood, and said, "Warren! You don't have to keep bowing."

Warren looked up at her and straightened up.

"*I'll* tell him when he can stop bowing," Conroy roared.

Warren bowed again and rolled his eyes at the ground. How could such a dopey guy be a king? Inbreeding really was interesting. It was lucky for Julianna that her mom was from outside the Royal Gene Pool. And, no, they didn't know about genetics in Fritillary.

"Dad, for goodness sake, just let him stand up so we can get on with whatever you have to say. He's *injured*. I'm not talking to you while you're having a power trip at my friend's expense."

Conroy growled, "You there. You may stand."

Warren stood and looked at the ground uneasily.

"Sit down, Warren," Julianna said. He got the distinct feeling that, while she was trying to make him comfortable, she was also trying to undermine Conroy.

Warren glanced at Conroy, who gave an irritated shrug, trying to pretend he didn't care that his daughter was humiliating him in front of a nobody. Warren sat down by his banjo and resumed looking at the ground. Being in the presence of the king was no fun.

"Okay, Dad, what did you want to say?" she asked.

The King looked around, determining that no one was in earshot. "We need to make sure we're all on the same page about all this. The curse and all that."

"What is there to sort out? I mean, gossip's already swirling around about how Farland messed up the curse."

"Yes. Exactly. I just need to make sure, as the only three people who know the truth about—*Warren*—being the counter-curse, we're in agreement what to tell people if they ask." He paused and looked from Julianna to Warren and back again. "So, Farland messed up the curse. That's it. And not a word about my other daughter. Not *one* word. Even to each other."

Julianna's curiosity got the better of her, and she stopped being aloof long enough to ask, "So, seriously, no one knows about her?" Now that the conversation had turned in this direction, there were a lot of questions she knew Warren had but was afraid to ask.

"No one. Well, no one but her mother, of course. Her mom knows about her because she was pregnant with her," Conroy astutely pointed out.

"Do they know that there's a way to break the curse?" she asked and looked at Warren.

"Nope. They don't. If they knew the curse could be broken, her mom would start asking around and people might get suspicious."

"But you're going to tell them now, right?" Julianna persisted.

Conroy gave a little wince. "Well, I would if I could. But they disappeared a few years ago. The place they were hiding was abandoned last time I was able to get out there for a visit."

Warren and Julianna gasped in unison, "What?!"

"Yeah. Disappeared. I haven't heard a word from them."

"Did you send anyone to look for them?" Julianna asked her dad while looking at Warren's shocked face.

"Of course not!" Conroy answered as though she was an idiot. "What reason could I give my spies for sending them to search for two random commoners? No, I figured if they wanted to disappear, that was their business. At least it meant I didn't have to fuss with child support anymore. And it wasn't like the visits were any fun, anyway, so no loss on my end. Margaret—my ex—when she got pregnant, she figured she'd be queen. But when I met your mom and married her, and Margaret found herself living in hiding with a kid who couldn't go out in the sunshine, she got *so* mad. All she did whenever I visited was whine, whine, whine. Good riddance, really."

Julianna and Warren gaped a bit.

Julianna swallowed, and prompted, "And now that we've located the guy who can break the spell?"

Conroy sighed. "Yes. I see what you're saying there. Yeah, I was thinking I could maybe tell a spy about it. See if he can track them down."

"*A* spy? Just one?"

"Of course. If it's just one, and word gets out about my other kid, I'll know who told. The spy, or one of you two. The more people know, the more of a chance there is that someone will find out. And then it's just a matter of time until your mom finds out."

Julianna knew there was no point trying to talk him into just admitting about the previous relationship and resultant child. But, really, it was so irritating. All this convoluted nonsense just because he couldn't admit to the Queen about Margaret.

The King was quiet for a bit, sipping his tea, and Julianna was too mad to string together a coherent sentence, so she was quiet too. Of course, Warren wasn't about to say anything.

"Hey, is that *another* fire?" Conroy asked as he gazed out over his vast empire. He sipped some tea.

Julianna didn't bother answering, since of course it was.

"Well dear. Are we all set? We just tell everyone Farland messed up the curse and that's why you can be out in the sunshine. And there's no need to mention anything about your sister. Right?"

"Right, Dad," Julianna responded.

Conroy gave Warren an arrogant stare and a quizzical eyebrow-raise. "You agree?"

Warren nodded and mumbled, "Yes, Your Majesty."

"Good. If word gets around about my other daughter, I'll have you killed, lad."

And off Conroy swooped, dropping his mug of nearly-untouched tea in the grass for the servants to tend to.

Warren's stared after him, not sure whether he was more shocked, horrified, or confused by those parting words. He looked with fear at Julianna.

She shrugged and rolled her eyes. "He wouldn't dare."

He cleared his dry throat, and asked shakily, "You sure?"

"I wouldn't let him kill you, Warren," She said with enough confidence to make him feel slightly better. Then she tossed aside her parasol and stretched out in the grass again. "He wouldn't want to make me mad—I can blackmail him about Margaret now, after all. And also, you're the person who can break my big sister's curse."

"He doesn't seem all that attached to her, though," Warren pointed out. "Seemed happy that she'd disappeared with her mom."

"He won't kill you," she reiterated. "Next time I see him, I'll be sure to threaten him about telling my mom his secret."

"Cool. Thanks. Could you also ask him what your sister's name is? I've been wondering."

"Sure," she answered and opened her eyes to look at him. "You must be really curious about her, hmm?"

"Very," he answered.

"I wonder... When you see her, do you think you'll fall in love automatically as a side-effect of the curse, or not?" she mused. "Wouldn't it be great to just meet a person and BAM! fall in love just like that?"

He nodded. "Yeah. It would." Warren was very anxious to meet this mystery lady; according to the terms of the curse, if they fell in love, her curse would be broken. Warren had never been that great at meeting ladies. For one thing, he had rarely met any of them while living on the pirate ship. And for another thing, he wasn't a fan of the usual small talk and awkwardness that precedes a meaningful relationship. But he was tired of being single; and if ever there was a good shortcut in the getting-to-know-you process, it was this magical sentence: 'Hi, my name's Warren, and I'm the dude who can break your curse.'.

"Well, I'm sure you'll get an opportunity to find out sooner or later! Fritillary's a pretty small country. They'll track her down."

"I sure hope so."

She watched him from her place in the grass. He was brooding again. She didn't like to see him brooding. So she thought of something to take his mind off his worries. "Hey, are you hungry? It's time we went in. I don't want to get a sunburn, after all."

"I'm starved," he said eagerly. He never turned down an opportunity to eat as much as he could of the excellent food that was on offer in the castle.

"And after we've eaten, we can see about getting you an audition with the Royal Theater in town."

"That would be really cool," Warren said with a grin; being friends with a princess definitely had its perks. He hopped up out of the grass, then offered her a hand up with his non-broken arm.

She waved him away. "I don't want to hurt your shoulder."

Warren grabbed his banjo, Julianna grabbed her parasol, and off they strolled to get a snack from the castle kitchen.

JANE WALKED ONTO the dock at the Apamea Bay Marina and strode to the spot where the pirate ship was tied up. She looked up the gangplank and saw Captain Maximus McManlyman chillaxing on a deck chair, apparently reading one of those romance novels he so loved. She was pretty sure she saw him turn his head her way a tad, spotting her out of the corner of his eye and pretending he hadn't. "Oh boy, here we go," she muttered, and walked up the gangplank.

McManlyman did a pretend double-take when she got near. "Oh, hi!" he said. "I didn't see you there." He kicked his feet off the footrest, stood, and clomped over to her.

She said, "My business in Apamea is done, so we can get going whenever works for you."

"Great!" he said. "How'd it go?"

They're going to help us," she said. It felt surreal. Just the previous morning, she had come unannounced to the Capital, and met with some members of the Apamea Council who had been able to make some time for her. The Council members had been very excited to hear what she had to say. So excited that they'd managed to throw together a meeting with all the rest of the members for the following morning. Just hours later, they had agreed (by a vote of 7 to 2) to help the Order of the Orange Star in Fritillary. Jane told McManlyman, "We just have to go back to Fritillary, gather up representatives from all the chapters of the Orange Star, come back here, and talk turkey." It would take a lot of time to organize Mortimer and Steph and all the other leaders of the chapters from across Fritillary, but with luck they'd all be sailing back to Apamea by spring.

"Hey, that's cool," McManlyman said. "Congrats. Oh, look what I did today!" He rolled up his billowy sleeve, revealing a heavily-tattooed arm.

She ignored the fact that he was blatantly flexing his gigantic muscles. "What am I supposed to be seeing?" she asked as she surveyed the tattoos. An anatomically impossible mermaid, a treasure chest, a few swirly designs that were obviously meant to disguise the names underneath that had to be of ladies that he'd had fallings-out with.

"Right here!" he said helpfully and pointed with his other hand. On his strapping deltoid, under a big, glaring skull-and-crossbones, was an orange star. And scrawled over it read: REVOLUTION!

"Oh man, *seriously*?" she asked. "You got a tattoo."

"Yeah. Because the revolution means so much to me. I care a lot."

"Well, it's your arm," Jane answered. "Look, will we be able to get going today? I'm anxious to get home and get the ball rolling."

"Yeah, we can get going any time," McManlyman said, then gave his burly muscles another unnecessary flex before rolling his sleeve back down. He looked around, spotted his first mate in the rigging, and barked, "BIGGBY!" Then he tipped his pirate hat at Jane and stomped off to get the crew moving.

McManlyman ran a streamlined operation, so the ship was ready to go in a jiffy. Jane went to stand at the bow (that's the pointy bit at the front), and as the pirates sailed off toward the horizon, she leaned against the railing and took a calming breath. It was finally happening. The Order of the Orange Star would soon have all the help and resources they needed.

Revolution was coming to Fritillary.

AN EXCERPT FROM
Wistful Musings from a Crow's Nest

BY CORRINE KENSINGTON

I'm a sad, lonely lady,
In this crow's nest tonight.
Thinking matters most weighty,
I'd like to take flight.

I'd fly over the ocean,
And land on the shore.
For that's where (I've a notion),
There must be dudes galore.

I'm not talking bloodthirsty
Pirates I know.
But fellas who're worthy,
Souls pure as the snow!

I've been known to date pirates
If they're nice to behold,
But when we'd go on dates,
All they talk of is gold.

Hard lessons have taught me,
If love's to be found,
Picky I must be,
Though men do abound.

I'm dreamy enough to get
Any old catch,
But a guy won at roulette,
Would be a bad match.

So as much as it irks me
I guess I must wait,
For who Fate has in store
For my marriagey state.

Come on mystery fellow
I hope you're attractive,
In danger not yellow,
And, heath-wise, you're active.

Be clever and funny,
Complexion not pasty,
Your temper be sunny,
Your cooking be tasty.

I'm tired of waiting,
So let's make it snappy.
On the record I'm stating:
We'll be so, so happy

ACKNOWLEDGEMENTS

Thanks to Will, who is the most supportive partner a writer could ever dream of.

Thanks to my parents, Pat and Steve. If you hadn't supplied me with zillions of books as a kid, I would never have become a writer.

Thanks to the rest of my family: Anna, Julia, Katie, Niko, Nick, Ben, Stephanie, Mike, Stella, Tristan, Holly, and Bill.

So many thanks to Lindy Ryan for reading this book and thinking it would be a good fit for Black Spot Books. I always thought I'd be too protective of this particular story to trust it in the hands of any publisher, but I had zero hesitation with you.

Thanks to Lindy Ryan for the editing, Najla Qamber for the absolutely beautiful cover, and Nada Qamber for the equally beautiful interior.

Thanks to Jennifer Flath for being an amazing friend. Writing can be a solitary thing, so it's lovely to have an author pal like you to navigate the writing world with.

Thanks to my pals at Spaceboy Books.

How to Break an Evil Curse is the first writing project I ever took seriously and put out into the world to be read by strangers. I wish my beta readers had any idea just how much they meant to me on my first foray into the world of writing. All the hugs to Shaunn Grulkowski, Dustin Honour, Marie Howalt, Angela Jackwitz, Ryan Norris, Alyn Spector, Joseph Waters, Ryan Watt, Shannon Vest, and Cameron Duke.

ABOUT THE AUTHOR

Laura Morrison lives in the Metro Detroit area with her husband, daughters, cats, and vegetable garden. She has a B.S. in applied ecology and environmental science from Michigan Technological University. Before she was a writer and stay-at-home mom, she battled invasive species and researched turtles. Her novel, Grimbargo, is published with Spaceboy Books.